To Margie

You have always been my b_ggest supporter, stood in my corner, you never judged, and you never let me down. You never gave up on me even in my darkness. You are the guide that counseled me through this life and your service as my spiritual adv_sor has meant more to me than you will ever know. I can only hope th_s book will immortalize you as the spiritually supernatural woman I had the pleasure of calling my aunt.

I'll see you on the other side. I love you.

"When you pass through the waters, I will be with you;
and through the rivers, they shall not overwhelm you;
when you walk through fire you shall not be burned,
and the flame shall not consume you."

Isaiah 43:2

STREET THERAPY

Summer 1992

Abraham picked up the basketball, squeezing it between his twelve-year-old hands. The pounding of the 2x4 took its toll, but not once did he cry out in pain. His father definitely knew how to scold and the beatings throughout the years had evolved.

Does he really think that beating me is gonna solve anything?

Running away had its perks, but the streets were unrelenting as drugs and gang bangers roamed about. Besides, Grandma and Margie would be heartbroken if he never returned home.

On the other hand, the basketball rim across the street gave him life. Mike set it up for the neighborhood kids to play on rather than wandering the streets. The gangbangers were doing drive-bys every other night and drugs were only two blocks over on South Flores Street, but Mike did his best to do his part in the community and little did he know that he was making a difference for one street kid across the way. Abraham admired Mike's attempts, looked up to him even, in a neighborhood that was overflowing with thugs, and despite the conditions, Mike was known as "The Weather Man," as he was oblivious to the cloudy forecast.

Abraham popped a jumper from three-point range and drilled it on his first attempt. He scowled at the ball as it hit the concrete. He wanted to pound on his dad as he had done him, but the circular object had a way of changing things. He was too small and not strong enough to mount a counteroffensive. Pummeling the basketball on the street would have to do for now, and along with the rim, it was this court that kept him from fleeing to the adjacent streets of delinquency.

Pancho, a street kid who used to play basketball, succumbed to the other side of South Flores, and three months in, he was already trying to sell Abraham a handgun.

"Abraham, you never know, you might need it one day…" Pancho insisted.

"Nah, I'm good, man. I don't need it, but thanks. I'll stick to streetball," Abraham said.

Those were some good times, Abraham thought.

"Maybe, I should just go with Pancho…" he said to himself.

He dribbled the ball a few times out to the three-point line, turned around and popped another jumper. The ball swooshed through the hoop.

As a child, he never excelled at sports. While playing baseball and basketball early on, Abraham was the least likely to get playing time and often the kid who was picked last. Feelings of inadequacy and discouragement were constantly present during this time of growth. He was the smallest kid on every team he had been on, not to mention, with skills that were the poorest. His father would constantly drill him and push him, but he just wasn't as skilled or developed like the other kids. He could see the frustration in his father's eyes and the feeling of failure, knowing that he had let his father down by being the worst player out there. The embarrassment left him not wanting to go to another practice again. Even at nine-years-old, he knew that every time he stepped on the basketball court or baseball diamond, it was utter humiliation for him and his father. And every time, he wanted to crawl under a rock as if he never existed.

"It doesn't matter what I do, it always results in a beating," he said with disgust.

Now, one month out from his thirteenth birthday, the tables were turning. It was the first time he picked up a basketball with skills that were developing at a rapid pace.

Basketball began to take on much more meaning. To the world, basketball was a global phenomenon. The USA Dream Team was busy displaying total dominance, in succession with Michael Jordan's second straight championship, and everyone took notice of a game that was fast becoming the most popular sport on the planet.

But on one particular street, there was one teenager who needed the game more than ever, and to this young adolescent, basketball was the world.

The streetball court served as a sacred house of hoops. His home was only steps away, but to him, stepping on the pavement was like stepping into another world. It was a world where problems and pain didn't exist. A world that carried no worries or shame. A world where his father's eyes would not look at him with embarrassment, but of disbelief of how far he had come in a place that would allow him to let out his anger and aggressions with no consequences or repercussions. A world in which Abraham was fueled by emotions, simply measured not by penalties, but with individual victories. He would study Michael Jordan's moves; just as every other kid in the world did, turning weakness into strength.

Basketball soon became an outlet, a best friend, and a mentor at various times. Sadness, despair, and difficulties were erased once Abraham touched the ball. Confusion was replaced with calmness. The court granted him the ability to think clearly when things went awry. There was not a person who existed in the world that Abraham could talk to, but there was an inanimate object with a circular silhouette that could give the best therapy.

✟

Gloria stepped into the bedroom and noticed a peculiar object sitting on the bed. Considering the latest events, a stuffed bear was an odd thing to be lying against her pillow. The bear held a heart with its paws and a card hidden just behind it. She figured it was from the boy under heavy scrutiny, nevertheless, one that she loved. She gently opened the envelope and upon reading the words inscribed on the front, a twinge fell upon her heart. It read:

I Love You and I'm Sorry!

It only took one glance for her emotions to overpower her. The woman who showed no emotion suddenly began unraveling. The heartfelt card carried words in blue ink and the penmanship she recognized to be from her conflicted son.

Mom,

I'm sorry for running away. I didn't mean to hurt you. I just wanted to find answers. How do I make this abnormality easier to deal with? Please forgive me. I don't know what else to do. I love you.

Love your son, Abraham

Tears streamed down her cheek before she could even close the card. She knew exactly where to find her son and comforting him would be a challenge at best. Her words were futile going up against something she didn't understand, much less, something she could not help him with.

"There is only one person who can help him…" she whispered, "…and it's not me…"

She placed the card back in the envelope gently and gathered herself. Her feelings rarely made it to the surface and when her son needed her most, she was going to face him, emotionally compromised.

✧

Abraham dribbled to the top of the key and rose, releasing the ball from his fingertips. The ball clanged on the back end of the rim and bounced straight up into the air. He rarely missed a bucket from his sweet spot on the basketball court. Taking his time, he retrieved the ball and turned toward to the top of the key, once again. Much to his surprise, Gloria stood quietly on the sidewalk.

"Hey dude," she said, softly.

Her eyes were red and swollen. One glance at her and his eyes began to tear up.

She read my card...

Gloria never cried, nor did she ever get too excited. Her happy medium of staying in between the spectrum of emotions was like an art and a science.

"Hey," he said.

Abraham quickly walked to the curb to sit down and brace himself for the onslaught of emotion.

Gloria inched closer to him and planted herself on the curb, placing her arm around him.

"I love you, Abe," she said as tears streamed down her face.

Abraham hunched over as his own tears began spewing out. His five-foot three frame jerked uncontrollably and there was no stopping it. She managed to break him down instantly with only four words. It was the first time he had ever heard her say such a thing. For her to openly say her feelings aloud meant that she was in bad shape.

"Don't ever do that again..." she said. "You're my son..."

Tears continued to flow as his mom continued to speak words that had never left her mouth. As she held him, he hugged the basketball tightly.

He did not have the power to calm himself down enough to tell her the two words he wanted to say the most. *I'm sorry.*

She can hear me, he thought. *I don't know what to do. I love you...*

Gloria grasped him tighter. She heard his plea and could do nothing but console him the best she knew how. Comforting others was not her strength; nevertheless, her son needed a savior.

"You need to talk to your dad..." she whispered.

Abraham and Gloria cried together on the sidewalk. Her left arm held him close, and he cradled the basketball closer than he ever had.

Abraham composed himself enough to utter a few words. "I'll figure it out…"

"Abe, I've seen this before…" she sighed. "You're special…people are going to hate you, turn on you, belittle you…and they won't even know why," her words, heavier than she could bear. "I love you…I worry…because I'm afraid…that the world will reject you…because you're different…" Gloria forced her words out into the universe. She had seen what he could become, and the kind of man the world would potentially meet. She witnessed a future full of chaos and a future full of hope. Which one he would become would depend on his heart and soul and his choices. The choices of a man highly favored by the light, and the choices of a man tempted by the dark.

"You have a good heart…don't let the world turn it ugly." Gloria could only do her best as the inevitable was out of her hands. He had to face the wilderness, just like everybody else.

"I'll find a way…"

"I know you will…"

"I'll figure it out…I never give up hope."

"And that's why I believe you'll make a difference…don't get lost, Abe. You're my only son…"

Gloria embraced him like she once had twelve years prior. She dreaded the journey he was about to embark on, but unbeknownst to her, it had already begun.

"Come on," she said. "I'll call Margie."

"Why?" he asked with a puzzled look. "Margie knew I was gone?"

"She took the day off when we couldn't find you. She wanted to take you somewhere once we found you. I'll let her know you're alright."

"Where?" he asked.

"Somewhere that you need to go is all she said…"

He wiped away his tears. His emotions began to level out and, if he learned anything from the Batman, it was to recover quickly and move forward. Spiritually, he began forming a firm foundation, but his current mentors were from the Justice League of America. His research and reading material taught him more than any human being in the real world could, and these mentors taught him to better himself.

Rising from the sidewalk they heard shouts and yells in the distance. Pancho turned the corner in full sprint. His 205-pound frame carried him as fast as his legs would take him.

"Abraham!" Pancho yelled with urgency as loudly as his out-of-breath lungs would allow. "They're coming! Get down!"

An engine roared thunderously, and even a street over, the sound intimidated the neighbors in a three-block radius.

"Come on, Abe! Move!" Gloria demanded. "Get behind the truck!"

A few steps away sat his father's 1986 Chevy pick-up. The black truck boasted a mean exterior, and her hope was that it would shield them from the oncoming barrage.

The car skidded making its turn onto the street. The driver pressed on the gas fiercely, gunning for the house that had been targeted for retaliation. The gray colored Buick Regal picked up speed and with windows rolled down, two Uzis protruded from the four wheeled death machine.

"Moreno! You motherfucker!" one of the men yelled.

The Uzis pierced the midday air. The gunfire hit with extreme precision striking the house and truck. Bullets clanged on the metal frame of the truck. The dings echoed loudly as the glass windows shattered.

Abraham glanced at the speeding car and, for a split-second, made eye-contact with the passenger. The man harbored darkness in his face. His dark menacing eyes emitted hate and his grizzled beard dangled off his chin. His look was that of a man determined on exacting revenge. Abraham recognized the look of vengeance, as he had seen it a thousand times in his dreams.

This time, it was real, and the shock and awe of guns blasting were now being burned into his psyche.

"Tell your dad, we're comin'!" the man yelled. "And we won't stop!"

The rapid fire of bullets left his ears ringing and the blasts left a billow of smoke. Gloria lay on the pavement in shock of the ambush, and amid the madness, a body rested, dangling off the sidewalk and onto the street. Pancho was down.

Abraham rose quickly to check his friend's vitals.

"No, Abe! Stay down!" Gloria yelled, grabbing his ankle. She held on to it with all her strength. Abraham fell to the ground and in that moment, it was obvious this was only the first round of attacks. It was clear this faction sought revenge, nor would they hold back.

I have to train harder...

His father had not planned on the return of an old nemesis. A life which he left long ago, decided that it would not leave him.

His past had returned...to settle a score.

DARKNESS

The room was engulfed in darkness, suffocating in silence. The stench of mildew slithered throughout the space, and an eerie feeling surrounded it, like passing into another realm. The doorway was the only thing that separated the real world from the cold, black dimension that the central figure was cloaked in. Faint energy emanated from him, as he was consumed in darkness. His soul, deprived of light, was the essence that allowed him to manifest into the powerhouse he once was, but the fire that personified him could not enter. He sat alone, cold, and confused, for the darkness had taken hold. His defenses were down, and the blazing inferno that once burned proudly now looked deserted.

Each element of life he stood for was erased, and the glow in his eyes that had reigned for years nearly ceased. He was a shell of his former self. Sustaining the bombardment of tortured shadows took its toll. The darkness was a constant, delving into every pore of his body. The metamorphosis was well underway.

The darkness became more powerful with every waking moment he remained in this dimension. The odds of it relinquishing its grasp were slim, as it proved unforgiving. There was no person who could step so far into the realm of darkness and return fully resurrected. For some, this dimension of suffering was not a choice, but for those who became it unknowingly.

People die in this place.

Slowly and surely, he began his journey with darkness and death, hand in hand. The potential and greatness he possessed were dying with him as well. The darkness rejoiced in song, for if no light could enter, then there would be no tomorrow.

This manifestation did not abruptly happen. It surfaced from all that came before, triumph and tragedy, pain and love, misfortune and fate. The rollercoaster sent him drifting into a downward spiral. He partially prolonged his date with destiny, and this current title bout danced in darkness.

The shadows surrounding him needed no introduction. Being seduced by the darkness carried a price, and it could not be easily dispatched like an ordinary man. Avril had taken him to the limit once, but she was nowhere near what Abbadon had introduced to him. Brawling with that kind of darkness came with a cost.

"What am I fighting for?" he whispered somberly to himself.

The depth at which he was falling knew no bounds. His thought process functioned at a normal level, but the inevitable was upon him if he continued in this malignant state. On the outside, he sat statuesque, still as night, but on the inside, he began running his emotions on a higher state of consciousness. He reminisced on the life he had before, before the dark times, before the sickness, before the emptiness took hold of him. He remembered the light, the love, and everything that made him exist in near superhuman form. A rebellion, although in its infancy, was beginning to take shape. The time would soon come to challenge the Darkness, but not without sacrifice. With his soul on the line, he searched for a higher power, one that felt so far away.

"If God is for me, who can be against me?"

The light yearned for a resurrection, but the Darkness showed no mercy. This cloaked figure was bound to break in its wrath. Equipped with the power of persistence, he contemplated a high-powered assault from the gravitational forces that the black hole boasted. If he was to have a chance of defeating the Darkness, this battle would have to be fought on many different fronts, with the victor eventually emerging through time.

For now, he remained a figure shrouded in shadows. The light struggled to create a spark in this dimension where it was not allowed to exist. His soul, once filled with fire, had succumbed to the darkness, and he longed for a distance from this desecration. He waited for a sign of hope to reignite the fire within him. He waited and waited with each passing second…for a spark that would never come.

BEFORE
THE
STORM

braham's cocoon-like state was disturbed by rustling footsteps and muffled voices coming from the other side of the door. He finally stirred; his thoughts scrambled by hours of staring into oblivion. The voices became clearer as he regained consciousness. It was possible that a customer had come to see Grandma, but it was already late for visitors.

"Él está aquí. *He is here*," Grandma said, in exchange with the stranger.

"In his room?"

"Yo creo que sí. Él podría estar dormido. *Yes, I believe so. He might be asleep*," Grandma cautioned.

The voice belonged to a woman he hadn't had contact with for the past few days. Her voice sounded different from what he remembered.

On the other side of the door, the woman stopped, gathering herself. She took a deep breath and stood up straight. Hesitantly, she turned the knob to the right and gently pushed, causing the door to slowly squeak open. She approached timidly, inching her way into the darkness, trying to see through the shadows.

"Abraham?" she asked, looking for him.

It was his greatest love, the one he had known like no other. Her soul was cut from the same cloth as his. Surprisingly, she had come over at eleven o'clock at night, which was not typical of her. Strategically, she had learned plenty from the man she intended to rescue.

"Are you asleep?" Liv's sweet voice brightened the darkened room, but he was not strong enough to feel it.

She refused to turn on the lights in case he was asleep but decided to ask anyway. She rustled around in her purse, pulled out her cell phone, and pressed a button. The light from the phone was bright enough for her to navigate the darkened room.

"Baby?" she called out to him. "Baby," she said again, walking over to him.

There in the darkness, he sat in his chair, motionless and silent, looking down into obscurity. She would never have known he was there if it weren't for the light emanating from her phone. He sat still, camouflaged in the darkness, as he had become a part of it.

"Baby, what are you doing?" she asked, her tone filled with worry as she hunched over in front of him, desperately searching for his eyes.

"Just thinking," he said in a muffled tone.

"Why are you sitting here in the dark?" she questioned.

"I feel like…I'm falling…"

"Baby, what's wrong? I don't understand," she said, her voice shaking.

"…and I don't know how to stop…" he replied quietly.

He remembered the thousands of times she had called him "baby," and he had always liked the sound of her gentle voice. It had been soothing, as had her presence, but now it was different. As she kneeled down before him, trying to make sense of his strange ritual, her hands failed to comfort him in the way they had before. He was semi-aware of the events unfolding before him, but his lack of emotion was uncharacteristic.

"Baby, aren't you excited? You're about to close on your new house!" Liv said, desperate to bring him out of his funk.

"I need to leave this place…I promised my Grandma I wouldn't go far."

"I know she doesn't want you to leave, but living four houses over isn't bad," Liv said, trying to lighten the mood.

"I don't want her to see me like this anymore..." he said.

"Abraham, you're not alone. You have people who love you. We can help you. You need to breathe..." Liv said, sensing his anxiety. "I feel something is really bothering you. Are you sad?" Tears rolled down her cheeks. Her empathic abilities kicked in. "I don't understand why you're so cold and numb. I love you, please tell me what's wrong?"

"I feel lost..."

"Oh, love..." she said, relieved that he finally spoke. "...you're Abraham, the 'S,' the Instructor! You're a lion, you're the sun, and you're the fiercest leader I know. You'll find a way..." Liv did her best to lift his spirits, but her instincts sensed the odds against her.

"I think I'm having trouble because it's something new...I haven't dealt with his death fully...and I don't know how. I've never experienced this before, so I don't know how to get all the way through..." he said. "Before...I could always find a way, and now, I'm struggling...I'm all over the place..."

"Have you talked to God about it?" she asked innocently. "Would you say you're a bit angry with Him?"

"...I'm losing my way. I used to be resilient...recover within twenty-four hours, and if something or someone didn't serve the greater good, then I'd walk out in ten seconds flat..."

"My soul can comfort you, but it won't heal you. Healing comes from within, and you know this..." Liv said.

"I thought I could recover, just like I've done countless times, but this is different. I took a hard hit...and I didn't even know it..." Abraham turned away from her. Although the shadows hid direct eye-contact, he refused to face her, even in the blackness. "Losing someone you love is hard...he was my best friend...my brother. This is a place I've never been before..."

"Abraham, it's okay...we'll get through this...it's been a rough few months. You never give up hope, remember? Isn't that your code?"

"Yeah...I never give up hope...maybe hope is giving up on me..."

"You know that's not true. How can you say that?" Liv struggled to reason with him.

"You of all people know that words are powerful. They can build people up, just like you always do for others, or they can bring people down. Don't speak life to negative nonsense."

"I'm sorry, my feelings are all over the place and some are even missing…I don't know how to love anymore…"

"You're full of love…and you know how to channel it." Liv placed her hand on his cheek.

"That's what soulmates do for each other, remember? We teach one another and we learn from each other," Liv said.

"I feel like I was so full of light…" Abraham sighed heavily. "…did I fight so hard and give all the light I had, and now it's like a blackout? Nothing left…"

Liv cupped both of his hands in hers. "Abraham, you fought for the right reasons."

"But at what cost? I'm falling…and I can't stop."

"Then Abraham, you get back up! You fight harder!"

"The Angel of the Abyss is dragging me down…"

"Abaddon, you mean?" Liv asked, though she already knew the answer.

"I'm angry and I'm hurt. I admit it." Abraham lowered his head in defeat. The Darkness clasped onto him and held on tight. He struggled not to break under its wrath, but doubt and guilt piled onto him. "I'm tired of waging war…"

"Abraham, we don't even have a choice. War is always upon us. Spiritual warfare is ongoing…" Liv placed her right hand on his heart. It had been damaged, and his aura was fading. "This kind of war doesn't end, you know this. You have fought to keep hope alive. Don't give up!"

Liv then placed her hand in his. Hope had always been a constant in their relationship, and she counted on hope to bring him back this time. Each bout was more treacherous than the last, and she needed hope to keep her spirits lifted as well.

He grasped her ring finger and, with his thumb, gently rubbed the stone on her ring.

"Do you remember when you got that for me?" she asked sweetly.
He nodded slowly, reminiscing about a time so long ago.

✝

Abraham and Liv walked onto the site with a slew of people from the tour bus.

"Ok, everyone, welcome to our factory in beautiful Honolulu, where the finest jewelry is made in Hawaii! You might be asking yourself, 'what makes this factory so different?' Well, because of the volcanic activity, this factory is the only one in the world that makes jewelry from black coral. It is so rare that the reefs in Hawaii are the only place in the world where black coral is found. As you can see behind me, through the glass windows, our employees are hard at work putting together these fine pieces of jewelry. Folks, please feel free to look around as this is also a jewelry store…" The tour guide whisked away as tourists flooded the store. Abraham shot a wide-eyed glance at Liv.

"Did you hear that!? Black coral is found only here! I didn't even know that was such a thing."

"They have some nice pieces. Wow, black stones and diamonds look really good together," she said as she perused the glass cases.

"Dang, this one is expensive! Fifteen hundred bucks!? Black coral ain't no joke! I should get a handful of these and sell them back in—"

"Baby! Oh my gosh! I love that ring, right there!" Liv pointed to a tiny ring underneath the glass. Her eyes lit up with wonder, and Abraham admired her without making it too obvious. She was oblivious to her surroundings, and he smiled at her, nevertheless. He didn't mind. His plan was to be in the moment without a care in the world, and now, he was watching it unfold before him as her light brown eyes screamed in amazement.

"Would you like to take a look at that one?" An older gentleman asked from behind the counter.

"No," Liv said.

"Yes," Abraham interjected.

"No, it's okay, thank you," Liv said with a conflicted look on her face.

"Yes, sir, please. We'd love to take a closer look at it," Abraham said, looking straight into her eyes. "We're gonna look at it, okay?"

Liv sighed with excitement. "Okay."

The older gentleman smirked at the young couple. From the looks of it, it certainly was not the first time he had seen an indecisive duo quarrel over a closer glance at the black coral.

"It's a gorgeous piece. Not too big, not too small..." he said, reaching for the elegant ring.

"Can we see it in a size six and a half, please?" Abraham kindly requested. He grinned at Liv, winking at her subtly.

Liv smiled, rolling her eyes and shaking her head. Here we go, she thought, his adventurous whims.

"I do believe we have that size," the gentleman said.

"How much is that ring, sir?" Abraham inquired.

"And here we go...this ring is three hundred and fifty dollars. Try it on, young lady," he said to Liv.

Liv's eyes widened as she was in awe of the piece. "Baby, it's beautiful...but it's expensive..." she whispered.

"Well, do you like it?" Abraham asked. He couldn't hold back his huge smile. Caressing the back of her arm, he could feel the charge of excitement flow through her.

"I love it!" She cuddled the oval black coral stone in the middle. On each side, it carried two small diamonds. Both diamonds sparkled, complementing the black stone like it was the star of the show.

"Sir," Abraham turned to the gentleman, "we'll take it."

"All right, no problem...would you like to wear it out, young lady?" the gentleman asked.

"Yes, sir!" Abraham and Liv responded simultaneously and in unison. They turned to each other and laughed at their synchronicity.

Liv pulled him closer, whispering in his ear. "It's too much, it's okay, baby...you don't have to..."

Abraham sighed at her request. He grabbed her hand and kissed it. "I know you love the ring and I know you really want it and I'm gonna get it for you…"

"Why would you do that?" she asked innocently.

"This…" he pointed to the ring, "is for being good to me."

She smiled, admiring his antics.

"That was when times were simpler…before the darkness…before I lost my way…" As much as he didn't want to admit he had changed, that memory served as a testament to his current state.

"I refuse to believe…that the man I love…so full of life…a man of God…a lion, with a heart full of fire…sits in front of me, as a stranger…" she sniffled, "…burned out and cold." Glancing over to his desk, an award plaque glimmered in the faint light. It read:

Teacher of the Year
2004-2005

She admired the plaque and resented it at the same time. "I can't compete with that, can I? A year has passed, and you've gotten worse and worse. The only thing to bring you happiness is your class of Pre-K kids…I wish it was me that could still do that for you…"

Hope kept him alive and now she sensed he was losing his grip.

"What can I do to bring you back? Anything?"

Teaching Pre-K was the life support he needed to stay holding. Jealousy ran through her thoughts and throwing the award to the wall would make matters worse. She glanced at the 8x10 picture hanging on the wall. Her white and red hibiscus Hawaiian garment draped her body gloriously. He wore his white polo with red stripes to match his white Air Force One high tops that was capped off with a red swoosh. *We were happy,* she thought. They both smiled as hula dancers stood on each side of them. Jermaine's Luau in Honolulu seemed like a distant land that he never fully returned from.

"Abraham, you made it…you have everything! You have a career, a fancy car, a house you'll move into next week, and you have me by your side! You came from nothing and made yourself into a person destined to change the world," she said. Perspective was a tactic she used previously, but now she was reaching farther into her bag of tricks.

Her words triggered memories of the man he once was, a man he could barely remember, much less, one that he could still be.

"What good is it…for a man to gain the world…yet lose his own soul in the process?" he mumbled. Abraham rummaged through his failings. "I know how he felt, now. Not being able to feel…not being able to love…" he said somberly, "…have I now become him? I don't know who I am anymore."

"He did this to you…but you're still good, Abraham…" *He's still alive in there,* she thought. "I can bring him back," she whispered. "I stood by you through all of it, but I can't stand to watch you like this. Abraham, you're better than this. You're a good man, so full of love, a love that knows no bounds. I don't believe that these shadows have overtaken you. Come home to me…please," she said softly.

"I didn't pray *for* him, and I didn't pray *over* him…in those final moments…I did nothing…just let him slip away. I couldn't save him in life, and I did nothing for him in death…how am I supposed to live with that?"

"Is that what your faith has taught you!? You used to ask me, what am I made of?" she reminded him. "What are you made of? You're better than this!"

Abraham slowly rose from his chair with a blanket draped over him, doubling as a cloak.

He stood in the dark. A man without purpose.

"Have you talked to Margie yet?" Liv asked, her voice laced with desperation. *If I'm going to bring him out of this, I can't do it by myself,* she thought.

"No. I don't want to bother her with this," he replied stubbornly.

"She's your advisor, Abraham," Liv implored. "She's always been there for you. You don't have to go through this alone."

"I can fight this on my own," he insisted, his voice tinged with frustration.

His damn ego, she thought. "Abraham, don't underestimate the darkness…you're not thinking clearly." Her frantic attempt to reason with the man she loved was no use.

Liv's heart shattered into a million pieces. She knew he was slipping away, and she didn't know how to bring him back. "Please, don't leave me," she begged, tears streaming down her face. "I love you, Abraham. Please come back to me."

But her words fell on deaf ears. He remained unresponsive, lost in the darkness that consumed him. Liv clung to him desperately, hoping that her touch would somehow bring him back.

Her worst fear was upon her. She hoped he would say something to keep her heart holding together, but that hope was dying fast. Her sniffles were loud in a room filled with silence. She was losing her grip on the man she loved and so she grabbed onto the left side of his body, one arm on his chest and the other on his back as she rested her head on his shoulder blade. Her sideways hug played tug of war with the darkness that clenched onto him tightly.

"You're not taking him. You won't win," she whispered fiercely to the darkness, her grip on Abraham tightening. But the darkness only seemed to grow stronger, suffocating him in its embrace.

The Darkness wrapped around the other half of his body. "This time, I will succeed," it whispered to her in the darkened room.

LIGHT
OF THE
WORLD

A figure draped in a glistening white garb passed through the shining golden gates. The Light radiated with such brilliance that an ordinary man would have been blinded, yet the figure remained unfazed. The calm tranquil beams summoned the figure, and it was considered the highest honor to seek counsel and orders firsthand from the Light.

The messenger bore massive feathery white wings on its back and walked humbly, sauntering through the soft delicate ground. Its cherub rosy face radiated humility and gratitude as it addressed the Light.

"Lord, what shall we do?" the messenger asked.

"Watch over him. He will be tested, but not more than he is able to withstand."

"Our adversaries are after him and will make full efforts soon."

"Yes. His choices will determine his steps. They will make him stronger, or they will break him. This test is administered to all my children."

"Lord, you sent him to do a mission…is he meant to succeed, ultimately?"

"His choices will lead him to destiny or darkness. Only he can choose to come to Me."

The Light gleamed without a flicker, and its strong, soothing presence gave the messenger a final order.

"And only then will he be blessed beyond measure…"

SPRING TRAINING AND TACTICS

IV

Spring 1988

Abraham swung the bat as hard as he could, and a cracking sound echoed into the outfield. The baseball bolted out to center field, farther than he had ever hit a ball before. He walloped seven or eight in a row into right, left, and centerfield.

Ray showed up just in time to catch the spectacle. Although it was only practice and not an actual game, Abraham felt powerful and confident. The bat felt amazing in his hands, like a magical wand that could shoot out flares at will. He wished it was his own bat that was serving up the magic. The one Ray had bought for him just days before felt like a waste compared to the mystical connection he had forged with the practice bat.

Coach Castro grinned at Abraham's uncharacteristic display. The team had been used to him striking out every time he came up to bat. Coach Castro pitched much like an eight-year-old would; not too fast, but not too slow. "Chato!" he would say after every hit, whatever that meant. Maybe it meant he was hitting them right on the nose, or maybe it meant he was just getting lucky. Abraham didn't care. He was on a high he'd never felt before, and finally, Ray got to see him full of electricity, belting out ball after ball as if he were bulletproof.

"Alright, let's pack it up! Moreno's getting too cocky!" Coach Castro said as he could see Abraham's eyes light up.

The team huddled around Coach at the pitcher's mound. The sun dipped further into the horizon, and it was a day that Abraham could finally have a good night's sleep, knowing it was possible not to be the worst player on the team.

"Y'all did good today. Get some rest for tomorrow's game...and Moreno, bring that swing with you tomorrow," Coach said with a smirk.

Ray waved Abraham down, his brow crinkled. The black truck accompanied Ray's presence with the same ferocity. Abraham swooped around to the passenger door and before he could open it, he noticed a dusty footprint on the sidestep of the bed of the truck.

Oh man, one of my friends climbed in to get the ball that flew into the back of the truck the other day...he's gonna think I lied...

"Which bat were you using?" Ray asked.

"Rene's," Abraham said.

"I bought you a fuckin' bat and you don't even use it!" Ray scolded.

The truck filled with expletives during the seven-minute ride home.

Abraham hopped out of the truck as slowly as he could without being obvious. He was ready to receive the rage monster that was coming in the form of Ray.

Ray gave him a wallop to the backside. "Why didn't you use the bat I got you?" he asked, again. Abraham shrugged his shoulders. The truth was, he had forgotten the bat, and it was a good thing he did because he would have never felt the power of confidence. But that didn't matter to Ray. It was no use explaining to him, either. Taking unnecessary hits was what he had grown accustomed to.

Ray delivered another blow to Abraham's back. It was 7 pm, and the neighbors surely noticed the debacle. It was as if Ray wanted to embarrass Abraham in front of his friends next door. Surely, they peeped through a window as Ray's voice bellowed enough to spur a peek through the blinds. The confidence bolstering through him less than a half-hour before dwindled to a showcase of humiliation.

Abraham lowered his head deep into the pavement. The pebbles at his feet were as small as he was now, and he didn't dare look at the nearby houses in case he made eye contact with one of the street kids. Ray's obnoxious rant failed to cease.

Just yell at me inside the house…hit me where no one has to watch…it's like he loves to put on a show…he doesn't have to shout for everyone to hear…showing off like he's so tough…look strong, Abraham…don't show weakness…act like it doesn't hurt…

Abraham refused to look at anything but the ground. He crumbled inside, but he didn't show a sign of how badly bruised his spirit was.

This isn't right…my dad should be happy for me…not beating me in the street for not having my bat…I finally did it…I didn't suck today…

"Get inside the house!" Ray yelled.

Abraham slinked into the house. He just wanted to go to bed and sleep the embarrassment away. Ray never missed an opportunity to demonstrate his power of authority, even at the cost of his son's spirit.

Abraham crashed onto his bed. He closed his eyes, and just as the tears welled up inside his eyelids, they quickly subsided as anger replaced them. Dusk surrounded the bedroom when he heard his name.

"Aba!" Ray called. "Come here."

Abraham scraped himself off his bed. *Here we go. Another round.* He crept into the living room. Ray's eyes were gentle and a far cry from the angered behemoth earlier.

"Why didn't you tell me the bat was in my truck?" Ray asked.

Abraham barely nudged his head.

"I'm sorry, dad. You should've told me. I didn't know you left it in the truck," Ray said. The guilt slithered out of his mouth, and the words were hollow like a dead tree. Abraham had grown all too familiar with Ray's antics, but he was beginning to formulate tactics to evade such encounters.

Another beating was sure to come. Ray missed the dusty footprint on the sidestep of the black Ford truck. It would only take a day or two at most for him to find it. He'd surely be out on the street again, humiliated for all to see. In the meantime, he would practice building himself up for the next round.

Batman always has a way out…Superman is always strong enough to take a hit…

Preparing himself for onslaughts meant life would certainly be a treat.

If my own dad can beat on me for no good reason, then why would I think anyone else would treat me any different?

COLLISION COURSE

The temptation was too strong for Ray, and he quickly stepped out of the house. The mechanical beast, an M3 BMW, glimmered in the driveway. Ray had already tasted its power and was now addicted to joyriding the silver sports car. "Why wouldn't I?" he thought to himself. "Abe's not driving it around a whole lot anyway."

"Ray," Gloria said, her concern evident in her tone. "Don't take his car. It's not yours to cruise around in."

"Don't worry," Ray replied confidently. "I'll be right back. He won't even know I'm gone."

"Okay, but if something happens, I already warned you," Gloria said.

Despite Gloria's warnings, Ray had a habit of overlooking boundaries for immediate gratification. He was notorious for his recklessness, and his stride as he walked over to Grandma Marcella's was more of an arrogant strut than a casual stroll.

"Grandma," he burst through the door, "I'm gonna take Abe's keys."

Grandma Marcella shot him a look of disapproval. "Es mejor que no lo tomes. *You better not take it,*" she warned.

"Grandma, I'm just going for a ride!" Ray exclaimed. "You and Gloria need to relax already, damn!" Ray grabbed the keys and rushed out of the door, jumping into the M3. He inserted the key into the ignition, and the engine roared to life. He boasted his presence on the street as he backed out of the driveway, revving the engine brashly. His exhilaration reached new heights as the back tires screeched violently, and he zoomed down the street with reckless abandon.

Abraham heard a tune that had worn out its welcome and hobbled over to answer his ringing cellphone.

"Hello?" he answered, his tone already irritated.

"Abe, I already warned your dad. He's at it again," Gloria's voice came through the line. "I told him not to take it."

"He took my car!? What's his deal? It's not his to be cruising around in!" Abraham barked, frustration seeping through his voice.

"Calm down, he said he was coming right back," Gloria tried to placate him.

"Fuck that! It's not his! What part does he not get about that? And what's up with the new name!? It doesn't make sense!" he shouted.

"Abe, it's his past…you know he had a hard upbringing, and it's for safety, too," Gloria reminded him.

"Safety? I don't think that's gonna make a difference. I'm sure they can still track him," Abraham replied sarcastically.

"You know how it is, Abe. He had to change it, so he compromised by changing it as little as possible. He said he doesn't need to hide from anybody," Gloria explained. "Anyway, I just wanted to let you know."

"Does that mean a war is coming?" Abraham asked.

"I hope not, Abe," she replied softly.

"If he'd stop living reckless, then *Ray* wouldn't be in this predicament!" Abraham hung up and threw the phone like a fastball onto the couch.

"Hey, is the deal still on?" Ray barked into his cell phone.

"Yeah, Ray. Are you on your way?" The voice on the other end was all business, not interested in small talk.

"I'm in my son's car. It's bad ass, dude! You should see it, bro! I'll be there in ten minutes. As soon as I get there, I'm gonna need to--" Ray slammed on the breaks. The screech of tires blazed onto the pavement. The smell of burning rubber left a trail of smoke. The M3 swerved left and right, fishtailing off the exit ramp. An eighteen-wheeler in front was at a complete stop, backed up from the evening traffic. Ray managed to regain some control, but it was too late.

BOOM!

The M3 never stood a chance.

Abraham paced back forth in the driveway like a lion waiting to pounce on his prey. His emotions unraveled and anger assimilated his consciousness. "Now is my chance to confront him and make him pay…" His brow furrowing and his eyes darkening. "…it's my turn to rip into him like he did me."

The Darkness called to him, tempting him with the promise of power and control. The deal for his soul had tipped the balance in the Darkness' favor, and it reveled in Abraham's anger, using it to transform him into the agent it craved him to be.

A black crow cawed just above him as it sat on a branch of the oak tree above. The Darkness did not shy from taking various forms and it had a front row seat to the show it carefully orchestrated.

As he paced faster and faster, the walkway leading to the driveway felt like a lion's pen, and Abraham was ready to pounce. The venom of anger seeped into his veins, and his heart pounded with fury.

"This is the moment where he will break," The Darkness cawed. *"Sire, will be pleased."*

In the distance, the M3's engine roared, and Abraham recognized the intricacies of the car's power. The vehicle was more than just a means of transportation—it was a friend, a loyal companion. The pair had shared countless adventures, and if the M3 could talk, it would have been privy to many secrets that could potentially alter Abraham's life. Even though mechanical issues had occurred prematurely for the three-year-old vehicle, it remained steadfast and dependable, which was why Abraham had given it the nickname, "Steel."

As the M3 turned the corner, Abraham surveyed the damage immediately. "Mother fucker!" he swore under his breath. The once-provocative curvature of the hood was now smashed back into itself, creating a horrible 90-degree angle. The kidney grills were cracked and hanging on for dear life. The rattling noise underneath the hood left Abraham bursting with rage.

All those times he embarrassed me, scolding me in front of the neighbors and all my friends...yelled at me, whipped me on the street for all to see...never giving me a chance to explain...it's my turn, mother fucker. Now, I'm gonna do the scolding for all the neighborhood to see...

Ray opened the door and stepped out of the BMW.

"What the fuck?" Abraham demanded.

"Dude, this truck came out of nowhere and—"

"They told you not to take it, and you did!"

"Well, I—"

"No, I don't want to hear it! It's not yours to take! Who's going to pay for it to get fixed? You?"

No, Abraham. Stop. Don't do this. You can level out...

"Your mom will help you, man, come on..."

"No, she didn't wreck it, you did! She shouldn't have to pay for the damage. *You* should!" Abraham shouted.

"It wasn't my fault...the damn truck, it—"

Grandma rushed outside, further escalating the debacle. "¿Que paso? Yo te dije no te llevas! ¿Qué hiciste? *What happened? I told you not to take it! What did you do?"*

Ray attempted to explain. "Grandma, I'm glad you asked. The floor mat was sticking up and got stuck on the gas, and when I pushed the brake, it didn't stop …"

Furious at his excuse, Abraham struggled to control his emotions. "You shouldn't have taken it!" he barked.

It was no use. Wrath overcame him. His self-talks could only peep out a sentence or two these days and within a split-seconds notice, the recovery washed away. "It's all fucked up! And *you* fucked it up! I worked hard for this shit and you wanna fuckin' joy ride for fun and then shit happens and you can't do shit about it!"

"Dude, I'm sorry. Damn," Ray said.

Abraham continued to lash out, unrelenting. "You're going to pay for all the damages!"

"I told you…your mom will help you," Ray replied.

Infuriated, Abraham countered, "She shouldn't have to!"

The scolding Ray received took its toll, igniting his fury. "*This motherfucker! He doesn't know who he's fucking with!*"

Abraham's vitals spiked. "Now what the fuck am I gonna do without a car!? I have to get to work in it! You don't have a job you need to get to, but I do!"

The neighborhood noticed the commotion. Finally, he could reprimand his father and embarrass him. Finally, he had his revenge. Abraham held his emotions in check all these years, and his chance had arrived to allow them to spew all over the street and sidewalk. He sprayed Ray with noxious words.

Ray, however, underwent an instantaneous transformation. "Who do you think you're talking to, boy?"

"What?"

"I'm your dad! I don't let anyone talk to me that way, not even my son! You have something else to say to me?" Ray crept closer to Abraham, standing toe-to-toe, his left eye peering into Abraham's.

Abraham seethed with anger. "Yeah, don't ever drive my car again!" he snarled, with Ray three inches away from his face. *All I need is for this motherfucker to swing! Come on! I can take him, now! I'm not that little boy, anymore, that he used to beat on!*

Less than three years prior, Ray significantly outweighed Abraham by nearly fifty pounds, but Abraham had closed the gap to a twenty-pound difference thanks to his training. Both men, standing at five foot seven, were nearly evenly matched, apart from Ray having fought more bouts than his younger counterpart.

"It's happening…he's transforming…" the Darkness cawed with pleasure.

Abraham inched closer, his chest puffed up, and he stood his ground.

"I do whatever I want!" Ray said.

"And I'm gonna do whatever the *fuck* I want!" Abraham countered.

Grandma Marcella sensed the reckoning. "No te vas a pelear! *You better not fight."*

Ray put his palms on Abraham's chest and pushed him away as hard as he could. The force knocked Abraham back five feet into the driveway.

Enraged, he set his sights on attacking. "You fucked up now, Ray!" Abraham charged back, but just before he could strike, Gloria ran from the house.

"Abraham, stop!" she screamed. She stepped in between the two men. The escalation had drawn both lions to beat each other down.

"Fuck him!" Abraham yelled.

"Ray, stop! Y'all need to stop!" Gloria shouted.

"Fuck you! You're a pussy! You've always been a pussy! I'll kick your ass! You ain't shit!" Ray retorted.

"Get the fuck out of here! Fuck you!" Abraham countered.

"Mijo, no te peleas! *Love, don't fight!"* Grandma shouted.

Gloria guided Abraham away, back into Grandma's front yard and into her custody. The fight was over…for now.

VI

THE BASEMENT

Bob was his name, or so the neighbors thought. He never said hello, never gave a wave or any kind of salutation. He appeared to be in his sixties and dressed simply - jeans and a button-down shirt that was always tucked in. A ring of gray hair crowned the top of his bald head, and he had the look of a humble man. A humble, but mysterious man.

After dark, things turned creepy. Racket and flashes of light escaped from his house, along with wails that sounded like the abominable snowman. Whispers throughout the neighborhood spread wild theories. Mark said it was Bigfoot in the basement and that Bob was conducting experiments on the beast. Ms. Carpenter said it was the infamous Chupacabra down there, and its roars kept her up at night because it slept during the day. Others said that Bob was a cannibal and when he couldn't smuggle in fresh meat, he kept bear cubs to feed on in case of a drought.

Abraham hadn't the slightest clue, but whatever was down there flaunted wicked intentions, nor was it there by accident. At night, it became ferociously unstable, and these days, dusk fell rather quickly on the Alamo City.

The sound of clanking chains grew louder, piercing the stillness of the night and echoing throughout the surrounding houses. Light shimmered from a window at the bottom of the house, where the enigmatic monster was caged in the basement. Secrets were stashed away in that basement, where dreams were vanquished, and hope was lost. The struggle spilled over from the basement, onto the dew-soaked grass, and into the neighboring house, enveloping an occupant cocooned in darkness. The beast seemed to sense the presence of the darkness surrounding Abraham, and the dying soul within him. Each breath that Abraham took was indicative of a man dying a slow death, and the hope he held onto for so long was now fading away. He had once fought for its cause without hesitation, and defiantly overcame doubt so that hope could live. But now, hope was drifting onto life support.

A vicious roar interrupted his defeated thoughts, sparking fear in the neighborhood. Abraham had grown used to the growl and even welcomed its pleas. He and the beast shared an uncanny predicament, both chained by anger and darkness, unable to break free. The beast flailed with urgency, struggling to reach the surface. Whatever was in that basement would surely make its way to the ground level and, in time, eventually meet the man who remained blanketed in darkness.

It was meant to be this way. Soon, they would meet, but not without struggle.

VII BUELA THE WISE

He whispered to himself as he stared into the mirror, "This is not who I am." He took a moment to examine his physical changes before entering the kitchen, where Grandma was cooking breakfast. He didn't want her to worry. Aunt Margie had left her dresser and a large mirror in the dining room when she moved out a few years prior. He wondered if she had left it on purpose to show him what he had become.

He had never experienced such depths of depression before, and he was rapidly losing altitude. His sense of direction was off, and like a ship lost at sea, he didn't know which way to go. Happiness and sadness no longer existed in his world. He was just passing through time. Most of the passionate emotions he once felt were the first to go, and every aspect of his life and well-being was slowly deteriorating.

His appearance reflected this deterioration. His once strong and healthy physique was now a thing of the past. He was soft in places that were once hard and indestructible, and his psyche had been severely damaged.

Maybe, I'm not meant to make a difference...

As he scanned his body up and down, he could see the physical and psychological changes even through the tank top and basketball shorts, which had become his primary clothing preferences. Muscle had been replaced by flab, and his strong persona had been assimilated into the mediocre operation of the rest of the world. What he saw in the mirror disgusted him.

The aroma of eggs and bacon wafted from the kitchen, beckoning him out of his room for a midday brunch. He entered the kitchen sluggishly and took a seat at the tiny table.

"Hey, Grandma," he said.

"Mijo! Ya te levantaste! *Love! You woke up!*" Grandma exclaimed.

"Grandma, I'm on summer break. I have two and a half months to do nothing."

"Tienes que salir y hacer algo. *You need to get out and do something.*"

"Grandma, what do you mean?"

"Ve a tomar un poco de sol y ponte fuera de la oscuridad. *Go get some sun and get out of the dark,*" she said to him.

"The dark?" he asked curiously.

Grandma Marcella stirred the pot of beans on the stove and began to explain without missing a beat, "Si vas a permanacer en el oscuridad, entonces te acostumbrarás. *If you're going to stay in the dark, then you're going to get used to it.*"

Her words hit too close to home. Had she guessed his current condition? Had she experienced this kind of darkness before?

His thoughts became scrambled as the front door swung open and slammed vigorously behind the guest who entered. "If it's Dad, I don't need to hear his lip today," he whispered to himself. The visitor walked into the kitchen, but the smell of perfume gave her away immediately.

"Hey, Ma! What are you making?" the visitor questioned as she glanced at the table. "Oh, it's for the little boy! Tu hijo! *Your son!*" Margie would make her occasional appearance at Grandma's house, and, after all, she had only been four years removed from residing there.

"Are you taking care of my room, little boy?" she asked.

"It's *my* room now."

"You're ready to leave the nest," she said with a laugh. "When do you move into Joe's old house?"

"Next week."

"About time, little boy. You need your own space. It'll be good for you. It's been vacant for twenty years…you better clean it up real nice, little boy," Margie said.

"Mijo, no te vayas. Quédate aquí conmigo. *Love, don't go. Stay here with me,*" Grandma Marcella said.

"Don't worry, Grandma, I'm not far away," he said. Grandma Marcella had been there his whole life. Deep down, he couldn't leave her. He had found a home suitable to continue his journey and keep her close. She practically raised him, and together they made a great team.

"Ma, he needs to get his own place. Let him be," Margie said. Aunt Margie was the mom he needed, and she too played an integral part in his life. She listened to his doubts and fears, the only one who ever did. His secrets were safe with her. Ever since he ran away, she was the one who had been his confidant, his rock, when the world turned upside down. Her wise words comforted him, and they resonated deep into his soul. She was spiritual, not the overzealous forceful type, but the quiet and confident spiritual warrior. He had witnessed her supernatural feats, and one thing was certain: she had God on her side.

Margie is right. I need to leave this house. Something is coming…

The Darkness…
I see it in my dreams.
Unrelenting…
Projecting anger…
It's in my mind…and I can't get it out.
The fighting…I'm tired.
Its poison has seeped into my soul…

I need to break free. I can't drag Margie and Grandma into this. I have to do this on my own.

"Hey, maid!" Margie called to him. "You need to cook your own food." Margie turned to Grandma Marcella. "Ma, let him cook his own breakfast! He should be *your* maid!"

Grandma Marcella laughed as if she had gotten caught being mischievous. "¿Quieres comer? *Want to eat?*"

"No, it's ok, Ma. I brought barbecue from Bill Miller's."

"El no quiere comer! Estoy forzándolo! *He doesn't want to eat! I'm forcing him!*" Grandma shouted as she served Abraham a plate of eggs and bacon with a side of *frijoles*, just the way he liked it.

Margie sat across from him, pulling out her meal from the bag. Between bites of barbecue, she snuck in a few glances unbeknownst to him. "Grandma says you've been in your room all day. What's going on?"

"Nothing's going on...I just want to be by myself," Abraham replied.

Margie studied him further. *He's not telling me the truth.* "And Liv? You better be treating her good, boy!" she added.

Abraham shook his head solemnly.

Margie knew better. He might fool Grandma, she thought, but he doesn't fool me. "Do you remember when I took you to the Oblate church?" she asked.

"Yeah...why?" Abraham replied.

"This right here," she said, pointing in a circular motion at him, "is what that reminds me of...when you ran away. You were twelve-years-old..." Margie's tone switched to a serious one. She lived more in the spiritual realm and was aware of the darkness. "Did Grandma ever tell you the story of the Lechuza? Did she tell you I saw one?"

"No, y'all never told me..." Abraham paused. Disclosure of the legend that Margie spoke of meant that his descent would further. "I mean, I know a little bit about the story, but I didn't know you saw one..."

"It was outside the window of my room, *your* room. It was big and ugly..."

"Like, how big?" he asked.

"As big as you, but it had a woman's face, and the body was like an owl. They say they come to bring evil, so I prayed as soon as I saw it. I kept saying, 'I rebuke you in the name of Jesus,' and after a few seconds, it flew away."

"What does that mean...'I rebuke you in the name of Jesus?'" Abraham asked.

"Anytime you feel evil around you, that means the devil is near. Spiritual warfare is real, little boy, and when that happens, you say it, and the devil will flee because God is always with you, fighting for you, if you let Him..."

"I rebuke you in the name of Jesus," he whispered, trying to remember it. "So...why an owl? How did this story even come about?"

"Well," Margie said as she chewed on a piece of brisket. "A lady sold her soul to the devil, and in exchange, she became a witch. A little old lady during the day...and an ugly owl at night..."

"Mijo, no te quedes en el oscuro. *Love, don't stay in the dark.*" Grandma Marcella warned.

"Don't let it win..." Margie said, pointing at him. "It's okay to fall...nobody's perfect. Just don't stay there."

"I'll recover. I've done it before, and I'll do it again," he whispered. His ego answered, but his spirit resided in the dominion of defeat.

"And don't sell your soul. Sometimes we forget what we're doing, and we get lost and confused. That's when thoughts get distorted. Sin becomes normal, and we mistake evil for good. That's the most dangerous way to be. Look at the fall of Satan...even he was once an angel," Margie warned. "Pray, think good thoughts, and when you think you're falling, ask God to come into your heart. He's always with you."

"I'll try..."

Abraham listened intently to the two women who helped raise him since the day he was born. His half-eaten plate was uncharacteristic, and he surrendered his fork as he pushed the plate aside. He sat still, as time, and more importantly, the world, passed him by.

Margie pointed her finger at him. "Don't sell your soul, little boy. Don't sell your soul..."

VIII SHADOW HUNTER

Abraham's heart raced as he surveyed the dark alley, searching for any familiar landmarks. It looked like a place he'd been before, but he couldn't quite place it. Shadows flickered along the walls, whispering secrets that he couldn't comprehend.

He patted himself down, feeling the unfamiliar weight of black clothing against his skin. He couldn't recall owning this set of clothes.

This has to be a dream...

The faint glow of a streetlight beckoned from the other end of the alley, illuminating fresh graffiti along the walls. Abraham couldn't make out the words, but he could sense the tension in the air. Garbage and decay mixed with the acrid scent of urine assaulted his senses.

Two dumpsters loomed on the right, and whispers seemed to emanate from one of them. Abraham took a few cautious steps forward, steeling himself for what lay ahead.

A figure in black emerged from behind the dumpster, sporting a fancy fedora and a long coat that trailed along the ground. The man's eyes burned with a fierce intensity as he approached, and Abraham couldn't help but feel a sense of familiarity.

"I've been waiting for you," the stranger said calmly.

Abraham tensed, his hand instinctively reaching for a weapon that wasn't there. He couldn't shake the feeling that this man was dangerous.

"What do you want?" Abraham demanded, his voice firm.

"The darkness doesn't shy away from people like you," the stranger replied, extending a hand towards the shadows. "In this alley, you can become one with the darkness."

Abraham took a step back, feeling a creeping sense of fear. "I don't understand."

The stranger smirked. "I can play on your fears, or you can join me and avoid the pain."

Abraham weighed his options, his mind racing with possibilities. *I can take him. My chances are good.* Was there any other way out of this dark, twisted world?

"I need to get out of here," he whispered, his eyes darting around for an escape.

But the stranger wasn't finished with him yet. "The darkness is all you see," he said with confidence. "And soon, it will be all you know."

The voice had a familiar quality to it. Abraham had heard it before, and it made his skin crawl. It was a mix of a low growl and a human voice, but the balance between the two was anything but natural.

This is not an ordinary man.

Abraham braced himself, knowing that he was in for the fight of his life. The darkness was closing in, and he wasn't sure he'd be able to escape its grasp.

IX THE RETURN

Flares of light flickered under the door of Grandma's sewing room, casting luminous shapes onto the dim hallway. The sound of shuffling footsteps grew louder and closer.

"He's in there," Grandma whispered to the stranger. The footsteps stopped just behind the door.

Abraham couldn't help but think of Liv. She had never given up on him, even when all seemed lost. In the last couple of years, he had taught her that hope was tangible, something real. And she had fought to keep him afloat, even as he sank deeper into darkness.

She pushed the door open slowly, letting the light flood in and illuminate the slumped figure in the chair.

"Always sitting in the dark...I should've known," she said.

He raised his hand to shield his eyes from the sudden brightness. His vision was growing worse every day.

"Liv?"

The stranger laughed lightly. "No, not your little girlfriend...it's an old flame."

"Avril?"

"I thought I'd find you like this..." she said.

"It's been a while. What are you doing here?" he asked, suspicion lacing his words.

"I came to pay a visit. The last time we saw each other, I almost ran you over."

"Pinning me against Liv's car wasn't your best moment..." he replied.

"Oh, I know. We both have a lot of not-so-fine moments in our past."

"So, what brings you here? Did you come to finish the job?"

"I came to tell you that you were right..."

"Right about what?"

Avril let out a sigh as if a heavy burden had been lifted off her shoulders. "That night when I saw you with Liv, I did something really stupid. My sister saved me before I could do any real damage...and the diagnosis was exactly what you had always claimed it to be..."

Abraham stood up and closed the door, plunging the room back into darkness.

"Is that all you came to tell me?"

"No, I also came to say that I'm sorry for everything I did to you..."

He took a moment to process her words, and the silence filled the room.

"I was messed up, and I did a lot of things that you didn't deserve."

Her confession stunned him. This was not the Avril he once knew. The old Avril would have never admitted such tendencies. The revelation softened his heart for the moment. The Darkness had made an appearance back then too, and the assault left him with guilt as well.

"I did a lot, too...it wasn't all your fault...and I'm sorry..."

She heard his words, his voice, and his delivery. His tone was not the one she was used to. "Your voice sounds different. You're not you...I can tell," she said as her eyes surveyed him up and down as best she could in the darkness.

The moonlight pierced through the blinds. Full moon, he thought. The ring on his left hand glimmered and the flicker of it caught her attention.

"Did you marry her?" Avril asked.

"I…I wanted to, but…" his response exited his lips slowly and he searched for the words to muster up an answer. "It just…I don't know. It just didn't happen…"

"Maybe you should try talking to her again…"

He sat in silence. The truth stung him more than he let on. "Nah…she doesn't wanna talk to me…" he said. Abraham glanced at the shimmer of his ring in the pale moonlight. The ring matched Liv's. The International Market in Waikiki housed Hawaiian treasure, and he made sure to christen their unification with a matching set of hand-carved hibiscus silver rings. Liv accepted her second ring in Hawaii at Abraham's request, but this one meant more to him than she would ever know.

He shook his head quickly, struggling to refocus on the "now" and not on "what could have been." Avril had come in peace, but his instincts told him otherwise. "I'm glad you're doing better," he said. Testing the water, he played detective, questioning her reasons for seeking him out. "You're more normal than you've ever been…if you were like this back then, it might've worked…"

Avril's eyes widened at his claim. "I still love you, Abraham…I always will…" Her words were heartfelt. He believed her. Her aura radiated calmness rather than the buzzing he was accustomed to. "But things are the way they are meant to be…"

"The higher levels of serotonin have definitely changed you," he said, slightly glancing at her. "…for the better."

Avril slinked to a spot on the couch, and she made herself comfortable. His persona caught her off guard. Even now, he kept her on her toes, without the psychotic tendencies.

"So, maniacal, huh?" he asked.

Avril let out a chuckle, her initial response vastly different from years prior. "I remember that's what you used to call it," she said.

"Are you okay with what the doctor found?" Abraham asked.

"Yup," Avril answered, unashamed of her current state. Acceptance of it had been a long time coming. "I just came to tell you that. And thank you for always trying to help me, even when I didn't want to hear it." Sincerity had always been one of her strong points.

Abraham scanned her vitals, surprised to see that her anxiety levels were lower than he had ever monitored before. "Your heart is beating a lot slower than it used to…"

"How do you know?" Avril asked, then remembered. "Oh, right, you can sense it…I forgot.'

"And you wonder why you couldn't get a tactical edge on me?" Abraham snickered. "The only way was to run me over in your car, right? I'm just kidding, Avril. It's actually pretty funny, now."

"I'm sorry, Abraham, I was a little crazy," she laughed. "At least we can laugh about it now."

Reminiscing on the past usually brought hurt feelings and arguments to light, but this time was different.

Avril picked up her purse signaling her exit cue. "Well, it's been fun, but I better get going…"

"You don't have to," he said, viewing her curves in the dim light.

No, don't do it, Abraham thought. Giving her false hope would be his undoing. Any slight move had potential of going back to square one and any progress Avril made from being away would be for nothing.

"Do it," the Darkness pleaded, "She wants you to."

"No," Abraham countered, "It's not right."

"You have nothing to lose," the Darkness declared firmly.

I can't go backwards, he thought.

Avril rose from the couch and strolled toward the door. "What did you say?" she asked, hearing his mumbles.

"Nothing…"

"Well, it was good seeing you, Abraham."

"Wait," he said, "Don't go, yet…"

SOULS PART

The two-mile hike was a quest he hadn't undertaken in a couple of years. Collins Garden Park held nostalgic memories for him, especially the basketball court where he had spent countless hours in his younger days.

Now, a newly placed bench at the corner of Garland Street and North Park Boulevard marked the latest addition to the renovated park. It became a gathering spot for deep conversations between two kindred souls. At Liv's urgent request, Abraham arrived at the park, dressed comfortably in a black polo, khaki shorts, and a pair of Air Jordans. Meeting during daylight hours called for casual attire, a departure from his usual worn-out basketball clothes.

As he settled onto his regular spot on the left side of the bench, he noticed Liv's black M3 rolling up onto the side of the road, with half of the car parked on the grassy area. Liv stepped out of the vehicle, and Abraham stood up to greet her, his arms extended for an embrace.

"Wow, I wasn't expecting a hug from you...you haven't bothered to give one in a while," she remarked, a touch of surprise in her voice.

"My grandma says I need to get out of the dark...and I'm trying to remember who I was before all this...gotta go back to the beginning kinda thing..."

Liv took her place on the right side of the bench while he returned to his spot. Her purple sundress beautifully complemented her figure, and the hibiscus print reminded him of their "honeymoon" in Hawaii. He sensed her frequency, and it was sporadic, fractured even.

"Abraham, I need to tell you something," Liv began, her voice filled with a mix of apprehension and sorrow. She took a deep breath, her eyes drifting to the sandy dirt surrounding the bench. "I don't even know how to say this…"

"Well, do your best," he said.

Avoiding direct eye contact, she turned her gaze away from him. Her silence spoke volumes, and tears streamed down her face as she stared into the void.

"It's okay," he assured her, his sincerity evident. "You can tell me."

Finally, she mustered the strength to face him, but her eyes were already red and swollen from crying. "I know that we've both been a little off lately," she began, her voice trembling. "I had a miscarriage…" Her spiritual stronghold cracked at the mere utterance of her heartbreak. "…I didn't even know I was pregnant."

"What? Why didn't you tell me when it happened?" Shocked by the revelation, he turned to her, his weakened state giving way to anger.

"I didn't realize until it was too late," she replied through her tears. "I thought it was just my period…there were huge clots…I went to the doctor, and she confirmed it…"

"What the fuck!" his voice reverberating through the treetops. "You still should've told me, Liv!"

"How could I? You don't listen to anything I have to say! You stay in the dark, in your room, and everything I've tried doesn't work! You've fallen into darkness, and you don't even know it…"

"This would've changed things! Maybe it would've made me better! All I talked about in Hawaii was for my baby to have a baby!"

"Abraham…you don't let anybody save you! Your damn ego thinks you can do this by yourself!"

"You know what…" he yelled, "…you're right! I taught myself to rely on no one! And you know why? Because no one has ever been there when I needed them! No one has ever made the effort to talk to me or work shit out...all I've ever gotten is deaf ears, people incapable of giving me advice and people walking out when I needed them the most..." he said with a snarl. Blanketed in anger, his face turned tomato red. His eyes glared with a fiery glow, ready to devour.

"Look at you! You've forgotten all your 'training,' as you say! You're not a sob story, Abraham. You're better than that, and you've proved it many times over! So, nobody was there to help you cope with your special abilities! You think I can't feel you!? You think you're going through the darkness by yourself!? You're mistaken! I can feel everything...your pain, your hardship, your gift, and your curse...I know you can feel people...it's called being an empath...and the other things you can do are unexplainable, and you have them for a good reason...God gave them to you because He knew you could handle it...not to waste them...and definitely not to wallow in self-pity...you think I haven't educated myself? I had to! You know why? Because I love you! *We* have gone through this together! But no, you *choose* not to have my help because your ego says otherwise!"

Dumbfounded at her rebuttal, the fury paused momentarily, tears dropping like a steady rainstorm. He hadn't anticipated such a counterstrike from her, nor was he prepared for it.

"You're something special, and you're throwing it away...you have people who love you, people who want to help you, regardless of whether they are capable or not, and you have Margie...she is the only one who can get you through this...because obviously, I can't..." Her tears fell with her sudden realization.

"I'm sorry, Liv...you're right. I don't know how to stop this...it's eating me alive...and I'm so far away from home," he sighed heavily. "I feel unstable. And I feel...anger...rage..." he paused, struggling to admit a hard truth. "...and even hate. This is not who I am."

"I don't know you anymore." Liv barely managed to squeeze the words out, the lump in her throat overtaking her. Her questioning ceased; no words could escape through her cries. She coached herself into a few deep breaths as her sobs began to level out.

"Liv...I still believe in One Fine Day...I'm just...I'm all messed up right now," he said.

"You have PTSD, Abraham. It's obvious. Your emotions are all over the place, and these negative emotions...they're your repressed memories that have never surfaced. Abbadon did his work well...ever since you came back, you've been different...and believe me, I hate him for that...but these are things you needed to work on, nevertheless." Liv exhaled her words onto him. "Working them out is the only way that you're gonna get better and I can't be there to see you through...I gave you everything I had...and you're too destructive. You're killing *us*!" Liv's voice trembled with a mix of frustration and concern.

Abraham took a moment to absorb her words, realizing the harsh truth in them. It had been almost a year of struggle, but finally, her message broke through the walls he had built around himself. "I know," he whispered, his voice heavy with remorse. "And I'm so sorry."

"People often end up becoming what they hate the most. You need to let it go, Abraham. This battle isn't yours alone—it belongs to God. Let Him fight for you," Liv pleaded.

"I don't want to lose you...I know you think I don't care...or love you anymore," he said.

Liv sighed, trying to compose herself. "Yes, that's exactly what I think because your actions speak louder than words. All we do is argue now, and I hate it. You've changed so much," she said as she began to calm herself. "For months, I've begged and prayed for answers that you can't give..."

"My soul misses yours..." His anguish seeped from his soul, and he felt the weight of his mistakes. She was right. She had always been right. And now, he began to fight...

I need her...
Abraham, fight harder!
You can beat this. The Darkness doesn't stand a chance...
You have the greatest Power on your side...
You always find a way...
Be better!

In the park, surrounded by the shadows of trees, he coached himself, embracing the void and seeking a glimmer of hope. As the sunlight filtered through the branches, casting rays of light upon his surroundings, he felt a resurgence stirring within him.

The light was making a comeback.

Be better…for her!

He refocused on Liv. "…what can I do to make it better?" he asked.

Liv, on the other hand, wandered off into oblivion, her emotional reserves depleted. Everything she had in her psychological bag of tricks was spent. She wrestled with her own dilemma, hesitant to reveal it, yet knowing it was necessary. "You can't. I can't do this anymore, Abraham…" she confessed, tears streaming down her face. "I'm sorry…"

Her words struck a blow to the flicker of hope that had begun to rekindle within him. "With all the other girls, I could only go so far, and I know why now," he admitted, his voice trembling. "I don't want to lose you…I need you on this one…I can be better."

"Abraham, I tried…I can't do this anymore," Liv whispered as tears gushed from her eyes. "I'm sorry…" She reached for his hand, slipping a peculiar-shaped object into it before closing his hand gently. "I won't be needing this anymore…"

As he opened his hand, he saw the key to the black M3 resting there. The spark that had ignited moments before disintegrated, leaving behind a void. The silence enveloped him, and a sense of unease grew in his stomach, causing his breath to quicken. Watching Liv walk away without turning back crushed his heart. Her mind was made up. Hopelessness dived into his soul, and he began to feel the emptiness.

Another loss…
God, what are you trying to teach me?
Is she not my soulmate?
Why does she want to give up on me?
This is a time when I need her the most…

Why would You do this to me!?

Defeated, Abraham slumped over on the bench, placing his head in his hands. As Liv hurriedly walked away, he refused to believe that she was leaving him forever. The sound of her sobs echoed in his ears, piercing his heart.

This can't be it…it can't be over. Not like this…

His descent into darkness deepened, as the internal battle between the spark within him and the encroaching Darkness intensified.

We need to bring on more for him to break…he's still fighting. The crow cawed requesting further bombardment from his cloaked minions.

Liv turned back before crossing the street. Her eyes were red and tears streamed down her wet cheeks. "Soulmates don't always end up together…"

Her words pierced him like a million knives, and the weight of his own actions crushed him. The woman he loved had walked out of his life, and he blamed himself.

This is my doing…

The words echoed in his soul, shattering his facade of emotional invincibility. He had boasted of it for many years, a claim now obliterated by Liv's departure.

Impervious to emotional pain…

The Darkness reveled in his vulnerability, sensing an opportunity.

The black crow cawed with anticipation, its presence an ominous reminder of the looming darkness.

"Let her see your rage," the Darkness cawed.

"No!" He rose from the bench like a man possessed, striding towards the M3. "I don't want it!" he shouted, hurling the car key onto the gravel. "Keep the car!"

Abraham stormed off, his anger burning like a raging inferno, never looking back to see if she heard his demands.

The two-mile hike back to Grandma's house further deflated Abraham's spirits. He trudged along, kicking pebbles aside as they crossed his path, his brow furrowed as he replayed words, emotions, and scenes in his head.

Soulmates don't always end up together...It's not too late to fuck shit up...I can wreak havoc like everyone else...I'll just start packing like Pancho or Tommy Gun...nobody gives a fuck...I'll own these streets...fuck everybody!

The sinister thoughts attracted dark spirits, multiplying around him until they formed a suffocating presence, guiding him towards a dimension devoid of light.

An hour later, he finally caught sight of Grandma's house.

Maybe I can calm down once I get to the house...

As he approached, he noticed a couple of unfamiliar cars parked in front, one of which bore a striking resemblance to the one he had just left behind.

Liv...she brought it back...Stealth M3...she already ripped out my heart, what more does she want...she just dumped it here after I told her to keep it...

Abraham glanced into the driver's side, finding it meticulously cleaned, devoid of any loose ends. A sense of comfort washed over him when he spotted a light blue SUV in the driveway, knowing that his spiritual advisor, Margie, had come for a visit.

5:30...Margie's usual after work visit. I'll have to tell her...she'll probably ask about the car anyway...

A crow landed on an oak tree in Grandma's front yard, cawing fiercely, as if anticipating another clash of souls.

Unbeknownst to Abraham, an ambush awaited him, orchestrated by unseen forces.

The crow cawed once again, its call laced with intimidation. *We're going to break you...*

In search of much-needed water and Margie's presence, Abraham barged into Grandma's house.

Margie can save me…calm me down…

Sweat dripped from his chin, smearing his shirt, but he paid it no mind. He could be drenched in blood, injured beyond rehabilitation or even dead, at least it would make his heart stop bleeding.

As he entered the living room, he caught sight of two occupants sitting on the couch through the screen door. His mouth fell open, his heart sank, and shock struck him like a ton of bricks.

Liv and Margie sat silently, their conversation coming to a halt upon Abraham's arrival.

"What are you doing here?" Abraham asked, his voice trembling.

Liv remained silent.

"What are you doing here?" he yelled, his voice rising.

"Hey, calm down," Margie tried to intervene.

Abraham looked at Margie, sensing that she knew. "Did you tell her?" he shouted at Liv.

"Hey! Don't talk to her like that! You need to calm down!" Margie exclaimed.

"Did she tell you what she did to us!? What she did to me!" Enraged, Abraham sensed the breaking point coming on.

Listen to Margie, listen to her!

Overpowered by machinations of the wicked, he drifted further into darkness.

Listen to me…she came to spur your rage…let her have it…

The Darkness whispered, coaxing his psychotic tendencies back to life.

He turned to Liv, waiting for her to speak, but she sat sobbing in silence, her eyes fixed on Margie.

Abraham paced back and forth in front of the couch, the intensity building within him, hovering over Liv in an attempt to intimidate a confession.

"Back off of her!" Margie yelled.

"Don't tell me to back off!" Abraham shouted back at Margie.

"Don't you talk to her like that!" Margie said. "I'm not gonna let you treat her like this!" Margie rose from the couch, her eyes blazing with vigor as she challenged him. Her gaze cut through him like a hot knife through butter. "You better not lay a hand on her," she warned. "I'm going to stay with her," Margie said, sitting back down on the couch next to Liv. "Liv, don't worry, I'll stay by your side. Come on, I'll take you home."

"No. She's not going anywhere!" Abraham said.

"Mijo, calmate. *Love, calm down,*" Grandma pleaded, desperation flowing in her voice.

Oblivious to his surroundings, Abraham failed to notice Grandma's plea.

"You need to back down!" Margie's voice grew firm, shaking his confidence. He had never heard Margie, the spiritual warrior, speak to him in such a way, nor had he ever shown her his rage before.

"Fuck off!" Abraham yelled.

Liv sprang from the couch and stormed out the front door. Abraham ran after her, quickly catching up. Her speed walk was fueled by panic as her tears turned into anger.

"Abraham, stop! Leave me alone!" she cried.

"No, fuck that! You should've never come back here!"

"Stop following me! I'm going to get a ride!" Liv pulled out her phone and began dialing. "Go back to your grandma's...I don't want to be around you!"

Her resistance enraged him further. Without hesitation, Abraham grabbed her phone and slammed it on the concrete. The phone shattered into a thousand jagged pieces in the middle of the street.

"You asshole! Fuck you! Stay away from me!" Liv ran back to Grandma's house, where Margie awaited in the front yard.

I went too far...

Abraham's mouth dropped open, his eyes widened at the sight. Shock incapacitated him as he stared at the broken plastic and mechanical pieces on the pavement. He froze, realizing the gravity of his actions as he watched Liv walking back to the house he grew up in.

It was then that he awoke from the anger-induced coma, witnessing the anger and disappointment on Margie's face. Her glare pierced him, and the weight of his actions burdened him beyond repair.

What have I done?

Regret flooded his being, but it was too late. As much as he wished he could turn back time by just two minutes, he knew this moment could never be undone. The disgust from the people he loved the most burned him alive. The scowl subsided, and he stared down the street at Liv and Margie, never wanting to return to the hell he had created for himself.

It was a side that he hid from the world, and now Margie had witnessed the manifestation of his darkness. Margie consoled Liv, wrapping her arms around her.

The damage was done, for the time being. Abraham turned in the opposite direction and walked away from the only life he had known—the life of the good man he once was.

SPIRITUAL ADVISOR

I prided myself on being impervious to emotional pain. How foolish was I to think that? I'm not. I'm only human. I'm susceptible just like everyone else. Building myself up to be spiritually sound brings new meaning…and new questions. This time, the forces of Darkness have helped me realize that I am not impervious to their schemes; rather, I am heavily targeted. This revelation brings new challenges…challenges that I'm not ready for…

The past three days had been spent in seclusion, a result of the recent showdown that triggered his newfound inclination for solitude. The public debacle had unfolded in various scenarios in his mind, each with its own set of potential outcomes. The shame of being perceived as a madman was something he simply couldn't bear. What hurt him even more, though, was the dark side of his personality that Liv, Grandma, and Margie had witnessed; a side he was reluctant to acknowledge.

As Abraham folded wrinkled clothes scattered across the bed, a gentle voice broke the silence. He turned to face Margie, who had somehow managed to sneak into his abode.

"It's good to see you in daylight. Look at this pigsty," Margie remarked, surveying the chaos of boxes and garments strewn about.

"What do you expect? I'm moving into my new house. It's bound to look like a total mess," Abraham replied.

Margie had a remarkable talent for making amends. Grudges were nonexistent in her life, and if she had any enemies, they never made themselves known. She made herself at home in his new residence, her fashion sense remaining constant with her dark jeans, a nice blouse, and sandals. Only her perfume varied, as her extensive collection allowed her to wear a different scent every day of the year.

Her unwavering concern for Abraham persisted, even when he least expected it, and her gifts of knick-knacks seemed endless. "I brought some crosses so you can place them on top of your doorways, to keep evil and negative energy away." Margie had witnessed a sinister version of her only nephew, and she came prepared for the battle ahead.

"Thank you, Margie," he said somberly. His eyes welled up with tears, and he struggled to contain the flood of emotions within him. "I'm sorry."

"Grandma is worried about you…she had to take her blood pressure medication to calm down after you left," Margie revealed.

"No, she didn't," he chuckled, trying to lighten the atmosphere.

"It's not funny. You scared her," Margie said.

His face straightened immediately upon hearing her words. *Grandma's my whole life. I'd die if anything happened to her.*

"I wanted to check on you…to make sure you're okay," Margie said gently, recognizing the demons that haunted him in broad daylight. "What's going on?"

Abraham swallowed the lump in his throat and forced the truth out of his mouth. "I've been…" he said, hesitating. "…it's been hard lately. I'm trying really hard to hold it together and it's not working…and every time I try to be good, it's like I forgot how to be. I'm struggling, Margie." His eyes glistened with tears, and his voice trembled. After a moment to compose himself, Abraham continued, "They're coming after me in my dreams…they're not good."

Margie's concern was evident as she inquired, "What kind of dreams?"

"It's hard to explain...I can see them, Margie," he said, his voice tinged with frustration. "In the dreams, it feels like I'm being hunted..."

"By a creature?" she asked.

"No, it's like a shadow, I mean, like a shadowy figure, but it's a man." His brow crinkled as he attempted to recollect details. "The creatures...I see at night. Not with my eyes, but with my mind's eye."

"Your third eye...that's how you can see them. What do they look like?" Margie asked, her curiosity piqued.

"They come in different shapes and sizes...and more of them are starting to show up. The ones that have been coming the last couple nights, they're different. It's as if they're sending in bigger and stronger ones," Abraham described.

"Start from the beginning. Tell me everything you've seen," Margie urged.

"Well, at first, smaller ones were coming...two or three at a time. But now, the bigger ones are arriving. The bigger ones, though, only come one at a time. The other night I woke up and it was standing over me. It was big. It was probably about seven feet tall. It was bulky and wide like the Hulk. I couldn't see the face, but it was an ugly-looking monster. It felt like it was trying to intimidate me. This one was different from the other ones."

"In what way?" Margie asked.

"The others were small, stealthy agile creatures, but his one was like, I don't know, like brute force." he said.

Margie nodded, her eyes gleaming with a potent resolve. His description of the beings had her full attention, and she did not fear them in the least. "That means you're still strong, and there's still light within you. They won't give up. They'll keep coming."

"What do you mean, 'they'll keep coming'?"

"Listen, souls are fought over every day. We're unaware of it, unable to perceive it, but it happens. They want what you have...homes aren't burglarized when they hold no value. Gifts can be used to create or destroy."

"Why are they fighting so hard *now*?" he asked.

"Because you're still powerful. You have a lot of light left in you. They won't stop 'till you turn…this is spiritual warfare, boy! This is not something you can just fight off like the flu or with your fists," Margie countered. Her spiritual wisdom had been lacking in his life, causing him to lose sight of its importance. She was the medicine he desperately needed, the guiding presence. "We don't wrestle against flesh and blood, but against powers and rulers of darkness and against spiritual forces of evil in heavenly realms…we need to cleanse your house. I know someone who can help."

"What do you mean 'help?'"

"Little boy, trust me. Even though we live in the world, we don't wage war as the world does. The weapons we fight with are not the weapons of the world, rather they have the divine power to demolish strongholds…so, get it together! We're gonna need to pray hard."

"Like war…first you test for strength…and then you test for weakness…that's what the creatures are doing…" Abraham believed Margie and her spiritual reasoning. She'd never given a reason to doubt her. "…praying is not the same…" he admitted.

"You need to put your heart into it. Believe it. Speak life into your prayers. Have faith. Psalm 91 repels anything that's evil," Margie advised, her words sinking in.

Abraham absorbed her wisdom and nodded gratefully. "Thank you, Margie. In the meantime, what should I do?"

"Well, that's why I brought these…" Margie reached into her grocery bag. She pulled out several items, revealing seven crosses. Two of them had a beautiful wood finish, while four were long and slender, crafted from palm tree branches and folded neatly to form tiny crosses. The last one was a smooth metal cross with a silver tint. "It's no secret. I know what you're battling."

"What *am* I battling?"

"Dark forces," Margie replied with a sense of conviction.

"Margie, I need—"

"Stop," she interrupted, her voice calm but forceful. "Calm down. Your mind is racing. Try to quiet your thoughts. You're going to need help, but first, you need to breathe and calm yourself down. Try meditating..."

Abraham welcomed her advice, closing his eyes and taking slow, deliberate breaths.

"You have two problems here. This house has been vacant for twenty years, so whatever is inside has likely been here for a long time. Second, whatever is here has latched onto you. Don't bring Liv--" Margie caught herself, realizing her mistake. "I'm sorry. Have you spoken to her?"

His eyes teared up heavily at the mention of her name. The wounds still haunted his psyche. "No," he whispered. "She's gone."

The toll of war had claimed casualties, and Abraham found himself unraveling to the point of self-destruction—a state he was unfamiliar with.

Margie's eyes widened, a mix of concern and alarm crossing her face as she grasped the gravity of the situation. "This is worse than I thought...the devil is taking control of you. I've seen it. The person I saw the other day...that wasn't you...that was someone I've never seen before, and I don't ever want to see him again." Margie took a deep breath and exhaled slowly. "Satan is outwitting you...you're strong at psychological warfare. You've used that to your advantage for harm, but now you must use it for spiritual battle. Satan is not stronger than you. Outwit the bastard. Do you hear me? Fight this son of a bitch hard..."

XII   FOUR EVER

Abraham sank to one knee, a position he hadn't assumed in quite some time, desperately seeking a connection with the Lord.

"I'm at my breaking point, Lord. Grant me strength, courage, and guidance…help me to think straight." He released a heavy breath. "She's right…I *am* losing my way. I need you right now…more than ever. I said some ugly things to her, and I'm sorry. I feel lost…I don't know what I'm doing…help me get her back…please, God…"

Margie said to breathe…and to calm my mind.

In the barren emptiness he called home, he searched for answers. The dining room had been invaded by unpacked boxes, reflecting the psychological chaos he felt. Thoughts and things, all over the place.

A gentle knock resonated from the porch. Gloria smiled and waved at him through the screen door, her other hand gripping a leash as Thunder panted loudly on his inaugural visit to the new house.

Abraham rose from his prayerful position. "Thunder!" he called out. "Hi, Mom. come in," he said, opening the door for both of them. Thunder bounded up and down excitedly, while Gloria struggled to control the leash as the bulldog's antics bucked out of control. "Thunder, stop!" she yelled. "He's happy to see his brother," she explained, pointing at Abraham. "So, how are things going?" she asked.

"Eh, it's going," he responded.

"Margie says you have some problems of the spiritual kind."

"Yeah, we had our conference yesterday," he snickered. "Are we having *our* conference today?"

"I noticed you got the M3 back." Gloria had her methods of opening drama-induced conversations, and he knew the re-appearance of the M3 would raise some questions.

"Yup. Got left…again. What else is new?"

"What happened, Abe?"

"Same ol' shit…" he said.

"Abraham, you better not be mean to her."

"Nah, there are other things going on. Margie briefed you, so you know there's much more to it. I've just been thinking…my relationship with Liv was different."

"You have a deep love for her," Gloria acknowledged. "She's a nice girl."

"Being with her…was special…and I broke through barriers, that I never could with anybody else," he confessed. "I had to."

"Had to?" Gloria asked.

"I've always had a problem with relationships…and now I know why, so I wanted to ask you…" He hesitated, considering his fragile state. "…why did you leave me? When I was four years old…why did you *leave* me?"

Twenty-two years had passed, yet that memory remained etched vividly in his mind, replaying as if it happened only yesterday.

💣

September 1983

The massive big rig surged forward, aiming directly at its target. The eighteen-wheeler executed tactical maneuvers, strategically engaging the Trans-Am that stood in its path. The sleek black car, known as KITT, raced fearlessly towards the truck, a red glowing light above its bumper shifting from right to left. KITT was no ordinary vehicle—it could talk, drive itself, and possessed a distinct personality.

Closing in on the colossal eighteen-wheeler, the sleek Trans-Am maintained its resolve, coming within a mere thirty feet of the behemoth. Then, in a last-second move, it turbo-boosted over the towering truck, thwarting the imminent victory the truck had anticipated.

The General Lee, with its Confederate flag painted on its roof, accelerated alongside the big rig, diverting its attention. With daring proximity, the General Lee forced the eighteen-wheeler to veer towards the right, causing it to tip over and crash onto its side.

Manipulating the scene with his four-year-old hands, Abraham slid the truck on its side as if it crashed on the asphalt of a major interstate. The rectangular tan rug in Grandma's house transformed into the setting for the interstate showdown he envisioned.

"Mijo! Voy a cocinar almuerzo para ti. *Love, I'm going to make breakfast for you,*" Grandma said.

"Okay, Grandma!"

Abraham tidied up his Hot Wheels and turned on the TV. His favorite show, Pinwheel, was about to start—a program he never wanted to miss. Grandma's house was a safe-haven, a playground, and a dine-in restaurant all rolled into one.

Grandma Marcella strolled into the living room to check on him and make sure he wasn't climbing up the grandfather clock. Instead, she gave him a big hug as he sat on the sofa chair. "Mijo! Te amo mucho! *Love, I love you so much!*"

Abraham raised his tiny arms and wrapped them around Grandma's neck. "I love you too."

Gloria entered the house, indicated only by the sound of the steel door closing behind her.

"Mija, ya te cabaste a trabajar? *You're done working?*" Grandma Marcella asked.

"No, I'm here to take Abraham," Gloria said.

"No lo lleves. *Don't take him,*" Grandma pleaded.

"Come on, Abe," Gloria called to him.

"Where are we going?"

"To the daycare…"

"I don't wanna go to daycare. I wanna stay with Grandma. Pinwheel is starting…"

"Come on, we'll just go see it and I'll bring you back." Gloria attempted to reason with him.

"But Pinwheel is starting…" Abraham glanced at the TV as he reluctantly walked toward the door, the familiar tune of his favorite show playing in the background.

Pinwheel, Pinwheel, spinning around.
Look at my pinwheel, see what I found.
Pinwheel, pinwheel, where have you been?
Hello, how are you, and may I come in?
Pinwheel, Pinwheel, spinning around.
Look at my pinwheel, see what I found.
Pinwheel, pinwheel, breezy and bright.
Spin me good morning, spin me good night.

A Victorian house with a pinwheel on top appeared on the screen, its charm shining brightly as the animated characters' smiling faces graced the scene. For Abraham, being torn away from that happy place didn't sit well; his stomach churned, and his instincts dove into emergency mode. He felt the sun setting on the characters he had grown to love.

"We're just gonna go see it?" he asked.

"Yes."

"And then you'll bring me back?"

"Yes."

"You promise?"

"Yes, I promise I'll bring you back."

"Okay," he said. "Grandma, I'll be back."

Gloria escorted Abraham to the car. As he sat in the passenger seat, an overwhelming sensation came over him. *We're not coming back,* he thought. His appetite for grandma's breakfast soon disappeared. "Mom, we're coming back, right?"

"Yes, Abraham, I already told you."

The car ride only intensified the unease in his stomach. His senses were on overload, knowing that this was a one-way trip. Though he wouldn't be able to navigate back to Grandma's on his own, he figured the daycare was relatively close, considering the short time it took to arrive.

The car pulled up to the alleged daycare, and Abraham shook his head in disgust after viewing it from the outside. "I don't wanna go inside."

"Come on, Abe. After we go inside, I'll take you right back to Grandma's," Gloria prodded.

Reluctantly, he jumped out of the car and headed up the sidewalk. Gloria rang the doorbell of the daycare, which looked like an ordinary house in the middle of a neighborhood—far from the Victorian house he had imagined. Cars whizzed past them on the busy street, and he recognized the distant McDonald's sign.

"Hi, come on in!" a lady answered the door, greeting them.

"Hi, I'm Gloria, and this is my son, Abraham."

The lady welcomed them into the house. She was short and heavyset, with dark curly hair, and her presence lacked kindness. Her half-smile gave way to a stare that seemed to burn through Abraham's skull.

"I'm Darla, and this is Irene. She and I run the place," Darla said, as Irene entered the room.

Abraham glanced over at the rug where a group of kids were huddled together, watching TV. Some of them gave Abraham a stone-faced look, as if they were under strict orders to behave. There were about eight kids ranging from four to eight years old, and an eerie silence hung in the air.

"This is Abraham," Gloria introduced him to the two ladies. Darla and Irene approached him, their glares making Abraham freeze. Panic surged through him, but he couldn't find his voice to tell Gloria it was time to leave.

"Come on over to the kitchen," Irene said, placing a hand on Abraham's back and urging him forward.

"Okay," Gloria replied, "I have to go to work."

As Gloria headed for the door, Abraham's fight-or-flight response kicked in, leaving him with no choice. He was right; this was a one-way trip, and his chances of returning to his grandma dwindled to zero.

In a last-ditch effort, Abraham clenched onto Gloria's dress, gripping it so tightly that Darla and Irene couldn't pry him away. Gloria chuckled with embarrassment.

"Abe, I have to go to work," she pleaded with him.

"Noooooooo, don't leave me here!" he yelled, his four-year-old lungs releasing a torrent of tears, shouts, and cries. Yelling as loud as he could made no difference. It was as if he was in a mental hospital being forcefully escorted back to his quarters.

Irene held his right arm while Darla grasped his left, struggling to release his tiny hand from Gloria's dress. They pinned him against a child-sized table. "She has to go!" they repeated.

"Noooooooooooooo! Ahhhhhhhhhhhhhhhhhh!"

The other children mistakenly interpreted his behavior as a full-blown tantrum, but it was far more than that. It was a fight for survival against these strangers Gloria had left him with. Abraham fought with every ounce of his being, desperately trying to cling to hope. "Don't leave me!"

But despite his best efforts, his preschool tactics proved futile, and he knew he was losing the battle. Darla and Irene overpowered him, while Gloria showed no signs of coming to his rescue. Finally, they pried back his tiny fingers, allowing Gloria to escape his grasp, and as she walked out the front door, all hope drained from Abraham.

Abraham sobbed uncontrollably, tears streaming down his tiny face, calling out for his mother even though he knew she wouldn't come back to save him. He hoped she would turn around realizing she made a mistake by leaving him there.

He waited.

But time passed, too much time, and the realization sank in that she wasn't coming back. Irene and Darla placed him on top of the table, glaring at him from a distance and demanding that he cease his crying. "Shut up!" they yelled. Aside from their harsh commands, no comforting words escaped their lips. "You're stuck with us now, so shut up with all your crying!"

The other children remained on the carpet, not extending an invitation for him to join them. As the moments dragged on, a feeling of awkwardness settled in. He found himself in an unfamiliar place, surrounded by strangers and with kids who offered no help. Irene and Darla chatted in the kitchen. Abraham had no idea what action to take next. He wept softly, trying not to alert his captors, desperately hoping for a miracle.

Irene caught wind of his whimpers and immediately scolded him. "I said shut up already! You know what? We'll make you stop!" She yanked him off the table and opened a door beside it, forcefully throwing Abraham into the closet. "We're not letting you out 'till you get quiet!"

"AAAAAAHHHHHHHHHH!" he screamed at the top of his lungs, his voice echoing through the cramped space. The closet exuded a musty scent, and the assortment of objects beneath him offered no respite, only discomfort. It seemed to be a mishmash of baseball gloves and boxes, but it didn't matter though. Desperation filled the air as he frantically waved his hand in front of his face, only to be greeted by an impenetrable darkness. His sobs ceased and after a hard-fought battle, he closed his eyes. In the blackness, he felt his mind wander off, wishing to never wake up.

"Abe, you needed to go to school," Gloria said.

"But did you have to do it *that* way?"

"You act like it was some sort of trauma."

"Mom, you *left* me. It *is* trauma," Abraham reasoned. "Do you think at four years old I knew what was going on? Did you really think I knew you were coming back? Do you know how mean those ladies were to me? They weren't real caregivers or teachers…they just wanted me to shut the fuck up and comply like all the other kids. I was too little to give them a fight."

"I'm sorry, Abe. I had to get you over there, and that's the only way I knew how…"

"And I understand. I know you did your best, so don't worry. I don't hold it against you. You didn't know," Abraham exhaled a heavy sigh. "I'm a Pre-K teacher…I know how those kids feel when they come through my door. They're scared and crying…and I try to do for them what was never done for me. I sure as hell do my best to calm them and soothe them and comfort them and let them know that they're safe. I try to be the person that I wish I had when I was four…because I know the repercussions of having the opposite."

"And that's why you are a teacher…because you know what that's like, and that's why you're their hero. You're Superman to them."

"For the last couple of years, I've told myself that. This is where God needs me to be…that this is why it happened so long ago, you leaving me, because in the grand scheme of things, I was always meant to be an early childhood teacher. God meant for a part of me to stay four years old."

"Yup, that's for sure. We can't pry you away from looking at toys at the store, even now," she said with a giggle. "And you're good at it. How many awards have you won?"

Abraham raised two fingers, making a peace sign. The awards didn't matter though. Something more severe was at stake. "But where there's light, there's also darkness."

"What do you mean?" Gloria asked.

"The repercussions of that one event…hampered my relationships. Every person I've been with, I could only go so far. They would be so far ahead of me, wanting me to be their boyfriend, wanting to marry me, and they waited for me to catch up…but I could never pass a certain point. All of them were ready to take the relationship to the next level, but I couldn't move forward to join them…and so they left me."

"Okay, so what does that have to do with you being four years old?"

"If my own mother could leave me, what makes me think that another woman wouldn't?"

Gloria nodded. "I see."

"You *left* me, even after you promised you wouldn't. The moment you walked out that door, I had no idea what would happen to me. I honestly thought I would never see grandma again, and I felt so hopeless. I didn't think anybody was coming back for me," Abraham exhaled softly. "Psychologically, I realized that I've always had this fear of being left, and I didn't know it because it lived in my subconscious. But with Liv, it was different…my love for her outweighed my fear. That's not to say I wasn't scared because I was, but I had to evolve and break barriers painfully and even dangerously, and the one time I take a chance…she still left."

"Abe, things don't always work out," Gloria reasoned.

"It was my fault…but, the thing is, with all that's happened in the past year…" he struggled to keep the lump in his throat from leaping out. "…I'm finding myself to be emotionally unstable."

"That's why I came over…to check on you. And your brother, Thunder, wanted to see you," she said, laughing.

Abraham took a seat on the newly delivered red futon. Thunder hobbled over and instantly sniffed Abraham's leg.

"Hey, Thunder." He scratched the top of the dog's head.

"Life is hard, Abe. Just pray and have faith. Make the right decisions and don't get sucked into this idiotic world. Treat people the way you want to be treated…the golden rule, dude. Hold onto hope."

"Hope…" Abraham said the word aloud, struggling to find his resolve. Deep in his soul, he knew it would take more than just words to bring about a miracle.

"Do you still have that poem that you wrote when you were little? About hope…"

"If you mean around the time when I ran away, then yes, I still have it."

"Maybe you need to read it…keep your head up. Don't give up on Liv just yet. Don't lose sight of what really matters when things go dark."

"I'm trying not to," he said. "I know good things come out of even the darkest places…I'm still hoping for a miracle. That one single event when I was four led me to where I needed to be. It was always part of the plan…God's plan," he said, nodding his head. "That reminds me…I got you something for Mother's Day." Abraham reached to his left and picked up a rectangular box off the futon. He handed it to Gloria, who stood her ground at the doorway.

"Dude, you didn't have to get me anything," she said.

He handed her the gift. "Open it so I can tell you about it."

Gloria carefully opened the box, removing the bubble wrap that surrounded a figurine.

"It's a statue…an angel and a little boy?" she asked, puzzled.

The little boy hugged the angel, and she wrapped her arms around him, comforting him, carrying him, as his head rested on her shoulder.

"Yeah…that little boy is me…because a part of me stayed four years old, and you were the angel that took care of me."

Gloria admired the statue, intricately gazing at it. Her eyes became glossy, and the redness replaced the white in her eyes before he could finish explaining what the statue meant to him.

"I know I give you a hard time, but you leaving me didn't make me bitter…it made me better. You had an authoritarian parenting style…high on rules, low on love, you know? But it worked."

"How so?"

"You have a soothing presence…and you have a kind voice. I know you did your best. You gave me all that you had…and that's what counts. I love you."

"I love you too, Abe. Thank you."

Thunder was displeased that Abraham took his attention off him. Thunder dealt a head butt to Abraham's shin, cueing him to continue rubbing the top of his head. The canine wasted no time cavorting to the side of the futon after his requests were ignored. He lifted his leg, and out came a shower of yellow urine on one end of the couch.

"Lovely," Abraham said to his canine brother. "Anything else you'd like to whiz on, Thunder?"

XIII

DARK SIDE OF THE SUN

Abraham pulled into the crowded parking lot, filled with dozens of cars. Reaching over to the passenger seat, he picked up a handwritten paper with the title emblazoned at the top. "Hope," he whispered, glancing at the words he had written a lifetime ago.

> *The pen and the palm wrote curvy lines that sloped*
> *And were fueled by inspiration of a thing called hope*
> *And that began the journey that the duet was to embark*
> *On the path of light, to escape the clutches of the dark*

It had been some time since Abraham last laid eyes upon the Volcano, yet now, with his faith dwindling, and his power fading, he sensed Liv's presence and it guided him to the place where they had once celebrated their union.

This is a solo mission, he thought, unaccustomed to venturing into the nightlife alone. "Liv, if I'm to have a chance, I need you with me..." His desperate attempts to reach her proved futile; her communications were down, and the sensation disturbed him.

Abraham folded the paper with the poem, tucking it into his back pocket. *Maybe this'll give me some good luck,* he thought. Exiting the M3, he made his way towards the club entrance.

"Abraham! Long time no see, buddy!" Gene yelled, greeting him warmly.

"Yes sir! Good to see you, Gene!"

"Look at you with the fresh threads!" Gene exclaimed, admiring Abraham's wrinkle-free royal blue button-down and new pair of Timberland boots. "Don't worry about cover tonight, you're good to go."

"Thanks, Gene! You're still the boss man!" Abraham entered the club, immediately scanning the venue for Liv. He posted up at the first bar on his right, ordered a drink from the bartender, and as the glass of whiskey touched his hand, he set off to explore the venue.

Navigating through the sea of partygoers, he discreetly studied faces and features. After one rotation, he spotted her by the cage where they had once danced and experienced wild nights together.

"She's with Evelyn," he whispered to himself. He noticed her wearing the signature seductive black shorts paired with black heels and her top was a black Bebe brand shirt that Abraham had bought for her back in the Fall.

Inhaling deeply, he exhaled nervously, his fingers tapping repeatedly on the whiskey glass. "I can do this…what do I say?" Abraham glided to his left for another rotation around the Volcano. He planned to buy some time so he could calm down enough to have a friendly conversation with the woman that had his heart.

The dance floor had an oval shape, with a pathway flocked with clubgoers encircling it. In the past, every face he encountered in the club was familiar, whether they were acquaintances, long-lost friends, or friends who had become like family. But now, as he looked around, he didn't recognize a single face in the crowd.

Returning to where he started, he mustered a hint of confidence. *I'll just ask her if she wants to dance, no big deal.* But then, a whisper escaped his lips. "She's gone." He scanned his surroundings from left to right, but she was nowhere in sight. Perhaps she had seen him and decided to leave, he thought.

With a sip of his whiskey, he surveyed the area one last time. His inability to sense her meant her vibrational energy was low. Either that or he was drifting off further into oblivion.

The Darkness had taken its toll on him. His senses were dulled compared to their former sharpness. The fog of the Darkness obscured everything: judgment, perspective, awareness, and insight. His intuition surrendered to the truth that manifestation thrives in the light and crumbles in the dark.

Setting his glass down on the bar, he made his way toward the exit. Casting one final glance at the dance floor, something caught his eye. In the middle of the dance floor, he spotted her. The scene was not what he expected, and it took him a few seconds to register the horrific view. His stomach turned into knots and his mouth went dry.

Liv was grinding against another man, her seductive movements mirroring those she once reserved for Abraham. Like a charging bull, anger coursed through him as he noticed the man's surreptitious grin. He found himself trapped on the lower level of the dance floor, the rope separating him from the upper area where she danced.

"Are you going to dance with me?" he asked.

"No," she replied firmly.

"Just one dance," he pleaded, his rage simmering in his gut. Her rejection fueled an impending eruption.

"I said no!" Liv yelled.

Abraham stormed off the dance floor, overwhelmed by a flood of emotions. He clung to the last remnants of clarity by walking away, avoiding what would surely be a chaotic scene in the middle of the nightclub. *I'll get her back for this.*

He hopped into his black M3, consumed by unchecked rage. All he needed was a moment to contemplate his next move. In the meantime, he accelerated, the engine roaring as he sped off.

The M3 smoothly merged onto Highway 90. An expanse of road stretched out before him, lasting for three miles. His foot grew heavier on the pedal. *Fuck it. If there are any cops, I'll see 'em.* The speedometer climbed, surpassing the limit, and then began its descent to the right.

90 mph

Fuck her.

100 mph

Who the fuck is that motherfucker she's with…

110 mph

She won't get away with this.

120 mph

I'm gonna catch her and find out what the fuck is going on.

130 mph

Fuck it! Go faster!

140 mph

I knew she was fucking off!

The pedal pressed against the floor, propelling the M3 to 150 mph. The M3 Stealth boasted greater power than its silver counterpart, and with each passing moment of the ten-minute drive, his recklessness multiplied. Heavy breaths pounded through his nostrils, and his heart raced as if it might burst from his chest, leaving him completely powerless in controlling either. His thoughts raced through countless scenarios where Liv was no longer his.

The M3 drifted onto Nogalitos Street, and as he weaved through the streets of the south side, his mind fixated on sinking deeper into darkness.

Abraham maneuvered stealthily through her neighborhood.

Her curfew is 1:30…I'll catch her.

The M3 came to a halt beneath a massive tree, its shadow concealing him even further. Parked on the next block, facing her house, he prepared for an ambush.

Just leave, Abraham. You don't need to do this…

His knee shook uncontrollably. Adrenaline coursed through his veins like rapid gunfire.

Nah, fuck that, it's payback! 1:30…I'm fuckin' calling her!

His face contorted into a scowl, his eyes piercing the darkness of the night. The desire for revenge consumed him. The Light called to him, but it was a voice he no longer recognized. The spiritual soldier he once was now dissipated, and he became highly decorated in the dark.

He dialed her number, only to be greeted by voicemail.

"Where the fuck are you?" Abraham yelled into the phone.

A few seconds passed. He pressed the side button of his phone, illuminating the time display.

1:31.

His leg shook violently as he glanced at the time again.

1:31. She should have been home by now!

He called once more. Straight to voicemail.

"You fucked up now! I'm gonna throw it back in your face!" Vengeance was an urge he had never felt before. Now, he bathed in its destructive fury.

A block away, headlights shone in the distance, growing nearer until they finally stopped near her house.

It's go time!

Abraham brought the M3 to life, discreetly moving to the next block. Keeping the headlights off, he cruised at 15 miles per hour.

Once he caught a closer glimpse of the betrayal, he parked across the street and prepared to confront them both.

As he attempted to flank them, little did he know he was about to venture deeper than ever before into a realm for which he was ill-equipped and untrained in combat.

Forces gathered around Abraham, unseen by human eyes. With their advantage, they stood firm, ready to unleash havoc upon him. These Forces were skilled tacticians, having conquered prey countless times over. Hovering a few feet above the ground, their black cloaks concealed an arsenal of darts. Eager to strike, their leader waved, signaling the battalion to stand down.

Abraham circled around Liv and the would-be suitor, causing Liv to look on in horror. Her eyes widened, and her mouth dropped at the sight of him; it was as if she had seen a ghost.

Abraham wasted no time with the interrogation. "Are you two together?" he asked the man she had danced with. The young man shook his head with a smirk and looked away, refusing to utter a word to Abraham. Anger surged through him, making him want to pummel the smirk right off the man's face.

Infuriated, Abraham turned to Liv, shouting, "Are you two together?"

"What are you doing here?" she asked.

Gripping the trash can in her front yard, Abraham repeated his question, "Are you two together?" Silence hung in the air as Liv refused to speak. The fury inside Abraham reached its peak, and he flung the can toward her front yard. It rolled across the grass, its lid swinging open, scattering garbage across the lawn. From within the mess, a group of wasps emerged, swarming around Abraham. Consumed by rage, he paid no attention to the venomous assault.

"Abraham, stop!" Liv shouted.

"The more you fuck up the worse it gets. I don't think you realize that and now I'm gonna spit it back in your face. You really fucked up now!" His rage consumed him, spreading like a disease.

Unbeknownst to Abraham, the leader of the Dark forces observed his every move. The wasps served as a disguise for the impending onslaught, their stingers served as perfect three-dimensional weapons to inflict supernatural pain. The wasp contingent awaited orders to strike.

Abraham scowled at Liv, his face contorting like a man possessed. His anger swelled, and the leader of the Dark forces waited for the opportune moment to attack.

"I hate you!" Abraham spat out words he had never spoken before, his emotions spiraling out of control. "You fuckin' left me when I needed you the most! I *hate* you!"

His armor is off! The leader motioned to his battalion. *Attack!*

The swarm of wasps hovered above Abraham, their fiery darts not of human origin but forged in a realm unseen by the three-dimensional world. Although invisible, the stings were agonizing, capable of tarnishing a human heart and corrupting it.

Years of buried trauma surged to the surface, and Liv witnessed the explosion unfolding before her eyes.

"Abraham, stop!" she pleaded. The man she had danced with leaned against his car, silently observing, his arms folded.

"Soulmates don't always end up together? That's what you said, right? Fuck you!" Abraham's words lashed out as he stormed off toward his M3. His body moved with furious swings, while Liv's cries echoed through the darkened street. He reached into his back pocket and retrieved a folded paper. Jumping into the M3, the engine roared to life. Gripping the paper in his left hand, his blood boiling, he rolled down the window and let the paper fly out into the night. He sped off, fading into the blackness. The poem and the hope he carried floated away into the dark of night.

XIV THE FIRST TEMPTATION

Early June 2005

God, I don't know what to do…how did I get so far away? I need *you…*

The sunset painted the sky in hues of pink and orange, creating a breathtaking backdrop. Abraham relished his favorite time of day. To him, it was a moment of reflection, a time when life held deeper meaning. There was something special about the day's triumphs and failures converging, and the contemplation of how to make tomorrow better.

These days, the encroaching darkness signaled a transformation into the beast he had recently become, intensifying his predatory instincts and unleashing chaos and rage. The Volcano, a place that housed debauchery, embraced Abraham as he joined its fiery pit. This time, his thoughts were consumed by the raging fire.

"If Liv's here, I'm gonna make sure she sees me," Abraham confided in Rodrigo, his longtime clubbing partner. The memory of her dancing with another man was seared into his mind, every detail vivid, and it made him feel nauseous whenever it resurfaced.

"You make sure she sees you dancing with some hot ass girl. Don't worry, we're gonna meet some right now after this shot of patron!"

Rodrigo said. He effortlessly attracted the attention of curvaceous women, who gravitated towards him without a word being spoken.

Without delay, the duo made their way to the main bar.

"Sam! What up, baby boy?" Rodrigo greeted the bartender. Sam had been running the main bar at the Volcano for the past two years and had become familiar with the regulars.

"Yo! What up, Drigo?" Sam poured the clear liquid into three shot glasses before Rodrigo had a chance to respond.

"Patron poison from the best bartender in the Alamo City! Cheers, my brothers!" Rodrigo declared.

Sam was no stranger to joining his customers for shots. His blue-tinted mohawk added to the image of a warrior ready for combat as if he were fitted with seven-inch blades atop his head.

"Sam," Rodrigo called, raising two fingers. Sam refilled two of the shot glasses.

"Don't worry 'bout it, Drigo. I got you," Sam assured him.

"That's why you're the man." Rodrigo turned to his partner in crime. "Cheers, brother!" Rodrigo raised his shot glass, and Abraham followed suit. The glasses clinked together, and both men downed the shots without hesitation. "Don't worry, my brother," Rodrigo said, slinging his arm around Abraham. "You're gonna hook up tonight…trust me on that."

Abraham released a heavy sigh. Venturing into uncharted territory at half-strength didn't suit him well, but Liv had left him with no choice.

"You're right," he acknowledged, nodding his head. "I need to live my life, with or without her."

"Hey, check this out. So, you remember that girl, Mari, right?"

"Yeah, from last week?" Abraham asked.

Rodrigo laughed, a mischievous grin spreading across his face. "Yup, that's the one! Been bangin' her all week, and tonight, she's bringing her friend. Word on the street is she's pretty fuckin' hot!"

"Is she really hot, or are you just saying that so I can be the wingman?"

"Dude! Mari showed me pictures of her, and if I weren't banging Mari, I'd be banging her! She's smoking hot!" Rodrigo exclaimed.

"Go for it, man. There's your threesome," Abraham said.

"Nah, Mari said her friend doesn't go for a lot of dudes. They gotta be like sophisticated and shit. She's more on the stuck-up side, but I think she'd go for you."

"You know what, she's probably two-hundred pounds with a mustache," Abraham said skeptically. He remained unconvinced by Rodrigo's claims. "But…I'll give it a chance. She better be halfway decent, bro."

Rodrigo's back pocket buzzed, and he pulled out his cell phone to check a text message. He glanced at the screen and shot a look at Abraham. "She's here."

"Handle it, bro. I'm gonna go take a wiz. I'll be back," Abraham said, slipping away to the restroom just as Mari approached Rodrigo.

"Where's your friend? She didn't come?" Rodrigo asked.

"She wasn't going to, but I had to drag her out. She's on her way in…she just went to change her top," Mari replied.

"In the car?" Rodrigo asked, surprised.

"Yes," Mari said, laughing. "She keeps a whole wardrobe in her trunk!"

Mari's golden heels elevated her to a modest height. Even with the four-inch heels, she barely reached five-foot-two. Her striped romper outfit exuded a throwback disco vibe.

Abraham returned from the restroom to find Rodrigo raising both eyebrows, silently conveying a message. "My bad, bro." Abraham understood his discreet communication.

This isn't a good idea, Abraham thought, shaking his head with widened eyes, exchanging the same concerned look with Rodrigo. Forcing a hookup wasn't his style. He decided to wander around the club alone, giving Rodrigo and Mari some time together.

"Oh, look! There she is! She's at the bar," Mari pointed out.

"She seems like she doesn't even want to be here," Rodrigo observed. "I told my boy he'd at least dance with her." He continued to watch her dismissive gestures. "She's scowling!"

Mari motioned for her friend to join the group, and she reluctantly complied after downing her whiskey on the rocks.

"This is my friend, Lili," Mari introduced, motioning towards Rodrigo. "And this is Rodrigo, the guy I told you about," she said, placing her hand on Rodrigo's chest.

Lili barely smiled and whispered a quiet "hi."

"You look like you could use another drink. What would you like? Anything you want," Rodrigo offered.

Lili glanced at the club's entrance. "I think I'm okay for now. I don't plan on staying long."

"Oh, come on! Just one more! It's on me!" Rodrigo sure knew how to put on the peer pressure with a party vibe all at once.

Lili sighed. "Okay, just one. Whiskey, straight up."

"Lili's about her business! And a cherry vodka sour for you, right?" Rodrigo asked, pointing at Mari.

"Ewww, no! Vodka and Sprite. You forgot already?"

"I was just playin' with you. I was testin' you," he said with a laugh.

A couple of guys walked past Lili, gawking at her. "Hey, beautiful," one of them said just loud enough to be heard. Lili rolled her eyes in disgust. "I can't believe you come to this place. There's nothing but aimless kids getting drunk like it's a full-time job."

"Relax, girl. Let's just have a good time. Rodrigo brought a friend along, maybe he'll entertain you with some educated conversation, Ms. Entrepreneur!"

"If he's anything like these guys, no thank you!" Lili said, pointing to a group of gawkers with clothes three sizes too big.

Abraham approached, looking for Mari, but there was no sign of Rodrigo. Standing next to her was a girl wearing red heels and tight-fitting jeans. She had a curvy yet slender physique, and her red top accentuated it. *This can't be her friend,* he thought. *Maybe, it's some friend she ran into here.*

As he got closer to them, he realized it was indeed her. *Walk tall, look sharp,* he coached himself.

"Hey," he said to Mari.

"Hi, Abraham!"

"Drigo?"

"He's somewhere at the bar over there," she said, pointing to where Rodrigo and Sam were taking another shot. "This is my friend, Lili. She's not having a good time, but I told her you were a nice guy with an educated mind," Mari said, laughing to break the ice.

"Is that true? You're not having a good time?" Abraham asked sarcastically, squinting his eyes.

Lili's eyes widened at his displeasure. She looked down at his chest and then back up to his eyes, avoiding judgment. "I can leave if that would help? I mean, I don't mind. I was actually planning to leave anyway, so…" Lili countered.

"You know what, not necessary. My main man and I will escort you to a cozier spot in the dance club. Perhaps a VIP section is in order? What do you say, my lady? Shall we?" Abraham capitalized on the opportunity to play an actor of sorts. After all, he had plenty of practice in the Pre-K classroom.

Lili looked at him with a stone-faced expression, glaring at him as if he were the biggest idiot to enter the Volcano. His clean-smelling cologne caught her attention, and his wavy spiked hair, lightly styled with gel, looked pillow-soft. She wondered how it would feel if she ran her hands through it. His piercing eyes seemed to look into her soul. Her ability to stall for further assessment paid off.

Abraham waited for her response, staying in character. He was used to it from dealing with four-year-olds. Never let 'em see you sweat, he had learned. Her straight dirty blonde hair piqued his interest, and she didn't take her light brown eyes off him. It was like a staring contest in the middle of the dance club, neither giving an inch.

Rodrigo approached with four shots in both hands. He stopped five feet away, looked at Mari, and mouthed, "What the fuck!"

"Well, it seems I may have some time to spare. Since it's still early, I'll give you sixty minutes to sway me to stay longer. And if you should prove successful," Lili said, lightly brushing her hand on Abraham's shoulder as if removing dust, "Then you may have me for the rest of the night. I should warn you though, many have failed."

Inside, Abraham couldn't help but burst into laughter. *She's quite the actress herself,* he thought, captivated by her smooth milky white complexion. If only he could get close enough to kiss her cheek.

"Fair enough. Let me escort you to our finest table. Is there anything else I can do for you, Ms. Lili?" Abraham said with a hint of amusement.

"No, that will be all, thank you!" Lili smiled, and as her smile widened, she erupted into laughter. "That was pretty good, Mr. Abraham, but my sixty-minute timetable stands." She playfully jabbed her index finger into his chest.

Abraham smirked at her gesture. "Right away, Ms. Lili! Oh, and don't worry about your sixty-minute timetable."

"Why's that?" Lili asked.

"I only need five," Abraham said confidently.

THE NEXT DEGRADATION

XV

Late June 2005

The Volcano had become a ritualistic adventure every weekend for Abraham. He had grown accustomed to the vibrant nightlife, and each visit brought forth a new wave of potential suitors that he found increasingly difficult to ignore.

Abraham handed Rodrigo a shot of clear liquid. "Here you go. Buyer's choice," he said.

Rodrigo grinned. "And what a fine choice it is!" he exclaimed. "Down the hatch!"

The two men positioned themselves to the side of the dance floor. Sunday nights at the club attracted the regulars of San Antonio, lured by the nostalgic beats of 80s throwback music.

"Eleven thirty…three numbers already…I'm bangin' all of 'em tonight!" Rodrigo boasted unabashedly about his sexual escapades.

"Don't get ahead of yourself, now," Abraham cautioned.

"It's been done before, bro. You gotta set it up like a factory…one after another. It's a lotta work, lemme tell ya."

"Dang, I don't think I could pull that off," Abraham laughed.

"Oh, trust me, you ain't that far off," Rodrigo warned. "This chick has been eyeballin' you all night." He discreetly pointed over to a group of girls, with one facing them head on.

"Who?" Abraham asked, surprised.

"Blue dress…she's fuckin' hot, too!"

Abraham glanced over at the woman in question, pretending to survey the club while stealing glances to better assess her physical attributes.

Five-foot-four, three-inch naked heels, royal blue skin-tight fitting dress, straight black hair to midback, red lipstick just the way I like, voluptuous, oh, and the legs…smooth with nice muscular curves and thick thighs…

"You're drooling," Rodrigo laughed.

"Dude, she *is* fuckin' hot! She can't be lookin' at me…she's probably lookin' at you."

"That's an impressive girl, right there…she's checkin' you out hard. I wouldn't lie to you," Rodrigo said.

"Alright, let's put it to the test. We'll walk by," Abraham decided, driven by curiosity. The club was packed, making it easy to brush past her.

With purpose, Abraham closed the distance between them, fortunate that she and her friends were positioned near the entrance to the dance floor, creating a steady flow of foot traffic.

Their eyes locked.

Abraham flashed a half-smile, curious to see if she would take the bait.

She seductively smiled back at him, sipping on her drink.

Taking her response as an invitation, he placed his hand on her lower back.

"Hi," she purred, her alluring tone signaling him to proceed further.

Abraham had intended to fly by and gather intel, but Rodrigo had other plans. As Abraham drifted by, Rodrigo submerged himself with the four other girls in her company.

"Where's the party?" Rodrigo shouted, dancing as they surrounded him.

Abraham turned to see his partner enveloped by the most attractive girls in the club. Chuckling, he shook his head at the sight. *No surprise there,* he thought.

"Who's your friend?" the exotic-looking girl asked Rodrigo.

"That's my boy, Abraham!" Rodrigo answered.

"He's cute. Can I talk to him?" she asked Rodrigo, her eyes locking onto Abraham.

"*Can* you?" Abraham responded with a question of his own, taking over the conversation.

She smiled flirtatiously, tugging on his shirt, and pulling him closer. "Let's go dance," she demanded.

Her eyes were dark brown, with a nice round shape to them.

"What's your name?" Abraham asked.

She leaned over to Abraham's left ear and whispered softly, "Maria." Her Mexican accent flared with sexiness. "You don't remember me, do you?"

Abraham crinkled his brow, studying her features further. "You do look familiar…have we met before?"

"I had a class with you in college…psychology…we talked a couple of times. You sat in the back, and I sat in the front of the class…"

"I *do* remember now," he chuckled. "I never knew your name."

"When we talked, I remember saying to myself, 'why isn't he asking me out?'"

"Really?" Abraham asked, much to his surprise.

"You're like the only guy who has never asked me out!" she laughed.

"Sorry, I'm not trying to make history here."

"C'mon, let's go," she said. Maria grabbed his shirt and dragged him onto the dance floor on the upper level.

His thoughts drifted to memories he desperately sought to purge. *This is where Liv danced with that guy…*

Maria immediately brushed her backside against him. He felt the rotations of her hips on his pelvis. Her dress was thin enough that he could feel its firmness. His hands rested on her waist, stopping just above her glutes.

She thrust harder against him, placing her hands on top of his, waiting for him to take control.

Liv used to do that to me…

Liv invaded his thoughts, but the anger fueled his instincts. *Fuck it!*

He mustered up the courage to lower his hands onto her and caressed her backside. Maria wiggled further into him.

Rodrigo made his way to the dance floor with Maria's entourage of women. His eyes widened at the sight of the show Abraham and Maria put on in the middle of the club.

Abraham grabbed her arm and twisted her around, clutching her waist with both hands and pulling her body against his.

Maria gasped, surprised by his aggressiveness, yet welcoming the pleasure. She closed in on his left cheek, panting against his skin.

Rodrigo nudged Abraham's back with several elbows, signaling an emergency. Abraham glanced at Rodrigo, who spoke in a hushed tone. "Liv's here," Rodrigo informed him.

Abraham lost his breath as the words reached his ears. His heart raced, and a wave of shock hit him. Refocusing, he gathered himself to not show any physical signs of the onslaught of emotions.

Liv and Evelyn crept up on the dance floor. Abraham scanned with his peripheral and felt her presence behind him. Oblivious to Rodrigo's warning, Maria continued to dance on him.

Without hesitation, Abraham twirled Maria around, gripping her hips and pressing her backside against his pelvis. She danced seductively, enticing the attention of a few onlookers whose eyes widened in awe.

Abraham placed his hands on her curves, gently exploring their alluring contours.

Liv tapped Evelyn on the forearm, and they both gasped at the sight before them. Liv's face turned pale, her eyes transforming into cold stone.

Abraham caught a glimpse of Liv's defeated expression in his peripheral vision.

Determined to divert his attention, he spun Maria around again. This time, she leaned in close to his cheek, and he moved in, capturing her lips with his own.

Liv and Evelyn attracted the attention of a couple of regular nightclub patrons. As they approached, Liv danced provocatively, captivating the gazes of the men around her. In no time, the eager group of males closed in, and Liv and Evelyn danced purposefully with their newfound partners.

Maria wrapped her arms around Abraham's neck, gently resting her hand on the back of his head as her lips moved across his cheek.

Adding insult to injury, the DJ switched to a song that Abraham and Liv seductively danced to many times before. "Rapture" boomed from the giant four-foot speakers that surrounded the dance floor. As the song played, lyrics blasting, she screamed internally as the words burned her insides.

I'm mesmerized in every way
You keep me in a state of daze
You're kisses make my skin feel weak
I'm always melting in your heat
Then I soar like a bird in the wind
Oh, I glide as I'm flying through heaven

Mi amore, don't you know
My love, I want you so
Sugar, you make my soul complete
Rapture tastes so sweet

Liv's eyes burned with anger as she watched the exchange, her internal world shattering into pieces. She stormed off the dance floor, with Evelyn following closely behind, leaving their dance partners in the dust.

Maria temporarily released her grip on Abraham, but little did he know that she was just getting started.

Moving closer to Abraham's left side, Maria's lips grazed his cheek. Her Spanish accent oozed sensuality as she whispered into his ear, "I want to go home with you."

XVI
THE LAST TESTAMENT

Early July 2005

The Darkness devoured him, its infiltration akin to a stealth mission, and his heart and soul existed in a world commanded by its presence.

His latest conquest awaited him in bed, eager to have him all to herself. Abraham reached for a towel on the floor. *This is the one I used earlier,* he thought. The rendezvous a few hours prior was still fresh with the scent of pleasure.

"Abraham," she said with a smile.

"I can't," he interrupted before she could speak further.

Natalie had made it a habit to come over for a nightcap, enjoying the privilege of late-night invitations, thanks to her proximity to Abraham day in and day out.

"I just want to lie with you for a little bit," she pleaded.

"Get out," he demanded.

"Gawww, you don't have to be so rude! Do I have to leave *right* now?" Natalie's voice grew increasingly high-pitched.

"I don't want to cuddle. I'm hot-blooded…I'm just gonna sweat all over you."

"I was going to massage you but forget it! I wanted to talk to you about something…it's really important!"

"What is it?" he asked.

"I was going to leave my husband, and I—"

"Don't..."

"What do you mean, 'don't'?" she asked.

"Look, if you're going to leave him, then leave him for you. Don't leave him for me because I'm not going to be with you."

"You're so mean. Abraham, I love you, and I know you love me."

"Just leave," he said, firm in his resolve.

The Darkness performed its work with proficiency. Instead of exerting further effort, it admired its latest creation, a formidable force, as the former man of God caused chaos, disseminated lies, and deliberately inflicted pain.

He belonged to the Darkness now.

"Fine, just let me get my stuff," Natalie finally conceded to his demands. "And don't worry, I won't bother you at work tomorrow!"

Sexual encounters had become a nightly routine, but contrary to their previous significance, they now served as mere escapades. Feelings and emotions that were once necessary for him to drop his clothes were now a thing of the past. Seeking pleasure and fulfillment had replaced them.

Natalie quickly gathered her clothes and rushed to the restroom. He could hear her rustling around, clumsily bumping into the walls, opening and closing cabinets, and even the can of shaving cream clanking against the sink.

What the heck is she doing in there, he thought.

The bathroom door swung open with force. "Is this what you've been doing when I'm not here?" she asked, her anger evident as she held a condom wrapper in her hand. "This isn't the one you used with *me*!"

"Hey, we're not together."

"You're an asshole. I love you, and you don't even care!" The lump in her throat grew, and tears streamed down the swollen parts around her eyes. "...I know you want to be with me...I could be so good to you. I'll treat you like a king."

Abraham sighed heavily. "I'm seeing other girls, and I'm not going to be with you. I'm sorry...just leave."

"You're such an asshole! I hope you never have a daughter because one day she might go through this!" Natalie stormed out of the house, slamming the car door shut. He sensed her hesitation as she reversed her vehicle out of the driveway and into the street.

Reconciliation isn't in your favor...just go, he thought.

Amidst the tension, a buzzing noise grabbed his attention. His cell phone clamored incessantly from the couch. The screen lit up, revealing the identity of the caller.

Avril...what does she want?

With suspicion lingering, he answered. "Hello..."

"I need to talk to you," Avril said.

"Now isn't a good time...I'm busy."

"It's really important." The shakiness in her voice put him on high alert.

"Look, I don't want to talk right now. I'll call you later," he said.

Her next words shook him to his core, and they were words he would never forget. It marked the first time in his life that the consequences of his careless actions were becoming all too real. At that moment, the world stopped.

"Abraham...I'm pregnant."

XVII   CHOICES

His dark domain enveloped him like a second skin, deepening the already uncontrollable downward spiral. Seated in his office chair, he maintained an immaculate stillness.

"What are we going to do?" Avril asked, her voice tinged with hesitation, yet the answer already resided within her gut—a reality she had never wanted to face.

"We're not ready," he replied. "We're in no position to have a kid…"

I can't have a kid. I love Liv. I don't want to lose her. I want a life with her.

Abraham fought to regain his focus on the present, but the latest predicament served as damning evidence of his recklessness. His thoughts betrayed him, and he couldn't break free.

I can't, God. The Darkness is breaking me…it's too strong.

"There's only one other thing we can do. Do I need to make an appointment? Do you have the money to do it?" Avril asked.

Abraham's gaze fixated on the wooden floor. Countless thoughts raced through his mind. *I can't go through with this. My life's over if I do. I don't want to be with Avril for the rest of my life. I'm not ready to be a father…*

"Abraham? Are you there?"

"What do you think we should do?" he countered, hoping that if she voiced her opinion first, he might find some solace.

"I don't know…it's whatever you think we should do…" Her voice quivered, as if she were as shell-shocked as he was.

"Give me a second," he said. Abraham closed his eyes, expending the little energy he had left to satisfy his selfish need for answers. His senses instinctively revealed what he had foreseen long ago. The premonition was now unfolding, but not in the way he had imagined.

His mind raced. He had seen his little girl in a dream, knowing even then that his firstborn would be a girl. Back then, her mother remained unknown, but nonetheless, he had seen her, and it had filled him with unprecedented joy. But it was just a dream—a dream from which he could wake up, free from the burdens of responsibility and heartache.

Even now, a flicker of elation persisted, though those feelings would never surface. He knew what he wanted, but it wasn't with the person he wanted it with.

And then there was Liv…

He yearned for everything with her—a family, a home, a marriage, a few kids, and a couple of cats, just because they were her favorites. That was the life he wanted.

You're throwing it all away, he thought. *Liv still has my heart…If I do this, she'll never be with me again…*

"I guess…" Abraham faltered, reluctant to make the final decision. "…go ahead and make the call…and see how soon you can make an appointment."

This is not right…God, what am I supposed to do? I fucked up…and now I'm going to have to pay…how am I going to get out of this one?

He had given her his request, and it provided temporary relief, but the reality would soon set in. He was nearing a crossroads and either direction would change his life forever.

The Darkness understood precisely the catalyst he required, and it basked in glory. Luring Abraham to cross the line into darker regions brought the plan closer to fruition.

He was coming, and the Darkness waited for him at the door of desecration.

XVIII   FALLEN

Fire illuminated the sinister cave, housing several entities. At its center, a strategically placed throne commanded attention.

Seated upon the throne, a statuesque creature slouched, chin resting on a clenched fist. Its form bore a mixture of red, black, and brown hues, blending together in a faded complexion—a testament to a weathered warrior ravaged by battles.

"Do you have him?" the monstrous creature growled, its words echoing throughout the cavern.

A scrawny, skeletal minion knelt before the creature and its imposing throne, draped in a black cloak that almost camouflaged it amidst the darkness. "Sire, we are close to capturing him, but…he has started to resist."

"What do you mean, he's starting to fight?" The creature lifted its head, disturbed from deep contemplation.

"He has never displayed such formidable resistance before. Although he is nearing complete transformation, he is becoming increasingly aware…"

"You fool! Intensify the pursuit! Summon reinforcements and ensure he crosses over! He should have been under our control by now! Strip him of his armor!" Annoyance laced the creature's voice, and the flames surged in response, their fury reaching new heights within the cave. The creature rose from the throne, towering over the intimidated servants.

"Yes, Sire, we will persist in our assault." The minion bowed its head in submission before the terrifying monstrosity.

"Claim his heart...a mere nudge is all he needs..." the creature demanded. "The next time I see you, his soul better be consumed by darkness."

"Yes, Sire," the minion acquiesced with a lowered head.

The monstrosity settled back onto its throne. "And he will be ours..."

XIX  ATHENA

Doubts crashed into him, intensifying with each passing moment.

This is wrong. We shouldn't be doing this...

The nurse had informed him that no one was allowed in the room during the procedure. Protocol dictated that only the patient could enter the room where countless lives were taken. With no waiting rooms or places to dwell, he decided to leave the building.

Abraham wandered over to the neighboring taco hut, Cristian's Tacos, a local favorite. He convinced himself to at least have one taco, even though he hadn't eaten in days. Waiting was not one of his strong suits. *Idle hands do the devil's work,* he thought, attempting to convince himself that the damage hadn't already been done.

Finding a booth with an enormous window, he stared at the two-story structure adjacent to the taco hut, wondering what horrors might be unfolding within those walls.

Horrible things...things that people like us decide to do...

Tears welled up in his eyes.

Maybe...there's another way...

He stood up for a moment beside the booth.

I should just go over there and stop this before it's too late...

He sat back down and clasped his hands together.

God, forgive me…give me the strength to do what's right…

His heart waged war.

I can easily correct this slip-up…but it's not the right thing to do…

A kind older woman approached the booth. "Hi, what can I get you?" she asked with a warm smile.

"Uh, let me get a water and a chorizo and egg taco," he replied.

"Just one taco?"

"Yeah…just one," Abraham confirmed, stealing a glance at her name tag. *Esperanza…of course that would be her name…Hope..*

Abraham glanced over at the building next door.

God, your signs are never subtle…the Spanish twist is new…

He felt the presence of the Lord in the taco hut.

Okay, I'm going to eat this taco and then head over to stop it…

Esperanza brought him the solitary taco and a glass of water. "Here you go. Enjoy!" she said cheerfully.

"Thank you," he replied, and devoured the taco.

All right, God. Gimme the strength to go over there and stop this…

He reached into his front right pocket and extracted his wallet. Sliding out a ten-dollar bill, he left it on the table. As he did so, a card slipped out of his wallet and landed on the table.

His brow furrowed at the unexpected sight. *There's no way this could've fallen out on its own. My favorite prayer card…it's tucked way too deep in my wallet…*

Flipping the card over, he read it.

> *I was regretting the past and fearing the future.*
> *Suddenly my Lord was speaking:*
> *"My name is I Am"*
> *He paused.*
> *I waited.*
> *He continued.*
> *"When you live in the past with its mistakes and regrets, it*
> *is hard. I am not there. My name is not I WAS."*
> *"When you live in the future, with its problems and fears,*
> *it is hard. I am not there. My name is not I WILL BE.*

"When you live in this moment, it is not hard. I am here. My name is I AM."

Hellen Mallicoat

I'm living in the future…

Tears streamed down his face as he walked out the door of Cristian's Tacos, overwhelmed by the weight of what lay ahead.

I know she's a girl…I just know it…and I know what I'll name her…Athena…

A surge of determination propelled him forward as he left the restaurant.

Okay, God. I know what I need to do…

He took a deep breath and rehearsed what he'd say to the nurse upon entering. As he rehearsed the words, the insistent buzzing of his cell phone disrupted concentration.

No, it's the devil trying to distract me. Wait, what if it's important…I'd better check, just in case.

The screen illuminated with a new text message, and hope flickered in his heart as the name pooped up.

Avril? Maybe she didn't go through with it after all.

He opened the message and read two words that dropped his knees to the asphalt.

"It's done."

He cupped his hands over his face, his body jerked uncontrollably as tears gushed out.

God…forgive me…

WARFARE

Avril lay sound asleep, her body weary from the toll the procedure had taken.

The weight of mental anguish began to make its appearance by nightfall. The once-familiar silence now became deafening, amplifying the turmoil within him.

Feeling the palpable stillness, Abraham reached for a pen and a pad, seeking solace in the act of writing. He flung himself onto the futon, embracing the familiar comfort it offered, and allowed his emotions to surge through his pen. The enveloping darkness of the house served as a backdrop as he vomited words onto paper.

It all comes to an end...

God forgive me
There will be no delivery
So much sin in me
That could burn from here to infinity

We can't go back
The procedure was done,
As she faded to black

I was too late, and I suffered this fate
And so, it ends…
The most beautiful thing I could ever create

God forgive me, for I know not what I do
I understand that it was a gift from You
God forgive me, this mission has failed
Bless my baby, for my baby has sailed

The negative energy dissipated for the moment, but his senses warned it was just the beginning. The volatile emotions he felt were bound to resurface, crashing over him in relentless waves. Even the therapeutic act of writing could only offer temporary respite. Abraham released a heartfelt sigh and slumped over on the futon. In his weariness, the pen slipped from his grasp, clattering onto the wooden floor below.

The ensnarement of emotions carried him into a dream state, and it was a place where he least expected to be entangled in combat. It was exactly where his adversaries strategically orchestrated an ambush, and on the battlefield, the Darkness awaited.

THE RECKONING

Abraham stepped into the living room of his new house, but this time, he wasn't alone. A tiny visitor clung to him, their connection unbreakable.

"Hi, dada!" the little one exclaimed, beaming with a smile.

"Hi, baby!" he said to her. She looked exactly as he had imagined, just like she appeared in his dreams. *My daughter…this is my little girl.*

He cradled her in his right arm, carrying her with him everywhere around the house. Yet, despite their closeness, he struggled to get a clear view of her. No matter how hard he strained, his neck refused to cooperate. He could only catch glimpses of her from the corner of his eye, and she was beautiful. With her dark hair mirroring his own and her chubby, round face, she was a precious sight.

Tears streamed down his face. *I'm so sorry, I should've never done what I did.* Shame devoured him. His soul was overtaken by remorse, his heart shattered into countless fragments of regret.

Before he could plunge deeper into sorrow, an evil presence surrounded them. An ominous black arm reached out, threatening to snatch his daughter away. Instinctively, Abraham shielded her, cradling her tiny head against his chest. The arm suspended in midair, slowly decloaked the rest of its body as it transformed into a humanoid figure.

The entity approached with fierce determination, positioning itself on Abraham's left side, one inch from his face.

Desperately averting his gaze, Abraham found himself unable to escape the entity's presence. Its voice, a deep growl, pierced his ear. "You killed her."

The sinister utterance sent shivers down Abraham's spine, as the foul beast warned him of a terrifying truth. The entity was no mere human. "You failed her," the voice growled, its menacing tone resounding. "You belong to us now. We *own* you."

XXII

BEGINNING OF THE END

Abraham jolted upright from his pillow, his hand instinctively reaching for his phone. With a single press of a button, the dark room was illuminated.

4:01 a.m.

The Darkness circled around him. It monitored his reaction to the latest injection of fear and anger, and this time, guilt.

He stumbled towards the bedroom, peeking inside only to find it empty.

Avril was gone.

She left. We could've talked about it at least.

Stumbling back to the futon, he reached for the pen and the pad. The ink discharge wreaked of hopelessness. The Darkness robbed every ounce of hope it could get, and now, he was running thin. A horde of unpleasant thoughts spilled onto paper.

Abraham Moreno, esteemed early childhood teacher, died last night of heart complications. He was 25 years old…

He penned the final sentence and then transferred the cryptic transmission from paper to text message. His finger hesitated before finally pressing the send button. He laid his phone to rest and as the light shut off, so did he.

XXIII

APOLOGIES BEFORE EULOGIES

10:27 a.m.

In a matter of hours, Abraham had his first visitor. He left the door unlocked in anticipation of guests.

Ricky entered the dimly lit house. "Hey, dude...I got your text. Thought I'd come check on ya," he said.

It had been quite some time since their last communication, and a lot had changed over the course of four years.

"What's going on?" Ricky asked, his concern leading him into the dark corridor.

Abraham sat on the futon in silence, struggling to find the right words.

Ricky sat down next to Abraham. "You know I'm not good at this," he said.

"Yeah, I know," Abraham replied in a low voice, barely audible. "Nevertheless, I had to send it to you."

"What made you write that?"

Abraham let out a heavy sigh. "Time is given to all of us...we never know how much of it we have left."

"We haven't been close in the last couple of years," Ricky paused, his voice filled with remorse. "I'm sorry, brother, for what I did. I should have never said those things. You're like my brother. You *are* my brother."

Abraham heard the sincerity in his voice and noticed tears welling up in his eyes. "In sixteen years…this is the first time I've ever heard you apologize. I forgave you…a long time ago. I always wondered why you would do that to me, but it doesn't matter now. All I have ever done is take care of you and love you like a brother."

"My family is always here for you…you know that," Ricky said.

"I know they are…and I love them as if they were my own," Abraham said from amidst the shadows. "Thanks for coming by. I love you, brother."

"I love you too, brother. If you need anything…call me."

"I'll be all right."

"I know…you always find a way." Ricky swiftly made his way out the door, just as quickly as he had arrived.

Maybe not this time, Abraham thought.

12:32 p.m.

Jason burst into the house, causing the screen door to slam shut behind him. "What's wrong? Why did you send that text?" he asked.

"I don't know, I just…" Abraham hesitated, fully aware that he couldn't deceive Jason. "…you know I'm a writer. It was on my mind."

"So, what's going on? Why would you think of something like that and then send it?" Jason pressed, eagerly awaiting an explanation. "Bro, talk to me."

"Have you ever done something…that changes your whole life? Something you wish you never did…and you can never go back?" Abraham gathered himself. He leaned back on the futon and took a deep breath, exhaling his disgust as he stared at the popcorn ceiling.

He had known Jason for nine years, their bond growing exponentially over time. Abraham found solace in knowing that two of the people he loved most were now connected as family: Jason married Lisa, and Margie married Lisa's father, Richard. Even if they were unaware, he needed Margie and Jason now more than ever.

"You know, it's a small world...in our band of brothers, we're legit family now. You probably see Margie more than I do," Abraham said.

"Margie asked if I've talked to you lately. Now, I know why..." Jason's voice trailed off, sensing the weight of the situation.

"There's going to be a time...real soon...when I'll need your help. I can't tell you when or how, but that time is coming..."

Jason sat down beside him on the red futon. Abraham held many secrets, and his plea was enough for Jason to understand that he wasn't ready to reveal them just yet.

"I'll be there," Jason assured him.

"Whenever that time should come, I'll let you know."

Jason reached over, placing his hand on Abraham's shoulder. "I'll be there."

XXIV FATHER OF LIES

Margie was well-versed in navigating the clandestine channels of the curandero world. "There's someone I want you to meet. I've been going to her for a few months…maybe, she can help." Margie said, her history of rescuing him from dark moments fresh in his mind. She possessed an uncanny ability to extricate people from the depths of despair.

As they drove down Pleasanton Road, Margie veered into the parking lot of a nondescript *tiendita* on the south side. Although he had passed by this place countless times, he had never set foot inside. Margie seemed to possess an intimate knowledge of hidden enclaves dedicated to spiritual warfare.

Upon entering, it resembled any other curandera shop he had visited in the past. The tienda was replete with aged trinkets—statues, candles, oils, and an assortment of weapons and remedies catering to the spiritual realm.

"Hi, can I assist you with anything?" a young girl inquired.

"We're here to see Yadira," Margie responded.

"She's currently with a customer, but I'll let her know you've arrived."

As Abraham perused the store, an aisle laden with figurines caught his attention. Amidst the cluttered shelves, he was captivated by a three-inch statue of Jesus, emanating an aura of divine glory. The outstretched arms of the figurine beckoned to him, bearing circular marks resembling droplets of blood.

With hesitation, Abraham reached out to grasp the statue.

"Abraham," Margie called, motioning for him to join her.

Turning away from the statue, he admired it briefly before complying with Margie's gesture.

"She's ready for you," Margie said.

Abraham stole a final glance at the statue, entranced by its presence, as he walked away.

Come back to me…

Abraham halted in his tracks, unsure if what he heard was a whisper or merely a voice echoing within his mind. He glanced to his left and right, searching for the source.

Let me fight for you…

He peeked over his shoulder at the statue. *I'll come back…*

He proceeded to the rear of the store, disappearing behind a heavy curtain. Behind it, he discovered nothing more than an aged storeroom, teeming with stacked boxes reminiscent of the chaotic disarray in his own home. Seated behind a small table was an older Hispanic woman, who promptly fixated her gaze upon his entry. Her brown complexion bore faint wrinkles, mostly around her eyes, suggesting she was in her mid-fifties. With jet-black hair, he speculated that she probably dyed it.

"Please, have a seat," she said, her voice gentle and devoid of the harshness he had expected. "I haven't seen you before…do you know Margie?"

"Yeah, she's my aunt," Abraham replied.

"She's a kind woman…very generous," she added.

"Yeah, she's the best." Abraham placed his hands on his lap, studying Yadira's workspace.

"What's your name?' Yadira asked.

"Abraham."

"Abraham...interesting," she said, flashing a smile.

What the hell does that mean, he thought.

"I'm Yadira. I'm sure your aunt told you. So, Abraham, what brings you here?"

"My aunt brought me to see you and, I'm gonna be honest, I have no idea why."

"Is there something you'd like to know or find out?"

What the heck is this? Margie brought me to a witch doctor...great. "Not that I know of."

Yadira observed him, taking in his facial features. "Uh-huh," she uttered every few seconds.

Abraham was accustomed to awkward silences and behaviors. He dealt with them frequently with his Pre-K students, and his counseling skills allowed him to engage in uncomfortable exchanges.

"Let me see your hands," she said. It was more of a demand than a request.

Abraham reached across the table and offered her both hands. He studied the tablecloth, noticing the Native American designs reflecting the Aztec culture. Perhaps this practice was a ritual passed down from her ancestors, he thought.

Yadira took hold of his hands, scrutinizing his palms. She briefly flipped them over, as if ensuring they were made of flesh, before returning them to their original position.

Abraham curiously noticed the intricacies of her ritual. *What's she doing?*

Yadira placed her palms on his, oblivious to his gestures. "Your energy..." she said, her voice becoming more animated. "Oh, my."

"What does *that* mean?"

"Well, there's a lot going on here." The energy transfer continued to speak to her. "You've recently experienced a major change...something new...you spend most of your time alone..."

"I just moved into a new house..."

"I can sense it...it's an old house."

"It's new, but old, whatever..."

"There's a small space in your house, not quite a room. When you walk out of the bedroom and go to the restroom, there's a small area, and then there's another doorway."

Abraham listened intently. "That's the closet. It's a long walk-in closet. At some point, it was a minor addition to the house." *How does she know what my house looks like?*

"Has anything strange happened in that house since you've been there?"

Abraham furrowed his brow, deep in thought. "No, not really…"

"This might sound strange, but I believe you'll understand. Do you *feel* anything unusual about the house?"

"Yes…I have…on several occasions."

"Describe it to me," she said.

Abraham recollected the events she wanted to hear. *I can't tell her the truth…she'll think I'm crazy.*

Yadira sensed his hesitation. "Abraham, it's okay…I know you have unique abilities…"

"What did you say?" he asked. Yadira's words were meant to reassure him, but they surprised him more than anything. "What do you mean?"

"We'll address that later. First, tell me what you felt in there," Yadira said, capturing Abraham's interest. She appeared genuine, dispelling his initial perception of her as a phony. *If I engage further, she'll tell me more as well.*

"I can feel when they're close…it's an evil presence…like they're after me or something…" he confessed.

"Have you seen them?"

"Yeah, I mean, no. Kinda. I see them with my other set of eyes if you know what I mean…"

"Your mind's eye,' Yadira affirmed without missing a beat. "Who lived in the house before you?"

"No one. It's been vacant for about twenty years…"

Yadira nodded. "That makes sense…"

"Why are they in there?" Abraham asked, his curiosity mounting.

"They made their home there...and they didn't appreciate it when you moved in. But they've been waiting for you..." Yadira began putting the pieces of the supernatural puzzle together.

"What do you mean 'waiting for me'?"

"They're trying to bring you down, to hinder you from fulfilling your purpose. Otherwise, they wouldn't be fighting so fiercely. The choice is always yours," Yadira explained.

"Do you feel like yourself lately?" she questioned.

"Not at all, honestly," Abraham admitted, recalling the unsettling events of late.

"They're filling your head with lies...doubts...fears. They're attacking your mind, your thoughts," Yadira warned.

Spiritual warfare. "They're all lies...to get me to submit...to give up hope."

"These entities in your house were sent for a reason, just like you were. You possess unique abilities," she paused. "...seeing the future, communing with the departed, and so much more. But it's not about the abilities themselves, it's what you're destined to do with them that frightens the devil. As soon as you start fulfilling the purpose God created you for, the enemy will dispatch special forces. You must be on the right path, or else they wouldn't be targeting you so heavily."

Abraham recalled a recent sermon by Pastor Levi, which emphasized the enemy's stealthy infiltration into people's lives. "He's the Father of Lies...and I've allowed him a seat at my table."

"You can change that, but you'll need help. Abraham, you have the power to make a difference, but you must believe in it again. Until we close this portal in your house, you have to pray and have faith that God is with you," Yadira advised.

"Portal?" Abraham questioned, his concern mingled with confusion, though his intuition warned him of a supernatural malevolence lurking within the closet.

"They're entering through the closet...they're using your past to torment you. Make peace with your past."

"That's why I keep the light on in there all day and night. I had a strong feeling that was the case, but I wasn't sure of it till now."

"This form of warfare is supernatural. There are no rules of engagement, and they will exploit the things you hold most dear. Your father...your daughter...your mistakes...they will not hesitate to take everything away from you..."

"I don't have a daughter..." Abraham countered.

Yadira paused for a moment, then replied, "You were going to...I'm sorry."

"How did you know that? Nobody knows that!" he snapped.

"I didn't mean to upset you. Your grief is understandable. I have a way of perceiving things all at once. Please forgive me," Yadira said.

Abraham sighed, consumed by anguish. "What did she...um..." His voice trembled, and a lump formed in his throat, momentarily silencing his words. "What did she look like?"

Yadira studied him. ' She bore a striking resemblance to..."

"Never mind," Abraham interrupted before she could reveal more. "I don't know why I asked. You don't have to tell me."

"I can sense your grief," Yadira empathized. "You're grappling with unresolved feelings towards your father. You want to save him, but you're unsure how...make peace with your past."

Abraham nodded in agreement. "We need to close this portal...the sooner, the better."

"I agree. I'll contact Margie to arrange a day and time for us to gather at your house before it's too late. We don't want to leave it to chance, and have it open any longer than it has to be."

"Too late?" Abraham questioned.

"We're dealing with real evil here. It's a doorway to darkness."

XXV

CROSS TO CARRY

Make peace with my past…

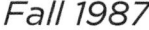

Fall 1987

Michelle sat cross-legged on her bed, as silent as a mouse. Her homework rituals were as precise as clockwork, while Abraham shifted to the desk beside her bed, hoping for a mathematical miracle. The desk had a vintage charm with its metal frame and wooden top. Abraham's math book lay open, as he struggled to multiply using his fingers. Third grade brought a myriad of challenges, including multiplication, a concept he just couldn't grasp.

The multiplication sign looks like a cross laying down…my grades are getting bad…I need to figure this out before anyone finds out…

Ray burst into the room without warning and headed straight to the desk. He scanned Abraham's work. "That one's wrong. Do it again," Ray said, pointing to the first problem on the paper. Abraham erased it and rewrote it.

114

$$14$$
$$\times \underline{12}$$

Ray's eyes bore into the loose-leaf paper and Abraham's skull simultaneously. Abraham hesitantly jotted down a 6 on his paper. Ray's heavy hand swooped down, striking Abraham's chest. The blow caught him off guard, causing both him and the desk to jerk back forcefully, and his pencil flew out of his hand.

He must know about my grades.

"Do it again!" Ray yelled.

Disoriented from the strike, Abraham struggled to recall the multiplication procedure. This time, he wrote even more slowly, as if tiptoeing through a minefield.

"I'm good at math, and you should be too!" Ray scolded.

Abraham made a second attempt, only to forget the zero in the hundreds place. Ray's hand swooped down again, knocking Abraham and the desk back against Michelle's bed. Michelle, on the other hand, remained focused on her own schoolwork, observing the math debacle unfold.

This is just the first problem…c'mon Abraham, get through this.

The third attempt, plagued by doubt, only worsened matters. Abraham had forgotten to place number one in the ones place for the final answer—a simple oversight with severe ramifications.

Ray made his way to the door. "Go stand by your bed," he commanded as he walked out of the bedroom.

Abraham stumbled out of the desk and leaned against his bed, facing the wall. From the corner of his eye, he caught a glimpse of Ray grabbing a belt off the rocking chair just outside the bedroom. Without a sound, three lashes fell upon him, but he refused to cry out.

"Now do it again and do it right this time!" Ray's voice boomed.

Abraham completed the first problem and proceeded to the next. Right from the start, he copied problem number three instead of problem number two.

Ray pointed at the bed. "Go stand over there." He picked up the belt and delivered three more lashes to Abraham's backside. With every blow, Ray grunted while Abraham, determined not to make a sound, stood his ground as much as an eight-year-old could.

Ray remained silent as Abraham returned to the desk. *This one should be easier.* He regained his composure and scribbled problem number two.

$$23$$
$$\times\ \underline{10}$$

He jotted down the first digit of the answer but immediately flipped the pencil over to erase it.

3...no, it should be a 0...

"Go," Ray pointed to the bed. Abraham limped over to the side of the bed. Ray swung his arm back and unleashed three more powerful lashes. The cycle continued until all ten problems were completed.

Abraham finished five minutes before bedtime, and for the first time, he looked forward to a good night's sleep. Michelle had dozed off as soon as the lights went off, but Abraham needed at least thirty minutes to calm his racing heart. Falling asleep with his backside and the back of his legs throbbing was a problem he could live with.

He closed his eyes, tossing and turning while the pain persisted. After thirty-three lashes, he mustered the strength to convince himself to rest. *Go to sleep, it's over.* His mind raced. *I got hit for not knowing math?*

Ray whispered to Gloria in the living room just outside the bedroom. "I hit him hard...I'm going to tell him sorry..."

Ray sneaked into the darkened room. Abraham, wide awake, pretended to be sound asleep.

"Aba," Ray whispered. "I'm sorry for hitting you." He waited for a response, but after a few seconds, he left the room.

I don't want to hear sorry...fuck that! You can't come in here and expect everything to be okay. I did nothing wrong!

Abraham contained the anger welling up as best he could.

"He's asleep," Ray whispered to Gloria.

Fuck him! Mom didn't even come in once. I have to watch it 'till I get old enough, big enough, to stand up to him. I guess I'm by myself 'till then. Maybe I could live with grandma…nah, they'd never let me. It's a lot of years 'till I can be on my own and leave. Sister Pino said everyone has a cross to carry. Maybe this is mine. Isn't my dad supposed to love me? Isn't he supposed to help me? Maybe one day we can be close…yeah, just like Rene and his dad…but he's mean all the time…and he's really mean to mom sometimes. Never mind…I'll hold it together 'till I get older. God…I just want to go to sleep. Aren't you supposed to love your dad?

In the early morning hours, Abraham forced himself out of bed, feeling an urgent need to relieve his bursting bladder. Navigating through the darkness had become second nature to him. Waking Ray up in the middle of the night for no good reason, especially if he was in a grumpy mood, was always a recipe for trouble.

As he pulled down his shorts, a sudden soreness in his legs caught his attention. Sitting on the toilet, he winced, feeling a dull ache in his bottom. Curiosity got the better of him, and he flicked on the light for a brief moment, examining his surroundings. After pulling up his shorts, he twisted his neck, imitating an owl's movement, trying to catch a glimpse of his body. Within a few hours, he noticed an array of purple bruises scattered across the back of his legs and bottom.

He's never hit me hard enough to give me bruises before. I better not tell anybody…I don't want to get in more trouble…I'll just stay away from dad…is he mad at me for not being good in math? Am I embarrassing him for not being good enough?

In an attempt to quell his racing thoughts, he quickly turned off the light. However, the questions continued to plague him.

Abraham, you're not good enough for basketball…you're not good enough for math…you're not good enough for third grade…maybe I'm not a good son…God, aren't you supposed to love your dad?

XXVI TRIAD THUNDER

Abraham vividly recalled the memory as if it had happened just yesterday. The psychological aspect helped him process it, but the Darkness knew how to strike, and Yadira's words rang true.

It's spewing out…I have to take control of these emotions…my training wasn't for nothing…or maybe the enemy is exploiting my tactics…

Reflection had once been a daily practice, but now it seemed distant, overshadowed by the encroaching darkness clouding his judgment.

Never let anyone tell you, that you can't do something great…never let anyone rob you of who you are…never let circumstances dictate who you're meant to be…

Self-coaching had become a rarity, but the triggered memory sparked an evolution within him that had served him well throughout the years.

You're better than this…go back to the beginning…take control of yourself…

His hands shook uncontrollably.

Athena, forgive me…my sweet baby girl…I need to work through this…who can I call? Maybe Michelle can calm me down.

With hopeful anticipation, he retrieved his cell phone, desperate to reach out to her.

She'll remind me of who I once was...

"Hello?" A sweet voice answered on the other end.

"Michelle..." The sound of her voice caused his entire being to tremble, and tears immediately streamed down his cheeks, falling from his face.

"What's wrong?" she asked, concern evident in her voice.

Abraham sobbed uncontrollably, his words choked with anguish. Michelle felt utterly helpless in the face of his distress. "I'm struggling, Michelle...I'm not gonna lie to you. I used to be good, Michelle...I was so good before. I'm all messed up, now."

"Abraham, what's wrong? Talk to me. Dad said y'all got into a fight," she said as worry laced her voice.

"I wanted to kill him, Michelle...I've never felt like that before. I've done a lotta horrible things...and I can never take them back."

"Abraham, calm down. Tell me what's going on?"

"I made mistakes that I can never fix."

"It's okay, people make mistakes. You've been through a lot lately."

"No, Michelle...it's not okay," Abraham wept, tears flowing profusely. Michelle could sense the agony in his voice. "There's no excuse...I know I'm better than this."

"Awww, Aba, I wish I was there to help you," she said.

"Me too, but I know I have to do this alone..." he sobbed.

"Aba, you're not alone. It's going to be okay. Let Margie help you."

A few houses down, Paulina skipped on the sidewalk.

"Be careful, Goose!" Gloria shouted, trailing behind her.

"Look, there he is!" Paulina exclaimed, pointing at Abraham sitting on the porch.

Abraham scrambled to compose himself, hastily wiping away his tears as Paulina approached him. "I have to let you go. Paulina is coming and I can't let her see me like this."

"Okay, call me later. Give Paulina a big hug for me. I love you," Michelle said.

Paulina skipped all the way up to the porch, dressed in her finest clothes for the occasion. Her overalls were now shorts instead of pants, and she wore a new pair of pink converse, adding to her collection.

"Happy Birthday, Abraham!" Paulina shouted.

Abraham pretended to sneeze multiple times, as if trying to explain the redness in his eyes caused by his tears. "Thank you, Goose! Do you remember when you used to call me Ham?"

"No," she laughed. "Ham…that sounds funny! Why are your eyes red? Were you crying?"

"No, I have rowdy allergies today," he said. "You're getting so big, Paulina. You're already a big girl…seven-years-old!" He desperately tried to change the subject.

"How old are you now? Sixteen?" Paulina asked.

Abraham chuckled at her assumption. "I'm twenty-six today…" He appreciated her innocence. *Athena would have looked like her, I know it.* He hugged Paulina tightly. *Abraham, stop…rewire your thinking.* He couldn't help but be reminded of what could have been when Paulina was around.

"I love you," he said to her.

"I love you, too."

"Guess who I was just talking to?"

"Who?"

"Your sister!"

"Michelle!" Paulina screamed.

"Yeah, and you used to call her 'Shell.' Do you remember?"

"Yes," she laughed. "What did she say?"

Abraham held her hand as they walked together toward Gloria's house. "She said she loves you and she'll see us soon. You know what I told her you and her remind me of?"

"What?"

"A Triad Thunder…"

"What's *that*?" she asked, curious.

"It's like…a lot of power, kind of like how thunder is really powerful, and triad means three. You, me, and Michelle…that's three. You both give me power…and hope." Abraham did his best to explain what Paulina and Michelle meant to him as they walked back to Gloria's house.

"Come on, Abe, we have your cake," Gloria said, motioning them inside.

Abraham held Paulina's little hand, switching her to his right side. "Here, Goose. Walk on this side of me. Stay on the inside of the sidewalk. In case a car drives off the road, they'll hit me first," he said.

"Hey! Don't say that!' she said. "Come inside, Abraham. The cake looks good!"

Thunder bolted toward Abraham and Paulina. Like a wild horse, the bulldog jumped in Paulina's direction, grazing the side of her leg and nearly knocking her down.

"Thunder!" Paulina yelled.

As they entered the house, the cake was in plain sight, resting on the table.

"Happy birthday, dude! Your favorite!" Gloria exclaimed, a triumphant smile on her face. "Ice cream cake!" She pointed excitedly to the Oreo rendition of the frozen delight.

Abraham scooped up a piece of cake with his finger and playfully smeared the icing on Paulina's nose.

"Ahhh!" Paulina shrieked, her laughter uncontrollable.

"Here, have a taste," he offered, guiding his fork toward her face.

"No!" she said, quickly moving her head to the side, narrowly headbutting him in the mouth as she hopped onto his lap.

"For real this time," he reassured her, a warm smile spreading across his face.

Her innocent brown eyes and infectious giggles lifted his spirits in ways she couldn't possibly comprehend. He leaned down and planted a gentle kiss on the top of her head. *I wish she was my own daughter. I could probably take care of her and raise her way better than dad can. No, don't think that way...be in the moment with Paulina...let her give you hope...*

As Abraham fed her another mouthful of cake, she had only one comment to add on his birthday.

"Yummy!"

XXVII THE WAR ROOM

The church was enveloped in a serene silence, as St. Leo's stood strong against the passage of time. It had come alive during the Prohibition year of 1919, and for Abraham, this sacred place had a remarkable ability to revive his spirit.

Choosing the last pew to the right, he swiftly pulled out the kneeler and sank to his knees. His pleas extended towards the tabernacle, where a radiant light shone upon the figure of Christ suspended on the cross.

Returning to this sanctuary felt different this time, not solely because he dared to enter in shorts and tennis shoes, defying the customary reverence of God's house.

Time seemed frozen within the church walls, untouched by the passing years. Abraham recalled his elementary and middle school days, and the interior appeared exactly as he remembered. Banners adorned both sides of the cross, exchanged with each season. Now, resplendent green silk banners cascaded in the backdrop. On the left banner, a white cross with intertwining vines took center stage, accompanied by elegant white italic lettering that read, "I Am the Vine." The right banner showcased a mighty tree, its roots visibly entwined in the soil. Above the tree, a graceful white dove soared. Below it, the white italic letters spelled out, "The Tree of Life."

Not a speck of grime marred the pristine black piano, and the six white candles on the tabernacle emitted a gentle flame. The illuminated cross, against which Jesus hung, emanated a warm glow.

I wonder if Father Richard is still here...

It had only been a year and a half since their last heart-to-heart, and somehow, Abraham's situation had worsened since then.

Where do I start? Abraham smirked. *Have I forgotten how to pray?*

He closed his eyes, hoping to recall a long-forgotten ritual.

It's been a long time since I've been in here...so much has happened since then...but You already know that...

He clasped his hands tightly, convinced that the strength of his grip could somehow deepen his prayers, or at least he yearned for it to be so.

I never thought I needed a war room...I know why it's necessary now...

A single piano key reverberated through the church, its sound echoing in the hallowed space. Abraham scanned the area around the tabernacle, but there was no one seated at the piano, nor any visible signs of movement.

Another high-pitched key rang out.

Followed by another.

Ushers, maybe? They're just fucking with me...

A low-pitched key resounded. He surveyed the empty church, the fine hairs on his arms standing erect like tiny sentinels on high alert.

The lights flickered on and off like lightning strikes, and the scent of sulfur infiltrated his nostrils, overwhelming the church. If an evil presence lurked within, it had breached the sanctity of holy ground, instantly conjuring worst-case scenarios in his mind.

They're here for me...

Emerging from behind the tabernacle, a figure dressed in black from head to toe rose into view.

The Man in Black...

His heart raced.

War had become a wretched and treacherous battlefield that wore out the spiritual soldier he once was long ago.

Get back on the clock. He coached himself, preparing for the impending confrontation.

With cautious steps, the Man in Black moved around the tabernacle until he stood directly in front of it. Though his eyes remained concealed in darkness, their intensity seemed to pierce through Abraham's skull. Wrapped in a trench coat and wearing a fedora that concealed his features, the Man in Black emanated an enigmatic aura.

What's he doing here?

The Man in Black descended the steps of the tabernacle with measured strides, his feet landing softly on the maroon carpet that led straight towards Abraham.

I'm in freakin' church…what the fuck? Just ignore him…

"You can't ignore me!" the Man in Black bellowed, his voice echoing through the church.

What the fuck? He knows my thoughts…

"It doesn't feel good to be on the other side, does it?" the Man in Black taunted, his movements resembling a panther closing in on its prey. "Reading people's thoughts…"

Our Father who art in heaven…

"You can't get rid of me! And you can't pray your way out of this."

Fighting back the rising panic, Abraham clenched his eyes shut and maintained his kneeling position, his body rigid. *No, this is a dream…just like the last one I had…this dude ain't real…*

The Man in Black's voice sliced through Abraham's thoughts. "This, my friend, is not a dream."

"You have no power here!" Abraham shouted, hearing the approaching footsteps.

"Oh, no? Then how am I here? Let me enlighten you," the Man in Black sneered with arrogance. "It all started with the single most important event that brought us to this point…you let your best friend die," he whispered. "But wait, there's more. You committed adultery, betraying the love of your life. You seek revenge against the man who humiliated and beat you down…your father, a real piece of work. We've done wonders with him, by the way. And yet, even now, you hold on to a glimmer of hope for him, but that's a tale for another time." The Man in Black paced back and forth down the aisle, delivering his dark sermon. "Deep down, I know you harbor a desire to inflict pain upon others. How can you ever redeem yourself from all this wickedness? There's no hope for you because…here's the one that will eventually push you over…"

He can't get to me…

"Oh, yes, I can," the Man in Black sneered. "Because deep down, you believe, without a shred of doubt, that you're not nearly as good as you think you are. And as for your unborn daughter…you made the choice to end her life. She never stood a chance…because you took it from her!"

Fuck…here we go…I'm gonna have to fight…he's not gonna stop…God, I need you…

"God can't aid you, not even within these walls," the Man in Black declared. "And if you refuse to join me, then you *will* have to fight…but know this: everyone who has challenged me has come to realize one undeniable truth: I am unbeatable."

Abraham rose from the pew, striding confidently to the center of the maroon carpet, his gaze locked with the Man in Black. *I'm out of shape, but I think I can take him.*

A soothing energy whisked from behind, cloaking him in a comforting embrace, like a warm blanket draped over his shoulders.

I Am with you. Let me fight for you.

The whisper echoed in his mind. With newfound resolve, resorting to normal fighting styles was no more as he fought now with head and heart, together.

"You have no power here!" Abraham shouted.

"You have no idea who I really am." The Man in Black charged toward Abraham at full speed, but instead of engaging in a typical confrontation,

Abraham readied himself, preparing to lunge forward with all his might, akin to a football player delivering a blindside hit.

As the Man in Black closed in within five feet, he suddenly vanished into thin air.

What the fuck? Where'd he go?

He scanned the church, his hands trembling, his breathing heavy, searching every nook and cranny for any sign of his adversary.

Abraham sank to his knees, taking a moment to collect himself, relieved that he wouldn't have to fight today.

I thought I'd be safe here...

At that moment a swirling energy buzzed around him, growing louder and louder.

A low-pitched growl emerged from thin air behind him.

"I know what you've done. You believe closing the portal is the only way to stop us, but there are other methods. This fight is inevitable."

Abraham turned his head slowly, his body crouching stealthily like a rabbit evading a hawk. *Where is he?*

"The Great Darkness has come."

The Man in Black reappeared beside Abraham, grabbing the back of his shirt and hoisting him off the ground. With a swift motion, he swung Abraham around in a full circle, launching him towards the cross at the center of the church.

Abraham soared through the air, propelled by the force of the Man in Black's throw. He tumbled and rolled across fifteen pews, finally coming to a stop. Despite the impact, he quickly rose to his feet, anticipating another attack. But to his surprise, the Man in Black had vanished, dissipating into nothingness.

"This isn't real...the enemy is infiltrating my thoughts..."

XXVIII SPIRITUAL WARRIOR

Gripping the wooden shaft firmly with both hands, Abraham raised his arms above his head and swung the axe with fierce determination. The tree stump stood no chance against his assault. Its hollow bark housed an infestation of ants, bees, and countless other eight-legged creatures.

As pieces of bark scattered into the grass, Abraham grimaced at the sight. While chopping down the eyesore wasn't the issue, his anger seemed uncontrollable. The act of releasing frustration was his goal, but with each strike, his fury only multiplied.

The infuriating insects fueled his rage, and every blow from the axe felt like a step closer to dismantling their creepy-crawly empire.

Yet, he knew deep down that his recent battles were ones he had no chance of winning—at least not in his present condition.

The devil is beating me down…

The losses were mounting. The thought of continued failure consumed him, and the tree bore the brunt of his wrath.

A deluge of sweat dripped from his cheeks and chin. Throughout the past few months of living in the shadows, this was the first task he was determined to complete.

He tightened his grip on the axe, raising it high before bringing it down with a thunderous blow. The trunk cracked open, creating a crevice large enough for him to fill with leaves and old bank statements as fuel for the fire. Pouring paperwork into the fire pit had become a ritual, but this time, the tree trunk would become a victim of the pyro party.

With a single strike of a match, a flame ignited an old credit card receipt. The flame grew, evolving into a roaring blaze, as it voraciously devoured the multitude of numbers and letters on the abundance of paperwork. It reminded him of old times—the flames rising higher, reaching the lower branches of a nearby tree.

A fire rises…
…that was so long ago…
…what used to be…
…I barely remember what that felt like…

Engaging in deep thinking wasn't a novelty. He relished introspection, but dwelling in self-pity and depression didn't sit well with him. Yet, reminiscing about what he used to be only exacerbated his downward spiral.

The creaking sound of the backyard gate slowly swinging open broke through his thoughts, alerting him to an unannounced visitor. He heard the clank of the latch. Gripping the axe tightly against his chest, he prepared himself.

Visitors had become a rarity these days. To the world, his whereabouts remained unkown and his cell phone hadn't rung, indicating that the person behind him had arrived uninvited. He readied the axe, preparing to strike.

I'll kill this motherfucker…

Under the gentle footsteps, dried weeds crunched quietly as the trespasser crept closer. He closed his eyes, ready to wield the hefty axe.

"You're trespassing," he said.

"Easy there, tiger. Don't chop me up!" a gentle voice responded.

"Kay?" He swiveled his body, confirming that his ears weren't deceiving him.

"Abe! It's been so long!"

"What are you doing here?"

"I was in the neighborhood and thought I'd check on you. How are things?" she asked.

"Eh, you know…holding. In the neighborhood? You live ten million miles away," he chuckled.

"Thought I'd surprise you! How's work going?"

"It's good. I got a promotion. I just got word of it the other day. When I report back in August, I'll be the Assistant Director of the early childhood center I work at."

"Oh, that's great news! Congratulations!"

"Thank you…I love what I do. I guess I'll give it a shot and see how it goes."

"That's good. I don't think you'll like it though," Kay spoke truths that most people were unaware of. Abraham admired her transparency, and her foreshadowing was seldom wrong.

"Why not?" he asked.

"You'll miss the kids too much."

"I already do," he admitted.

She observed his body language, solidifying her instincts that had originated hundreds of miles away. His hunched posture betrayed him. "You sound different…your speech patterns aren't as lively and animated as I remember. You've regressed," she said, venturing straight into the depths of his psyche.

"Is it that noticeable?" he asked.

"Let's just say your energy levels are way off, and you appear…unbalanced."

"Thanks for the support," he said, jokingly.

"I felt your distress call, and I don't mean the one over the phone. You're always trying to act like everything's okay."

"I'm surprised the telepathy worked this time…*things* are not working so well as of late. I knew if anything, you'd be able to hear the call…and here you are."

"And I heard you loud and clear…why do you think that is?" Kay understood the dynamics of dilemmas and conflicts.

"It's a Jedi trait. I don't know...I just felt compelled to send a distress call...I didn't think you'd actually come."

"God always has a hand in what's meant to be," Kay said. "Just because I live far away doesn't mean I can't visit, right? Nine hundred and thirty-three miles can't keep me away from my fave cousin," she chuckled.

"I figured a phone call would be in order, but a visit is much better," he replied with a faint smile.

"Abe," she said, her voice gentle. "Look at me. It's okay."

His eyes welled up with tears. He struggled to maintain his resolve, focusing on suppressing the flood of emotions that threatened to overflow.

"All of our conversations before today revolved around faith, hope, and love...this isn't the Abe I know. It's normal to have moments of weakness and to break down...but remember who you belong to...your Father, the Almighty God, will never abandon you."

Abraham fell into silence, appreciating her intentions.

"When I saw you last year, you were filled with so much life, even a hero..."

Abraham dropped his head.

"You have the ability and imagination to see the world differently...to never give up hope. The devil is stealing that from you, right now, even as I speak. Don't let him! Fight him hard. It's not like hand-to-hand combat, another man standing in front of you whom you can counter, no. This force is unseen and can come at you in any manner, at any time, and when you least expect it. This battle is unlike anything you will ever face. You need to be spiritually aware...a prayer warrior. Pray. Protect your heart. Your spiritual training begins now. Don't be fooled by the wiles of the devil. He prowls like a lion, ready to devour." Kay sensed his brokenness. "Abe..." She studied him intently. "...do you trust me?"

His instincts hesitated, but he knew better. *The darkness is making me doubt. Come on, Abraham, trust her.* Urgency resonated in his thoughts. "I do," he finally surrendered.

"Let me take you somewhere..."

"Where?"

She leaned in for an embrace, and it had been months since he had welcomed a hug. "Just trust me."

TRANSFORMER

>

CONFORMER

Abraham settled into the passenger seat of Kay's car. "Denver, huh?" They zoomed past the enormous stallion statue located just outside the airport—an impressive thirty-two-foot blue horse, reared up on its hind legs.

"That's Blucifer," Kay chimed in. Its piercing red eyes cut through the misty fog. "It reminds them that evil is everywhere."

"Was this part of your Jedi training?" Abraham asked.

"It was, but I didn't know it at the time. Darkness can be elusive, hiding in the shadows. It strikes when you least expect it to. It slithers into your life unexpectedly, pretending to be everything you've ever wanted. As I slowly began to learn that…Denver became part of my spiritual training." Kay spoke with unwavering confidence. "When my mom died, I went to a special place…do you remember when she passed?"

"Yeah, I remember. I was eight-years-old…my dad went ballistic, on a rampage. He loved her a lot…and I remember I never saw you after that…"

"I was thirteen, and looking back, I was emotionally unstable. In the years following her death, I was looking for comfort in all the wrong things and all the wrong people. I was overwhelmed with grief of losing my mother and of never having a father, until I realized that I have everything I need in my *real* father." she paused, ensuring Abraham understood her meaning. "The Lord, my God. Jesus Christ, my savior."

"You know, I always wondered…why did you change your name when you were little?" Abraham asked.

Kay giggled at the question. "My birth name was Katy Veronica Rodriguez. My sister chose it because she saw a cop on TV named Katy, and she wanted our mom to name me after her—a symbol of justice. My biological father added Veronica because he liked the name, though my mom suspected it belonged to one of his girlfriends, because they didn't know anyone named Veronica. When my stepfather adopted us, we had the chance to change our names. Mom wanted my middle name to be Grace since I was born on Thanksgiving, and I agreed…and that's how I became Kay Grace."

"I see. The mystery of how Kay Grace came to be is no longer a mystery. It only took seventeen years." Abraham laughed. "And what about this guy?" He pointed to the symbol on the hood of her sleek silver sports sedan, recognizing the unmistakable markings from his favorite childhood cartoon. "Good to know we're riding in an Autobot."

"Abe, when it comes to the world, would you say that you conform or transform?"

"I'd like to think…I'm tipping the balance to transformation. Despite recent events, especially in the past year, I've always strived to evolve, to become better than what I currently am. It's a contradiction, I know."

"That's how I know God's not done with you yet. A powerful light is hard to extinguish. Evolving involves transforming. Do not conform to the pattern of this world but be transformed by the renewing of your mind. Then you will be able to test and approve what God's will is…His good, pleasing and perfect will."

"If I remember correctly…the book of Romans?"

"Romans twelve, verse two," she confirmed.

"We should take you to Bible trivia night," Abraham joked. "You have it down to the chapter and verse."

"Memorization without application means nothing. Aspiring to live it daily is what helps me remember verses."

"I'm ready to transform back into the good guy I once was. I'll put these countermeasures into practice." Abraham motioned toward the hood of the car. "What does he transform into?" he asked.

"A dragonfly," she half-jokingly replied. "They remind me of the living beings described in Ezekiel chapter 1." Kay pulled up the Bible verse on her tablet while she drove. "Here, read this—Ezekiel one, verses eleven through fourteen."

Each had two pairs of outstretched wings – one pair stretched out to touch the wings of the living beings on either side of it, and the other pair covered its body. They went in whatever direction the spirit chose, and they moved straight forward in any direction without turning around. The living beings looked like bright coals of fire or brilliant torches, and lightning seemed to flash back and forth among them. And the living beings darted to and fro like flashes of lightning.

"Interesting…" Abraham said. "…a spiritual Autobot…I love it!"

"Just wait till you see where Dragonfly takes us…the closest to heaven you've ever been."

XXX GRACE

Abraham hiked to the platform overlooking the majestic Rocky Mountains. "On top of the world!" Abraham exclaimed. His connection with Kay allowed for a few lighthearted moments, but deep down, he knew the truth.

I'm so far from being on top...

"Okay, here it is, babe," Kay said, wasting no time. When it came to sharing the Word of the Lord, she held nothing back. Amidst the vastness of the snowy mountains and the gray sky, she began her sermon. "There will always be darkness inside us. That's just how we were born. It's easy to be jealous, envious, selfish, vengeful, you name it, but it's the light that helps us through it all. God the Father. Jesus Christ. The Holy Spirit. They are with us from the first day we are born."

She subtly observed Abraham, searching for any sign that he understood. "You *are* good, Abe. You *are*. The enemy has extracted emotions from you that are not natural to who you are. It sunk its teeth and grasped its claws onto you. That's why these suppressed feelings and memories have erupted into the world. You've held them at bay, but evil has helped bring them to the surface. We all have darkness inside us...it's the ability to keep the darkness at bay is what makes the difference. That is the key. The light…only the light of Christ can bring you through. In Him, there is no darkness…"

Abraham kept his gaze fixed on Kay. She emanated sweetness and sincerity, her unwavering faith shining through even in the midst of darkness. Her dark hair swayed in the breeze, and her radiant complexion seemed to reflect God's favor upon him.

Despite his outward appearance, she sensed his actions were driven by autopilot. The subtle differences were not lost on her, and she had witnessed this inner energy before. There was darkness within him, and the foe that had overtaken him couldn't deceive her.

"Why did you bring me here?" he asked.

"When my mom passed away, I never truly healed. It wasn't until I turned thirty, seventeen years after her death, that I came to this very spot, yelled at the top of my lungs, and poured out my heart to God. I had nothing and no one…I was all alone here in Denver," she paused, giving him time to process her words. "I brought you here to start the process of moving forward…but you have to let go first. Give it all to God, Abe. Let Him fight this battle for you."

Abraham absorbed Kay's reasoning, allowing the truth to settle within him. She remained patiently silent, ensuring her words penetrated his soul.

Pikes Peak commanded reverence. Abraham focused on his breathing, taking deep, deliberate breaths. After a few moments of centering himself, he looked at Kay. Her eyes seemed to penetrate his very being, filling him with a long-forgotten strength.

The sight of snow was unfamiliar to him. In San Antonio, summer lasted for eleven months of the year. As he gazed at the pure, untouched blanket covering the mountaintop, his eyes wandered farther, reaching the nearby peaks and those stretching as far as the eye could see. In that moment, a sense of grace descended upon him.

The Lord is working through him, Kay thought. Her words had been powerful, but it wasn't her alone. God brought him to this place.

"God is the one using me as one of many instruments…to bring you back to the light."

God always finds a way.

Kay was not one to indulge in theatrics, but the gravity of the situation must have been immense for her to bring him into the clouds.

What does she know that I don't?

Doubt resounded within him, a familiar companion during the past few months.

Let her speak life into you.

He reasoned and argued with the darkness for so long that he yearned for a breakthrough.

"You wield a lot of power. You have a purpose. It is no accident that you are here." she calmly stated, and for once, he believed someone who recognized his potential. "All your talents and gifts are intended for a greater calling beyond yourself—mind, body, and soul. By serving others, you will connect with your true purpose. And believe me, someone, somewhere, is depending on you to do what God called you to do." Her words pierced through his desolate state. "When God makes a man great, he breaks him to pieces first and God uses broken people all the time. You know why? To help other broken people."

"I'm stuck, Kay. I can't forgive myself for what I have done..."

"Listen, the most formidable adversary you will ever encounter...is the Darkness. The devil knows how to hit you where it hurts the most. He knows what's most important to you. The perfect storm. He hit you where it mattered most. The enemy always attacks what is valuable."

"I've been so blinded by the dark that I don't even know how to get back from all the sin I've committed."

"Abe, God loves you! He has forgiven you for all your sins, and nothing can separate us from His love. Nothing! Not even death or life, neither angels nor demons, neither the present nor the future, nor any powers, either height nor depth, or anything else in all of creation, can separate us from the love of God that is in Christ Jesus our Lord."

"I do know His love is immeasurable, but why do I feel hopeless inside?"

"The enemy uses tricks, mind games, to make you believe you're not good enough. It's all in your mind..." she said, pointing to her forehead. "There is only one thing Satan can target and that is your mind. His weapons are lies...so you need to fill your mind with the Word of God."

She's right...

The truth was simple. He was a captive in the darkness.

Kay continued, "You are highly favored. The devil always targets those who walk in God's favor. He does not need to pursue those already lost in darkness...no, he goes after the ones who dwell in the light." She nodded her head, a faint smile adorning her face. "The darkness doesn't stand a chance. Spoiler alert..." she said, her smile widening, "...God wins. The thing is, people tend to forget that, and when they forget, that's when they get lost."

"I've forgotten what that feels like...to have that kind of supernatural power...the power to believe."

"All that you've been through, all that came before, is preparing you for who you will be tomorrow. Today is all that matters because today you can choose who you'll be tomorrow...do not let Satan's lies devalue who you are. You are a child of the Most High King. Act like it. Abe, I believe in you! You have the power to change the world. Remember who you are and be the person God made you to be!"

Abraham sighed heavily. "You're right...I've forgotten who I am..." The weight of the world burdened his shoulders, and letting go of it was the problem.

"Don't worry, Abe. You're still a good man...he's still in there...he's just overcome by the darkness. All you have to do is call out for Jesus. He's always with you, and He's only a whisper away..."

Abraham closed his eyes, concentrating on Christ and the sacrifice at the cross. *Jesus, I need you...*

"The Darkness does not retreat without a fight. The good news is you can beat it. The mind is powerful...you *know* this...you're a writer...your thoughts, your words. The real fight is you versus you." Kay spoke truths and knowledge from the greatest book known to man.

"None are taken back from the darkness, not without giving one up in return," Abraham whispered.

"What did you say?"

"Oh, nothing...it was just something I read in a comic book. I don't know why I remembered it. Wonder Woman was telling Aquaman about a saying from the Amazons, and it turned out the Atlanteans had the same saying. None are taken back from the darkness, not without giving one up in return."

Kay typed up the saying in her phone, possibly for further research.

Fourteen thousand, one hundred feet above the earth...the mountains are glorious...my Father created them...and He created me...to be the best version I can possibly be...

Kay joined him and admired the view. Her five-foot frame loomed larger than life compared to the mountains that accompanied them. "He created all this," Kay said as she motioned to the mountains. "The mountains, the clouds, the sky, the stars, the universe, the rocks, the snow...and He didn't forget to create you. How great is our God that He created us, specks in the universe, in His image? Didn't you write once about the consequence of choice? Now, the choice is yours, Abe...a worker of the light or an agent of the dark. Always remember, He created you for a purpose."

"Maybe this is as close to heaven as I'll ever be," Abraham said with a laugh.

"Or maybe...this is a preview of what's to come." She raised both of her hands in praise to the heavens. "Perspective...that's something that you lost, but it's also something that you can easily regain." She inhaled slowly, mindful of the thin air. "Clear your mind. Open your heart again."

"Thank you, Kay. I feel better already, but I know the hits are still going to come…"

"Are you ready for your final exercise? Stand up. Yell as loud as you can, at the top of your lungs. Make this mountain shake. Get it out of your system. Let it go."

Abraham raised an eyebrow. "I don't want to start an avalanche…that wouldn't be well."

Kay met his gaze with a confident smile, waiting for him to unleash. *Okay, she's serious,* he thought. *Here we go.*

He took a cautious breath of the dry air and let out the loudest yell his lungs could muster. Like a lion roaring to assert dominance in the wild, Abraham's voice echoed through the mountains, a proclamation of his return to a Kingdom hidden from earthly sight.

"This is your first step toward becoming who God meant for you to be. You're about to do damage to the Darkness and this is where you have to rely on God's power and not your own." Kay said. Their bond had grown stronger over the past few years, and the mountain top had cemented their relationship as brother and sister. "There's something that might help you. My mom told me about it right before she passed away. It's hidden in Grandma Perla's house. I have a feeling it'll help."

"Is it a treasure?" Abraham asked.

"It's an old book…and it's been passed down in our family, or so I've heard. Go look for it. If it's still there, it should be hidden in Uncle Zeke's secret room. Let me know if you find it. It's for you to use…and to further your training."

"Training?"

"Yes," Kay replied. "As you put it, it's part of the Jedi Order. You have to know where you've been in order to know where you're going."

"Copy that," Abraham said, returning the smile.

"Abe, before you go, I want you to remember something," Kay said earnestly. "2 Timothy 1:7. 'For God has not given us a spirit of fear, but of power and of love and of a sound mind.' Purge anything that isn't from God—fear, anger, hate. It's up to you, Abe. It's you versus you."

XXXI   EXPULSION

"It's a beautiful day. Thank you for coming with me to the park," Margie said.

The transformation of Concepcion Park had resulted in a significantly altered landscape compared to its previous state. There was now a pathway that led down to the river, unlike the last time, when Abraham stumbled down to near death.

"It's coming along nicely," Margie said.

Despite the presence of large boulders and safety nets sectioning off certain areas, the park thrived. Young and old engaged in exercising activities. Runners, cyclists, and fishing enthusiasts were dotted along the riverbank.

Laughter and cheerful shouts of children filled the air as Margie and Abraham strolled past the playground. A couple of kids waved at them, acknowledging Margie's serene and spiritual aura. She dressed in her usual attire: a purple t-shirt, jeans, and biblical-style sandals imitating her spiritual ancestors. Abraham dressed as if he came out to play one-on-one on a hot ninety-degree day with a cutoff, basketball shorts and untied tennis shoes.

Near the playground, a food truck had set up shop, accompanied by a few tables adorned with colorful umbrellas—green, red, blue, and yellow. The sight of children playing and the laughter echoing throughout the park sparked a glimmer of hope.

There is more to this world than sorrow...it's going to be okay.

The river water rushed along the banks, its currents raging with a fierce and unforgiving nature. This time, Abraham had the advantage of observing from a higher ground.

Taco enthusiasts savored their meals at two of the tables, while the one with the blue umbrella remained unoccupied. Perhaps it was luck that they found shade beneath Abraham's favorite color.

Maybe this is a sign of things changing for the better.

"They don't have burgers here, little boy, so you have to get something else," Margie said.

He laughed at her demand. "It's good that I'm a big taco guy, then."

"Remember Yadira from last week? The one I took you to see for help," Margie asked.

"Yeah, why?"

"We have an appointment with her today at four."

"Wait...we have to go back and see her?" he asked.

"No, she's coming to us. She knows someone who is going to cleanse your house. I think she said his name is Reggie."

"So, they're gonna come to expel whatever is in my house?"

"Yeah, so make sure you eat a good lunch, because I don't know how long it's going to take."

Abraham took a deep breath. "Okay."

"It's time to put your armor back on, little boy."

"Armor?"

"Yes, Armor...from the Bible. The Belt of Truth, the Breastplate of—" Margie's explanation was interrupted by a soft tune emanating from her phone. The ringing became louder, catching the attention of nearby joggers, as it played a disco-themed ringtone.

"Hello," Margie answered. "Oh okay, no, don't worry, we'll be right there." She glanced at Abraham with eyes widened. "C'mon, let's go!"

"What's going on? I thought we were gonna have lunch?" he asked.

"It's Yadira. She's already at your house. We gotta go!"

"I thought you said four o'clock. It's only one..."

"Well, she's early. It's okay, we'll eat later," she said. "I don't believe in coincidence. The devil is trying to make us cancel our appointment…but we're not!"

✟

The energy crackled throughout the house, sending a palpable buzz in the air. Margie and Abraham sensed it the moment they stepped through the door.

"They know something's up," Margie said.

It was as if the entities dwelling within knew they were on the brink of expulsion. Abraham glanced at his right arm, where the hairs stood on end like tiny needles piercing through his flesh.

Yadira entered the house, accompanied by a middle-aged Hispanic gentleman. "Hi, Margie. Abraham, good to see you again," Yadira said. "This is Reggie."

"Nice to meet you." Reggie said, shaking hands with Margie and Abraham. His calloused grip felt as solid as stone. An exchange of energy passed through Abraham, signaling a lack of trustworthiness emanating from Reggie. With his dark complexion blending into his face and neck, Reggie sported a bald look. The logo of the *tiendita* where Yadira worked adorned his gray t-shirt's upper left.

Reggie held a trash bag in one hand, while in the other, he gripped a dog carrier that housed a rooster, which wailed uncontrollably. "Did you manage to gather the items?" Reggie asked.

"Yes," Margie replied, handing him a pack of cigarettes, a lighter, and a wad of cash.

If these are items to go to war with, then we're in trouble, Abraham thought, a flicker of concern crossing his mind.

"Alright, let's get to work," Reggie declared, tearing open the pack and lighting a cigarette. "Yadira tells me you have a horde of goblins running amok in here."

"Too many to count," Abraham said.

"We're going to take care of that. I'll set up in the kitchen and call for you and Margie when it's time." Reggie wasted no time in coordinating the ritual.

Yadira and Margie dispersed, each entering a different room. Yadira murmured gentle prayers under her breath, the words partially audible to Abraham. Margie silently recited her own prayers, her lips moving soundlessly as she sprinkled holy water from a small plastic container she had obtained from the San Juan Basilica down in the valley. She made her way to the corners of each room, splashing water and offering prayers. If he had to guess, it was likely the verse Margie often recited, perhaps one from Psalms, Abraham speculated.

Abraham ran through the list he compiled in his head in the meantime. *Expel the demons...forgive everyone, including myself...make amends with the people I've wronged...and I'm gonna try one more time with my dad...the Man in Black spoke about the Great Darkness...but God can help me bring back the Light...God, help my light shine...*

"Abraham," Reggie called out, breaking his train of thought.

Abraham entered the kitchen cautiously. The carrier was empty, and Reggie had hidden the rooster inside a trash bag, presumably dead, as the wailing had ceased.

"Turn around," Reggie said.

Abraham turned, facing away from Reggie. *I trust Margie, so I guess I trust him...*

Reggie whispered what sounded like a prayer. Abraham noticed light red splatter stains on the baseboards. Drops sprinkled onto Abraham's hair, neck, and back. *Rooster blood.*

"You're good," Reggie said.

Abraham proceeded into the living room and heard crackling noises coming from the attic. All four occupants of the house froze, their movements halted by the sound. The rustling continued above, resembling the footsteps of a small but fast creature.

"Reggie," Yadira whispered.

Reggie didn't respond. Instead, he continued sprinkling the remnants of rooster blood, his eyes fixed on the ceiling, waiting for an ambush.

144

"They're coming out," Margie said. She continued praying, holy water flying from her fingertips, splashing against the walls. Margie was fierce; not even the Darkness stood a chance in denting her spirit. She carried out her business in Abraham's home, every action performed for God's glory.

Abraham faintly heard Margie's whispered words.

He that dwelleth in the secret place of the Most High...

He couldn't make out all the words, but the ones he did hear sounded powerful.

The growls from the closet grew louder. Initially, they sounded like cries of pain, but now they grunted with anger.

Boom!

The house went dark. The loud bang reverberated through each room.

"Shhh!" Yadira said, raising her hand to signal everyone to stop. Abraham wondered if they were meant to hear something specific. "They're trying to break free."

Abraham froze. Despite the blackness enveloping him, his senses heightened.

The creaking sound of Yadira's small feet sliding on the wood floor...
The acrid smell of cigarette smoke wafting through the air...
The sensation of energies brushing against his skin...

The mingling of earthly and spiritual energies flooded the living room. There was a war raging, and Abraham sensed it, standing in the midst of it. He concentrated on deciphering which energies belonged to whom or what.

The enemy dispatched countless troops, but the light weakened the minions of darkness. Abraham focused on creating a projection, a shield of spiritual energy around himself, or at least tried to envision one. He closed his eyes, and as he did, the entities flew past him. Too many beasts filled the airspace, desperate to make a last stand in the territory they had claimed for the past twenty years.

Abraham felt taps on his arms, then his shoulders, and finally his chest and back. *They're getting physical. C'mon Abraham, hold it together! They can't hurt you.*

The blows came harder, piercing like daggers. The entities swirled around him, resembling a tornado with debris striking every part of his body.

"Abraham!" Margie shouted. "Fight them hard! Don't give in!"

Abraham shielded his face with both arms, gradually crouching down in an attempt to withstand the onslaught.

God, help me...

The swirling entities enveloped him, spinning faster and faster like hurricane winds. Then, in one final deafening gust...

Poof!

Abraham absorbed a blow to the chest, knocking him onto his back. The tornado ceased, and the lights flickered back on, leaving only silence.

"Abraham!" Margie shouted, scurrying over to him. "Are you okay?"

"What the fuck was that? Did you see that?"

"Are you okay?" Margie asked, concerned.

"Yeah...that was crazy! They fuckin' punched me!" Abraham picked himself off the floor. "It felt like...something went through me...what now?" he asked.

Margie, Yadira, and Reggie entered the living room after the commotion. The three of them glanced at the ceiling and the four walls, expecting an encore of sorts.

"It's over..." Reggie said. "...you should sleep good tonight."

Relieved by Reggie's comforting words, Abraham let out a deep breath. "Thank God!"

"Try not to wear any black or dark clothing. It attracts them," Reggie warned.

A ringing noise sounded, like a dog whistle inside Abraham's ear. "Do y'all hear that?" he asked.

"Hear what?" Yadira questioned.

"A high-pitched whistling sound."

The three guests looked at one another. "No," they said.

A deep bellow echoed, audible only to Abraham.

"This war is never over…you are not a child of God. You. Are. Mine."

XXXII GENERATIONS

The shadows concealed the two men, rendering them almost invisible. Only the occasional flare of a neon-orange cigarette pierced through the veil of darkness. Ray exhaled a puff of smoke, his customary duties as a neighborhood watchman unfolding like clockwork.

Leaning against the sleek black M3, Abraham and the car seamlessly blended into the night, a fact that had grown comfortable to him in as of late.

The paths of father and son intersected, the tranquility of the nocturnal hours subdued any inclination for confrontation. Ray drew another drag from his cigarette, the ember momentarily illuminating the surrounding darkness with a fiery orange glow.

"You know," Ray spoke calmly, "I'm not a bad guy…I just do what I gotta do…to protect my family. Is that why you despise me?"

"I don't hate anybody…" Abraham countered.

"Dad, I don't understand. Do you know why I call you 'Dad'?" Ray inquired.

Abraham easily identified Ray's patterns. Rambling was one of his traits after hours. "You told me, once."

"It's because you're the boss."

"If that were true, we wouldn't be having this conversation over and over."

"I've always been there for you!" Ray's gestures grew animated, perhaps meant to evoke a sense of conviction.

"Are you trying to convince me or yourself?" Abraham prepared his arsenal of rebukes, ready for a full-fledged refutation. "I can't even begin to tell you how many times you let me down…countless."

"Okay, tell me when?" Ray challenged.

"Pshhh, you got time?"

"It wasn't that many times.".

"Too many to recall. Remember that time when I was in sixth grade and I had that model of the U.S.S. Enterprise? I tried building it on my own…" Abraham recalled the details as he transformed the memory into spoken words. "It was pissin' me off. I was frustrated and I just couldn't get it to stay…" Abraham shook his head, recalling the debacle of fusing the dual engines to the lower half of the ship. "You told me you'd help me the next day after you got off work. I wanted to believe you. So, the next day comes, and I waited and I waited and I waited. I waited all day until 4 o'clock, and then, it got dark…9 o'clock and still nothing. You never showed up."

"Why do you resent me? Is this why you're mad? Over a model toy?"

"No, you're missing the point. That was one of countless times you let me down…and it was a stupid model toy, yes, but it taught me a lot."

"To hate me?"

"Dad, if you couldn't help me with the little things, what makes me think you'd be there for the important ones?" Abraham took a breath, not only to compose himself but also to allow Ray an opportunity to comprehend his perspective.

Ray retaliated with a rebuttal of his own. "Grandma spoiled you. She catered to you and did everything for you…"

"No, that's where you're wrong. Grandma saved my life. Without her, I would've ended up in jail or dead a long time ago. She gave me the unconditional love that I needed. She saved me…and I'm sorry if you resent that. Maybe it's because you had no one to save you…"

"Yeah, but she's not your mom and dad...*we* are!"

"Then, where were you when I needed you? Huh? Where were you?"

"Dude, you're always gonna hold that against me!"

"No, Dad, honestly, I don't. I've learned not to need you, and I've trained myself to be resilient, to adapt to change, to welcome it, and if necessary, to cut toxic people out of my life in ten seconds flat...because if my mom and dad can leave me behind, what makes me think a stranger won't..." Abraham spoke calmly, his words hanging in the midnight air.

Ray froze, confronted by his son's confession. His life had been far from drama-free, and the consequences of his actions as a thirty-two-year-old were now coming back to haunt him.

"Oh, and in Mom's defense, she only did it that one time...but that was during a crucial time...in early childhood...and she didn't know any better..." Abraham chuckled, able to find humor in it now, although it had been pandemonium at the time.

Despite Abraham's laughter, Ray remained lost in his own thoughts, absorbing the weight of his son's revelation.

"Do you regret the way you grew up?" Ray asked.

"No...I don't regret it at all. I loved the way I grew up."

"Why?" Ray inquired.

"Because it made me grow up fast. Everything you did...or didn't do...made me better. It taught me to rely on myself and it taught me how to evolve."

"I could've taught you all that...and probably even better. I always told you that, but you never listened."

"Actions speak louder than any words you've ever said to me. You didn't teach me anything..." Abraham paused, reflecting on his own words. "...no, I take it back. There is one thing, actually...you taught me what *not* to be."

Ray remained unusually calm. This was the moment he would usually retort, deny, and shift the blame, but only the cool breeze whispered through the air.

"All those beatings I took, all the times I saw you beat on someone, all those times when you ridiculed me in front of my friends, family, baseball teams, basketball teams, all those times you treated mom like shit, all the times I had to drive Mom to pick up your car from the next neighborhood because the cops were looking for you, all those times I found drugs lying around, all those times you told me 'fuck you,' 'you ain't shit,' 'you're a pussy, and you always have been,' 'I'll kick your ass,' 'give up on school and get a full-time job' because I couldn't make the grade, and all those times you threw your own son under the bus just so you can look good…those moments taught me a lot…"

Ray descended from the top step by the doorway, his steps measured as he walked down the path. "When you were two years old, and Michelle, she must have been around five…I told your mom to take you and your sister to the back room, and I stayed in the front room with the window open, holding two Uzis in my hands. No one came that night, but I'll be damned if anybody's gonna try to hurt my family…"

Confession time? Abraham thought. Ray's words sank in. He had been at war before—countless times, as far as Abraham knew.

Abraham had witnessed it once, and that memory felt like a distant echo from the past.

"I remember the drive-by…the gunfire…all the bullet holes…and then you left for a few weeks…when we needed you the most.. "

"Let me ask you this…did they ever come back?"

"Not that I know of," Abraham replied.

"My sins came back to haunt me…and the last thing I wanted was for anything to happen to my family. That's why I left…to make sure that would never happen again," Ray said.

"When you *left*? You say it like it only happened once. You left so many times, it felt like I didn't even have a Dad. That was a habit you never could break," Abraham said.

Ray leaned on the front yard fence, his head bowed as his arms folded atop the gate. "I'm sorry…I wasn't there for you," he admitted. For once, Ray didn't retaliate with anger. "I don't want to make the same mistakes with Paulina that I made with you."

Abraham's eyes widened in shock upon hearing words Ray had never spoken to him before. *Is this for real?* he thought.

"Is that why you became 'Ray'? Mom said I wasn't ready to know back then. I remember when they came for you…the look on that dude's face…the darkness…the rage…"

"I'm not perfect. I did what I had to do."

"Admitting when you're wrong is the only way to move forward, and it's not just about admitting it…it's about changing. I forgive you, but you never change, Dad. How long before you want to try and kick my ass, again? How long until you tell me how much of a fucked-up son I am?" Abraham spoke the truths that had hardened his formidable shell over the past twenty years. "You chose partying and women and having a good time over us…and believe it or not…I understand. You were seventeen when you had Michelle and twenty-one when I was born…you didn't get the chance to do all the things a normal twenty-something would have. I'm not justifying what you did…but I *understand.* Mom was the real parent, she was a single parent, so please stop claiming you were there for us when you weren't…and when you were, it was a shit show."

"Get over it. I can't change the past. I'm not perfect, Abe."

"I'm not perfect, either. I, too, have done some horrible things. Things I can never take back, but I'm not asking you to take them back. I'm asking you to change your ways, learn from them, and become better. Otherwise, history will repeat itself, and Paulina *will* suffer…and I don't want her to suffer. She deserves better."

"I've done a lot of bad things, Abe…" Ray confessed. "I can't tell you everything I've done because it's better if you don't know…who I've been associated with…but I did it so that my family can be safe."

Abraham kept his thoughts to himself, but it was no secret. He knew Ray had been involved in unimaginable things. Connecting the dots wasn't hard in this case.

Ray's confession triggered memories of an old friend. Despite his efforts to push away the thoughts of a year ago, Abraham was quickly reminded of the last time he would ever see his best friend, with only a few traces of goodness left in him.

"The last time I heard a confession like that…my best friend died," Abraham revealed.

"Donnie?" Ray asked.

Abraham gazed deeply into the shadows, beyond the backyard and over the tree line, where only space, and time, existed.

He finally brought it up, Ray thought. " I saw it on the news…I didn't know it was him at first, because they used his real name. I had no idea he was like that…he was an evil dude. That manhunt made headlines. You were there, weren't you?" Ray asked, though he already knew the answer. "You saw the life fade from his eyes…"

In that moment, Abraham replayed the scenes in his head as he had done countless times, and it never got easier. It only grew darker each time.

"I told your mom I knew you had gone over there…and then, I really knew when I saw the changes in you. I know this because I've seen the light dim in someone's eyes," Ray said, his gaze fixed on his only son. Abraham maintained a calm demeanor, unmoving with folded arms and a face etched with anguish. Only his eyes shifted steadily, their whites glistening in the moonlight. There is still light in him, Ray thought. "What did it feel like…to take a life?"

"I didn't…I couldn t…" Abraham paused, overwhelmed by grief. He was now ready to admit a terrifying truth. "…he would've killed me…" Those words had never left his mouth, but in the darkness, in the still of night, he finally gave them a voice. "…and I don't know what's worse…knowing that I did nothing to save him…or that it should have been me who was supposed to be killed…"

Ray listened. His son had endured terrible things, things he hadn't the slightest inkling of. Perhaps his ego had blinded him, or perhaps the hardships of life had beaten him down to the point of not recognizing the severity. The best conclusion Abraham could come up with is that it was a combination of both.

"That is where your darkness comes from…I've been there…sometimes you never recover, but I know *you* will. You'll always have it inside you…this dark force, but it's a lot like an alcoholic. They may stay sober for the rest of their lives, but they'll always be an alcoholic. It's just controlled, that's all. You're resilient and you're well equipped to overcome anything. I have always said that my kids will be greater than me, and your kids will be greater than you...evolving to be better. This is the way of life, or so it should be."

Ray extinguished his cigarette, tossing it to the ground and crushing it beneath his foot like a bug. He carefully made his way back to the top step, leaning against the screen door. He glanced over at Abraham in the dimly lit driveway. "When you see yourself, what do you see?"

Taking a deep breath, Abraham answered honestly. "I used to be good...and I'm not anymore..."

"When I look at you, I see three people. The person you were, the person you are, and the person you can become...the first, was a man who loved the world and knew no evil. The second, is a man consumed by darkness, and the third will be so great that you owe it to the other two who came before. When these three meet, it will be more powerful than anything you have ever known and greater than anything you have ever faced. This manifestation of all three will be a testament to your true power."

Abraham nodded as he absorbed the information. "Power," he whispered. His thoughts led him to a question that only he could ask in the pale moonlight. "I've been told that before. I don't know what I'm meant to do, but I know I fooled myself into thinking I was meant for more...and now, it feels like I'm drifting away."

"The demons have a hold on you right now, but trust me, one day the third version of you will be the one to break free from their chains."

"Is that why the Darkness comes for us?"

"It's a strong possibility," Ray said. "Your Uncle Zeke was the strongest of us...Phil and I could do some shit, but Zeke...he could achieve out-of-body experiences and manipulate people like puppets."

"I remember the stories...about Uncle Zeke from a long time ago...is there anybody else that has it?"

"No, not that I know of..." Ray pulled out another cigarette, but this one had a peculiar shape. It was smaller and bulkier, emitting the familiar aroma that Abraham had encountered countless times. "Your Uncle Zeke always talked about some book that had stories of other family members and the things they could do…he showed it to me a couple of times…" he said as he lit up the cigarette. "But I never read any of it."

"What did the book look like?" Abraham asked, hopeful that Ray's description would align with Kay's claim back in Denver.

"It was a brown leather book. It kinda looked like an old school photo album. Zeke used to keep in his old little hideout, that secret room he made, at your grandma's house."

It is true, he thought. "So, the book is still at Grandma's house?"

"Not anymore. If it was there, it's long gone by now," Ray said. "Grandma's house burned down last week. Didn't your mom tell you?"

"Burned down? How?"

"Somebody burned it down and it wasn't an accident…" Ray revealed. "There's nothing left of her house…but it doesn't matter, because that power lives on."

Stunned by the unfortunate news, Abraham's hopes were reduced to ashes.

If only I could have read that book, it might've made a difference.

Ray sensed his son's disappointment. "You don't need that book…you have that power, too," he said, sniffing the aroma of the cigarette.

"I don't have it anymore. It left me…"

"It's because you don't believe anymore…"

"I'm fighting hard to believe again…"

Ray inhaled deeply from the modified cigarette, held the smoke for a moment, and exhaled with ease. "When the demons come…at night…that's when they fight the hardest. It's a battle for something that can't be seen…a battle for your soul…"

As the clock struck 1 a.m., the night air remained silent while Ray delivered his discourse on the darkness. "Abe, I can't fight this war for you. A man has to go into battle alone…spiritually, but as long as I'm alive, no one will mess with you on this earth. And, even when I'm gone, no one is gonna mess with you, because my boys will watch over you. They got your back, always."

"I've always believed that fighting should be a last resort...only for self-defense..."

"Ohhhhh man, this is just the beginning...little do you know...you're about to face the fight of your life."

The truth brewed within his core, and he understood that Ray spoke with unwavering certainty. He wasn't ready. Just like when he fought Abaddon, he wasn't ready for war.

"Maybe you need a teacher...I figured you'd get through on your own, just like Zeke and Phil and I did. But I'm no teacher."

"I think I managed pretty good on my own. No offense, but you wouldn't have been a good teacher."

Ray listened as he pinched the shrinking cigarette, exhaling after holding the smoke in for much longer than he should have. Choking on the smoke, he nearly coughed out a lung.

"Come on, I want to show you something," Ray said, opening the door quietly like a prowling ninja. "Shhh, your mom's asleep." He carefully opened the door, and they slinked past the tiny living room, venturing into the miniature game room. The room showcased a record player, posters of NBA players from the '90s, and a dart board.

Ray reached for a set of metallic objects. On the ends of these minuscule spears were fins decked out in all black.

"Darts?" Abraham asked.

Ray showcased his daggers, seasoned from battle. "Let's play a few games."

"Nah, I don't feel like it. I haven't played darts since I was little..."

"You were like twelve...shooting bullseyes...you thought you could beat me at Cricket. You never *could* beat me..." Ray reminisced about a time long ago when glory spilled at his feet daily. "Your Dad was the best in the city," Ray said, often referring to himself in the third person, especially when it came to his dart skills.

Although boasting was second nature to Ray, the truth was on his side in this case.

Abraham noticed the new upgrades around the room. Shelves near the ceiling surrounded the entire space, adorned with trophies of every kind. Tall ones, small ones, a few plaques, and each one depicted either a man shooting a dart or a 3-D dart in all its golden glory. Most of them were enshrined with a "1st place" marking. Ray, the man requesting a one-on-one match with his son, was one of the most highly decorated dart players in the city.

"I'll go easy on you." Ray shot a few warm-up rounds, and with each release, his concentration grew fierce. "Just one game."

"Alright, I'll give it a go. Just one game…" Abraham said.

"I'll let you shoot a few warm-ups." Ray backed away from the line, allowing his son to take command of the dart board.

I just need three rounds of warm-up…nine darts…

He took his time releasing each dart, remembering the style he used to pierce the board with success.

"You ready?" Ray asked.

Abraham nodded.

"Do you remember how to play?" Ray asked.

"I think so."

Ray pointed to the Cricket board. "Remember, you've got to hit three 20's to close…and three 19's, three 18's, three 17's, three 16's, three 15's, and three bullseyes. The outer ring on the board are doubles, and the skinny ring close to the middle are triples. You've got to close all the numbers and the bulls and be ahead on points to win. Let me erase the board."

Abraham glanced at the marked-up scoreboard. The previous game was a landslide. Whoever the challenger was, they were getting their ass beat, he thought.

Cricket

C	20	C
/	19	/
/	18	X
	17	C
	16	₵
	15	
	Bull	

"Who lost?" Abraham asked.

"Your cousin Zander," Ray laughed. "He's been coming over to play. We didn't finish that last game though."

"Wait…it's been a while since I've seen those markings. A slash means a single, an X is two singles, and a C means the number is closed, right?" Abraham asked.

"You got it," Ray said, calmer than usual. Darts always had a way of sprucing up his calmness and concentration. "And don't forget, you can score on any number that's not closed. So, if I leave the 20's open and you hit it, that's 20 points. If you hit a triple, then it's 60 points."

"I remember…I'm ready," Abraham said.

"I'll go first…" Ray stepped up to the line with ease and confidence. He let the first dart fly.

Triple 20.

With one dart, he shut down that number.

He let the second dart fly.

Triple 19.

On two darts, he closed down two numbers, leaving five more to go, including bullseyes.

He let the last of the three darts fly with grace.

Ray missed the Triple 17 by a millimeter. He clearly hadn't lost the fire or the skill to compete.

Abraham stepped up to the line. Up until a few moments ago, he hadn't thrown a dart in fourteen years. With a significant disadvantage, he went for his old bread and butter. His concentration grew exponentially in a matter of seconds. He released the first dart into the air.

Outer ring of the bullseye.
That's one bull...need two more.

Tactically, aiming for another number entirely, if successful, would level the playing field. He was close to the red bullseye, but the green outer ring still counted for something. Abraham took a deep breath.

Inhale.

Exhale.

His face was stone. He released the second dart.

Outer ring of the bullseye.
So close. Third time's a charm.

He could feel it. This one was it. Not only would he hit the bullseye, but he'd also be up on points.

"Dang!" Ray couldn't contain his excitement any longer. "You're shooting lights out already!" Ray was obviously impressed, otherwise he wouldn't have a need to complement. "Let me give you some tips. This is what I do..." Ray positioned himself beside Abraham, as if he was shooting a dart. "Keep the dart in front of you," Ray said, demonstrating the technique.

Okay, keep the dart in front of me...like a goal...don't lose sight of it...

"Aim and follow through," Ray instructed, extending his arm toward the target.

Okay, aim and follow through...make a decision...and don't look back...

"Breathe," Ray advised.

Relax...and let God handle it...

Abraham released his final dart into the air. It glided gracefully, finding its intended target with precision.

Bullseye.

"Duuuuude! You closed out the bullseyes with your first three darts, and you're up by 25!" Ray shouted.

"Shhh! Mom's asleep!" Abraham whispered.

"Oh, right, I forgot…" Ray calmed himself down. "Dude, that was amazing!" Ray tended to exaggerate, and his outburst made it seem as if Abraham had performed a miracle.

Abraham, on the other hand, was overwhelmed with a surge of power he hadn't felt in ages. And for the first time in months…he smiled.

XXXIII FLASHPOINT

Memories collided, various time periods intertwined, forming a kaleidoscope of events. The onslaught triggered emotions that would typically go unnoticed.

I've never had flashbacks before...what's going on?

His ability to regroup proved to be one of his strongest traits, and now it was coming into play.

Okay, Abraham, remember your training...what's the root of the problem? C'mon, think! Liv said I have PTSD...PTSD triggers emotions...unresolved issues...acting out...let's come to terms ..I can't control the outside world, I can only control me...the Darkness has infiltrated my thoughts, exploiting my weaknesses...my thoughts are the key...rewire...accept all that happened before...forgive yourself for everything you've ever done...forgive yourself in order to move forward...remember you're better than this...it's not about who's stronger, it's about who's smarter...remember your tactics...it's not about strength, it's about strategy...Satan is not stronger than you...

February 1997

Gloria spoke in a hushed whisper, her voice barely audible. She never hesitated to talk on the phone, but she positioned herself facing the wall, using her body as a shield.

Abraham homed in on her words, sensing the concern in her tone.

"Okay...okay...I'll pick it up," Gloria murmured before hanging up the phone.

Abraham pretended to be engrossed in the television, feigning interest in the movie rather than the conversation Gloria desperately attempted to conceal.

"Abe, can you give me a ride?" she asked.

"Where?"

"Just down the street," Gloria replied. "I have to pick up your Dad's car."

Keeping secrets wasn't her strong suit.

As they arrived, the street swarmed with police, their red and blue lights flashing callously in the darkened neighborhood. Three patrol cars encircled the green Jaguar. Gloria cautiously stepped out of the car. "I'll see you at the house," she said. She approached the gathering of police officers. Abraham lingered for a moment, maneuvering past the commotion to catch fragments of the conversation that led to such a spectacle.

"We know you know where he is. Tell us where he is..." a tall, muscular officer interrogated Gloria.

"I don't know where he is. I just came to pick up the car," she responded.

"Why are you covering for him?" a short, husky officer pressed.

"Look, I just came for the car," Gloria asserted, resolute in her mission as she slipped inside the Jaguar. The crime-ridden neighborhood was no stranger to police presence, and for whatever reason, Ray had left the Jaguar behind. There was no sign of him.

What happened that he had to leave the Jaguar? What mess did he get into now?

Abraham approached the stop sign, with Gloria following closely behind him.

💣

Spring 1991

"Go see your dad," Gloria said with disgust.

Great…he's asleep. I'm gonna get beat worse now. I'm surprised he's even here this morning.

Abraham dragged his feet to the bedroom and nudged his father's arm. Ray turned over, half-asleep, his eyes barely open. "What?" he growled like a grizzly bear disturbed from slumber.

"I went skateboarding with my friends," Abraham said quietly. There was a perimeter he was not allowed to breach, a one-block radius, and crossing that line meant punishment. Most of the time, he was clever enough to get away with it, but there was the occasional slip-up.

Ray slowly rolled out of bed. "Go to the back and get me a two by four."

Abraham made his way to the backyard where a pile of wood lay near the fence. He reached for the paddle that was probably used the last time. By the time he reached the deck, Ray was waiting for him, eyes half-closed.

"Turn around," Ray said.

Abraham stepped to the edge of the deck and faced the backyard.

"Touch your toes,' Ray commanded, adding another order before the punishment commenced.

Abraham did as he was instructed. The thrashings had evolved since the first paddling. He never winced or made the slightest sound. He absorbed every beating in silence, wondering if Ray would hit him as hard as he could to break him. And so, the toe-touching was a new step in the punishment process.

Ray swung the board as far back as he could, like a batter aiming for a homerun.

Thwack!

The new technique didn't allow Abraham to brace for impact. He absorbed the full force of the two by four without flinching.

Ray reached back and swung again.

Thwack!

The pain ran down his backside to his calves. He held his position, not a single noise escaping him.

Thwack!

The usual was three and out. Ray tossed the paddle off the deck to the ground.

Abraham followed Ray back inside the house, doing his best to hide the pain. It seemed to worsen as he walked with a straightened back, even though he wanted to hobble. He did his best not to break, at least not in front of anyone.

💣

November 1989

Abraham quietly ate his cereal at the kitchen table, observing his parents as they prepared for work—a rare sight for him since they usually left the house before he and Michelle woke up. The sleepless night had taken its toll on him. In a few days, Gloria would be leaving, and that meant he would be in Ray's custody for a daunting six weeks.

As Ray playfully took a gentle hit to the gut from Gloria, her giggles filled the room. Abraham couldn't help but smile at the sight of his parents engaging in a lighthearted play fight. *What am I going to do without her for a month and a half?*

Gloria playfully nudged Ray's arm as he buttoned up his shirt, but he ignored her playful advance. He continued fastening the buttons without retaliating. Gloria tickled his belly.

"Enough!" Ray yelled.

His hand rose, and then…

January 1994

Gloria refused to budge. Her orders were final. "Abe's staying at that boarding school! He made the choice to go and he's going to stick to it! And that's it!"

Ray took offense at her demand. He had grown accustomed to giving orders, and Gloria's defiance challenged his wishes. "Send him to public school! Put him at Burbank! We don't need to pay tuition anymore! He hates it and he's failing anyway! Put him in public school!"

"No! He's staying at the school he chose to go to! He has to learn…you make a choice, and you stick to it!"

"Fuck it!" Ray said, storming towards the door as he typically did during combative arguments. He snatched a set of papers from the table and hastily scribbled his signature. "Here! These have been sitting here for too long!" He flung the papers back onto the table, causing them to flop on top of one another, only the staple holding the packet together.

Gloria's eyes focused on the bold heading of the document: Final Decree of Divorce.

"It's done!" he yelled.

May 1998

"Just give up already!" Ray said. "C's and D's…might as well just get a full-time job. Forget about school. Your grades ain't cutting it!" Ray stormed out of the house.

This is why I don't tell you my grades…what the fuck does it matter to you? I pay for my own tuition…and I'm not giving up!

October 1989

Ray arrived home at nine o'clock. Abraham was clicking buttons furiously on his game controller, engrossed in beating the robot boss. He hadn't noticed Ray entering the house.

"Turn that off. It's time for bed anyway. Let me watch T.V." Ray said.

"It's Friday...Mom let me stay up and play."

"Well, I'm here now, so get off," Ray insisted.

Abraham sighed, realizing he had to disconnect. The robot boss had almost met its end, and it had taken him the entire evening to reach the final stage.

Ray slumped on the couch, and Abraham caught a whiff of alcohol emanating from his father. Abraham clicked off the Nintendo, his brow furrowing as the TV went black.

"What's the matter?" Ray asked.

"Nothing," Abraham muttered.

"What's going on, dude? You seem pissed off," Ray pressed.

"I almost beat the robot boss in the game."

Ray nudged Abraham. "You can play all day tomorrow."

Good, because you won't be here to kick me off...

Ray tapped Abraham on the arm. "What, dude, you want some?" Ray playfully propped up his fists in a boxing stance.

Abraham cracked a smile. He could never defeat his dad in boxing, no matter how many times he watched Rocky. Nevertheless, he raised his fists.

Ray sprang forward, delivering a 1-2 combination of open-handed jabs. Abraham countered with a strike, but his hand missed its target.

Ray unleashed a second wave of combinations, each strike landing successfully. The blows knocked Abraham back into the kitchen area.

Preparing for a third wave, Ray poised himself. Abraham did his best to bob and weave. Ray grazed Abraham's forehead.

It worked!

Anticipating a 1-2 combination, Abraham felt fingertips graze his cheek.

Ray laughed, but the snicker trailed off as he focused. His son had gotten better at evading punches. His fingers curled into a half-fist.

Abraham bobbed hard to his right.

Ray threw a multitude of punches, with less than half connecting. The balance shifted in Abraham's favor. *He can't punch me if I make him miss.*

Ray's laughter ceased, and his hands and arms moved faster. A jab connected with the side of Abraham's head, knocking him off balance. He desperately tried to recover, but he left his ribs exposed as he swooped under a second jab. Ray landed a punch directly on his son's gut, and the impact of Ray's wedding ring squarely hit Abraham's rib.

Abraham felt a twinge, accompanied by a faint cracking sound. Ray laughed; his victory solidified as his son crouched on the floor.

Christmas 1998

Grandma Perla entered the room, her demeanor filled with somberness. Her eyes fixated on the maroon carpet, as if carrying burdens too heavy to share. Finally, her saddened eyes met Gloria, Michelle, and Abraham. "Your father is coming...I'm sorry. He just called."

Michelle's eyes shot daggers at her mother and brother, her unmistakable frown revealing her disbelief. "Are you serious?"

"He's bringing her..." Grandma Perla was forced to disclose the uncomfortable truth. "...the girlfriend."

Gloria let out a sigh, struggling to maintain her composure. Though she appeared composed on the outside, Abraham knew the truth.

"We'll just go to the movies," Phil interjected, attempting to redirect the heartbreak. "I heard 'Meet Joe Black' is good. And after that, we can go to Europe! You all can see where I live in Germany…there's no drinking age there, Abe."

"I can't believe him! It's Christmas!" Michelle's contempt was impossible to conceal. "We have to leave Grandma's house because our own Dad is coming."

"Come on, let's go," Gloria said calmly.

Abraham remained silent. He had grown accustomed to his father's recklessness, but a new element had emerged. His father could never truly break him. The only thing that shattered his heart into pieces was seeing his mother and sister angry and heartbroken, and now, for the first time, he cracked under his father's influence.

Before they could escape through the door, the revelation took a turn that left Gloria and Michelle in a bewildered frenzy. Grandma Perla, aware of the truth, didn't want them to witness it firsthand. "She's already showing…"

Michelle's anger surged through her eyes as tears welled up.

"She's pregnant…"

Spring 2000

The group anxiously awaited the arrival of Robin and Chris, creating an unusual amalgamation of street ballers that swarmed the inner-city street. Jason, John-John, Johnny, Ricky, and Abraham seamlessly mingled as the rhythmic bouncing of basketballs reverberated on the pavement.

"Y'all ready to take these fools at Concepcion?" John-John asked, his confidence oozing. "We're not losing one game today. We got the best right here," he declared, pointing at each member of the group.

"You know it!" Ricky chimed in enthusiastically.

Jason chuckled at the bold statement, his calm demeanor unwavering as he stood on the curb. Johnny replicated Jason Kidd's mesmerizing moves while conducting basketball drills up and down the street. Ricky practiced his shooting form, effortlessly releasing the ball towards imaginary baskets. Abraham skillfully spun a basketball on his index finger, counting the precious seconds before it inevitably toppled off, only to begin the routine all over again.

As a car approached from behind, they cleared the street to make way.

"What up, homeboys!" Abraham greeted Robin and Chris. "About time! Let's roll!"

The team dispersed, boarding three different cars, their actions filled with caution as a police car slowly made its way up the street. They discreetly slipped into the vehicles, the presence of law enforcement prompting them to be even more discreet. The police car veered into Abraham's driveway, raising suspicion among the group.

"Your kinfolk?" Robin asked.

Abraham remained silent, his expression revealing a hint of concern. The police officer emerged from the car and approached the front door of Abraham's house.

What did he do now?

July 2000

"Your Dad wanted me to give this to you," Gloria said, extending an envelope toward Abraham. "He said he's sorry he couldn't be here."

Abraham took the envelope and carefully tore it open, revealing a handwritten note. *This must've been all he had to write on.* "Is he still in jail?" he asked.

"Yup...on your twenty-first birthday," Gloria replied, her voice carrying an unwavering truth.

Her words hung in the air, not demanding a response from Abraham. He focused his attention on the note and began reading.

23 July 2000

Abe,

I'm sorry I couldn't help you celebrate your birthday yesterday. Under the circumstances, it can't be. I hope you had a good birthday with fun and joy. I feel you have reserved or private issues about us, but there's nothing I could do now, I did the best I knew how, then. Now is now and life is too short to be bitter or have a deep seeded resentment, but I guess I have no control. The day will come when I'm not around and maybe you'll feel better. Until then, here's wishing my one and only son a very Happy 21st Birthday. I love you always and I'll always be there for you.

Your Father,
Ray

Abraham crumpled the note.
He doesn't get it…it's not about that.
As he examined the contents of the envelope further, a newspaper clipping caught his eye, peeking out from between the folds. He carefully extracted the small piece of paper. It bore a bold title at the top, unmistakably torn out from the pages of the San Antonio Express-News.

The Time is Now

If you are ever going to love me,
Love me now, while I can know
The sweet and tender feelings
Which from true affection flow.
Love me now,
While I am living.
Do not wait until I'm gone
And then have it chiseled in marble,

Sweet words on ice-cold stone.
If you have tender thoughts of me,
Please, tell me now,
If you wait until I am sleeping,
Never to awaken,
There will be death between us,
And I won't hear you then.
So, if you love me, even a little bit,
Let me know it while I am living
So I can treasure it.

A tear streamed down his face.

It was never about resentment. I learned to not need you...and you don't seem to understand that...you inadvertently built me to not need anyone...

Guilt consumed him, and it was evident that his father experienced the same feeling.

Break free from the bondage...don't go around it, go through it...face it! The only way to move forward is to work out the past. I don't believe in going backwards, but fuck it, gotta plow through to the other side...

The psychologist within him yearned to gain an advantage over the Darkness, employing his tactical skills.

I know what you're trying to do...It's not gonna work...I can control my thoughts...they are not yours to use against me...

Caught off guard by the ambush, he excelled in psychological warfare on the earthly plane, but the spiritual realm posed new complications. Countermeasures reignited the simplicity of a Christian trait that he rejected in recent months.

Forgiveness.

If I can forgive my dad...I can forgive myself.

XXXIV IMPASSE

*G*od...*are you with me? I can't feel you...we expelled the Darkness...I don't know what to do...why do I still feel lost?*

The days seemed to blend together, lacking a distinct beginning or end—a meaningless tapestry of events punctuated by checkpoints of disaster.

294 days since the fallout with Liv...

249 days since I lost Athena...

212 days into this administration gig...

What the hell am I doing?

"Mr. Abraham...I miss you," a tiny voice cried out. Amelia limped into the office, her movements lacking energy.

"Hey, doll!" Abraham greeted her, his heart breaking at the sight of her sorrow. After all, she had spent most of her Pre-K life under his guidance. These days, he was rarely seen among the children, and the consequences of his absence affected both parties. Office duties were a far cry from what he was accustomed to, and their impact was immediately felt.

Abraham sensed Amelia's emotional pain and knelt down in front of her, enveloping her in his arms. "Rough morning?" he asked.

Amelia nodded, tears streaming down her face, mingling with her frown.

"It's gonna be okay, my sweet," he said, hoping to offer some solace. But deep down, he felt worthless without the comforting presence of his preschool children.

Amelia sobbed, clutching onto his neck with her five-year-old arms. "I want you to be my teacher," she said, burying her face in his chest.

"Aww, my love. I wish I *was* still your teacher. I'll tell you what...I'm gonna go check on you every day, okay?"

Amelia glanced up at him, her face lighting up with a smile from ear to ear. "Yay!" she shouted.

"Gimme a big bear hug," he said, embracing her once again.

She tightened her grip around his neck, her big brown eyes filled with delight.

"Bigger!" he said. "So it can last all day."

Things hadn't been the same since he left the classroom. It was a testament to his decline, and he couldn't deny that his promotion played a role.

I haven't made a difference...

Not in a long time...

If I'm gonna find my way back...being in the office isn't gonna cut it...

But...maybe stepping away from the classroom is good right now...they all remind me of Athena...

"Okay, my love, go be awesome! You're great and don't let anybody tell you any different!"

"I love you, Mr. Abraham," Amelia said.

"And I love you!"

Amelia skipped to her classroom, and he smiled. "Mr. Abraham is about love," Amelia said to her new teacher.

If only I listened to my own advice...

The love from his Pre-K kids kept him going, if only for the moment.

"Mr. Abraham is like Superman!" Amelia's voice faded as she walked down the hall to her classroom. Her teacher had probably heard enough of Amelia's claims that her former teacher was a superhero.

I used to be...

Abraham glanced at his new desk, only to find it already piled high with junk. Old toys that needed to be thrown out, file folders and binders filled with protocols, a laundry basket overflowing with infant onesies, and a freshly delivered magazine. He recognized the kid-friendly magazine, and on the cover was a picture of Christ in a white garment surrounded by children. The headline caught his attention.

God and Abortion

Why would that be here? He slipped his hand between the pages and flipped it open. A heavy sigh escaped him as he viewed the article. *God's probably gonna send me to hell after what I did.* He scanned to the bottom of the page where the magazine wanted to grab his attention. The article referenced a fictional story where a man questioned God.

"*God, why do you allow all this evil in the world? You allow suffering, hate, and disease. You send thieves, murderers, and rapists into the world. Why don't you send someone good? Somebody who will bring goodness and peace or find a cure for cancer?*"
"*I did...*" *God replied,* "*...but you aborted them.*"

The magazine fell to the floor, its pages flapping wildly on impact. Abraham cast the magazine aside like a leper. The emotional urge to yell at the top of his lungs and drop to his knees was momentarily subdued.
What have I done?
Guilt covered him like a preschool pajama suit, from head to toe. In that moment, as he searched for much-needed relief, a soft knock could be heard at the office door.
"Mr. Abraham, can I talk to you for a second?"
"Yes, Ms. Kelly, what can I do for you?" Abraham said, his reserves restoring his professional persona.
"Well, I just wanted to ask you...how am I doing...with my music class? I mean, be honest."
"Umm, it's not bad. I know it's challenging with the little ones." Secretly, he wanted to say her music class sucked, but he knew that

wouldn't be the best way to provide constructive criticism. So, he chose a more tactful approach.

"I'm trying my best."

"I know you are, Ms. Kelly."

"Also, can you please make a copy of this for me? It's a music sheet I wanted to practice with the kids," Ms. Kelly requested.

"Sure," Abraham said, turning his back momentarily to insert the paper into the copy machine.

Ms. Kelly examined him intently, studying him even. His senses intercepted her diagnostics, and despite the emotional damage he had endured in recent months, his instincts still worked like clockwork. She focused on his inner workings rather than his physicality.

"Mr. Abraham, are you a prophet?" she asked.

Abraham laughed at the question. "No, I'm far from it."

"Can you tell me what's in my future? What's in store for me?"

"Ms. Kelly, I don't know. I can't predict the future."

Abraham turned to retrieve the printout she had requested.

"Your color is indigo," she suddenly remarked.

"What? What are you talking about?"

"Indigo. That's your color. I see it above your head. It used to be wide open…" She raised her arms in the air like a cheerleader. "…and now, it's closed." She cupped both hands over her head. "Did something happen to you?"

"Possibly." *Her predictions are not far off…*

"I had this dream, and you were in it. You had an indigo flame above your head, and there was a large group of people in front of you. It was dusk, and, for some weird reason, you were all at the beach. You opened your hand, and an indigo flame ignited in your palm, and all of a sudden, everyone in the group had an indigo flame above their heads. Are you going to change the world? I think you're going to change the world…" Ms. Kelly shared.

"Who knows, Ms. Kelly…who knows."

"Oh, and in the dream, you were accompanied by an older man…he had a white beard…he was bald…and you were working together on something…I don't know what, but it was important," she continued.

"That's odd...I don't know anyone that looks like that...weird dream, Ms. Kelly."

"I think you *can* see things, Mr. Abraham...I really wish you'd tell me what my future holds."

"Ms. Kelly, I'm not a prophet...I don't know what your future holds, and even if I did, would you really want to know?" he questioned.

A soft knock interrupted their conversation. A young girl stood at the doorway, clutching her purse as it hung off her shoulder. "Um, I was told to come to the second-floor office...for an interview," the young girl said, fixing her glasses. The slight rubbing of her frames caused her nose to crinkle. She swung her hair off her shoulder as she waited for a response to confirm she was in the right place.

"Hi, come on in," Abraham said. "You must be the new hire I've heard so much about."

"I'm hired?" she asked. "I thought I needed to interview with you."

"You're a busy man, Mr. Abraham. Thank you for all your help," Ms. Kelly swiftly exited, as she had entered.

"No problem, Ms. Kelly," Abraham said. "And you..." He pointed to the candidate for hire.

"Elida," she said, pointing to herself.

"Elida, let's go downstairs to the Pioneer Room. We'll conduct the interview there and have you fill out some paperwork. Follow me," he said.

"Okay," she replied, smiling. *He's young to be a director,* she thought. *Not what I expected.*

Elida followed him down the stairwell, and he opened the door to the Pioneer Room on the first floor. It resembled an early 1900s living room, with a ten-foot dining table and vintage wooden furniture, circa 1920.

His description matched the picture that was given to her. *He's nice...I wonder why they want him...*

"So, Ms. Katherine tells me you have experience with infants and that you would be a good fit for the infant room. Can you start tomorrow?" he asked.

Elida's eyes widened. "Um, yeah...I can be here." *That was easy,* she thought.

"Great...you're hired. I'll leave you to it." Abraham handed her a packet of new hire paperwork. "When you're done filling this out, just give it to Ms. Betsy in the office...oh, and be here at eight tomorrow."

"Okay," Elida said.

"Oh, and Elida..." Abraham paused, waiting for eye contact from his new employee. "Don't let me down."

"I won't," she said, smiling.

Abraham closed the door and ran up the stairwell.

XXXV DECEPTION

Elida cautiously stepped out of the front door, ensuring she wasn't being followed. She discreetly reached for her cell phone and dialed the number, eager to report her success. "I'm in. He hired me. He didn't suspect a thing."

The voice on the other end wasted no time in issuing her next set of instructions. "Infiltrate. Find his weaknesses. You know what to do."

"Am I going to get paid? I completed the first step."

"You'll get your money. Just do what you need to do. You'll get the other half when the job is done." The deep voice, slightly muffled but unwavering, grew firm and merciless. "I need to dismantle him in every possible way."

XXXVI THE RAGE

"**H**ey, Kahuna! Check this out!" Cooter yelled.

"What is this?" Ray asked. The Big Kahuna was one of the many nicknames given to Ray. Many of them had been self-proclaimed in the same way Apollo Creed had given himself dozens of nicknames, and Ray wasn't shy of which ones were his own creation.

Cooter slid a flyer onto the bar top. "Tournament!" he said.

Ray shook his head, refusing to glance at the paper. "Nah, I'm retired."

"Ray, c'mon! This is the tournament of tournaments. You gotta enter!"

"I only shoot with my family now. There's my son over there. He's pretty good. He's a natural...just like his old man." Ray pointed to where Abraham stood, ready to fire a dart. "Aba! Come over here and meet this guy!"

Abraham released his last dart, hitting a bullseye. They were quickly becoming his favorite target.

"I told you!" Ray said to Cooter, pointing at Abraham's bullseye.

Abraham marched over to the bar and extended his hand, which Cooter reciprocated.

Above the bar, a three-foot trophy took center stage. Cooter's bar housed dozens of trophies, but this one outshined the rest. Occasionally, Cooter would polish the nameplate.

Cooter Carpenter
Alamo City Dart Champion
1982

Cooter had played darts his entire life. At one point, he even reached the professional ranks, and was considered the best dart player in the Alamo City, though that was a matter of debate. In his prime, he had defeated every contender except one.

"Good to meet you, young man. Your dad is the best dart player this city has ever seen. I see you're on your way to replacing him," Cooter said with a laugh.

"He's gotta long way to go. He still can't beat his old man, though," Ray said.

"Yeah, you were the best, Kahuna! That ain't no lie! Remember when you hit ton eighty after ton eighty and came back to beat Peter Henley? Man, that was one for the ages!" Cooter shouted.

"Abraham! You're next!" Zander shouted.

"I'll be back...let me finish this game real quick," Abraham said, stepping up to the line and pounded bullseyes once again.

"Your son...he has a lot of rage. Look at that scowl on his face...he looks a lot like you, Ray...when you were ready to pound on somebody..."

"Yeah, he's been dealing with some anger issues lately...but he ain't bad at darts, either." Ray grinned at his son's ferocity. *Maybe we can give this tournament thing a shot,* Ray thought. "Aba!" Ray shouted.

Abraham nodded, yanked his darts from the board, and headed to the bar top.

"Cooter says you have a lot of rage, but I said you're a natural just like your dad," Ray said, sliding a flyer toward his son. "Whaddya say? You wanna go for it?"

"Son, just focus your rage on that dart board…and I say y'all got a chance," Cooter said, flipping up a glass and pouring himself a straight whiskey.

"I don't think we're in any kind of shape to go into a big-time tournament like that. I just started shooting again. And who else are we going to get on our team?"

"We've got six months. That's plenty of time to get it together," Ray insisted.

"Y'all gotta shot, especially with this man right here," Cooter said, pointing to Ray. "What you gonna call y'all selves? You gotta have a team name…"

Abraham listened to Cooter's enthusiastic rambling. *They're talking like it's a done deal. This is crazy. We'll probably lose miserably. Well, it's not like I got anything else to do. Fuck it!* Abraham finally broke his silence. "Rage, huh? Then that's what we'll be…the Rage…from River City."

"Oh, I like that!" Cooter exclaimed.

"That's pretty good." Ray said, genuinely complimenting his son, for once.

"River City Rage," Abraham declared. "Alright…I'm in. Let's do it. Shit, I got nothin' to lose."

XXXVII WITCHING HOUR

The post-game party continued in the sanctuary of Ray's backyard. Countless hours of landscaping had gone into merging two backyards together, creating a personal haven for Ray—a place he called "The Park." It served as his nightly escape like popping a prescription pill, and having guests over heightened the experience. In this tranquil space, his depression-induced thoughts had a way of slithering away.

The late hours of the morning seemed to play tricks these days. Allegedly, 3 a.m. was when the demons came out to play, and this time, they had companions under the influence of Bud Light.

The muffled voices of Ray and Zander grew louder.

"Nah, Ray, fuck that!" Zander yelled.

The surge of anger prompted Ray to retaliate. "That was my mom, dude! Don't speak about her like that!" Ray scolded.

"You're right, I'm sorry…I'm sorry," Zander said, managing to calm his anger within seconds. Emotions fueled his fire of repressed memories, and alcohol stoked the blaze, turning his fists into weapons of fury. But when it came to family, it was different. Any mention of his childhood sent him into a frenzy, and visions of the hell he endured with his father felt like they happened yesterday.

"I'm not mad at her. When my dad was beating on my mom, she never came to help…and we lived next door! She knew what my dad was doing. We cried and yelled for her to help us, and she ignored us. We were little kids…we needed somebody to save us." Zander shook his head in disgust, his grip tightening on the beer bottle. Taking a swig, he squeezed the bottle neck and then hurled it to the ground, shattering it into several pieces on the cracked, water-deprived dirt.

The Moreno men, a volatile handful of them, could transform into rage monsters given the right combination of circumstances: mind-altering substances, machismo, and emotional instability.

"My brother wasn't well…he was mean…and he hurt a lot of people…" Ray said.

Zander paused, his thoughts drifting to his cousin. "Abe's become meaner…more volatile…he didn't used to be like that…he's becoming more like us…I noticed it at the bar earlier…"

"He's headed for a—" Ray began, but a ferocious roar in the dead of night abruptly interrupted his thoughts. It sounded like a starved monster, eager to feast on human flesh.

The low-pitched roar startled the two men, as if the beast could hear their anger, their rage, and sought to engage with them. Bedroom lights in nearby houses flicked on, one by one, as the wave of terror spread through the neighborhood.

"What the fuck?" Despite his intoxicated state, Zander's senses sharpened at the growl.

"What the fuck was that?" Ray asked, knowing well that Zander had no answers for him.

"There's a fucking monster out here…"

Ray pointed toward the neighboring house. "It's coming from next door," he said. "Let's get inside."

The beast's ferocity subsided, its growl diminishing to a low rumble that echoed through the air, lingering like the fading notes of a haunting melody. It reveled in the frenzy it had incited, drawing strength from the fear permeating the community. The creature's affinity for darkness was evident, and the mounting anticipation of its escape fueled an insatiable desire to unleash havoc.

XXXVIII   ROGUE

Elida settled herself comfortably on the futon, lying on her stomach with her elbows supporting her, her gaze fixed on Abraham.

He leaned against the doorway, one foot planted in the tiny living room and the other in the dining room.

"Are you seeing anyone?" she asked.

"No…" he replied. "…and I'm not looking for a anything either." Thoughts of Liv flooded his mind, and the pain associated with talking or even thinking about her still seared within him. "What kind of music do you listen to?" He wasted no time changing the subject.

"Mostly country."

"Country?" His face scrunched up. "Have you ever heard of Jaheim?"

"No, what does he sing?"

Abraham grinned. "Hold on, I'll play some Jaheim for you." He reached into the CD cabinet, retrieved a disc, and inserted it into the stereo. "He's only the best R&B singer ever. I have all of his albums."

The lyrics saturated the room.

> *Just in case I don't make it home tonight*
> *Let me make love to you for the last time, baby*

Want to cherish each moment like the last
'Cause baby, you're all that I have
So just in case

Think of how we made love almost anywhere
Haven't I taken you almost everywhere
Think of all the things that, that we shared
And imagine me not there, oh, oh

He pressed the power button on the stereo, turning it off as abruptly as he had turned it on.

As the tune ended, Elida had already mixed and poured various liquids into a large tub to accommodate a pair of size nine feet. She added one last solution, preparing a pedicure concoction that he desperately needed for his skin dried feet. "What happened?" she asked, noticing the sudden silence.

"Nothing," he said. The song stabbed at his heartstrings. Everything reminded him of her. If Liv resided in his heart, then she occupied a mansion from which he couldn't evict her. She had become a permanent resident in a place she left long ago.

"It's ready," she said.

He made himself comfortable on the couch and dipped his feet into the tub. "Oh, snap!"

"Cold?" she asked, giggling.

"Just a bit." The scene reminded him of the One who came to serve. "This is like the washing of the feet."

Elida sat cross-legged on the floor, gazing up at him with a blank expression.

"I take it you don't know the story…" Abraham remarked, acknowledging her perplexed state. "Jesus washed the feet of his disciples as an act of humility. He is the Lord of Lords, even as the Son of Man, he came not to be served but to serve."

"Interesting," Elida mused, pausing for a moment. "Are you a servant?"

"I used to be. Maybe, I still am…I don't know."

"Or maybe you should be washing my feet," Elida said, laughing. "I'm just kidding."

"No, I will. Really. I will be your humble servant." They both laughed before a horde of superheroes caught his attention as they flashed across the screen. "I used to watch this cartoon! It's Batman Beyond!"

"You're such a kid, Abraham," Elida teased.

"I know this episode! The Justice League makes a cameo, and they try to recruit Terry McGinnis, the new Batman. Superman even has gray hair. His suit is black and white because it takes place in the future when the original Batman is in his seventies," Abraham exclaimed, taking a deep breath.

"You're so excited about it," she said, smiling.

"Sorry, I love superheroes, especially when they team up. This is the one where Superman goes rogue."

"Rogue? Like he turns bad?"

"Yeah, but not because he truly is. It's a mind control thing in this episode. Superman isn't really bad."

"Mr. Abraham, are you a good Superman or a bad Superman?"

Half-jokingly, he responded, "That remains to be seen."

XXXIX THE CODEX

The wreckage contained piles of personal belongings, half-burned to ashes, and furniture barely recognizable.

Abraham and Zander scoured the debris, searching for the alleged book of secrets in the presumed location. The place resembled the aftermath of a bomb explosion, ravaged by the destructive power of the fire.

This doesn't make any sense. Abraham pulled out his phone, dialing a number he hadn't used in a while. "Detective Balderama?"

"Moreno! Are you ready?" came the voice on the other end.

"For what?" Abraham asked.

"To join the force…isn't that why you're calling?"

"You ask me that every time," Abraham laughed. "I regret to inform you the answer is still no. But I do need your help with something."

"Sure, go ahead."

"302 Pendleton…the house burned down last week. Can you find out the cause?"

"Okay, give me a minute. I'm pulling up the information now. Hmm, it says here that the house burned down due to arson."

"Arson?" Abraham's voice was filled with surprise.

"Did you know anyone who lived there?"

"Yeah, a relative, but the house had been vacant for some time.'

"I'm sorry to hear that. It says here that remnants of accelerant residue were found in multiple locations around the house."

"Hmm, that doesn't make sense...hey, thanks for the help. I appreciate it."

"No problem. Just remember, next time you call, I'm going to have to swear you in."

"Copy that." Abraham ended the call, his mind racing with questions. *Arson? Who could've done this? Why this place?*

Zander sifted through the burned pieces of wood, almost losing his balance on a charred 2x4. Both men ventured further into the epicenter, cautiously navigating the jagged debris. The last remnant of the standing structure collapsed to the ground.

Bang!

The crashing of wooden boards echoed through the neighborhood, causing both men to spring to their feet, assuming defensive positions as if ready for battle. In an instant, they spun around, pointing their guns at the lifeless wood.

"What the hell?" Zander gasped, noticing the firearm in Abraham's hand.

Wide-eyed, Abraham glanced at Zander's gun, surveyed the perimeter, then back at his own weapon.

Zander's brow furrowed, his confusion turning into a serious expression. *No signs of trouble or a fight,* he thought.

Both men discreetly holstered their weapons back inside their jeans, continuing their search through the charred beams, pretending they hadn't noticed each other's firearms.

"When did *you* start carrying?" Zander asked.

"I still have my connections in inner city..." Abraham replied. "I thought you *stopped* carrying?"

"Old habits die hard..." Zander patted his right hip where his gun rested discreetly under his garments. He wore a white t-shirt with a plaid short-sleeve button-down over it for further concealment.

"Help me out, Cuz...I found something," Abraham said, pointing to a charred wooden frame atop a hill of rubble.

The moniker "Cuz,' short for cousin, had become a common term among the males, a sort of code name they used to refer to one another. Ironically, Cynthia, a female cousin, was the one who coined the term, if Abraham remembered correctly, and it stuck. After all, she was the only tomboy willing to play tackle football with the boys in their horde of cousins.

Zander hopped over, and with their combined strength, they managed to flip over the pallet-sized wooden layer.

"What are we lookin' for, again?" Zander asked.

"The book that belonged to your dad. He had it in his custody for a lot of years."

"A book?" Zander questioned. "We came out here for a book? It probably burned to a crisp, Cuz...I hate to tell you—"

"I need to find it," Abraham interrupted, the urgency in his voice.

"Do you know what it looks like?" Zander asked.

"I think it's a brown journal that looks like a book..."

"A brown leather book?" Zander paused, his brow crinkling as if a memory had been triggered. "I've seen it before. It's not the kind of book you wanna find, Cuz. It unleashes all kinds of evil magic." Zander pulled his hands away from the burnt rubble.

" C'mon, man! That can't be true."

"My dad wasn't well...you know that. This book, if it's the same one you're talking about, corrupted his mind and he lost it." Zander glanced at the property next door, his childhood home now lying abandoned in ruins.

In an instant, the house changed color, returning to its original pink hue. The memory transported Zander from his five-foot-ten, two-hundred-and-thirty-four-pound frame back into his nine-year-old shoes. His older brother and two sisters screamed in terror, their cries echoing hopelessly. But it was futile. Their father shoved Alma to the kitchen floor. "Stay there!" Zeke shouted. Zander charged at his father like a raging bull, but his father flung him across the room with ease. His siblings trembled in fear, afraid they'd be tossed around like rag dolls if they made a sound.

"Don't hit my mom!" Zander cried out, desperately hoping for a passerby to hear their pleas as he peeked through the blinds. All he could see was Grandma in the backyard, glaring at their house before she turned and went back inside. Grandpa stood in the front yard, yelling from the fence. "¡No golpees a los niños! *Don't hit the children!"*

"Wait! I see something!" Abraham's shout brought Zander back to the present as he lifted a 2x4. Together, they uncovered Abraham's discovery. There, beneath the ash, lay a 10x12 brown leather book with gold-tipped pages. It remained unscathed despite the debris suffocating the sacred book. Abraham reached for it and examined the artifact, searching for any signs of desecration—burned pages, a damaged spine, a torn cover. Much to his amazement, not a single page showed signs of burn marks or had any sign of damage. *Totally intact.*

He clenched the book tightly. With his hand placed firmly on the cover, he prepared to open the highly sought-after diary. *Finally.* Using his fingertips, he brushed off the dirt and mud it had accumulated. To his surprise, the right side of the cover was engraved with words. Deciphering codes was one of his strengths, and this peculiar writing caught his attention. Instead of the writing going from left to right, it was vertical. He turned the book on its side and scraped away more dirt, revealing a picture of an object with markings underneath it. *Latin?*

"Cuz, don't do it…" Zander warned.

Abraham lifted the cover slowly, mindful of Zander's words. Before he could explore further, a strange voice interrupted them.

"Hey! What are you all doing? This is private property! You can't be here!" shouted a police officer. "You all need to leave immediately!"

"You ready to blast this fool, Cuz?" Zander asked, his fingers itching to go trigger happy.

"Are you crazy? Just be cool." Abraham cautioned. "I got the book, relax! Just chill."

"All right, this is your show, but since I helped you, I'll need your help on one of the nights I'm working. Is that cool?" Zander asked.

"Yeah, I got you, Cuz. Just don't blast this cop."

Abraham and Zander maneuvered through the debris, making their way towards the BMW.

"It's my grandma's house. We just came to see if there's anything salvageable," Abraham explained.

The police officer remained silent, his eyes fixed on them as they approached the car.

"Are you ready for the dart tournament in Vegas?" Zander asked.

Both men climbed into the Stealth M3, ignoring the officer's intimidating glare.

"I will be," Abraham said. "Why? You want to get your ass kicked this early in the day?"

"I don't mind getting a beer and giving a beating. Wurzbach Ice House?"

With unwavering confidence, Abraham glared at his formidable competition. "Let's do it!"

XL THE TRAIN HAS LEFT THE STATION

Abraham packed a pair of jeans in his duffle bag. *This should be enough,* he thought. "Three days' worth of clothes is good…probably only need them for one…" he whispered to himself. He zipped up the bag and fastened the two handles together. After eight years of ownership, the bag had traveled halfway around the world, and it was ready for another adventure.

A soft knock at the door interrupted his thoughts, resembling the sound of a baby woodpecker at work. Visitors were rare, and the knock didn't sound familiar. Abraham threw the duffle bag on the couch and cautiously opened the door. He recognized the unlikely visitor.

"Hey, what are you doing here?" he asked.

Avril smiled, standing opposite the screen door, and gave a wave. "Hey, I came by to check on you."

"Come on in."

"You moved far away from home," she said, giggling.

Avril entered the room and noticed the duffle bag lying on the couch. "Unpacking?" she questioned.

"No," he replied. "Packing…I'm going to Vegas tomorrow."

"Oh, don't party too hard out there. You know what they say about Vegas..."

"No, not this time. My dad and I are going to play darts in this big tournament. He wanted to give it a shot. Honestly, I think we'll be back home after the first day," he said with a laugh. "And, I don't know...I just thought it'd be good to get away from here for a little while, you know?"

"Are you sure about going to Vegas? That's like going into the lion's den...considering your condition. You'll either escape like Daniel or get eaten alive...and your faith is a little shaky these days."

"Another test...I got a lot going against me on this one..."

"Wait, did you say you're going with your dad?" she asked, wide-eyed.

Abraham let out a sarcastic laugh. "Yeah, I know. Any more than a day is pushing it."

"Good luck. You're gonna need it," she said. "I don't know what's worse...drinking in your condition or spending more than twenty-four hours with your dad..."

"Hence, a lot going against me...honestly, I'm not sure this is a good idea, but I feel this is where I'm supposed to go for some reason...and the drinking has brought out a dangerous side." The struggle to relay the truth pierced his emotional reserves. "It's ironic...going to Sin City after all the sin I've committed."

"Sin that *we* committed," Avril added.

"Is that why you came? To remind me of what we did?" Abraham turned his back to her, swiftly zipping up the side pocket of the duffle bag.

"No, Abraham. It's hard for me too. I regret what we did, and I wanted to stop by because I know it's hard for you too. *We* did this. I wish I could go back in time..."

Abraham fell silent, consumed by heartbreak that urged him to run away forever and begin a new life in a place untainted by memories of his gravest wrongdoings.

"What a getaway, right?" he sighed heavily, sinking into the couch beside his well-traveled duffle bag. "Vegas...the last place on earth I should be going to…" Shaking his head, he continued, "I'm all messed up right now…"

Avril stood by his side, placing a comforting hand on his shoulder. "It'll get better," she reassured him.

"I don't think we should be around each other anymore. I don't mean that in an ugly way. I just don't want to be tempted into doing things I shouldn't."

"And going to Vegas is going to help you with that?" she asked.

"That's what I mean…the debauchery, the booze, the women…it's not the best place to go when avoiding temptation…but maybe I need one final purge. I don't even know what I'm doing. That doesn't even make sense."

"Well, you don't need Vegas to have a good time. We can have one before you leave…if you feel like getting it out of your system. Sorry…but I never liked the idea of you being with another girl. I never have. It's always bothered me," Avril admitted.

"Always the jealous type…please, don't get all psychotic…" Abraham said.

"I couldn't help it back then…I'm sorry."

"Even now, I'm tempted to take you up on your offer, but I don't want a repeat of last time."

"I know what you mean…use protection this time…I got needs too, you know. I don't want you getting your fix out there in Vegas…with some random hookers…ewww," Avril grimaced in disgust.

Abraham contemplated her proposition. *Just do it…this'll be the last time…*

"Fine…but this is where our story ends…because I don't want to be messed up anymore…and I don't want to be ugly to anybody like I have been."

"That's fair." Avril paused. "You still love her…"

He pondered her words for a few seconds, acutely aware of whom she was referring to. "I do."

"Why don't you try being with her again?"

Abraham inhaled deeply, then forcefully exhaled. *Where to begin?* he wondered. The odyssey with Liv wasn't an easy one to let go of.

"I, uh…I don't think she…it's just not a good time right now…"

The Darkness seized the opportunity to creep in and out at propitious moments. *Liv's not here…she left you, remember? Give Avril what she wants…there's no harm in that…you're single…you can do whatever you want…go for it!*

XLI SKYWAY TO HELL

Two and a half hours with this dude in close proximity…this should be fun…

The plane jettisoned from the tarmac, and once it reached 30,000 feet, Abraham set up his workshop. His notebook lay open on the tray table, filled with words scribbled in blue ink. He gazed out the window, mesmerized by the endless expanse of blue skies, searching for his next inspiration. In the distance, a menacing black storm cloud caught his attention. The cloud illuminated with ferocity as lightning struck the farmland below.

"What'cha got there?" Ray asked.

"Something I've been working on," Abraham answered.

"Dude, I still remember that poem you wrote about your sister. That was good, man…really heartfelt."

"That poem got me invited to the writing club at Palo Alto."

"The community college you nearly flunked out of?" Ray chuckled.

"Still got a degree though."

"Yeah, but it didn't get you a job. What good is that?" Ray didn't hesitate in his quips, even if it started a knife fight.

"I have a job now." *Does this shit really matter?* he thought.

"It's a good thing they didn't have to check your grades," Ray continued.

"Doesn't matter. I'm good at what I do." Rebuttals were the fuel for escalated arguments—Ray could never admit he was wrong.

"All I'm saying is, you've always been a 'C' student, that's all," Ray said.

"What's your point? I'm doing good for myself now. That's what matters…not the grades I got in college algebra, literature, biology, or PE." *Geez, what a fuckin' dick!*

"I'm just saying, dude. You could've done better," Ray persisted.

Abraham decided to temporarily put his arsenal of counterarguments aside. Unleashing that kind of payload would only lead to further confrontation, turning their conversation into a verbal battleground. The last thing the passengers needed was to be caught in the crossfire of their dispute.

Abraham refocused on his writing pieces. *No sense in arguing with a fool. Just let it go.*

After fifteen minutes of snoozing, his father finally resumed the conversation. "Hey, let me read it, man?" Ray asked.

If he wasn't sleeping, it was necessary for him to socially engage with anyone nearby, be it human or animal. Perhaps it was fear of being alone or maybe he was just a butterfly. Instinctually, Abraham derived that a portion of his habits stemmed from childhood trauma. His impulsive behavior and lack of patience mirrored that of a five-year-old, and Ray always found a way to justify his flaws by blaming others.

That's on the subconscious level for sure, Abraham thought. *Oh, what the hell…just show him…*

"I had this idea a while back, and I've been working on it," Abraham finally said.

"Is it new darts? Because you need 'em," Ray said.

Abraham ignored the sarcastic remark. "Here, read it," he said, tossing a stack of paper stapled together.

"It's a story?"

"It's a book. I've had all these ideas come to me, and I started writing down different pieces that will hopefully one day be part of a *published* book."

"And I'm in it?" Ray perused the eloquent display of words. It wasn't long before he stumbled upon his name in the crossfire of a literary fiasco. To Abraham's surprise, Ray laughed at his own portrayal in the story. "I'm a dick!" he exclaimed, referring to the depiction. "It's pretty good, Dad. What do you plan to do with it?"

"Release it to the world one day…to inspire others…in hopes of making a difference." Abraham sensed a supernatural power flow through him, sparking his natural state of being. Words came to life when he put pen to paper, much like dry bones coming to life.

That's it…

The words…

The writing…

…the spark!

The plane shook violently, jostling from side to side and up and down like a roller coaster in free fall. "Oh, my goodness," one of the ladies exclaimed a few rows up. The turbulence startled some of the passengers, bringing them back to consciousness. "Whoa" was the word being thrown around, awakening the travelers from their drowsy state. *Nap time is over,* Abraham thought.

Distraction…I know what you're doing…and it's not gonna work. "Satan I rebuke you in the name of Jesus…" Abraham whispered to himself. This time, he did not hesitate to recite the words with conviction. *Just like Margie taught me.*

Ray extended his left hand, gripping the seat in front of him. "Aw, dude," he said, bowing his head and closing his eyes as if ready to vomit. "I shouldn't have drank so much last night."

Wait a minute…the pattern…

Deductive reasoning kept him sharp and alert, and the "spark" reignited the traits that laid dormant for so long. *Sin City…the perfect storm…just when I'm gaining momentum, I'm heading into hell to fight the devil and his army…fuck that…he already lost…we'll test it…we'll see how hard he's gonna fight me…when I get home, I'm gonna finish this book.*

The protocol of positive affirmations ran like clockwork. *This is going to be a good trip…*

XLII SIN CITY

"And we have arrived...Sin City, gentlemen. What happens here never comes back home," Phil declared with a touch of sarcasm, as if narrating the scene.

Let's see what this place has in store for us.

The team stepped out of the sleek, elongated limo, each member exiting one by one. Ray insisted on arriving in style, mirroring a modern-day incarnation of the Beatles' arrival in America. Carrying their bags, they surveyed the expanse of casinos, restaurants, and daytime debauchery. Pedestrians strolled by clutching yard-long margaritas in their hands.

"It's been a long time since I've played in a tournament. This one is big time. Are y'all ready for this?" Ray asked, glancing back at his team members. As a seasoned veteran, he had found himself in this position countless times, often emerging victorious with the championship trophy and monetary awards.

They gazed upwards, their eyes catching a glimpse of the Mandalay Bay sign perched atop the hotel. The sunlight shimmered on the windows, casting a radiant reflection onto the streets below.

Abraham, no stranger to the allure of Vegas, knew all too well the repercussions of what the city could do to a man. This marked his third visit to the city of sin, and he anticipated a familiar sense of indulgence, drenched in decadence.

"Let's do it," Phil interjected. Having only recently taken up darts, Phil exuded a confidence that surpassed his diminutive 5'4" frame. He dragged his rolling suitcase, catching up to Abraham. "This time we're going to get you fucked, Abe. Not like in Germany. You got no choice here, boy. You're not gonna leave a virgin." Phil's humor never ceased.

Abraham shook his head and chuckled. "Already took care of that before I came here, so we're good there."

"Alright, guys. It's showtime," Peter said. The quiet brother, Peter, emanated a gentle demeanor, a natural fit for his chosen profession as a school counselor. His calm disposition remained steadfast, and his soft eyes shined through his glasses, shielding them from the world.

"Zander?" Abraham asked. "When's he coming?"

"He'll be here tonight. He caught a later flight," Phil replied.

Ray walked beside his son as they set foot into Mandalay Bay. "Dude, this hotel is bad ass. Let's check in and get this tournament started!"

"You know we don't have a great chance of winning…and we're going up against the best players from all over the world…" Abraham remarked.

"It'll be a great experience…me coming out of retirement…and we can be a father/son team."

The excitement of Vegas never failed to disappoint. Despite the overwhelming odds, the experience had already proven to be rewarding in every aspect. The desert doubled as an environment for a spiritual fast from all the heartache in San Antonio. "Sounds like fun," Abraham said.

A buzzing noise jolted Abraham alerting him that he was no longer incommunicado after the flight. Text messages had become a rarity these days, and he retrieved his phone from his back pocket to read the incoming communication.

Kay G. (11:16 a.m.): Hello love, just checking in. Be careful out there in Vegas. "Be sober-minded: be watchful. Your adversary the devil prowls around like a roaring lion, seeking someone to devour." 1 Peter 5:8.

Abraham M. (11:17 a.m.): Copy that. I'll need some extra prayers to get through this weekend. Need to brief you on the revelation I had on the plane. I think I found my spark. I love you!

"Aba!" Ray shouted. "Dude, I just checked the schedule! You're up at 12:15. Go check into your room and get back down here."

"Alright, alright…relax!" Abraham said. *Oh shit, it's already getting real and I'm freakin' starving.*

"Yo, Cuz!" a voice shouted across the lobby. Zander approached Abraham and Ray.

"I thought you weren't gonna be here till later?" Abraham asked.

"Nah, I decided to fly in earlier…get a head start, scope out the competition," Zander said. With his brawny physique, he commanded attention. His sheer size intimidated most men, although they often underestimated him due to his protruding gut. The rest of his body was a combination of mass and muscle, and he was as strong as an ox.

"Aba, go get ready. You don't have much time," Ray urged.

"Alright, I'll see y'all in an hour."

Once the elevator whisked Abraham up to his room, Ray signaled to Zander. "Hey, dude, everyone's a rookie on the team, so I'm gonna need your help," Ray said.

"Nah, nah, nah, don't tell me what to do…I'm gonna do this my way," Zander snarled.

XLIII — NOT ON BREAD ALONE

Abraham approached the line, his stomach churning with a cacophony of growls. He instinctively placed a hand on his rumbling belly, feeling its emptiness. *I'm going on critical...*

Feeding time had come and gone, and now he had to endure the cricket match before he could satisfy his cravings with a mouthwatering cheesesteak or burger, or anything he could get his hands on.

He carefully positioned his foot, edging as close as possible without risking disqualification, aligning the tip of his size 9 Air Jordans precisely seven feet and nine quarters of an inch away from the bullseye.

His opponent, a lanky young man not much older than him, wiped the sweat off his brow. Condensation fogged up his eyeglasses, prompting him to remove them with a wince. He used his t-shirt to wipe the lenses before placing them back on.

He looks like a first timer too...here we go.

Dizziness overcame him, and the voice of temptation called out, coaxing him to give up.

You can forfeit...it's no big deal...it's only a game...nobody cares...you're hungry...there's plenty of places in here to get something to eat…walk away from the line…you don't need to finish this…it doesn't mean anything…

Abraham briefly entertained the voice's suggestion to quit.

You're in the desert! Go have fun! Your family will understand…

Abraham knew better, but a juicy succulent cheeseburger sounded good. *Maybe he's right…I don't need to play today…I haven't eaten since yesterday…*

There's plenty of bread around here… The voice kept badgering with temptation.

The mention of sustenance triggered a memory of the advice Margie had given him before he left. *Margie warned me…the devil will tempt me to do the wrong thing…to let people down…to be selfish…*

You don't need to listen to anybody…listen to yourself…that's what's most important… The voice relentlessly directed him toward pleasure. *You have the power to leave right now and go get that burger you crave…fasting is not for you…go eat!*

Abraham released three practice darts at the board, but they faltered mid-flight, falling short of their intended mark. He felt his strength waver. *I feel weak…maybe I should just step out of the match. Margie told me about the bread…*

The voice persisted, its insistent tone echoing in Abraham's mind. *It's an easy decision…just walk away…no need to second guess…you don't have to wait forty minutes to get that grilled cheeseburger…you can get it in forty seconds…*

Abraham furrowed his brow, his focus shifting to recall the scripture Margie had shared with him. *One does not live on bread alone, but on every word that comes forth from the mouth of God…*

With a determined resolve, Abraham drew back his arm, took aim at the target, and released his grip, sending the projectile soaring through the air.

XLIV   BULLSEYE

The bitter taste of defeat from the previous cricket match lingered in his mind. The lanky youngster had caught Abraham off guard, and he struggled to regain his composure. *I didn't come all this way for nothing. Concentrate. Give it everything you got.*

Now, he had a chance to redeem himself. The competition in the second cricket match had reached a whole new level, but this time he made sure to fuel up with a full stomach.

Abraham watched as three darts flew from his opponent's hand, each dart released only milliseconds apart. Triple 20, Triple 19, and Triple 18—his challenger easily closing out three numbers. Todd Bingelman, hailing from Oklahoma, proved to be a much tougher opponent.

He recalled his father's words regarding the game of Cricket. *"In a perfect game, a player only needs 8 darts. Triple 20, Triple 19, Triple 18, Triple 17, Triple 16, Triple 15, green ring around the bullseye and a bullseye."*

Todd hit the first three targets precisely. If he was truly as good as they claimed, then this game could be over in the next five darts.

Todd   Abraham

Cricket

	C		20				

C | 20

C | 19

C | 18

| 17

| 16

| 15

| Bull

"Alright, Abraham, go for the next three, hit some triples and close them out," Abraham whispered, encouraging himself.

He raised his first dart, taking aim at the triple 17. Strategy dictated that he had to close out the 17, 16, and 15 to level the playing field. With determination, he released the dart.

Triple 17.

Okay, Abraham, be cool. Concentrate. Triple 16, here we go.

Raising his second dart, he targeted the small green curved rectangle on the 16. With conviction, he let the dart fly.

Triple 16.

Oh shit! I pulled it off! C'mon, Abraham, one more and you got a chance.

Abraham lifted his final dart, focusing on the triple 15. He released it with all his might.

Single 15.

Damn! Now this guy is gonna close it out.

Todd   Abraham

		Cricket		
C		20		
C		19		
C		18		
		17	C	
		16	C	
		15	/	
		Bull		

Todd Bingleman glided toward the line with unshakeable confidence. Standing at an impressive 6'1", he possessed a commanding presence, characterized by his dirty blonde hair and piercing blue eyes. At first glance, he appeared to be a businessman who indulged in darts as a passionate pastime. Not only was he just one of the tournament's higher-ranking contenders; he was also one of the most formidable.

Without hesitation, he unleashed his three darts in quick succession, leaving Abraham no time to think about his next move. Each projectile found its mark on the board with precision.

Triple 17.

Triple 16.

Single 15.

Todd   Abraham

	Cricket	
C	20	
C	19	
C	18	
C	17	C
C	16	C
/	15	/
	Bull	

He didn't close out the 15's. Okay, strategy.

Abraham approached the yellow line, contemplating his next move. *If I knock out the 15's with a triple, then I'm up on points and I can try to close out the other numbers.*

He aimed and fired.

Triple 15.

The scorecard displayed 15 points for Abraham and 0 points for Todd. Encouraged, Abraham aimed his second dart at the triple 20, hoping for another stroke of luck.

Single 20.

Shit!

Undeterred, he raised his third dart, considering his options. *Okay, where should I go now? Pound the 15's, get up on points.* He focused on the triple 15 and released the dart with determination. A successful attempt meant that he would score 45 points and be ahead by 60.

Triple 15.

Oh snap! It worked!

Todd   Abraham

	Cricket		
C	20	/	
C	19		
C	18		
C	17	C	
C	16	C	
/	15	¢	
	Bull		

60

The scorekeeper glanced at the darts, swiftly jotting down the numbers on the scorecard. The tally now displayed Abraham with 60 points and Todd at 0.

Taking his place at the line, Todd exuded an air of calm confidence, his features locked in a determined, stoic expression.

Todd is too good to lose to me.

With a burst of anticipation, Todd readied himself and released his first dart, his aim honed to perfection. He knew he could capitalize on any target, save for the elusive 15's, and amass points effortlessly.

Double 15.

Okay, he closed the 15's. There goes my scoring opportunity.

Undeterred, Todd pressed on, swiftly launching his remaining two darts.

Triple 20.

Single 20.

Todd		Cricket		Abraham
	C	20	/	
	C	19		
	C	18		
	C	17	C	
	C	16	C	
	¢	15	¢	
		Bull		
80				60

The 20's presented ample opportunities for scoring. Abraham hadn't closed the number, and Todd skillfully exploited the target by hitting it four additional times.

Shit! He scored 80 points. I have to go for the bullseyes. Get back the scoring edge.

Abraham approached the line cautiously, his focus solely on the red bullseye. *All three darts gotta be in there or this game is over. Even the green ring around the bull will count.* With a combination of concentration and hope, his best allies, he released the darts.

Double bull.

Double bull.

Single bull.

Closed out the bulls and scored 100 points.

According to the scorecard, Abraham had accumulated 160 points, while Todd had 80 points. Only to the untrained eye, it appeared like a brutal gap.

Maintaining a facade of calm, Abraham collected his darts from the board. The scorekeeper announced, "One hundred points. Total points: one hundred and sixty."

Todd		Cricket		Abraham
C		20	/	
C		19		
C		18		
C		17	C	
C		16	¢	
¢		15	C	
		Bull	C	

80

60

100

160

Todd stepped up, and this time it appeared that he might have been rattled. His brow crinkled as he contemplated his strategy. He released his darts in rapid succession, akin to the bursts of an automatic weapon.

Single bull.

Single bull.

His final dart missed the target, landing on the insignificant 5.

Todd		Cricket		Abraham
C		20	/	
C		19		
C		18		
C		17	C	
C		16	¢	
¢		15	C	
X		Bull	C	

80

60

100

160

He missed! Oh shit! This is it! All or nothing.

Abraham strode forward with more confidence than he had ever mustered before, his steps steady and determined. He eyeballed the red bullseye and fired at will.

Double bull.

Double bull.

Total miss.

Todd   Abraham

	Cricket		
C	20	/	
C	19		
C	18		
C	17	C	
C	16	¢	
¢	15	C	
X	Bull	C	

80   60

                                                                                 100

                                                                                 100

                                                                                      260

100 points! Okay, Abraham, be cool. Act like you've been here before.

His eyes shifted to the scorecard, revealing Abraham's total of 260 points compared to Todd's meager 80.

A voice erupted from the enthusiastic crowd. "There you go, Abe! He can't win without scoring points!" Abraham recognized the excitement in Ray's voice. *Now he wants to be my cheerleader...* Center stage always changed things. *Now he's proud of his son,* he thought. *C'mon, Abraham, give him a break, Ray's trying.*

Todd unleashed a barrage of darts at the board.

Triple 20.

Triple 20.

Single 20.

Todd		Cricket		Abraham
	C	20	/	
	C	19		
	C	18		
	C	17	C	
	C	16	¢	
	¢	15	C	
	X	Bull	C	
80				60
140				100
				100
220				260

"One hundred and forty points!" the scorekeeper shouted.

Strategy…take him away from the bullseyes…score and he has to catch up on points.

The scorecard displayed 260 points for Abraham, while Todd trailed with 220 points.

"Abe, rack up the points! Get as many as you can!" Zander shouted.

"No, dude, don't tell him that! He needs to close and score," Ray countered.

"He needs insurance. Scoring will keep this other dude focused on trying to score instead of closing out the game!"

Ray and Zander volleyed back and forth like preschoolers on the playground.

These motherfuckers! Shut the fuck up so I can concentrate! Abraham refocused, shutting out the commotion. *I need a bullseye, a double 20 and a triple 19 to have a chance.*

He released his darts.

Bullseye.

Double 20.

Single 19.

Todd   Abraham

	C	Cricket	C	
	C	20	C	
	C	19	/	
	C	18		
	C	17	C	
	C	16	¢	
	¢	15	C	
	X	Bull	C	

80		60
140		100
		100
		50
220		310

Up 50 more points. I closed the 20's, so he's gotta go for 19's or 18's to score.

Abraham had reached a total of 310 points, while Todd trailed behind with 220 points.

Todd squinted his eyes, contemplating his next move. He needed to focus on either the 19's or the 18's to bridge the gap and emerge victorious.

Studying the dartboard intently, Todd settled on the bullseye. He took aim and released the dart, hitting the target dead center. Triple 19 would secure his victory. He fired at the rectangular green slit, only managing to hit the huge white space, single 19.

Undeterred, Todd prepared for his next throw. Determination etched on his face, he lined up the shot and let the dart fly. Once again, hitting the target directly.

Triple 19.

Todd		Cricket			Abraham
	C	20	¢		
	C	19	/		
	C	18			
	C	17	C		
	C	16	¢		
	¢	15	C		
	C	Bull	C		

Todd	Abraham
80	60
140	100
76	100
	50
296	310

The scorekeeper studied Todd's darts and scribbled down a number on the scorecard.

He scored 76 points.

Glancing at the scorecard, Abraham saw his score of 310 points while Todd had 296.

All I need is a double 19 and a triple 18. Here we go.

Stepping up to the line, he aimed for the triple 18. The 18 had always given him trouble due to its challenging angle—high and off to the right.

Here it goes.

He fired.

Triple 18.

Okay, just two 19's and we're good. Dad, told me to always aim for the triple.

He fired his second dart.

Single 19.

Shit! It's all right. We got one more dart. Light it up!

With determination, he set his sights on the thick, pizza-like slice of the 19 and let his final dart fly.

Single 19.

Game over!

Todd Bingelman, a gentleman of the sport, approached Abraham and stretched out his hand. "Excellent game, young man! You showed great poise out there. Good luck to you!"

"Thank you! Good game," Abraham replied, returning the handshake. In hindsight, the game had lasted a mere fourteen minutes, yet Abraham's eyes widened with the rush of adrenaline still pumping through his body. The small crowd let out a few cheers as the underdog pulled off an upset, as Abraham clearly had the unmistakable look of an inexperienced competitor. He glanced at the final score.

Maybe we do have a chance to win...

Todd		Cricket		Abraham
C		20		¢
C		19		¢
C		18		C
C		17		C
C		16		¢
¢		15		C
C		Bull		C
80				60
140				100
76				100
				50
296				310

XLV METAMORPHOSIS

Fall 1993

"**I** need to talk to you..." Gloria beckoned Ray with a stern motion of her index finger.

"What now?" Ray growled, devouring his dinner plate of rice, beans, and quesadillas.

"Are you going to agree to the name change?"

"Fuck them! I ain't gotta hide from anybody! These motherfuckers wanna come and get me, they know where to find me!"

"It's not about you! You wanna go get killed, fine, go and get killed! It's the kids that need protection...not you! Think, for once!" Gloria scolded him. She engaged in a fight that she would not waiver from.

"Fine, but I'll do it my way!" Ray flung the plate across the kitchen. It crashed against the wall and landed on the stove, shattering into pieces. He made a dash for the door. Just as he was about to make his escape, Gloria prodded him further.

"And your son?"

"What about him?" Ray asked, pausing near the door. He reached atop the grandfather clock and retrieved a small plastic bag containing a green, herbal-smelling substance—a go-to for stress relief.

"You need to talk to him...he's showing signs..."

"Of?" Ray asked.

"He's inherited certain traits…and he doesn't understand what's happening to him. And I can't help him…" Gloria pointed at him, her eyes piercing through his flesh, refusing to back down. "…but *you* might."

"I'll talk to him." Ray put on his Stevie Wonder sunglasses and placed his darts in his shirt pocket. The darts were sheathed in a leather wallet monogrammed with the initials "MRM" for "Mr. M."

"No, I need you to help him…guide him."

"What can I do? There's nothing I can do…he's gotta go through it!" Ray retorted.

"Damn it, your son is lost! He needs guidance…he needs you to help him deal with this!"

"He'll have to tough it out. I got bigger things to deal with."

"What else is new?" Flustered, Gloria continued, "When he starts acting out and fucking shit up, I don't want to hear it."

"Gloria! He's gonna be fine! Just let him be…stop fucking complaining already!"

"We're gonna lose our son! You *know* damn well how dangerous this is! He's changing into who he's going to be for the rest of his life!"

Ray reached for another bag atop the grandfather clock, this time filled with a white substance.

"And you need to stop fucking around with that shit!"

"Don't worry about it!" Ray said, his focus was directed solely on the task at hand.

"You're gonna destroy your life and our son's life by using that shit," Gloria said. Her usual sweet voice had been replaced by a tone of stone.

"Nah, he's better than that. Let him do this on his own. He's stronger than you think. You should pull him out of that boarding school already and put him in public school." Ray tossed the herbal bag back on top of the clock.

"No! He made his choice and he's going to see it through. He's not taking the easy way out. He'll never learn anything by doing that. *This* is what will make him stronger…learning to not give up when it's hard. And *you* don't understand that!"

"It's always the same shit. I got darts tonight anyway." Ray zipped out the door, moving on to his next stop.

"Among other things," Gloria said sarcastically. "Motherfucker," she whispered under her breath. She grabbed a stack of paperwork from the entryway table that had been sitting there for at least a couple of months. All she needed was a pen to finalize the agreement that read: *Final Decree of Divorce.*

"We're gonna lose our son and you don't even give a shit...I'll do it myself," she whispered.

XLVI INTO THE LION'S DEN

"**H**i, Mom. Guess what?"

"Y'all are winning?" Gloria's voice exclaimed with excitement. Abraham could see her smiling on the other end of the phone.

"Yeah, kinda. I mean, we're holding our own out here. We've definitely gone farther than we all thought. How did you know?" he asked.

"I talked to your dad earlier. He was so excited, Abe. I'm glad you and your dad are getting along and having a good time. That makes me happy."

"I can't lie, it's been pretty fun, and we actually might have a chance to make it far in the 501 match tomorrow...all of us are shooting together on that one. Honestly, we've been getting really lucky...and Dad was actually not that bad."

"Where *is* your dad? I've been trying to call him, and he's not answering."

"I have no idea. He's probably at the blackjack table. Michelle's not here to stop him, so he's having a field day. You remember what happened last time…"

"Yes, do *not* remind me. They argued for two days straight. That man, my gosh. And how are you doing?"

"Recovering…better, I guess," Abraham said.

"Oh, Abe…I know you've lost a lot this year…"

Gloria didn't know the half of it. *If she only knew the truth…*

"Liv loves you…" Gloria paused. "But…she may not come back, though…I just want you to be prepared."

Abraham remained silent. *I don't want to hear this shit*, he thought. Hope was in the midst of a resurrection, and speaking life to it meant there was a chance. "We were supposed to get married. We're actually married in the state of Hawaii, not legally, but kinda. We *were* married." His emotions wavered, and the dam he built to prevent them from flooding cracked. "Mom…" he said, choking on tears that desperately wanted to fall. "…I miss her…I'm mad at her for what she did…and for what I did…"

"Does she still have the ring?"

"She does."

"Then there's still hope."

"I know you did your best to prepare me for the world, but there are some things you just can't prepare for. You taught me to see things through, to stick to my decisions, to take accountability. I need to put those into practice again. I won't let your divorce be in vain. You stood your ground. You let Dad and I both know there's no easy way out. You were the real parent, Mom. I *will* make you proud one day."

"Give it time. You'll find your way. We all have a choice, and I know you'll choose the right path."

"I'm sorry for everything I've done. I love you, Mom."

"Okay, dude. Be careful, have fun and take care of your dad. You know how he gets. Love you, too."

After what felt like an eternity, the elevator finally ascended to the 63rd floor. Atop the Mandalay Bay stood the crown jewel of Sin City's nightclubs. Stepping out of the elevator bestowed a sense of exclusivity reminiscent of a speakeasy.

Abraham surveyed the nightclub, its dimly lit interior illuminated only by strategically placed fiery orange lights. He moved stealthily along the perimeter, embracing the cloak of darkness that suited him just the way he liked. Several people were lined up at the bar, so he discreetly slipped into an opening to order a drink. The bartender acknowledged Abraham with a nod. "What can I get you?" he asked.

"Double whiskey," Abraham said. The bartender whipped it up in seconds and placed it on the bar top. Abraham dropped a twenty-dollar bill, and discreetly whisked away. Casually sipping on his drink, he made his way to the balcony.

Happy couples, bachelor and bachelorette parties, and various groups, easily recognizable as vacationing partygoers, reveled in the vibrant Vegas nightlife. Unbeknownst to them, a highly volatile man moved among them.

He leaned over the balcony, viewing the streetlights below, sparkling like a thousand diamonds. In the distance, a live concert unfolded, captivating the crowd with singing, drinking, and dancing.

He looked to the night sky, and above him, the towering letters proudly displayed "Mandalay Bay." Just above the letters was the rooftop. *Huge letters and I don't mix well*, he thought. *The last time I was around them, somebody died.* The Hollywood sign, especially the colossal "H," was a landmark he had no desire to revisit. He retreated into the club, swiftly placing his empty glass on a nearby table as he passed the VIP section. A waitress rushed by, carrying two bottles in her hands. The swinging door she exited offered a glimpse behind the scenes.

Abraham signaled the bartender for a second double whiskey and rested his elbows on the bar top. Jason had introduced him to the Crown Royal Green Apple version of whiskey, so he practiced patience, pacing himself rather than downing the drink in seconds. He glanced at his phone. *10:27...crowd should be filing in.* A notification appeared: Missed Call - Kay.

I hope she's okay...I'll call her back as soon as—

A stranger bumped into his arm, nearly knocking the phone from his hand. Another patron slid into an opening at the bar. "You don't really think you'll win, do you?" a smug voice taunted him. "None of you stand a chance. They say luck comes and goes, and even fame lasts for only fifteen minutes…and you, Cinderella, are out of time."

Abraham turned to his right, assessing the intruder. *Six feet, long wavy hair, clean shaven, brown blazer, black slacks, and cocky as a motherfucker. Donald Anderson.*

Donald, hailing from California, ranked number eleven in the state. His team, The Outlaws, were not far behind in rankings, and Zander had given Donald's right-hand man a run for his money earlier in the day.

"The only reason you're talking to me right now is because you're afraid you'll lose. Trust me, your mind games won't work. You're not entirely confident that your team can beat mine."

"Listen, young chap, you have no idea how this game works. You and your team are just here on a whim…just to see how far you can go. I've seen it before. There's no real chance of you winning tomorrow."

"We do have a guy who's ranked number three in the state of Texas, and last time I checked, Texas is a pretty big state." Abraham thought a little fib wouldn't hurt. Ray had been ranked twenty years prior, but Donald didn't need to know the details.

"Let me guess…don't mess with Texas…is that what you're saying, rookie?" Donald quipped.

"Don't *fuck* with Texas," Abraham countered.

"Oh, yes. You mean that washed-up old fool. We'll make quick work of him…and you."

"We'll see."

"Young chap, trust me, your old man always fucks it up. I've seen the footage." Donald glared at Abraham. "You all are just a bunch of Mexicans entering a tournament on a whim because you think you have a chance. We'll see you all tomorrow. Enjoy the rest of your evening, Cinderella." Donald walked off with his glass of bourbon.

Fuck that dude! Abraham glared at Donald's team, and they stared back at him. He mouthed the words, "fuck y'all," and ordered a third whiskey. Ignoring everyone in his sight, he returned to the balcony.

The Strip shined like one giant disco ball. All the lights, all the people, all the darkness — the energies swirled around him. The atmosphere consumed him.

Abraham chugged the second drink within seconds and began sipping on the third. The Dark Energy seeped into his bloodstream.

Kay G. (10:31 p.m.): Hi Uncle Phil, it's Kay. Are you with Abe right now? I called him but he's not answering.

Phil M. (10:32 p.m.): Hi Kay, no I'm not with him. What's up?

Kay G. (10:32 p.m.): Can you please check on him?

Phil M. (10:33 p.m.): Sure. I'm sure he's here at one of the clubs. I'll go look for him. What are you feeling?

Kay G. (10:33 p.m.): Abe told me something the other day and it popped up in my head randomly…I know it's a disturbance in the force. Please go check on him. Find him, like right now.

Phil M. (10:33 p.m.): What did he say?

Kay G. (10:34 p.m.): None are taken back from the Darkness. Not without giving one up in return.

The balcony called to him, offering an escape from the relentless thoughts swirling in his mind. Overlooking the bustling Strip, it seemed like the perfect remedy.

Abraham, rewire…

A bat-like creature swooped by and landed on the balcony. The Nighthawk inched closer to Abraham, but he remained lost in his thoughts. He stole a glance at the nocturnal visitor, its gray and black stripes with white bars on each wing, and it looked at him as if to speak.

Oh, c'mon, Donald is right! You all are done! Especially you! You don't deserve to win, much less, live!

The Darkness favored creatures of the night, seizing any opportunity to gain an advantage, utilizing anything or anyone.

You know the alcohol makes you more like me…

Abraham fought to focus his thoughts on calmness. "You're better than that. You *can* control it. You're a good person…it doesn't matter what you did…it's what you do from now on that matters…" he whispered.

It does matter! Fuck all those people! Fuck Donald! You know you want to smash his head on the bar top…and you should for the way he spoke to you!

"No, I'm done here." Abraham swiftly made his way back into the club, determined to reach the exit. "I need to get back to the room before I get into trouble." He rounded the bar, placing his empty glass conspicuously for the bartender. Before he could release his grip, a forceful jolt against his back caused the glass to slip from his hand and crash onto the floor, shattering.

"Watch it, dickhead!" a voice shouted.

Abraham turned around, seething with disgust, ready to pummel the stranger. *Fred Stoltz. Fuckin' pussy that Zander almost took out.* Standing beside Fred, Donald wore a smug expression.

"Yeah, what you gonna do? You want to get your ass kicked? There's five of us and one of you. Watch your fuckin' step!" Fred snarled.

"Fuck you and your crew!" Abraham said, his nostrils flaring. *Fuck it, go to the roof...cool off.* Amidst the crowd, Abraham slipped through a door he had noticed the waitress using when he first arrived at the club. Surveying the back room, he found the stairs he hoped would lead him to the rooftop.

"Sir, sir! You can't go up there!" the waitress called after him, but it didn't matter. Abraham was determined to free himself from the Darkness.

The Nighthawk from earlier perched on the ledge, waiting for Abraham to arrive.

Rewire...c'mon Abraham...focus.

The desert breeze heightened the effects of the alcohol coursing through his veins.

The sound of a nasal peent from the Nighthawk grew louder, as if speaking to Abraham like an old friend. *Take out your anger...there's nothing wrong with that. It'll come out one way or another. You know what you did was wrong. I'll make it easier for you. Join me and this nightmare of guilt will be over. Just jump. Nice, quick, easy.*

"Don't engage. It's what the enemy wants," Abraham said to himself, determined to resist the temptation. The Nighthawk crept closer.

You know it's what you want. You want this pain to be over. You don't deserve to live...because you took a life that should have had a chance to live. You are not worthy of God's Kingdom.

"No, I'm not playing this game. I *have* a choice."

You sacrificed your choice when you killed your daughter. The Nighthawk's unsettling words continued to echo, but Abraham refused to succumb.

"NOOOOOOOOOOOOO!" A tortured scream erupted into the vast expanse of the Las Vegas desert. His drunken state hindered his protective countermeasures.

You know it's true. It was so easy for you to give up her life…if it was so easy, why don't you give up yours. The Darkness calculated its words carefully, aiming to exploit Abraham's pain.

"Maybe you're right." Abraham edged closer to the ledge and peeked over. "I should give up my life." He maneuvered between the wired barrier for an unobstructed shortcut to the first floor. A worthy gust of wind would easily knock him over, and he secretly gambled with those odds. The Crown Royal ran through his veins, the poison numbing his extremities.

Abraham outstretched his arms, mimicking the unfolding wings of a bird, but the goal wasn't to fly on this one. "Give up your life…so she can have hers back…" he whispered tearfully. The whiskey expedited the flow of tears streaming down his cheeks. "I never meant to fall like this…"

You know exactly what I mean. I take it you agree. Jump. If you fall, I will bring your daughter back. A life for a life. But you must give up yours in return.

The bread and butter of a darkened bargain.

Abraham considered but could only imagine a real offer in which his daughter came back to life.

Do it! After all the evil you've done. You took a life! Mother fucker, take your own! Do it!

Abraham closed his eyes. Tears continued to smear his cheeks and he surrendered, allowing the wind and the alcohol and fate to take its course.

All it takes is one little push…
The Darkness whispered, encouraging the drop into blackness.

A powerful gust swept in from the west, its force brushing his back, tilting him slightly, enough for the pull of gravity to take over.

He didn't resist. Defeated thoughts converged on him. The assault too much to bear.

You win.

His body leaned forward, gradually shifting into a horizontal descent. With arms outstretched, a flicker of hope emerged, as if, just maybe, Athena could live again. His body angled into a nosedive.

This life…is over.

XLVII EDGE OF DARKNESS

Phil burst into The Foundation Room, colliding with patrons. He tracked his nephew to the one place he knew he'd be—the party scene.

He relied on senses he hadn't used in some time. Jedi traits, as his nephew called them.

Inside, a VIP section occupied by Donald and his dart crew loomed near the balcony doors.

"Hey, have you seen my nephew?" Phil asked.

Donald smirked, hearing Phil but ignoring the question.

Fred stepped forward, positioning himself as a barrier. "Is it curfew time for that chump?"

"Listen, I'm just trying to find my nephew. I don't want any trouble. Have you seen him?"

"Fuck you and your nephew," Fred sneered.

"Oh my God!" Chaos erupted in the nightclub as shouts and screams pierced the air. Occupants on the balcony rushed towards the left wing outside. "Somebody help!" a woman screamed.

"This guy is trying to jump off the roof!" a man yelled, his voice carrying to the patrons inside.

Phil made his way through the club, closely trailing the waitress into the backroom area. The bar staff, consisting of waitresses and managers, sprinted up the stairs leading to the roof. The search party burst through the door and hurried to the ledge.

Phil's eyes widened. Horrified at the sight, he forced himself to steal a glance at the lifeless body, suspended upside down from the ledge. "That's my nephew! Bring him up!"

Abraham dangled right above the giant letters.

"Abraham!" Phil shouted. "Abraham!" he yelled, his voice growing louder.

"He's unconscious," a man called out. "His foot is caught in the wires!"

Suspended in midair, the barrier cables held Abraham's ankle. Phil reached for his foot, grasping it with all his strength. *C'mon, Abe.. don't do this to me...*

XLVIII HORSESHOES AND GRENADES

Phil gently tapped Abraham on the shoulder, trying to wake him from his deep slumber. "Wake up, boy," Phil said to his snoring nephew.

Abraham reluctantly opened one eye, revealing dark circles sagging beneath both. The exhaustion was evident, and the throbbing pain in his ankle served as a painful reminder of his near-death stunt. He'd lost control. The failure was a testament to just how far he had fallen.

How could God welcome someone into His Kingdom after destroying the most precious gift He could give anyone?

God certainly intervened on his behalf, and he was convinced of His unlimited power, even in the earthly realm.

Broken people can be redeemed.

To make that possible, he'd have to start somewhere, and the starting point was nowhere in sight.

Redemption?

There was only one answer he could come up with. *Out of the question.* But then, he remembered what God's work sometimes looked like. *Miracles are what they call them.*

Phil noticed the weight of silence enveloping his nephew as he contemplated the events of the previous night. "How are you holding up after your trapeze show last night?" Phil, with his natural ability to inject humor into any situation, attempted to lighten the mood.

"Never better," Abraham replied, his voice tinged with a quiet shame that Phil discerned all too well.

"Well, showtime is in an hour," Phil said, drawing open the blinds, allowing the sun's rays to bathe Abraham in its warm glow.

Time to rewire...

"Don't worry," Phil reassured him. "This stays between us."

Phil, Peter, Zander, and Abraham gathered just outside the ballroom. One member of the team was visibly absent.

"Where is he? We go on in twenty minutes," Zander said.

"I have no idea. I thought he was with you?" Peter replied, a hint of concern in his voice.

"I thought he was with y'all last night…" Zander paced back and forth, his brow furrowing deeper with each step.

Phil wandered over to the window, discreetly ending a call on his cell phone. He returned to the group, ready to brief them on the latest development. "Hey guys, I just got off the phone with Ray. He should be here in twenty minutes."

"That's cutting it close. We're gonna have to forfeit. That's fucked up! All this way for nothing…and this was his idea!" Zander said, shaking his head.

"Let's just pray he gets here on time, and if he doesn't then we'll worry about it then," Peter suggested, trying to maintain a sense of calm amidst the mounting tension.

"Where is he?" Zander asked.

"Indisposed at the moment," Phil replied. "I'll have to talk to the scorekeeper and see what our options are." Phil tried to reassure the team, knowing that dealing with Ray often meant preparing for the worst. He walked over to Abraham, who sat on a sofa, his head buried in his hands.

Abraham shook his head in disgust, replaying the events of the previous night in his mind. The outcome of the latest bout sank in, weighing heavily on him. "I failed."

Phil took a seat next to his nephew. "It's alright. It happens to the best of us."

I let the Darkness get the best of me. C'mon, Abraham, you knew this was gonna be a fight. The devil and his army…in hell.

"How's your foot?" Phil asked.

"It's good. Thank God those wires were there to catch me," he said, his hand instinctively reaching up to touch a dried blood scrape on the side of his head. "I can't believe I did that, Phil. Suicide…that's a one-way trip to hell, destroying the gift of life."

"You know, for a long time, I didn't believe in God. But after what I witnessed last night…you are highly favored. God gave you another day…let's not waste it. We're going to kick some ass today."

Phil's right…thank you God for Your protection last night…help me to make it count…don't let me waste it…

"Have you heard from your dad?" Phil asked, although he already knew the answer. Perhaps it was his way of broaching the subject of their highly volatile relationship.

Treading lightly between the history of father and son made for delicate introductions on the topic.

"No…and he has no idea what happened last night. I trust it *remains* confidential," Abraham said.

"I don't know what you're talking about," Phil smirked, understanding the unspoken agreement.

Abraham chuckled. "Exactly."

"Well, there *is* something I have to tell you. Since I seem to be the keeper of secrets on this trip, this one I have to share," Phil said, preparing to disclose his revelation.

Abraham leaned in closer just in case Phil needed to whisper.

"It turns out your dad went out last night, and, of course, in typical Ray fashion, got himself arrested. He just said he'd be here as soon as he could."

"He didn't say how he got arrested, right?"

"Nope. I don't know what he did, and I don't want to know. He didn't say, and I didn't ask. All he said was that Gloria bailed him out. He's a grown man. You know your dad."

"No surprise there,' Abraham snickered. "Moving on to more important matters…if he doesn't show up, will we be able to play with one man short?"

"That's what I'm about to find out," Phil said.

Phil remained calm as he utilized his mediation skills, particularly in tense situations. "Alright guys, here's the deal…we go on in approximately five minutes. If Ray's not here by that time, then we forfeit."

"According to the rules, we can play with four to six people and there's four of us here. Why can't we just play with four?" Peter asked.

"Because Ray is already signed up. Five members are on our team and all members have to be in attendance once the match starts. In four minutes, we may have to pack it up boys," Phil sarcastically replied.

"Fuck this! This is some bullshit!" Zander wasn't one to keep his thoughts to himself.

Phil approached his nephew as he laid his darts on the table. Abraham picked them up one by one, carefully adjusting the flights to ensure they were evenly spread.

"I'm sorry, son," Phil apologized to him.

"Don't worry about it. I'm used to it." Abraham heard 'sorry' in that context countless times, and the tone was always on behalf of his father. "He never shows up when it counts…you know that. Life goes on, right?"

"Yep, you got that right," Phil said. "On that note, three minutes to showtime. Either that or San Antonio bound. I'm going to talk the referee…try and buy us some more time."

1 minute till game time…

The announcer's voice boomed through the microphone, delivering introductions with the flair of Michael Buffer announcing a heavyweight boxing match. "And now, for the thousands in attendance and the millions watching around the world, ladies and gentlemen, let's get ready to ruuuuuuuuuumble!"

Abraham laughed quietly. Only five of the twelve people in the audience displayed any enthusiasm, clapping for the competitors. Whether it was thousands or just a handful, it didn't matter. *We're in Vegas,* he thought.

"Welcome to the Annual Fall Classic here at Mandalay Bay! Tonight's event is the 501 Team Championship Match. Please give a warm welcome to the Outlaws from Los Angeles and the River City Rage from San Antonio as they compete for the 501-team championship! Good luck!" the announcer declared.

The crowd of twelve cheered. Phil caught the referee's attention, who immediately approached him. "Where's your guy? If he's not here, it's an automatic forfeit."

"He's here, he's here. He's just in the restroom. You know, tournament jitters," Phil explained, using his acting skills.

"He needs to be out here now!" the referee insisted.

"Well, unless you want him to decorate your carpet with regurgitated lasagna, I'd give him a couple of minutes."

The referee shot a cock-eyed look. "As long as he's out here before the first dart is thrown, otherwise it's a forfeit," he said.

Phil hurried back to the team. "Alright, guys, let's hope for a miracle."

"What's the story?" Peter asked.

"Ray had a late-night dinner that didn't sit well if you catch my drift. We're going to line up over here. Abe, you're going to go first, and then Zander, Peter, me, and then Ray when he gets here."

The referee approached Phil. Glancing at his watch one more time, he finally delivered the bad news. "I'm sorry, fellas, it's a forfeit. Your guy's not here." The ref signaled to the announcer. "Go ahead and make the announcement."

Grunts and moans of disappointment from Peter and Phil echoed through the crowd. Zander turned his back, shaking his head vigorously. "Bullshit!" he yelled.

"Out of time, Cinderella," Donald said. His team burst into laughter at the utterance.

Zander glared at the entire Outlaws team. "Look at these dudes acting like they won the NBA championship. Calm down, this is only intermediates! Get the fuck outta here with your Harvard V-neck sweaters with diamond shapes and shit!"

Zander's right, we shouldn't even be here. Zander can pass for intermediate, my dad, possibly professional, and the rest of us, definitely beginners. It's alright, it was fun while it lasted…

"Wait!" Phil yelled. "Wait! He's here!"

Ray strutted to the floor, unashamed of his dramatic entrance. "Let's get this party started!" His voice grizzled after a night of heavy drinking.

"About fuckin' time." Zander said.

"Y'all know how to play this. First one to zero wins. Don't forget to double out for the win," Ray reminded them of the basics, but more like a crash course for dummies.

The players on each team lined up behind the marker on the floor. Ray sneaked over to Abraham before taking his spot. "Hey, dude, sorry I'm late."

"I'm surprised you made it this time. Anything for darts, right?"

"What's that supposed to mean?" Ray asked.

"Get to your spot. We're starting," Abraham said. Watching his father walk in without a care in the world sickened him. Memories of normalizing wrongdoings disappointed him just as much now as they did years ago.

The ref briefed both teams on the rules of engagement. "Good afternoon, gentlemen. We're going to be using the best of three format, which basically means the first team to win two out of three legs wins. Does everybody understand?"

"Enough talk, let's go!" Ray shouted.

Abraham glanced at Phil. "Is he still drunk?"

"Hey, whatever gets us a win," Phil laughed.

"Okay. Outlaws, you're up first!" the ref instructed.

Donald stepped up to the line, irritated. He hurled his darts with no hesitation, relying on brute force.

Triple 20.

Triple 20.

Triple 20.

The announcer blasted the microphone. "Ton 80!"

Outlaws		River City Rage
501	(180)	501
321		

Shit! Highest score right off the bat. C'mon Abraham, don't choke.

Abraham glanced toward the scoreboard as he approached the line, mentally rehearsing each move. *All three darts…aim for Triple 20.*

Abraham aimed, releasing his darts in rapid succession.

Single 20.

Triple 20.

Single 5.

The announcer's voice echoed through the room, but this time, the point total was a disappointing 85.

"It's alright," Ray said.

Outlaws		River City Rage	
501	(180)	501	(85)
321		416	

Fred Stoltz confidently walked to the line and shot a look at Zander. "This is for you, Mexican Mafia," he said.

Fred fired away.

Triple 20.

Triple 20.

Single 20.

"Ton 40 for the Outlaws!"

Outlaws		River City Rage	
501	(180)	501	(85)
321	(140)	416	
181			

Fred headed towards a flood of high fives from his team. "We'll make quick work of 'em," he exclaimed confidently.

Zander swiftly stepped forward, unleashing his darts with the rapid precision of an automatic weapon.

Triple 20.

Triple 20.

Single 20.

"Ton 40 for River City Rage!"

Outlaws		River City Rage	
501	(180)	501	(85)
321	(140)	416	(140)
181		276	

Robert Ziegler planted the brim of his black dress shoe to the line. He fired away.

Triple 19.

Triple 20.

Double 16.

"It's over!" Donald yelled.

"149 for the Outlaws!"

Outlaws		River City Rage	
501	(180)	501	(85)
321	(140)	416	(140)
181	(149)	276	
32			

Peter calmly placed his foot on the marker. Fixing his eyeglasses, he concentrated on the target.

Single 20.

Triple 20.

Triple 20.

"Ton 40!"

Outlaws		River City Rage	
501	(180)	501	(85)
321	(140)	416	(140)
181	(149)	276	(140)
32		136	

Doug Cranston moved up to the marker. With a smart-ass grin, he eyeballed the dart board, and fired away. All it took was one dart.

Double 16.

"The Outlaws have taken the first leg!"

Outlaws		River City Rage	
501	(180)	501	(85)
321	(140)	416	(140)
181	(149)	276	(140)
32	(32)	136	
0			

"Look at them over there...they look defeated already. We've got 'em," Donald snickered to his team.

"Alright, guys, let's regroup," Ray said to his team.

"We're getting our asses kicked," Zander shouted.

"Phil, you're up next. Give 'em hell!" Ray said.

The referee signaled to Phil to begin the second leg.

Phil stepped up to the line, but the first dart flew wildly out of his hand. "Oh, shit!"

Double 20.

"It's my lucky day," he said.

Triple 20.

Triple 20.

"Ton 60 for the River City Rage!" the announcer exclaimed.

Outlaws	River City Rage	
501	501	(160)
341		

Trevor Dukes stepped up to the line.

"That's their weakest player," Zander said.

Trevor fired away.

Single 20.

Triple 20.

Single 1.

"81 for the Outlaws!"

Outlaws		River City Rage	
501	(81)	501	(160)
420		341	

Ray confidently strutted to the line. His eyes pierced the dart board.
Triple 20.
Triple 20.
Triple 20.

"Tooooooooooon 80 for River City Rage!"

Outlaws		River City Rage	
501	(81)	501	(160)
420		341	(180)
		161	

Donald wasted no time, firing his darts immediately.
Triple 20.
Triple 20.
Triple 20.

"Tooooooooooon 80 for the Outlaws!"

Outlaws		River City Rage	
501	(81)	501	(160)
420	(180)	341	(180)
240		161	

Ray glided over to Abraham. "Alright, dude. Go for triple 20, triple 17, and then double bull."
"Let him handle it, Ray!" Zander shouted.
"Hey, I'm just giving some advice to my son," Ray said.

"Now you want to give advice?" Zander quipped.

"Hey, fuck you, dude!"

"Will both of y'all keep it down! Abe's tryin' to shoot!" Peter scolded.

Abraham fired away.

Triple 20.

Single 17.

Shit! I missed! Alright, be cool. Act like you know what you're doing. Do the math. 161 minus 60 is 101. 101 minus 17 is 84. Okay. Let's try to get to 32. Stay even.

Single 20.

"97 points for River City Rage!"

Outlaws		River City Rage	
501	(81)	501	(160)
420	(180)	341	(180)
240		161	(97)
		64	

Fred stepped up to the line and this time he refused to glance at Zander or anybody for that matter and fired his darts.

Triple 20.

Triple 20.

Single 20.

"Ton 40!"

Outlaws		River City Rage	
501	(81)	501	(160)
420	(180)	341	(180)
240	(140)	161	(97)
100		64	

"Close it out Zander!" Peter shouted.

Zander stepped up to the line. "Double 16, double 16," he said to himself. He aimed at the dart board extending and retracting his arm like a golfer practicing his swing and he fired away.

Double 16.

Double 16.

Outlaws		River City Rage	
501	(81)	501	(160)
420	(180)	341	(180)
240	(140)	161	(97)
100		64	(64)
		0	

"Fuck y'all!" Zander shouted at Fred and the rest of the Outlaws.

"And the second leg goes to River City Rage from San Antonio! We have a match here ladies and gentlemen!"

Abraham huddled with the team while Zander had some more words for the Outlaws. "Zander!" he called out, motioning for him to join the rest of the team.

"Their weakest links are coming up next…this is our chance to take it! Peter, give it everything you've got! Phil, you do the same. Score as much as you can, and I'll close it out," Ray said.

Finally, Zander arrived at the huddle. "Fuck those dudes!"

"Hey, get your head in the game!" Ray barked.

"Look who's talking, Ray! We had to wait for your ass, and we almost had to forfeit 'cause of you!" Zander retaliated.

"Would y'all cut it out already! Fuck! I'm tired of hearing this shit! Let's take care of business here!" Abraham said. *These motherfuckers!*

The announcer's voice boomed through the microphone. "This is the final leg to determine the 501 Team Champion! The Outlaws will go first!"

Robert stepped up to the line.

Triple 20.
Single 20.
Single 20.

"Ton!"

Outlaws	River City Rage
501 (100)	501
401	

Peter zeroed in on the triple 20.
Triple 20.
Triple 20
Double 20.

"Ton 60! River City Rage jumps out ahead!"

Outlaws	River City Rage
501 (100)	501 (160)
401	341

Doug sprinted to the line, the urgency evident in his steps.
Triple 20.
Single 20.
Single 1.

"81 points!"

Outlaws	River City Rage
501 (100)	501 (160)
401 (81)	341
320	

Phil approached the line. He closed his eyes, relaxing his mind focusing solely on triple 20.
Triple 20.

Triple 20
Triple 20.

"Ton 80!"

Outlaws		River City Rage	
501	(100)	501	(160)
401	(81)	341	(180)
320		161	

Trevor studied the scoreboard before walking up to the marker.
Triple 20.
Triple 20.
Triple 20.

"Ton 80!"

Outlaws		River City Rage	
501	(100)	501	(160)
401	(81)	341	(180)
320	(180)	161	
140			

"What the fuck?" Zander whispered. "I thought this guy sucked!"

Ray marched to the line, and like clockwork fired at several different targets.
Triple 20.
Triple 17.
Single bull.

"136!"

Outlaws		River City Rage	
501	(100)	501	(160)
401	(81)	341	(180)
320	(180)	161	(136)
140		25	

They got 140 left…that's an easy number to close out. All he needs is a Triple 20, Triple 16, and a double 16 for the win, Abraham thought.

Donald calculated his targets.

Triple 20.

Triple 16.

Single 16.

"124!"

Outlaws	River City Rage
501 (100)	501 (160)
401 (81)	341 (180)
320 (180)	161 (136)
140 (124)	25
16	

He missed! He fuckin' missed! Alright, Abraham, you're up. Don't fuck it up!

Abraham did his best to walk over the marker with confidence. *Hit a single 1 and then concentrate all your firepower on that double 12. Everything you got.*

"He's going to royally fuck it up," Donald whispered loud enough for Abraham to hear.

Psychological warfare…don't pay attention to any of that.

Tune out all the negativity…

Just concentrate…

Focus on the game…

Redemption…

Control your thoughts…

Mastery over self…

I failed last night…

But I can do better today, right now…

Win, lose, or draw…give it everything you got…

Be who God made you to be.

He inhaled as much air as his lungs could take in. He exhaled in a desperate attempt to calm his nerves. *Here we go.* Abraham launched the first dart.

Single 1.

That was easy enough. Now double 12.

Abraham reset his feet.

Breathe. Aim. Fire.

With one swift motion, he let the dart fly out his hand.

Double 12.

Outlaws	River City Rage
501 (100)	501 (160)
401 (81)	341 (180)
320 (180)	161 (136)
140 (124)	25 (25)
16	0

The crowd erupted in thunderous applause as Ray, Zander, Phil, and Peter swarmed Abraham. His family, who had argued and fought with each other just moments earlier, now boasted smiles and victorious yells to the crowd, their animosity and anger vanishing in seconds.

"I knew you were gonna do it!" Ray shouted.

"River! City! Rage!" Zander yelled, throwing his arms in the air.

The announcer's voice boomed through the microphone. "What an amazing matchup, ladies and gentlemen! These two teams competed till the very end! And now, I present to you the 501 Team Champions! Give it up for the Rage from—" The announcer abruptly stopped his congratulatory broadcast. "I apologize, ladies and gentlemen…it seems that we have a last-minute call here from Referee Joe Daniels."

The referee and the announcer huddled together for a minute in deep conversation. Abraham glanced at his teammates, and each one of them waited in confusion for the announcement.

Finally, the announcer returned to the mic. "It appears that the last dart did not count. The player overstepped the line. The referee has reviewed the tape, and the last dart does not count. If the Outlaws can hit a double 8, they will walk away with the title. If not, the River City Rage will have a chance to close it out. Outlaws, go ahead and get your next man to the line."

Fred Stoltz crept up to the marker, firmly planting his foot.

All he needs is one dart, Abraham thought.

Fred focused and then fired.

Double 8.

Outlaws	River City Rage
501 (100)	501 (160)
401 (81)	341 (180)
320 (180)	161 (136)
140 (124)	25 (0)
16 (16)	25
0	

The Outlaws high-fived each other, turning what was once a bleak atmosphere into a spirited celebration resembling a champagne party.

"Fuck that!" Zander said. "That's some bullshit!" He stormed off to the exit.

The remaining team members watched in disbelief as their hard-earned victory dissipated in an instant.

Phil and Peter exchanged glances.

"Well, he had a good run, guys," Peter remarked.

Ray, determined to defend his son, approached the announcer with a plea. "Is there any way we can review the tape? My son didn't overstep, it's not his first time playing." But it was too late. The champions reveled in their triumph, leaving no opportunity for reconsideration.

Abraham reviewed the scoreboard. He nodded at the numbers. *I gave it my best...there's no shame in that...*

Donald strolled over to Abraham, interrupting his thoughts. "Young chap," Donald said. "You played a helluva game out there." He stretched out his hand.

"Thank you." Abraham extended his hand. "Congratulations."

"You almost pulled it off."

"Almost only counts in horseshoes and grenades," Abraham said.

Donald smirked. "Good luck to you." He nodded and returned to his teammates, ready to revel in their victory.

Abraham sheathed his darts and focused his attention on a conversation near the entrance of the ballroom.

"Hey, dude, you didn't do anything I told you to do out there. I said to follow my lead," Ray complained.

"I told you I was gonna do it my way! I play leisurely, Ray. Darts are not my life. But if you ask me to come to Vegas for a dart tournament, then you better believe I'm here to win and I'm gonna win the way I know how! *You* asked me to come! Not the other way around," Zander retorted.

"If only you had listened to me, we wouldn't have had to go through all three legs," Ray said. "I was the best in the city!"

"I'm sure you were, Ray, but at what cost? I don't choose darts over my family."

"What the fuck is that supposed to mean?"

"Ask your son."

XLIX   KEEP THE CHANGE

The sunset dropped differently in Sin City. God's glorious array of colors on a painted canvas sky faded each night without notice. The backdrop of such majesty failed to overshadow the musings of Las Vegas.

Abraham gazed out the window, admiring his favorite time of day. Just under twenty-four hours ago, he had nearly descended into hell. Now, he praised God for placing cable wires on the ledge of the roof.

There are bigger things going on than winning a dart tournament...

He heard a sudden knock at the door.

Dad...I'll invite him in for a drink...

Sure enough, Ray entered the room, radiating his own triumph. "Hey, we did great out there! I'm proud of you, son!" Ray's grin stretched from ear to ear. "We should've won. I complained downstairs about the officials cheating, but they ain't going to do anything," he said. "It's all right, though...we went pretty dang far."

"We almost pulled it off!" Abraham hollered. "Going home with a thousand bucks is fine with me!"

"And you hit the game-winner! Well, you know what I mean," Ray chuckled.

Abraham gathered two glasses. "How about a drink for the River City Rage?" he said, pouring whiskey into each glass, filling them a quarter of the way.

"You're finally gonna have a drink with me?" Ray asked, the faint smell of tequila emanating from his breath. After countless times of asking his son to sip booze and party with him, Abraham finally complied.

"You were right…it was worth it to come here and give it a shot. I had a good time, Dad." Abraham handed his father a glass. "Cheers to the River City Rage."

"Cheers! Cheers to my son. I love you, Dad," Ray said, clinking his glass against Abraham's. "Hey, listen, I'm sorry for almost blowing it today. I wasn't sure if I was gonna make it to the match on time. I should've been there."

"Yeah, that *was* fucked up! I would've been really pissed off if you hadn't shown up. We all would've." Had it been one day prior, Abraham surely would have delivered an onslaught of expletives. But today was different. His eyes had opened to a new day, and perhaps a new life. For once, he laughed and shared drinks with the father who had let him down countless times. For once, an opportunity to peacefully imbibe with his father's camaraderie, free from turmoil.

Abraham poured more Maker's Mark whiskey into the glasses.

This is the beginning of a new life.

Ray downed his drink, grimacing. "Damn, that was strong!" He gathered himself before prompting a request. "Hey, dude, before we go, can I borrow a few bucks? I'll pay you back once we get home."

"What? You're joking, right? You have a thousand of your own, and you're asking for more?" Abraham sipped his drink before nearly spitting it back out.

"C'mon, man! I just gotta take care of some business, and I owe your mom. Dude, I'll pay you back. It's just a few bucks."

"When is it gonna stop, dad? Where does it end? You owe money to who?"

"Doesn't matter, don't worry about it…I'll pay you back."

"You never change…" Abraham shook his head in disgust, sliding his glass on the desk. He reached into his pocket and gave the small wad of hundred-dollar bills to Ray. "Just keep it. It's not like I'm ever gonna get it back from you anyway…"

"When have I not paid you back?"

"You've *never* paid me back!"

"Is this about money?"

"No, it's not. It's about you caring more about stupid shit than what's really important." Abraham sighed. *No sense in arguing with a fool.* He gazed out the window, down at the Strip, hoping that the fading desert sun would strengthen his resolve to calm himself.

"That's not true," Ray said. "I think I was a pretty good dad. Zander said I chose darts over my family…I didn't. Did I?"

"Honestly? You chose a lot of things over us. You were a good dad? Being visible at your convenience is not the same as being present. You have the two confused."

"I was *always* there for you…always!" Ray placed his glass on the table, his voice raised.

"Are you trying to convince *me* or yourself?" Abraham returned to the window, overlooking the city that nearly took his life. "You know, I thought we could be cool, like a real father and son, but I guess it's just not meant to be. I gave it a shot, and you always disappoint…always letting me down and blaming other people…you *always* have to *fuck* it up."

"Just because I need a few bucks? You make it seem like I'm robbing you or asking for your whole life savings. *You're* the one making this into a big deal!"

"You don't even see my point! This cycle stops with me. I'm doing my best to change…and I'm going to stick to that." Abraham shoved shirts, socks, jeans, and the rest of his belongings into the duffel bag. He zipped it up and placed the strap over his shoulder. "I'm done here. I tried, Dad…I really did."

"You never come over to talk to me…never! I'm wise, but you don't bother to ask for advice or anything. You want it this way," Ray said, handing back the wad of cash. "Here…use it to get home."

"Nah, I don't need it. Keep the change. That's the only change you care about." Abraham headed for the door.

"Can't even ask my son for a few bucks," Ray mumbled.

The sun breached the horizon. The Strip descended into the darkness of the night. Disappointment reigned.

Just walk away…it's not worth fighting over. God gave you another chance today. Don't make the mistake of letting anger rob you of the gift of today…

The swirl of anger and disgust rumbled deep in his stomach. "I didn't want it this way, Dad. You *made* it this way."

Vegas had taken a casualty. It had taken his father.

PRAYER

Writing is therapeutic. I've relied on this method all my life…words are powerful…prayer is powerful…words are my ally…prayer is my strength…

Abraham tapped his blue pen on the tray table. His heart was heavy, and he desperately needed to unload the emotional baggage that weighed him down.

The only way we'll be able to talk without arguing is through writing…

The flight back to San Antonio was three hours well spent.

Dad,

I know you don't remember a lot, so I felt that a letter would be the best way to explain things. First, I don't hate or resent you. Second, I love you. You're always going to be my dad.

You forget a lot of the things you've said and done. Please know that I do not hold a grudge for anything that you've ever said or done. I have now let that go. I'm not justifying what you did, but I do understand.

Growing up, you were never there for me, especially during the times when I needed you the most. All of our "conversations," even in adulthood, always ended up in an argument. Your ways "were always better." You proclaimed yourself to be "wise."

In retrospect, what did that teach me? It taught me that your actions were driven by ego and my ways were inferior just because I was younger, and the son shouldn't be better than the father. Your self-proclamation of being "wise" is a version where I could never speak my mind and if I had the opportunity to do so, it fell on deaf ears.

I have always been different, and my differences you see as weak, hence, you've said, "I'm a pussy, and I'll always be a pussy." Even at 26 years old, my 47-year-old dad wanted to "kick my ass."

The majority of my life, all I've known is that it was toxic to be around you.

I know you wonder why I don't talk to you or see you and mom. I want to make it clear that it wasn't my choice for things to be this way, because you said to me, "that I wanted it this way."

This is not what I wanted. As I explained to mom once, "you reap what you sow." Because you have never been there, I evolved and adapted. I moved on. I learned to not need you or rely on you, and it made me stronger.

And you wonder why I moved on without you in my life…

I didn't choose for it to be this way. You made it this way.

You hurt people that love you. No one is perfect and I too, have done some horrible things.

Please do not think I am criticizing you or bashing you or that I am speaking in anger. These are truths that I feel you need to know, and in these truths, I just want you to understand.

You have never taken accountability for your actions.

As I've grown older, I am constantly changing and evolving. One of the things that I have done in the past few years is do my best to "walk like Christ." I am not perfect, and I will never be like Christ, but I have strived every day to do that with my actions, and believe me, these days it has been extremely hard. I have fallen too, and although I struggle to get up, I know in my heart that Christ still lives in me...

I know you might say that you have Christ in your heart, but it is your actions that show it. If you truly have Christ in you, what are you doing every day to show that? It is a question for you to think about, and not a question that you need to answer for me.

I do my best every day to serve others as Jesus Christ did, and in doing so, I want you to know that I forgive you for everything.

I am not looking for a response, especially if you feel like you are going to respond negatively. I am done fighting with you. You may disagree with what I have said, and that is okay. I hope that you soak up these words as something positive.

Again, I do not hold a grudge or dwell on the past. I don't regret anything. I thank God for these trials because it made me better. Having you as my dad is the way it was meant to be, and after everything, I had a choice. I chose to be better. This is all part of God's plan, and for me, I am doing my best, however imperfectly, to live a life as a man of God.

This is not a letter to point out your flaws. I just want you to understand. I am trying my hardest to be a good person myself, so I am in the same company as you…flawed by the flesh.

I don't hate you or hold your past against you at all. I love you, dad.

You're always going to be my dad.

☦

The plane ride was as smooth as a feather, ascending above the wind before descending gracefully towards the ground. It was only right that a flight out of hell and up into the heavens serenely guided Abraham out of the desert.

Abraham M. (7:21 p.m.): Thank you for dispatching Phil when you did. I might not be here if you hadn't felt a disturbance.

Kay G. (7:22 p.m.): Matthew 18:20 "For where two or three are gathered, there I am with them." You are my brother, and I don't know what I'd do if I lost you unexpectedly.

Abraham M. (7:22 p.m.): God has given me another day, and I'm going to do my best to not waste it. That said, I have forgiven my dad for his latest fuck up. I tried, I really did, Kay. The bible says we must honor our mother and father … and I don't want to face God when my time comes, only for Him tell me that I didn't do everything I could have … that I could have done more, but I know now this is the way it is meant to be.

Kay G. (7:23 p.m.): Faith is a gift. We can't fault people who don't receive it. Romans 4:16 So the promise is received by faith. It is given as a free gift. And we are all certain to receive it, whether or not we live according to the law of Moses, if we have faith like Abraham's. For Abraham is the father of all who believe … the father of faith. Someone's disbelief is even more reason for us to thank God for giving us this precious gift of faith and whether or not your dad accepts it, is up to him.

Abraham M. (7:24 p.m.): And I can't keep doing the same things. He hasn't changed, but I know I need to. If anything, I learned to cut people off in a second's notice, especially toxic people, even if they're family … because of him. I've done everything I can, no matter the outcome.

Kay G. (7:25 p.m.): 1 Peter 2:9 "But you are not like that, for you are a chosen people. You are royal priests, a holy nation, God's very own possession. As a result, you can show others the goodness of God, for he called you out of the darkness into his wonderful light." You can't save your father, only God can. He is not for you to save. We all have one Savior. His name is Jesus, not Abe. We extend forgiveness but we can't force people to accept ours or even offer forgiveness back to us. That is between them and their God, not us and them.

Abraham M. (7:26 p.m.): You're right … it's not my cross to carry. Only Jesus can carry that.

Kay G. (7:28 p.m.): We can't tell people how to have faith or believe or walk right. That's a personal journey we are all on. I forgave my father not so I could have a relationship with him. I forgave him so that I could move on and let go of the expectation I had of him. I expected him to be what he didn't have in himself to be. And that's okay because what I didn't get from him, I found in God. God is my Father. I am His daughter, there is no middle man. No doubt or confusion as to where I came from. As my brother Jesus once said in John 8:14 "For I know where I came from and where I am going, but you don't know this about me." Had my father been there for me, loved me, raised me, never failed me, I probably wouldn't look to God as I do. If God planned him to be in my life, or a part of my life, nothing would have stopped him. But he wasn't and I'm good with God's plan ... and God has a plan for you, with or without your biological father.

Abraham M. (7:29 p.m.): You're absolutely right. The goal was never about helping my dad be the best he can be, only if he welcomed it. It was about me being the best I can be ... despite the cards I was dealt. I thought by trying to make amends with him, it would bring me closer to Christ, but he rejected it. I can't control that, and I can't control him. I can only control myself. I realized it was about me doing my best to love him like Christ does, even if it's from a distance. I'm at peace with it now. Thank you ... I love you.

☦

Abraham cupped his hands together and it had been months since he'd done so. The burden had been lifted. Kay Grace steered him away from the desert, but it was not her doing alone.

God, please guide my heart. Calm me, cleanse me, help me to be better. Lead me out of this wandering desert. In Jesus' name I pray. Amen.

LI GREATER IS HE

Abraham stepped out through the sliding doors and positioned himself along the curb. The San Antonio International Airport was abuzz at 9 p.m., with vehicles whizzing by. Within seconds, Margie swerved into the right lane in her baby blue SUV.

He opened the passenger door and jumped in. "Perfect timing!"

"Hey, maid! How did it go?"

"Oh, you know," Abraham said, tossing his bag into the back seat.

"I thought you were coming back with your dad?" she asked.

"I'm home a day early," he sighed. "Is that why you were on standby?" Abraham joked, but it held a glimmer of truth.

"I figured," Margie said. "I told your mom that you and him would come back on separate planes. You know your dad."

"I should've known better. It always ends this way … and each time I have hope that it will turn out differently. Not this time."

"Did you have a good time?" Margie asked.

"Uh, yeah, it was fun." How could he tell her the truth? *Oh, hey, Margie, I almost committed suicide, but yeah, I had fun.* It wasn't so much that she'd be disappointed, but he tucked his embarrassment close to the vest.

"I was praying for you to make it home safe … that the angels would take care of you over there." Margie knew. Somehow, she always did.

"How did you know I would need them? The angels to protect me..."

"I always pray for you and your sisters."

"I know that, but how did you know that I would need protection over there?"

Margie focused on the highway, taking a few seconds to answer. "I know what we're up against ... I know what's at stake." Dressed in her gray pajamas and wearing her glasses, which she only donned while driving at night, she concealed her true persona as the spiritual superhero she was.

"Thanks for picking me up. I know it's late." Abraham placed his hand on the center of his chest and slid it across like a magnet searching for a clue. His right hand came to a stop over his heart.

"What's wrong?" Margie's senses picked up on his distress.

"I felt okay on the plane, but I feel like crap now. My chest is tight."

"Did the devil come after you while you were in Vegas?"

"What do you mean?" Surprised by her sudden mention of spiritual warfare, he continued, "Why do you ask?"

"That city is the perfect hunting ground."

Abraham took a deep breath. "I made mistakes ..." he admitted. "My thoughts got the best of me."

"God's mercy ... is greater than your mistakes. The enemy gets you to give up by getting into your thoughts. But you're highly favored. God will surround you with the right circumstances and the right people to get you through. Listen ... pay attention to where He is trying to lead you. Fighting the enemy head-to-head is not working." Despite being at war, Margie spoke to him calmly as she always had.

"Digging out of this hole is hard. I'm slipping and falling too much ... and God is silent," he said somberly.

Margie not only kept his secrets, but she was also privy to the hard truths he shared with no one else. In return, she offered him honest candor he could bear. Her words were devoid of judgment but infused with love, and he accepted them without offense. "You are not prepared for this battle. All your psychological and physical training means nothing in this war. That's why you're losing … and you'll continue to lose until you learn a different style of fighting."

A different style of fighting … no more going head-to-head … no more mistakes … remember who you are … you're meant for more …

Margie resumed her counsel. "Jesus Christ is the only way to be free of this darkness. If you confess with your mouth that Jesus is Lord, you will be saved … Jesus is the light!"

As Margie spoke, she transferred spiritual power much like a transfusion, into his thoughts. "You're only beaten if you allow the devil to beat you. Greater is He who is in you, than he who is in the world…"

LII

HALL OF MIRRORS

"What's wrong? Do you not like the carnival?" Elida asked.

"No, it's not that," Abraham laughed. "I just … I don't know. I don't feel like myself." He placed his hand on his chest, rubbing it in hopes of soothing the tightness.

"Well, I thought maybe we could play some games, and you can win me a stuffed animal like high school sweethearts," Elida chuckled. She glanced at him with the affection of a lover infatuated with their significant other.

"You know that I'm not looking to be with anybody." His tone shifted, and the firmness in his voice put her on the defensive.

"You're still hung up on her," Elida said.

"Can you please not bring that up … I don't know why you always bring her up."

They strolled in silence. Elida managed to steer conversations toward Liv, despite several requests to keep the subject off the table. Her motives were unclear, and why she chose to hang out with Abraham was still up for debate.

I don't trust her … I don't trust anybody…

Incoming frequencies bombarded him simultaneously. The screams of the pirate ship swinging back and forth caught his attention. Children began laughing and crying at the clowns in white and red makeup. Several clowns waved as they crept up behind them. A couple laughing together at the soda ring toss game, sharing a kiss, captured Elida's interest. The sound of balloons popping at the dart game heightened his sense of awareness. Trouble lurked on the carnival grounds, and this time his intuition served him well.

"I'm sorry," Elida said. *I'm getting too close to him ... you have to do the job, or you won't get paid. Stop getting attached to him.* "So, why don't you feel like yourself? Are you sick?" Elida asked.

"No ... not physically."

"You can *feel* things, right?"

"What do you mean?" Abraham asked.

"Well, like the other day ... and it's happened more than once ... where I pick up the phone to call, and the phone rings, and it's you calling, or like when I feel down, and you text me to see if I'm okay in that exact moment, like you know what I'm feeling all the time. It's weird."

"Sorry."

"No, don't be. I think it's kinda cool that you can do that," she said, smiling.

Wait! If she can see it, then that means I'm healing ... my abilities are coming back ...

"Look, there's a basketball hoop." Elida pointed in the direction of the hoops lined with stuffed animals on both sides. "I bet you can't win one."

Abraham turned to her, both eyebrows raised, and eyes widened. "You don't know who you're talking to ... I'll take that bet."

The attendant noticed Abraham and Elida approaching as he tossed a basketball up and down with his hand. The scrawny kid couldn't have been more than seventeen years old. "Three shots for five dollars!" he shouted.

Abraham handed the young man a five-dollar bill.

"Here you go, sir," the attendant said, handing Abraham the basketball.

Abraham dribbled the ball a few times, getting a feel for its texture as if he were standing at the free-throw line. He gently let it fly off the tips of his fingers, and it spun nicely with a satisfying arc. The ball clanged on the back iron of the rim.

"Shot number two!" the attendant called out.

Go a little easier on this one …

Concentrating on the release, he shot it up in the air just a little higher than the last attempt. The ball swooshed through the net without touching the obviously rigged oval back iron of the basket.

"Winner!" the attendant yelled.

Abraham turned to Elida. "You were saying?" he said, his eyes widened with a triumphant smile. She smiled back, captivated by his confidence.

"I knew you would. I just wanted to get you to win me a stuffed animal," she said, pointing to the giant yellow Pikachu. "I'll take that one."

"Never doubt me again," he laughed.

A buzzing sound emanated from Elida's purse. She scrambled to find her cell phone, silencing the noise and discreetly placing it back inside her purse. "It was my mom … I'll call her back later."

Abraham handed her the stuffed animal. She placed it under her arm, and as she glanced inside her purse, Pikachu slipped out from under her arm and onto the asphalt.

She's lying … she's not a good liar.

A small four-year-old boy snatched Pikachu and ran off with it into a small structure with the sign, "Hall of Mirrors."

"What the fuck?" Abraham whispered. "This kid ripped off our prize! Let's go get Pikachu back, 'cause I'm not getting you another one," he said, jokingly. The chime of a bell diverted their attention as three notifications rang out in succession.

"It's you this time," Elida said, pointing to his back pocket.

Abraham reached for this cell phone. *3 New Messages – Kay*

It's probably her, Elida thought. "You go … I don't like the Hall of Mirrors."

Abraham placed his cell phone back in his pocket and ventured toward the entrance.

A monstrous growl, now all too familiar, summoned him to the playhouse.

Come inside … I've been waiting for you.

Abraham stopped dead in his tracks. *Another test. Control your emotions … and overcome your anger. God is with me.* He entered the dimly lit hall. The child's laughter bounced off the mirrors, echoing through the maze of reflections. Ten doppelgangers appeared, each looking in a different direction, distorting his features. The mirrors showed versions of him—long, tall, short, stubby, and even a curved, deformed version. *Which one is the real you, Abraham?* He examined the deformed version, studying it, but he didn't recognize himself.

You've been distorted …
you lost your way …
you forgot who you are …
you let the enemy distract you, almost destroy you …
remember who you are …
the real you is still in there.

The Hall of Mirrors was meant for disorientation, but instead they gave him a new sense of reality.

Truth vs. Illusion …
You are not broken …
You are not who the world says you are …
You are not what the enemy says you did …
You are a child of the Most High King …
You are worthy …
You are still loved …
You are enough …

You are powerful beyond measure …
You can do things through Christ.

Abraham pressed forward, navigating through the myriad of distorted realities that surrounded him, yet he remained focused on the path ahead. A mischievous grin adorned the face of the little boy as he watched him dart through the intricate maze, his laughter echoing and fading amidst the labyrinth of mirrors. A sudden flickering of lights seized the room, and with each abrupt blackout, a few fixtures succumbed to eternal darkness.

The Darkness stealthily crept closer, enveloping the surroundings in an ominous shroud that made objects increasingly difficult to discern. In the midst of this encroaching obscurity, the pitter-patter of a four-legged critter scurried past Abraham, its shadow and reflection causing the fine hairs on his arms to stand erect and goosebumps to form, stirring his heightened senses.

"Your mind is deceiving you," the Darkness snarled, its voice a chilling whisper.

Abraham instinctively reached for his cell phone, his fingers deftly finding the button that illuminated his path. The radiance cast by the screen pierced through the gloom, revealing the text messages from Kay. With a sense of relief, he clicked on the message and began to read.

> **Kay G. (9:38 p.m.):** Proverbs 28:1 "The wicked flee though no one pursues, but the righteous are as bold as a lion."

> **Kay G. (9:39 p.m.):** I felt you needed this.
> https://youtu.be/CHYcKWHcDEE

> **Kay G. (9:39 p.m.):** You vs. you

Abraham clicked on the video link. As Pastor Steven began his sermon, his words radiated every corridor of the darkened maze.

There is a way that God sees you because he formed you. There is a way that you see you. There is a way that others see you. And where you go from this point forward in your life is going to depend on which mirror that you believe ...

It's not how God sees you that determines where your life ends up, it's how I think God sees me that determines where I end up ...

And see the question is the right one. Who made you? But if you don't know that, you will hand other people your mirror to show you who you are.

When your mistakes are your mirror, you stay on the outside of Canaan even though you have the strength to go in. Not because you are small, but because you see small.

It's not how big you see God, it's how much you believe that God is in you.

God is trying to use your enemies to show you how valuable you are in His Kingdom. And why would you let your enemies hold your mirror anyway?

You've been living at "see" level. You've been looking in the wrong mirror. You've been consulting the mirror for your flesh.

You've been struggling with external issues, but what about what's in you? My Maker is my mirror.

When God sees you, He sees Himself. He sees His son. Christ is the image of the invisible God. And if He is in you, He is more than the world against you.

You've been going to the wrong mirror. You've been consulting physical, natural, relational elements, incomplete fragmented elements and you don't know who you are right now. And you're stuck between two realities. The message God gave me was ... your Maker is your mirror.

Light sliced through the maroon curtain, guiding Abraham towards the exit. Emerging from the Hall of Mirrors, he wore a wide smile that stretched from ear to ear.

Confused, Elia wondered if the playhouse had distracted him from his initial purpose for entering. "Did you have fun?" She tightly clutched Pikachu with both arms, and a laugh escaped her as she took in the sight. "That little boy came out of the mirrors five minutes ago."

The Darkness had employed cunning tactics to lure him into the hall, but its attempt to subdue him had failed.

The title bout tipped the scales in his favor. He'd lost several rounds to the Darkness, but God showed up when He needed Him the most. With the help of Kay and Pastor Steven, the Darkness stood no chance this time.

This round goes to me...

Families, couples, and carnival workers passed by, their faces wrinkled and perplexed, as Abraham laughed to himself. "I don't believe in coincidence."

LIII   VENGEANCE

His chest throbbed with palpitations, racing like a freight train hurtling across the tracks. "Something isn't right ..." he muttered, feeling his stomach churn. Abraham closed his eyes, searching for answers.

Ever since I came back ... I haven't felt the same ...

Meditation offered a pathway to finding solutions, and perhaps this time it would help him break free from the Darkness.

God, please guide me ... calm my heart ...

Despite his pleas, his heart continued to race, threatening to burst from his chest.

"God, help me break free from this bondage," he whispered. He focused on the Light.

Remember who you are.

Self-coaching exercises had become a resurrected practice from the days before the dark times. This new enemy had grown stronger and relentless. His instincts led him to the bedroom, where a long-forgotten artifact lay at the bottom of a six-foot high tandem bookshelf.

The shelves housed treasures, including a black hardcover journal safeguarding precious adventures and personal excerpts. Within the journal, loose pages, untouched for the past seven years, contained the evidence of his secret, penned by Uncle Phil. The quiet whisper of the journal beckoned to him.

Abraham placed a hand on his chest, feeling an unsettling rumble within. *Oh man,* he thought. *This is how the Darkness has a hold on me...*

He then realized the horrific truth, the revelation shaking him to his core.

It's inside me ...

Once again, he closed his eyes, hoping God would provide some sort of direction. *The journal ... God, I know you directed me to it. I hid this away for so long ...*

With an index finger, he gently pulled the journal from its place on the shelf, removing the documents that spanned the previous decade.
The e-mail ...

The printed email lay before him, its words etched on the paper, patiently waiting for him to read them once more and be reminded of his power. Gloria had created a hard copy of the email for him a long time ago, in her desperate plea for help. In that email, Phil had shared guidance and insight into his own evolutionary state.

He slunk into his chair and laid the journal in his lap. As he examined the paper, a surge of energy coursed through him, and he was instantaneously transported to another time.

10 March 1999

Gloria, Abe is extremely sensitive, does feel our emotions, and you could say, "is a heartbeat away" from us both. Primarily, he senses the closeness of his father.

I too, feel stronger towards Ray than Peter. My heart tells me that Ray is somewhat bothered, ashamed or embarrassed and is running away from his fears. He has difficulty adjusting to stability, to his new family, and his only outlet is to keep running but also hiding at the same time. Abe could feel drained because the more he thinks and feels the emotions the more physical strain. Nothing is more tiring than psychological and emotional stress. His dilemma is twofold: First, Abe feels inadequate because there's nothing he can do. Second, he wishes that he had a father. Although Ray contends that he was too young when he got married, never had a real life, and now that Abe and Michelle are grown up and able to understand, he has done his part, so he can move on. The problem is deeper. While Ray was growing up (with you), he said that he was a real father. But when Abe needed him the most, he wasn't there. The rumors that Abe heard concerning his father became a reality but at the cost of Ray's truthfulness. In other words, "he lied" to his only son only to preserve and protect himself. Now Ray runs away, Abe keeps growing and is left behind with the memories. Are the memories of truthfulness or lies? What role did Abe play? Ray kept pushing Abe to excel, is Abe considering himself a failure? Did he not meet his father's expectations? So, now Abe has another dilemma. He has a special gift of extraordinary perception. He may be feeling the hurt that his father feels. He certainly feels my illness. I am too weak to concentrate and no longer choose to mentally venture. It drains me out completely.

So, Gloria, ask Abe to choose a number between 1-10 and ask him if he knows what number I was thinking about.

Tell him that I said that I always think of him, and yes, we do have a special bond.

Abe's gifts are manifesting and if he believes, then he should be strong, not physically, but spiritually and emotionally; mind (mind over matter), words (of wisdom, truth, but also listening), and his actions (being responsible or accepting responsibility, helping others, extending an open hand, caring and passionate). There is no better gift than these fine qualities that very few possess.

Gloria, hope this helps. Please don't worry, Abe will be fine.

All my love,
Phil

The words written by Phil resonated deeply, and in a time of desperate need, they brought hope.

Words … it's always been words …

Words of encouragement.
Words of love.
Words of hope.
Words to help him remember who God created him to be.
The document contained a sentence that induced a supernatural power, and every time he read it, it reminded him of his purpose, and of his light. The words never seemed to disappoint. They were *alive*.
Abraham scanned the paper again.

He has a special gift of extraordinary perception.

Even though Phil had lived half a world away in Germany, distance couldn't hinder his recognition of the intricate qualities Abraham possessed. Phil's acknowledgment of his abilities fueled a relentless battle against the dark forces that had previously gone unchallenged.

The Darkness writhed and moaned. It crashed against the interior walls, desperate to reattach itself to Abraham.

It's working …

He re-read the line, restarting the process of believing he was more than the lies told to him.

The trials Phil mentioned were inconsequential.

What mattered was that his words reminded him of what he was capable of, which no evil force could ever extinguish.

Each time he read the letter, an overwhelming power surged through him.

A power only God can provide.

The Darkness wailed, its anguish echoing like an injured lion, as it struggled to maintain its grip.

They can't stop me … they can only try to turn me … to do their bidding.

To break free from its grasp, Abraham pressed on, reading the words aloud.

Expel the darkness and return to the light.

The Darkness clawed at his insides, desperately searching for something to hold onto.

I have to draw it out! I need to bring it to the Light. Only love can do that.

Abraham had forgotten how to love, but the memories of his past began to resurface, piercing through the coma of Darkness that had kept him imprisoned.

I love you, Liv.
I love you, Abbadon.
I love you, dad.

I forgive you. I hope you can forgive me ...
For being a horrible boyfriend and Hawaiian husband ...
For being a terrible best friend and brother ...
And for being an awful son.
I give it to you, Lord ...
... and I replace it with love.

The entity fought to latch on, but love ripped it from the clutches it once had. Abraham reread the passage, forcing the entity to escape its residence, where hope had previously resided.

God has not given me a spirit of fear ... but of power, and of love, and of a sound mind...

Abraham squeezed his eyes shut, focusing on flushing the entity out. His third eye observed the struggle, triangulating the rising blackness.

Light.
Love.
Forgiveness.

The entity spewed out toward the ceiling, hovering above him for a few seconds. A cloak of blackened fog emanated from it. It floated briefly in an offensive formation before scurrying away like a dog with its tail between its legs.

Abraham let out a sigh of relief. The effects of dispatching the entity were immediate. A sense of lightness occupied his chest, and his heartbeat returned to normal.

The front door swung open and closed forcefully. The floorboards creaked, despite the intruder's soft footsteps. Elida made her presence known at the doorway to the bedroom. She noticed Abraham sitting in silence, deep in concentration. Her senses picked up on the battle at hand. Furrowing her brow, she scanned the darkened room with a confused look. "It feels ugly in here..." she murmured. "I'm going to wait outside."

She felt it, he thought. Abraham let her walk out. *This is no place for anyone to get caught in the crosshairs.* He prayed, using the words Margie had taught him. *Satan, I rebuke you in the name of Jesus. You have no place here.*

He repeated the phrase twice more, taking sixty seconds of silence.

Closing his eyes, he scanned the area.

The room was clear.

A text message notification chimed on his cell phone.

Margie (8:11 p.m.): Time to put your armor back on.

Margie knows ... it's time to let the Light back in ...

The nightmare of possession was over for now. After years of fighting the Darkness, Abraham knew better. It would come back ... with new tactics.

LIV

THE EMPTY CROSS

Traveling on I-10 West for fifty minutes straight was not Margie's usual.

"You've been driving for almost an hour," Abraham said. "Relax, maid. We're here."

Countless trees, hills, and an abundance of greenery had kept his interest throughout the sixty-plus miles of highway. As they approached, a massive cross atop a hill came into view.

"Whoa, that's a big cross!" Abraham exclaimed. "Looks like a top-secret location."

Driving into Kerrville turned out to be quite different from what he had expected, especially with the sudden appearance of a 70-foot metal cross perched on top of the hill.

"I take it that's where we're going?" he asked, pointing to the colossal cross.

"That's right, little boy."

Margie took the exit and maneuvered her way up the hill, navigating a series of turns and ascending elevation. The car's hood tilted up to a forty-five-degree angle. The last turn was a sharp left, leading them into a parking area that leveled out. From there, a set of stairs awaited them, as the final ascent to the top of the hill had to be made on foot.

Abraham pulled on the door handle, and a gust of wind forcefully swung the door open.

"That's a sign ..." Margie said, smiling. "... you're meant to be here."

Margie had never believed in coincidence, and her faith remained unwavering. Circumstances never swayed her heart, as it was protected by the Lord, and worry did not exist within her.

They began climbing the stairs, each step bringing Abraham closer to the man he once was. Despite last night's victory, there was still much work to be done.

"Miracles happen here," she said. Her hair fluttered in the breeze, almost covering her face. She took her time ascending the stairs, and Abraham was in no rush either.

I trust her.

"They say all the snakes left this place once the cross went up," Margie shared.

"Then I shouldn't be here, then," he said with a laugh.

"Little boy, cut the crap with that kinda talk. That's not good for you," Margie scolded. She didn't believe in negative self-talk.

"I'm just kidding, Margie."

"Words are powerful! When you say words, good or bad, you speak life to them. You know this, you're a writer!"

Abraham glanced at the concrete path, noticing the tiles placed sporadically along the walkway, each etched with engravings. The bronze color of the tiles contrasted against the white concrete.

"Scripture," he observed, turning to Margie. "They have scriptures on these tiles…"

She sensed his spiritual energy awakening as he absorbed the words on the tiles. "Read them out loud. Speak life," she said.

> *"A new commandment I give to you, that you love one another, as I have loved you, that you also love one another." Jesus Christ - John 13:34*

"Unconditionally," he whispered to himself, his thoughts consumed by memories of Kay and her words of encouragement. "His love is unconditional," her voice echoed through the recesses of his mind.

"The path leads straight to the cross," he said.

"And along the way, you'll see different scriptures, stones, and other pathways …" Margie replied. "The road to the cross is not easy nor is it ever a straight path. Each scripture you see carved in stone will remind you of a different time in your life when you needed those words the most."

At the beginning of the walkway stood a six-foot bronze statue of Jesus, as if to welcome visitors to His glorious garden. He held a fisherman's net draped over his hands.

The Fisher of Men.

Positioned three hundred feet behind Jesus, the magnificent cross towered above them, guarded by rectangular white rocks on either side of the path.

As Margie and Abraham strolled along the trail, they noticed tiles with Bible verses in English, Spanish, and Hebrew scattered throughout the concrete.

"*That* is a glorious pose," Abraham said, admiring the statue emerging from the circular water fountain.

On top of a sandy-colored, six-foot cube stone, a white stallion stood proudly. Its muscles bulged as it reared its legs into the air. Atop the stallion sat Jesus, holding a ram's horn in His left hand and a sword in His right hand, pointing towards the heavens. He wore a crown with seven square stubs jutting out, and a royal cape outlined with gold trim flowed behind Him, gently fluttering in the breeze.

At the base of the fountain, the path branched out to the left, right, and straight ahead, leading to the seventy-seven-foot steel cross.

Margie surveyed the area. "Let's sit over here," she said, motioning towards the right. After walking thirty feet, the path came to an end, revealing another lifelike statue of Jesus. This depiction showed Jesus on His knees, with a towel draped over His midsection, and the disciple Peter sitting on a bench, facing the Messiah. In Jesus' right hand, He held His disciple's foot, and in His left hand, a washcloth.

"I thought you'd take me to the Oblate church again, like you did when I was twelve," he said, admiring the scenery. "I swear, I thought I was gonna get beat that day. It was weird. My dad didn't even yell at me."

"You know why?" Margie reached into her purse, rummaging around until she found a tiny yellow sticky note. "I wrote a note to God. When we found you, I asked Him to protect you."

His eyes widened at the sight of the tiny treasure. "You *still* have it?" he asked, surprised she kept such things. She handed it to him, and after thirteen years of hiding, the paper hadn't aged a day. The red ink had not faded, as if she had written it just yesterday. Abraham unfolded the note—a perfect yellow square, showing no signs of being tattered or torn, except for two faint fold marks indicating its concealment over time.

He examined the note, admiring her elegant handwriting

Dear God,

> *Please let me or my sister or mom find Abraham okay. Please Lord, let Abraham be okay and find him today and maybe this time his parents will let him stay with me, to solve problems or be there for him to help him out. We love you. Amen. Dear Lord, I hope his mom and dad do not hit him.*

"I can't believe you still have this," he said.

"God's power is supernatural," she said. "You have to *believe*."

"It's been hard, but I feel an awakening. I want to be the man I used to be ... a good man."

"Little boy, you will *never* be what you used to be. You'll not only be good, but you'll be better than you were before ..."

"You believe in me so much ..."

"*You* need to believe in yourself again," she said, pointing to his heart. "It begins with serving others. That's why we're here." Margie glanced at him. His body language shifted as he hunched over, took a deep breath, straightened his posture, and then repeated the cycle.

Doubt had its way of resurfacing unannounced.

Can I be better than I was before?

The repetitive nature of his movements foreshadowed the victory they both longed for.

"Look at this statue. Jesus washing Peter's feet. Serve others. This selfish, dark version of you is not who you truly are. You know that."

Abraham nodded with full confirmation. The inscription just below the statue spoke to him. The words of Jesus were powerful, and this particular Bible verse never failed to give him goosebumps.

> *"You do not realize what I am doing, but later you will understand." John 13:7*

The verse sparked a conversation with God, who had gone quiet. *I'm trying so hard to trust You ... I have to believe You have a reason for all of this ... I'm conflicted ... and I want to be free of this pain ...*

Margie motioned to him, interrupting the impromptu chat with the Lord. "I'm going to give you one of the most precious things I have in my life." She reached into her purse, once again, which could house three smaller purses for sure. Like a magician, she pulled out a tattered red leather book, barely holding itself together. "I want you to have this," she said. "*This* is my Bible. It was mine for a long time, and I used it to help me fight, and I'm giving it to you."

"This Bible looks old. How old is it?" he asked.

"*Old.* You're going to need Psalm 91 when you go into battle. These verses will help you fend off evil." Margie spoke with a combination of gentleness and confidence. "Ephesians is another book I marked off that you need to study."

"Ephesians?"

"Yes, little boy. It's time to put back on your armor so that when you get attacked, you can withstand it."

"Armor?"

"Spiritual battle is no different than any other battle. You need armor! You need weapons, and you need to learn how to fight. The only difference is that we fight unseen forces. In Ephesians 6:12, it talks about what we wrestle with, and it's not flesh and blood but against different kinds of powers. We wrestle against the rulers of darkness and against spiritual hosts of wickedness in heavenly places."

"I do know that these adversaries you speak of are unseen ..."

"But do you know how to fight them? That's the real question."

"This is where you need to put on your armor. The armor the Bible talks about is the Belt of Truth, the Breastplate of Righteousness, the Shield of Faith, the Helmet of Salvation, the Sword of the Spirit, and the Shoes of Peace. Right now, you're a soldier, a warrior. Your mindset is everything—the mental edge you need to overcome. But before you do that, you need to find peace within yourself. Victories will never happen unless you win the internal battle with yourself. Heal. Grow. Move forward."

"That's been my struggle. I *need* to let go," Abraham said.

"Let go of the anger. Let it *go*. There is nothing you can do to change the past. Let go of everything that doesn't bring any good into your life." Margie was never at a loss for words. Her spiritual nature flowed endlessly. "I brought you here so you can heal, move forward, and bring goodness to the world again."

"And that's all I want."

"What do you think will help you become a good man that you don't already have?"

"I just feel like I need a little more *oomph* to be a good man again. Like...a push to get over the hump kinda thing."

"God never runs out of miracles. You'll get yours. He's always on time."

"You think He's got one more miracle for me?"

"He's got plenty, so don't worry. You'll receive your miracle, and it will come in a way you least expect."

Abraham buried his face in both his hands. "Margie, I left a lot of wreckage ... I have blood on my hands, and-"

"DON'T! Don't say another word," she said, her voice firm, almost scolding. "Let it go. Everything God does is in your favor. Even when things are not going good or things are going all wrong, or even when you sin. He works things out, not to harm you, but to give you hope and a future. He makes all things work together for good, no matter what that looks like."

Margie's spiritual training served him well. If it wasn't for her, his service would be elsewhere, among the evil in the world.

"You're right. I need to rewire my thinking. I used to think so differently back then, and I've forgotten how to think in a positive light." Abraham reflected on the spiritual journey that led him here. "The trauma of being left and abandoned … I had trouble reconciling that because when I couldn't feel God, I thought He had left me too. I know better, but in my weakness, I succumbed to darkness. I was so beaten down that I forgot that when I am weak, He makes me strong."

"Come on, let's go to the cross," Margie said.

Abraham followed her as she stepped onto the original path leading to the cross. The tiled scriptures caught his eye, urging him to read them.

"For I am convinced that neither death nor life, neither angels nor demons, either the present nor the future, nor any powers, neither height nor depth, nor anything else in all creation, will be able to separate us from the love of God that is in Christ Jesus our LORD" Romans 8:38-39

Margie stepped into the hollow cross, studying its origins. Abraham quietly joined her in the corridor. A light of some sort hung seventy-seven feet above him on the cross's interior. He imagined what a sight it would be when illuminated at night. A beacon of Light.

"Why would they build a cross here?" he asked.

"This is why," Margie pointed to the plaque. Abraham skimmed the inscription.

A man was given this vision by the Holy Spirit. God commissioned this man to create a giant, 77'7" cross on Interstate 10, so people would come to Jesus. God had indeed set aside the ideal property, which looks just like the Biblical Holy Land, for His Garden Tabernacle. The site is 'high and lifted up,' 1,900' above sea level, halfway between the Atlantic and Pacific Oceans at the same exact latitude of Israel!

The corridor vibrated with spiritual consciousness. A profound calmness draped over him. His heart rate slowed considerably.

"Do you feel it? The energy?" Margie asked.

"Yeah, I feel like I'm high or something," Abraham said. "I'm adjusting to the frequency."

For the first time in a while, there was no need to rush, no irritation, no anger, and no sense of time. It was a perpetual realm of supernatural power, where problems and the world's afflictions ceased to exist.

"This is where you have to rely on God's power and not your own," Margie said.

Abraham caught sight of a tile behind Margie, just outside the corridor. He silently read it to himself.

"He was wounded for our transgressions, He was bruised for our iniquities; the chastisement for our peace was upon Him, and by His stripes we are healed." Isaiah 53:5

Margie placed her right hand on his shoulder. "Please, Heavenly Father, protect my nephew. Surround him with a hedge of divine protection as he continues to search for his path in the world. With Your guidance, Lord, help him become a servant for Your glory. In Jesus' name, I pray." Margie removed her hand from his shoulder and struck his heart with a backhand. "You are *healed*. Now, go and finish the work you started. Use your gifts. And go to Him!"

Abraham nodded. "I'll try."

"From this day forward, the Darkness will never stop coming after you because you hurt it … you damaged it by doing what you did last night. Your faith in God is no match for the Darkness. It's going to try to hit you hard. It will make you doubt. It'll go after your heart. And it will take away the things and the people you love the most. But you better keep fighting. Fight these motherfuckers hard!"

"The demons reopened these wounds and they waited for the right moment to exploit them. I have to make peace with that. The one who sent them, who orchestrated the chaos, I'll fight *that* motherfucker hard, and the rest will fall." His eyes gleamed with determination. The garden had worked its magic, healing his weary soul, restoring him to nearly full strength like a video game character powering up.

"When you feel presence of the enemy, do you remember what I told you to say?"

"I rebuke you in the name of Jesus," he said.

"Good. You remembered. Say it again."

"I rebuke you in the name of Jesus," he repeated.

"And the devil will flee," Margie said, her voice filled with conviction. "Let's go for a walk on this side of the cross." She gestured towards the left side of the garden. "There's a prayer garden here. People write their prayers on rocks and place them in the garden." Margie pointed towards the sign.

This Memorial Rock Garden was
inspired by the Holy Spirit

This garden was not planned by any man. It is the
creation of the Holy Spirit. God Himself touched the
hearts of visitors to this garden. They wanted to praise
Him and write out their prayer requests. Jesus Christ
said that the stone would cry out if we did not tell
people about Him. (Luke 19:40).

"Go ahead," Margie encouraged. "Pick any rock and write a prayer on it."

"But I don't have-" Abraham began, interrupted by Margie who pulled out a black sharpie from her purse and handed it to him.

Abraham laughed. "You always come prepared."

"It's not my first time here, little boy. I'm going to find one, too," she said.

Abraham lingered behind, scanning the area for the perfect rock.

Not too rough.

Not too jagged.

Not too small, either.

And there had to be enough room to be able to write his entire prayer just in case it was a long prayer. He picked up a potential candidate—a smooth jellybean-shaped rock but it was not big enough to write the prayer he was already cooking up in his head. Continuing along the dirt path, he came across a larger rectangular rock. Uncapping the sharpie, he began to write his prayer request. The surface was too rough, and the letters looked more like preschool emergent writing than actual words. *Okay, that's not gonna work. Moving along.* Further down he scanned a whole group of clean rocks waiting to get a prayer written on them. *There it is.* He dropped the other two potentials and picked up a heart shaped rock. *Perfect.* He inscribed a prayer he needed to leave in this Holy place.

> *"God, please take anything and everything out of my heart*
> *that doesn't belong to you and replace it with Your calmness*
> *and goodness. In Jesus name I pray."*

Capping the sharpie, he carefully placed the rock near an adolescent oak tree, leaning it in a manner that resembled a tombstone. He admired it for a few moments, and then made his way toward Margie. His movements felt lighter, sharper, and with a renewed sense of clarity, as if he had just finished a pick-up game of basketball.

In the distance, he caught sight of Margie writing on her own rock. "Hey," he called out playfully, sneaking up on her. Margie swiftly placed her rock in its designated spot and stepped away.

"Come on, walk with me. I need to leave a donation on the way out," she said.

"I love you, Margie. Thank you for bringing me here. This place is different ... supernatural."

"You needed to see this place. It's a place of healing … of power."

"Did you write your prayer rock for Richard?"

Margie glanced down at the path filled with scripture and grinned. "I've written several here for him."

"I don't know how you did it … losing a loved one is hard, especially a husband or a wife. You're strong, Margie. I'm not like you."

"He was my soulmate. Soon, I'll be with him again."

"Soon?" Abraham asked. "Why would you say that?" Abraham slowed his pace. It wasn't like Margie to say such things, especially after what she said about "speaking life" to feelings and events.

"I have something to tell you," Margie said solemnly.

In that moment of confession, the realization struck him like a ton of bricks. Margie did not bring him here for his healing alone, but for hers as well. His brown eyes flooded with seriousness.

"I went to the doctor last month," she paused for a moment, "And they found cancer in my lung."

Abraham crinkled his brow, confused at her admission. "Wait, how did you get cancer? You're fine, I mean you're healthy, Margie. How do you have cancer?" He did his best to make sense of this news. "How bad is it?" *God, please don't do this to me …*

"I have to go back for a follow-up, little boy. They'll let me know, and then I'll let you know."

"Have you told Grandma yet?"

"Yeah, she knows. She's worried. Can't help that, you know how Grandma is … tanta mortificada. *Extremely worried.*" Margie let out a chuckle. "She wants me to move back in. She doesn't want me to be alone, and she's been bugging me ever since Richard passed."

"I think that's a good idea. You shouldn't be by yourself. You can have your room back," Abraham laughed, failing miserably to distract himself from the confession at hand.

"It's *my* room, little boy," she said with a grin. "Anyway, I brought you here so you can heal … so both of us can heal. Spiritually and physically."

"Margie, what if-"

"God has a plan," she said, cutting him off from the words she knew would come next. "His ways are higher. Either way, it'll be fine." Margie smiled. "We're both in for a fight. That's another reason why I brought you here, little boy. You need to *learn* how to fight. Not with your fists, but with your soul. I won't be here forever, and I promise you, before I go, you will have learned to fight in the spiritual field of battle."

"I've never lost an immediate family member." Abraham was in the midst of losing control of his emotions. No matter how much progress he made, it was slipping away faster than he could comprehend the cancerous curveball. *God, please, please, I beg You … don't take her from me …*

"Hey, listen! Calm down. It's going to be okay," Margie reassured him.

"I can't lose-"

"Listen! I'll be fine."

Abraham darted back to the prayer garden where the rocks serenely rested. Frantic, he grabbed the first rock that would allow his writing to be legible. The rock was the size of his fist, and he didn't have time to search for a better candidate. As it was, time was not on his side. His handwriting kept up as best it could as his thoughts progressed at lightning speed. *Don't forget to put in Jesus name I pray.*

> *"God, please place your healing hands on Margie and take away any illness, in Jesus' name I pray."*

Margie pursued her frenzied nephew into the garden. "Hey!" she said. "Listen to me." Abraham turned to her, his face drooped to a frown. "This is all for nothing if you can't control your emotions. You have to concentrate on what we have to do and you're going to have to fight harder than you ever have …"

"I can't do this by myself. I mean, look at me. I thought I was getting better, especially here in this moment, in this place, and look at me! All it took was for one word of death and it unraveled everything I've been working toward."

"Why do you think I gave you my bible? Why?" she asked as if to quiz him.

"So I can rewire ... and fill my mind with scripture ... to learn how to fight, spiritually."

"You remembered what I said, that's good. You always need to remember that so whenever you feel lost or feel down or when you think you can't go on, let this be a reminder that I'll never leave you and if it gets really hard where you're in a bad place, just remember my voice guiding you ... 'get up, little boy ... because Margie loves you.'"

The sun dipped lower, casting a halo behind her. "You are in the most important fight of your life. The fight for life over death," she said reminding him.

"And you're gonna be with me ..." His voice shook. Tears formed on the edges of his eyes. Losing her meant he would break into a billion pieces, especially considering the condition he was in. *I'm not fully healed yet.* He struggled to engage his emotional reserves to level out the oncoming outburst of tears. "You'll be there to help me ... and give me counsel."

"Abraham, I always will be ..." she said, smiling. "... Always."

LV · DEATH IS DEFEATED

Calm down ... remember your training ... death is just a portal to heaven ... we are luminous beings ... death is a part of life ...

Abraham M. (10:56 p.m.): I'm a mess. I thought I was doing good, but I got a bomb dropped on me.

Kay G. (10:57 p.m.): What happened? Is there anything I can do to help?

His next words were simple, concise, and heartbreaking all at once. As much as he wanted to unleash the emotional deluge, Margie's voice echoed in his head. *Control your emotions.*

Abraham M. (10:57 p.m.): Margie has cancer.

Kay G. (10:58 p.m.): I'm so sorry, Abe. I know how much she means to you.

Abraham M. (10:58 p.m.): I don't know what I'd do without her ...

Kay G. (11:02 p.m.): Remember, death is not the end. It's not over when we die. We continue living, just not in the physical form and we live in heaven with Christ our Savior. If God's plan is to have Margie join Him in heaven, then rest assured, you will see her again. We will be reunited with the ones we love when we get to heaven. Have no fear. We don't grieve as those without hope. Do we weep for the caterpillar when the butterfly emerges from its cocoon? So the love you have for Margie will be transformed. For love is as strong as death. Death is nothing to be afraid of, it is simply the doorway that stands between us and our Maker, our Creator, our Father. Are you afraid to return home? Do you tremble at the door? Or do you come in, knowing you are always welcome. She has fought the good fight and ran her race well. We should all be so blessed to fulfill our life's purpose and return home. Though it seems her body is fading, her spirit is being renewed daily. As Scripture says, 1 Thessalonians 4:13 … we do not grieve like people who have no hope.

2 Corinthians 4:16 … That is why we never give up. Though our bodies are dying, our spirits are being renewed every day. We were never meant to remain here, just pass through, as my ancestors before me.

Song of Songs 8:6 … For love is as strong as death.

2 Timothy 4:7 I have fought the good fight, I have finished the race, and I have remained faithful.

1 Corinthians 15:26 And the last enemy to be destroyed is death.

2 Corinthians 5:4 While we live in these earthly bodies, we groan and sigh, but it's not that we want to die and get rid of these bodies that clothe us. Rather, we want to put on our new bodies so that these dying bodies will be swallowed up by life.

1 Corinthians 15:54-55 Then, when our dying bodies have been transformed into bodies that will never die, this Scripture will be fulfilled:
"Death is swallowed up in victory.
O death, where is your victory?
O death, where is your sting?"

Abraham M. (11:04 p.m.): I'm beginning to remember my spiritual teachings. I had forgotten about them for so long.

Kay G. (11:04 p.m.): Jesus has conquered death.
2 Timothy 1:10 but it has now been revealed through the appearing of our Savior, Christ Jesus, who has destroyed death and has brought life and immortality to light through the gospel.
John 11:25 "Jesus said to her, "I am the resurrection and the life. The one who believes in me will live, even though they die."
Hebrews 2:14 Since the children have flesh and blood, he too shared in their humanity so that by his death he might break the power of him who holds the power of death—that is, the devil—

Kay G. (11:06 p.m.): The enemy beat you down with your own thoughts that you have forgotten the code, your code, that you have lived by your whole life. What is it? Tell it to me.

Abraham M. (11:07 p.m.): I never give up hope.

Kay G. (11:08 p.m.): Do not listen to the enemy, Abe. Don't worry. Margie will be okay because Jesus has overcome death. Don't listen to the enemy.

Instead, listen to this.
www.youtube.com/watch?v=zDOVvsiB8Wg

Abraham clicked on the video link. Pastor Steven was now part of his spiritual army. He didn't know Pastor Steven personally, but he might as well have, considering how many sermons he'd listened to.

Do not listen to your enemy or agree to his demands. Just because my enemy speaks something does not mean I have to agree with it. It is not the voice you hear that determines the life you end up with, it's the voice you believe. And before the enemy can get you to agree with it, he has to get you to believe it. So, in order to get you to believe it, he'll get somebody to say it, and how many have found out you cannot believe everything you hear.

He fired up his laptop and typed a single word into the Google search bar: "Death."

The screen exploded with 1.5 billion search results, but he clicked on one specific link.

No one wants to die. Even people who want to go to heaven don't want to die to get there. And yet death is the destination we all share. No one has ever escaped it. And that is as it should be, because Death is very likely the single best invention of Life. It is Life's change agent. It clears out the old to make way for the new. -Steve Jobs

Abraham closed his eyes, absorbing the inspiring testimonies that had intersected with him in this moment. *God is always working in my favor ... even when it seems He is not ...*

He bowed his head.

Change agent ...

My life needs to change.

Hope ...

Live by your code again.

Love ...

That is my greatest superpower ...

Jesus ...
He has overcome death.

Kay G. (11:23 p.m.): God built you to be the supernatural spiritual force that brings hope to people. When sin has taken hold of your heart, it'll use your gifts, too, so come full circle and bring them back to the Lord. Love is as strong as death. The world needs your love. The world needs you to bring hope.

THE VALLEY OF THE SHADOW OF DEATH

LVI

How did I get here?

The thunderstorm pounded him, its ferocity unforgiving. Each raindrop pierced his body like a barrage of tiny daggers. Water saturated his clothing, turning his jeans stiff and heavy. His black V-neck clung to him like a second skin, and even his Timberlands felt like bricks. Abraham sought shelter under a massive oak tree, scanning his surroundings.

Alamo Plaza.

He reached for his cell phone in his back pocket, only to find it missing.

What the fuck is going on?

He sprinted towards the gazebo, the weight of the drenched clothes slowing his movements to a crawl. The feeling of being weighed down disgusted him, a constant reminder of his aversion to water.

Hopefully the rain dies down enough so I can find a way home...

The street was empty. The darkness combined with the relentless downpour, made for poor visibility. Abraham felt completely out of his element, realizing that building a fire to survive the night was unlikely.

What the hell am I doing here?

Being in the heart of downtown at 3 a.m. was an odd place to be. The buildings, businesses, restaurants, and streetlights were all dormant as San Antonio slumbered. Not a single car passed by, a sight that turned his stomach.

He had been brought here for a reason.

Everything is pitch black...

Abraham turned toward the Alamo. The spotlights that usually illuminated the structure caught his attention. But this time, they flickered once, and then twice, and finally died, leaving nothing but darkness in their wake.

Total darkness.

No office lights glowed in any of the buildings. The Tower Life building, known for its signature orange and green crown, stood dark and devoid of its usual radiance. The other high-rise structures followed suit.

The rain transformed into ice, and the gusts of wind dropped the temperature by at least twenty degrees. Cold breath escaped his mouth, dissipating into thin air before it could rise towards the tree.

Why am I here?

In the distance, a shadowy figure approached. Despite the furious downpour, it appeared to be a man walking along South Alamo Street. Keeping his head down and concealed under a black fedora, the figure treaded along the yellow line in the middle of the street. The rain blurred his features, but Abraham strained his 20/15 vision, determined to gather any description he could. The detective skills ingrained in his DNA operated like clockwork, urging him to note even the smallest details that could keep him sharp in the face of an ambush.

As the figure drew closer, Abraham observed a sleek, trim individual. The man never lifted his face, his eyes fixed upon the concrete as he stomped through puddles.

This man keeps coming after me … The Darkness … he doesn't give up …

The first two meetings, confusion and then fear smoldered his consciousness. Now, anger had taken hold.

The Man in Black halted in the middle of the street, provoking Abraham to confront him head-on. Leaving the comfort of the gazebo, Abraham ventured into the street, stepping onto the yellow stripe that divided the road, positioning himself directly in front of his adversary. Thirty feet stood between Abraham and the Darkness, creating a confrontation reminiscent of a wild west showdown, with both gunslingers waiting for the other to flinch.

"I *know* who you are now. Let me be…" Abraham attempted to reason with the Man.

"I never take a day off. I never stop my work. Ever!" The Darkness responded with boasting confidence. "I *know* you know me. You have become quite familiar with my shadows. I come late at night … when all is quiet, yet only you can hear me. You hear me calling you, don't you?"

The figure closed in, seemingly oblivious to the heavy rain. "You are one of the few who have ever been able to see me."

"What do you want from me?"

"For you to let go…" The Darkness circled around Abraham as he stood his ground. The heavy rain gradually transformed into a light drizzle.

Abraham clenched his fists.

"Come with me … you'll be doing yourself a favor."

"No. I know who you are, and you don't scare me."

"Do you really know me? Take a good look!" The Darkness swiftly removed his fedora and flung it away like a frisbee.

As Abraham locked eyes with his adversary for the first time, he involuntarily took a step back. His mouth dropped, his eyes widened, and his brow furrowed at the sight of the man's face.

"I'm *you!*" the Darkness chided.

Abraham examined the features before him. Every aspect of the entity mirrored his own: the wavy hair, the prominent nose, the rounded cheeks, the childlike ears, the eyebrows, and even the crooked teeth. The eyes bore a resemblance, but instead of kindness, they emanated forcefulness, dominance, and a morbid evilness.

"Surprised?" The Darkness asked. "You shouldn't be. This is your true self. Especially after all the lies, deceit, and murder you have committed. You have truly proven yourself to be one of our best!" The Darkness patted Abraham's shoulder. "Great work, by the way…"

"It doesn't matter what I've done. I have God with me, and I know He will forgive me."

"That's where you're wrong. You are too far gone! It's over. Come with me."

"You may have won a few rounds, but I'll never go with you. God loves His children, and He will never forsake me," Abraham declared defiantly.

"No, He has abandoned you. He has taken things away. Your gifts … these gifts from your God … have left you. You're on your own. God can't help you. He stripped you of your greatest weapons, and yet you still praise Him. You *still* want to go back to Him. Come with me. I will give you your greatest desires. I can bring Liv back to you. I can heal Margie. I can even bring Athena back to life. I can give you all that you have ever wanted. All you have to do is pledge your allegiance to me. Follow me, and all your hopes and dreams will become reality."

Abraham had grown strong. His resolve did not waver, and he was beginning to believe again.

No, God's got me … don't listen to the Father of Lies …

"I know what you're thinking. 'God's got me.' I've heard it countless times," the Darkness responded, unfazed by Abraham's conviction. He attempted to charm his latest victim before he could become a victor.

"I know the truth. All of God's children know the truth,' Abraham pressed on.

"And what is that?" the Darkness asked, mocking such a declaration.

"That you're a liar. We fall only when we believe the lies."

I can do this … the devil will flee …

"You think you can *win*? You can't beat me. I come in many forms … the stories you heard growing up, they're all true … La Lechuza…The Boogie Man…the monsters you see at night…hiding in the closet…under the bed … in your thoughts … in your head." The Darkness positioned himself directly in front of Abraham, preparing to go head-to-head. "I've even been the people you know…" In a millisecond, the Darkness morphed his appearance from a doppelganger to that of Tommy Gun.

The Gun grinned, his mouth forming an evil smile.

The Gun morphed into Abbadon.

Abbadon reached out to Abraham. "I was your brother, and you didn't save me."

Abbadon morphed into Ray.

Ray scowled. "Hey boy, you ain't shit and you'll always be a pussy!"

Each one carried darkness in their eyes.

Abraham stepped back, stumbling into a pothole and falling onto the soaked ground.

"Be careful, there," The Darkness said, mimicking Ray's voice.

Abraham crawled out of the pothole.

I know what he's doing and it's not gonna work.

"You might be all those things. You might've have won in the past…but not tonight," Abraham declared firmly.

The Darkness shifted back into its human doppelganger form, smirking. "Oh, don't be so sure. Your human flesh is no match for me. You'll come with me tonight, whether you like it or not." The Darkness taunted, pointing a stern finger at Abraham.

This motherfucker is threatening me … fuck him!

"Oh, wait. How could I forget your loved ones that you lost." The Darkness transformed into Liv's likeness.

Liv smiled, her voice dripping with bitterness. "Baby, we were happy together, but you threw it all away..."

Then, Liv morphed into a tearful five-year-old version of Athena. "Daddy ... why didn't you want me?"

Athena transformed into Margie. "You can save me, little boy ... but you won't."

"Ahhhhhh!" Abraham roared, charging towards the Darkness. Unyielding rage surged within him. He extended his arms, preparing to wrap them around the Darkness to bring him down. Before he could get close enough, the Darkness effortlessly tossed him aside like a rag doll.

Abraham regained his footing and, without hesitation, launched a left punch followed by a right. The blows struck the Darkness, but it merely grinned at Abraham's feeble attempt.

In response, the Darkness delivered the exact combination—a left punch followed by a right that sent Abraham hurtling ten feet away, skidding on the wet concrete. The drizzle switched into a heavy downpour.

Undeterred, Abraham sprang back up and retaliated with a powerful right hook. The Darkness promptly responded with a right hook of its own, knocking Abraham back once more.

He's mimicking my moves ...

Determined, Abraham closed in on his adversary, unleashing a left uppercut followed by a right. The Darkness showed no signs of damage, barely flinching. In turn, it delivered a punishing combination, its uppercut ringing in Abraham's head. He dropped to one knee, struggling to regain his composure.

This is not working ... my punches have no effect ...

Fueled by fury, Abraham intensified his assault, his punches growing stronger with every surge of rage. He launched a ferocious right hook, but the Darkness deftly evaded it. A left punch followed, and the Darkness smoothly ducked under it. Abraham orchestrated a rapid 1-2-3 combination—right, left, right—but the Darkness skillfully weaved and countered his strikes.

"The angrier, the better!" the Darkness shouted.

I'm giving him everything I got. His forehead creased with rage.

"Yes, let it all out!" the Darkness goaded.

I can't fight him like an ordinary man ...

The Darkness dusted off his shoulder, his garments intact. His black shirt remained untarnished, neatly tucked into his pants, and his black dress shoes unscathed.

"You're getting tired ..." The Darkness unleashed a thundering uppercut, causing Abraham to drop to the ground. A brutal kick to the stomach sent him flying into the Cenotaph monument, his body slamming against the marble structure. Blood spilled from his mouth as rainwater pelted down on him in tandem with the Darkness.

"Ahhhhhhhhhhhhhhhh!" Abraham yelled at the top of his lungs, driving his fist into the concrete.

The Darkness advanced towards its target. "You let your best friend die, and that set in motion a series of events that led you straight to me. You could've saved him, but you didn't. You killed your daughter and didn't even hesitate to give the order. You nearly took your own life ... and you know why? Because deep down, you know that God will never forgive you. You know you'll never enter the gates of heaven. I'm not in the gates, and let me tell you, I'm having a grand ole' time ... and you can too!" The Darkness circled Abraham. "You see, God makes you suffer first so you can have a chance to get in. But I can give you a worry-free life right now! Do you want to be rich? Famous? You can have it all! Women ... mansions ... cars ... the downtown penthouse ... I know how much you fancy those luxurious BMWs ... you name it. You don't have to suffer here!"

The realization sank in. *I'm not outmatched ... c'mon, Abraham ... dig deeper!* His heart and soul were the only duo strong enough to overcome the infectious combination of darkness and death.

Don't reject your gifts ...

The Darkness was elusive, like an airborne disease—unseen, untouched, and appearing without warning. It invaded his life like a parasite.

Unleash the fire! The same power that rose Christ from the dead lives within you ...

It was unbecoming, infiltrating every known fiber of his being, and Abraham had allowed this Entity to torment his soul.

I'm done letting it beat me.
The greatest battles are the ones fought within ...
This Sickness ... is an ongoing war ...
I have the weapons ... to defeat this darkness.

Abraham felt the light breaking through.

Fire back! Get up!
Remember who you are ...

The internal war raged on—a trial unlike any other a man could face in his lifetime—and yet it remained unspoken. But Abraham was about to speak life to a force that had already been defeated.

"Join me," the Darkness insisted. "I'll show you what it's like to be true royalty."

Jesus ... I need you ...

Margie guided him to utter the words that would banish the devil. Her spiritual training offered him a fighting chance at survival. The phrase materialized before him, crystallizing in this critical defining moment. "I rebuke you in the name of Jesus," Abraham said.

"I'll take that as a resounding no," the Darkness retaliated, resorting to countermeasures of an offer rejected. "We are coming full circle…you came from nothing, and you'll go back to being nothing. Death is imminent. We're almost there…just like I've done countless times before. Each one of your predecessors, taken away, defeated by death."

Abraham dropped to his other knee and gazed up at the Cenotaph dedicated to the defenders of the Alamo. Each of them had sacrificed their lives for freedom. In the face of insurmountable odds, 300 brave Texans confronted an army of 5,000 Mexicans. The monument stood nearly sixty feet high, depicting seven courageous men charging forward with guns and swords. Engraved on the gray and pink granite were 187 names.

The Spirit of Sacrifice…

Abraham refocused his thoughts on his spiritual training.

God didn't give me a spirit of fear, but of power…and of love…and of a sound mind…

Abraham glanced at the inscription. The Darkness shouted, but its voice faded into the background.

Erected in memory of the heroes who sacrificed their lives at the Alamo, March 6, 1836, in the defense of Texas. They chose never to surrender nor retreat; these brave hearts, with flag still proudly waving, perished in the flames of immortality that their high sacrifice might lead to the founding of this Texas.

Survival in this case was not determined by strength alone, but of the heart.

These men fought with heart...there's nothing to fear in death...it's a natural part of life...now use your gifts...give it everything you got...like Margie said, fight this motherfucker hard!

The Darkness sensed its victory within reach, but this man had faced it before. The thin line between revenge, psychotic tendencies, and malevolent tactics converged, exposing a glimpse into the boundaries of darkness. Now, his spiritual, physical, and mental training worked in harmony. The supernatural power that once coursed through him manifested within his spiritual composition.

God makes all things work together for our good...
It wasn't in vain...
I needed the dark to appreciate the light...
I needed to be in the dark in order to beat it...

"No one has ever defeated me!" The Darkness sensed the rebellion. "Even the few who managed to escape...I snuffed out their lives before they could see another day. It doesn't matter if you leave here, you're headed for death."

Abraham closed his eyes, and focused on slowing his breathing. He inhaled for four seconds, then exhaled for four seconds.

God is with me...

"It's beautiful," The Darkness continued, "You lose here and now...you'll never wake up and I take you with me. You *will* die in your sleep, and I will have my victory."

"My God has conquered death. I'll be fine."

"Is that your submission?" The Darkness asked, surprised.

"This is just a dream."

"To you, it is. But this is *real.*"

"God will take me...when the mission is done...and now I know what that is," Abraham said, his anger long dissipated.

"You are broken, just like the rest of this world."

"And God uses broken things all the time." Abraham rose to his feet, his spiritual strength renewed. He glared fearlessly at his doppelganger. He raised his arms in a circular motion, as if spreading his wings, cracking his back, preparing himself for another round. He felt like a Jedi emerging from meditation—calm and steady. The anger he had felt moments ago vanished into the night.

I never give up hope...
I love all people, even when they don't love me back...
My faith is my foundation...God has never let me down...

The Darkness struck Abraham with a powerful right hook. His face turned to the side from the blow, but he stood his ground, staggering a few steps back.

"In my weakness, You make me strong..." Abraham said. He threw a strong right hook, and to his surprise, the Darkness turned its face, stunned by the impact. The Dark doppelganger's mouth dropped open, its hand instinctively covering it, shocked by the force of the blow.

It worked! Scripture weakened it...

The Darkness clenched its fists, preparing for a counterattack. Abraham seized the opportunity presented by his opponent's momentary shock and unleashed a series of blows—a 1-2-3 combination—with unwavering grit. The Darkness staggered under the onslaught.

C'mon Abraham! Margie gave you the scripture to fight...say it!

"He who dwells in the secret place of the Most High..." Abraham recited, his voice filled with conviction.

"Psalm 91...that doesn't work on me..." the Darkness declared. "It's too late for you. You're too far gone."

"You can't fool me with your lies anymore."

The Darkness swung hard, landing a couple of punches to Abraham's face, followed by a forward kick. "You're a killer! A murderer! God will never let you into His Kingdom."

Abraham caught the Doppelganger's right leg with his left arm and swiftly struck the Darkness with a right hand. He delivered two more punches, grabbed the black shirt of his adversary, and headbutted him. Finally, Abraham lifted the Doppelganger, still holding its right leg, and threw it to the ground.

Reciting scripture, Abraham continued, "…shall abide under the shadow of the Almighty. I will say of the Lord, He is my refuge and my fortress: my God; in Him, I will trust." He swung back his right leg, kicking the Father of Lies, causing the Darkness to roll over on its back.

"No…this can't be happening. I own you!" The Darkness roared.

"Surely He shall deliver thee from the snare of the fowler and from the noisome pestilence."

Struggling to its feet, the Darkness removed the black button-down shirt and hurled it aside. Abraham stood confidently in front of the Alamo as the lamps flickered back on, shining upon the historic structure. The Darkness shielded its eyes from the blinding light.

"He shall cover thee with His feathers, and under His wings shalt thou trust: His truth shall be thy shield and buckler."

"You're making this harder for yourself. Now I'll show you my true strength. No human can withstand pure evil. There is nothing special about you!" The Darkness morphed slowly this time, taking on a non-human form. Its black outfit, torn and tattered, shredded as its new form emerged. The Entity grew to a height of seven feet, its skin changing from human flesh to a reddish-black hue. Shiny black horns protruded from its head, and its face transformed into a beast-like creature with snakelike eyes, skeletal-like nose holes, and lion-like lips filled with sharp, vampire-like teeth. Wings materialized from its back, stretching twenty feet from tip to tip, flapping violently.

Initial shock overtook Abraham, but with God's supernatural strength coursing through him, fear could not enter.

The Beast spoke, its growling voice caused the ground to shake. "You are weak!" The Beast turned its back to Abraham, and its giant wing backhanded him with a powerful slap. Abraham flew forty feet, landing on the grassy lawn in front of the Alamo.

Struggling to recover, Abraham scrambled up from the ground, reciting the verse that brought his words to life. "Thou shalt not be afraid for the terror by night, nor the arrow that flyeth by day."

The Beast buckled to its knees, its face grimacing in pain. "Ahhhhh," the Beast shrieked.

"Nor for the pestilence that walketh in darkness, nor for the destruction that wasteth at noonday." Abraham pressed on, goosebumps covering his body as the Holy Spirit worked through him.

The Darkness morphed from the Beast to its human form and back.

"A thousand shall fall at thy side, and ten thousand at thy right hand; but it shall not come nigh thee."

The Beast wailed, falling to its knees, and instantly switched back into human form. The doppelganger looked up at Abraham. "It will never be over! I will always take away the things you love. Always! You will always have to fight me! You will never rid yourself of me! I will *always* be there!"

"You have no power over me," Abraham said, his voice calm, almost a whisper.

"It's not over…I *will* see you again," The Darkness gasped for air. "If I don't take you today, you *will* die one day."

"Then I'll go on God's time…not yours. And I'm okay with that." Abraham locked both hands on the Darkness' throat, squeezing as hard as his human form would allow. "I rebuke you in the name of Jesus!"

The Darkness' eyes bulged. It reached for Abraham's forearms with each hand, but it was too weak to fight back as it struggled to draw breath. The Doppelganger grew still, the writhing of its head stopping as it fell back.

Abraham let go of his adversary, expecting the dark Doppelganger to drop to the stone ground. Instead, the Entity used the last trick it had left.

The Darkness vanished into thin air.

Abraham sighed in relief.

Death is defeated…

When he arrived, fear and anger had a strong hold on him, but now, he prayed as he gazed at the stars. No clouds were in sight, and the rain had ceased.

As he looked straight up into the night sky, he gave his last thoughts to the Lord.

Even though I walk through the darkest valley, I will fear no evil, for You are with me…Thank you, God, for another day…If I'm not dead, You're not done.

LVII   CHARLIE

The melodic chime of an incoming text message broke the silence, jolting him out of his battle-induced slumber. Its groovy disco theme sliced through the air, forcing his eyes open. Even though he had been living in his new house for months, it felt as though he was seeing everything for the first time.

Kay sensed the spiritual reawakening. She wasted no time for a debriefing.

> **Kay G. (8:03 a.m.):** For he has rescued us from the dominion of darkness and brought us into the kingdom of the Son he loves, in whom we have redemption, the forgiveness of sins. Colossians 1:13-14

He felt stronger, more alive.

The Darkness had been defeated for now, but it didn't mean he was immune to its deceptions. In a world governed by the Father of Lies, he clung to the spark of hope that amidst the chaos and confusion, anything remained possible, all because a humble carpenter had triumphantly risen from the grave.

I'm not gonna take anything or anyone for granted anymore. I'm gonna tell grandma I love her every day…and Margie…and my mom. Every single day. And Margie's going to be okay. God will find a way.

Abraham M. (8:05 a.m.): Mission successful. I can only assume you were attacked as well…

Kay G. (8:07 a.m.): I was…but not in the way you think. As believers we are targets for the enemy. It is not us, but the power that lives within us. The power of Christ. To attack you is to attack us all who are bonded together with our Brother and Savior, Jesus. Hebrews 2:14 Since the children have flesh and blood, he too shared in their humanity so that by his death he might break the power of him who holds the power of death—that is, the devil.

Abraham M. (8:09 a.m.): You knew the enemy would come after all of us?

Kay G. (8:11 a.m.): We're not done fighting just yet. And who can win this battle against the world? Only those who believe that Jesus is the Son of God. 1 John 5:5

Grandma was sure to have breakfast prepped by now. He threw on a black cut-off shirt over his tank top, while his royal blue Jordan shorts served as his typical pajamas. He shot out the door and walked four houses over.

The crisp fifty-nine degrees signaled winter in San Antonio. As he turned into the walkway leading to Grandma's house, a fierce roar bellowed nearby. "The beast…" he whispered. *That's odd…I've never heard it during the day.*

Bob roamed his front yard. He was somewhat of a mythical creature himself. Rarely seen, rarely heard, and avoiding the public eye. "Good morning," he said, surprising Abraham with his chipper greeting. Bob was well-groomed, contrary to what Abraham expected.

"Good morning," Abraham responded, puzzled by Bob's willingness to strike up a conversation. He had never heard Bob speak before, and his voice was surprisingly pleasant rather than the grizzled tone he had anticipated.

The beast continued to roar wildly, seemingly ready for breakfast too. "He must be hungry," Bob said, not bothering to hide the fact that Abraham heard the growl.

"Your dog?" Abraham asked, assuming that Bob must have been aware that the neighborhood was onto him, and that the presence of a wild beast in the basement was no secret.

"Would you like to meet him?"

"Sure," Abraham replied, with unmistakable surprise in his voice.

"Come around to the back, I'll go get him."

Abraham took a detour through Bob's driveway, making his way to the back gate with some reluctance. *It's daylight hours, what's the worst that could happen.* Curiosity got the best of him, as he would be the first to see the creature up close.

Bob unlocked the screen door, which slowly squeaked open.

Alright, let's see what this thing looks like?

Out of the house came a huge tan-colored, four-legged beast, running towards a grassy patch in the backyard. Abraham froze at the sight of the creature. *What the fuck! A lion!*

"How is *he* your pet?"

"Well, that's a long story," Bob laughed.

"I've got time," Abraham reassured him.

"Come on in." Bob motioned with his hand for Abraham to open the gate.

"Nah, I think I'm good."

"Charlie's harmless. I met him when he was a cub, took him in as my own, and raised him ever since."

"How did you get him here?" Abraham asked.

"I'm sure you have a lot of questions. You're actually the first in the neighborhood to see him. Believe me, I've heard all the horror stories about him, well, *us*," Bob chuckled.

Charlie lay in his sand pit underneath a towering oak tree. His calmness mirrored Bob's, as he nestled into the den.

"That's his favorite spot. It's like home for him," Bob said, pointing to the cave-like structure. It dipped slightly under the tree, with stringy roots exposed but not deep enough to fully hide Charlie.

"To answer your question…I smuggled him here, to the States. There's this tiny island, about sixty miles off the coast of Honduras. It's home to a small zoo for injured animals. The zoo takes care of the animals and keeps them safe from any kind of harm. Charlie used to live there until I took him in. Come on over, he's harmless." Bob strolled over to Charlie and caressed his mane as if he were a pet dog. The beast's head reached Bob's chest. "After I lost my wife, I traveled the world. Heck, didn't know I was going to bring somethin' back with me."

"Why would you want to take him from the island? Isn't he better off there?"

"Yes and no. His chances were always gonna be fifty-fifty…he was declawed and abandoned. Luckily, he was found, and the zoo saved his life. There's no way he would have survived in the wild. Charlie has no clue of the life he's supposed to live…the life of a wild lion. If he were to be set free, he would die."

"And Charlie has a better life here? I don't understand…"

Bob sighed heavily. "Considering the circumstances…yes. I love Charlie. He's like a house cat, only twenty times bigger. He sleeps most of the time. I play with him, feed him…and we keep each other company."

Bob wandered off into his thoughts. It was clear that there was more to his story, but Abraham didn't pry.

"Charlie has been deprived of a normal life. His lifespan will be short." Bob hugged Charlie, wrapping his arms around the lion's neck. Charlie yawned, revealing his formidable array of teeth.

"You're lucky I'm not one of the other neighbors. They're ready to call animal control," Abraham laughed.

"Aw, I trust you."

"You trust me, but you don't even know me…"

Bob's confession seemed odd considering it was their first conversation. *How does he know I won't report him?*

"I can't tell you how or why, but when I saw you out late one night, talking with your dad, I knew you'd be the first one to see him." Bob paused, combing Charlie's mane with his fingers, then continued. "Charlie can never be who God truly intended him to be. He's lived in captivity his whole life. The life he should have had…he'll never know. But he is loved, and he still thrives. You can bet I'm gonna make sure he has a darn good life. I'm tellin' you this because, for some crazy reason, something is telling me that you need to hear this…" The seriousness dripped off his face. "…be who God made you to be."

Bob spoke as if he were a messenger sent to guide Abraham on a path he was destined to walk.

Abraham opened the gate.

There's nothing to fear.

Charlie rose from his relaxed state and crept over to Abraham. Abraham stopped in his tracks and froze inside the gate. Charlie nuzzled his head against his waist. The sudden contact caused Abraham to stiffen up. He gathered all his willpower and forced his fingers to run through Charlie's mane. *This dude can snap me in half in two seconds.*

"He's a four-hundred-pound gentle giant…you got nothin' to be afraid of. He ain't gonna eat ya," Bob reassured. "Heck, you thought he was gonna gobble you up, I bet. He's not a devouring lion. Those are the ones you gotta watch out for. Charlie is one of the good guys. I like to think of him as the lion who takes care of the lamb. The lion of Judah. The One that triumphed over everything. This is one of God's miracles…this magnificent creature is alive in a place where he shouldn't be."

This lion is a version that I don't have to be…

"Abraham, I'm glad you met Charlie. God meant for this meeting to happen. You haven't been declawed. Don't waste your chance…to be who God made you to be. You still got time." Bob stretched his hand out.

"Thank you for that." Abraham shook Bob's hand. "See you later, Charlie." He exited through the gate, walked across the front yard and redirected himself toward his original destination.

Be who God made you to be…

Margie emerged from Grandma's house. "Hey, maid," she greeted, her tone filled with somberness.

"What's going on?" Abraham asked.

"Your mom is in the prayer room. She needs to talk to you."

"Is she okay?"

Margie opened the door for him, silently indicating the way as if he had never been inside Grandma's house before.

The only time Margie was ever this serious was when things were adversely out of control. A buzzing inside his head alerted him of a dark revelation that loomed.

He entered the living room.

What the heck is going on?

Passing through the kitchen, he silently prayed, "God, please let my mom be okay."

He walked through both of Grandma's sewing rooms.

Here we go.

Taking a deep breath, he placed his hand on the doorknob. Turning it slowly, he opened the door to find Gloria sobbing on Margie's couch—a place where countless spiritual conferences had taken place.

"Mom, what's going on? What's wrong?" Abraham rarely witnessed her cry, only a handful of times in his nearly twenty-seven years of life. It was at that moment she delivered the news he least expected. News that would surely test his spiritual resolve.

"Your father died this morning."

LVIII

WHEN ENEMIES MULTIPLY

Words were his ally…
But not this time.
He couldn't come up with the right ones to say.
Shock filled his flesh.

My dad is dead…

Abraham sat beside Gloria on the maroon conference couch. He placed his arm around her, comforting her as best he could. His father had been the love of her life.

The Darkness was right. It's going to hit me where it hurts the most. This fight will never end.

Tears welled up in his eyes. The Darkness had stolen his father overnight. Their last conversation replayed in his mind, and it had ended just like countless others before. The dart tournament had taken place months ago, but as he held his mom, it felt like yesterday.

The enemy exchanged lives…

He reflected on their final words, knowing he would never have another chance to speak with his father.

Had I known, I would've done things differently...I should've tried harder...

"I have to go to the morgue to identify the body," Gloria said.

"Do you want me to go with you?"

"No, Abe, it's okay. I can go by myself." Even on the darkest days, Gloria remained strong.

The triumvirate of Gloria, Margie, and Grandma were the strongest women Abraham had ever known. They possessed an incomitable spirit, like mystical Hispanic creatures, weathering a storm of tragedies and forging ahead unscathed. These extraordinary beings fueled a firestorm of ultimate willpower, and it took all three of them to mold Abraham into the man he knew he could become.

"No, Mom. I'm gonna go with you."

Returning to the realm of death held no coincidence. The Darkness wanted him to know it was still alive and well, eagerly awaiting his return to where Ray's lifeless body lay.

You couldn't take me, but you sure as hell made sure to take my dad...

Gloria nodded, signaling confirmation. Tears streamed down her cheeks, causing her face to crinkle. She listened intently as the medical examiner briefed her on the autopsy results.

"Mrs. Moreno, your husband had several substances in his toxicology report, but it does not appear to be a suicide attempt," Dr. Rosales explained.

"Suicide? I was told he was hit by a train."

"Yes, that is correct. The police wanted to rule out suicide, so they requested an autopsy. They have more information regarding the circumstances," the doctor clarified.

Abraham overheard the exchange of information but remained in a state of shock as he stared at his father's lifeless body. He forced himself to walk over to him.

His father was gone.

"This is my son," Gloria said to Dr. Rosales.

"I'm sorry for your loss. I'll give you a few moments alone," the doctor offered, retreating into the next room.

Ray's body lay covered by a white blanket, devoid of life. His face was expressionless and pale, and a wound on his head had been stapled together. The gash extended from just above his left eye, curving up past his hairline. Gloria sobbed quietly beside him and witnessing her pain broke him to pieces every single time. "Let's go," she said.

"Wait. I need to do something first. You go ahead. I'll be right out. I just need a minute."

"Your father had enemies," she whispered.

"I know," Abraham acknowledged. It was a truth he had been aware of for some time. *Enemies are multiplying faster than I can gather myself.* "I won't take long."

Years had passed since he last attempted to delve into another person's thoughts, much less someone who was deceased. Before last night, he wouldn't have dared to test his strength, but his confidence had grown significantly since facing the Darkness.

It's worth a shot. Just concentrate. Abraham coached himself, channeling his energy towards Ray. Reading thoughts and memories of the living was tricky enough, but connecting with the deceased was uncharted territory.

Here we go. He reached out to Ray with his index, middle, and ring fingers, making contact with the topside of his foot. He closed his eyes, waiting for a sensation or a glimpse into a memory.

Nothing.

"I had to try," he whispered. His attempts weren't always successful, but it was an art and science kind of practice. If Ray were still alive, he would probably claim that he could accomplish such a feat. Abraham examined Ray's face, which, for once, revealed no emotion.

"Try again," a gentle voice whispered, urging him to make another attempt.

With man this is impossible, but with God all things are possible…

Abraham extended his hand once again. A serene presence entered the room, and unlike the enemy, an aura of tranquility enveloped him, like a soothing blanket that encompassed his entire being. The Light began to operate through him. Within seconds he was transported to the scene.

Nightfall…railroad tracks cloaked in a drizzly mist…

The images bombarded Abraham. The location remained unfamiliar, defying any known region of the city.

Vast stretches of land sprawled out…adorned with knee-high grass that swayed in the breeze…

With focused determination, he homed in on the last moments of the scene, his third eye lens capturing the details with increasing clarity.

Ray brought the car to a complete stop…railroad gates descended…red lights flickering…distant train horn pierced the air…drizzle blurred the windshield…Steely Dan blared from the speakers…Ray's fingers tapped on the steering wheel, mirroring the guitar riffs…another vehicle hurtled toward the BMW…no headlights…the engine roared…black 4x4 truck…

Abraham struggled to maintain his composure, but he persisted in observing the scene, feeling like a ghost visiting from another time.

The black truck slammed into the rear of the BMW…a thunderous boom…shattered glass…a mangled bumper dropped to the pavement...taillights exploded into countless fragments...red plastic pieces scattered everywhere...the back end of the car crumpled...

Sweat droplets accumulated on Abraham's brow as his concentration wavered. *C'mon, Abraham, just a little bit more...focus...*

The scene came into full view, its surroundings becoming even clearer.

The engine revved...the truck slammed into the back of the BMW...tires spinning...a swirl of smoke in the drizzly mist...the wooden black and white railroad barrier snapped in two...the truck pushed the BMW past it...pushing the skidding the car onto the tracks.

"Motherfucker!" Ray yelled.

The truck quickly reversed...speeding off...the train blared its horn repeatedly...warning to avoid collision...

BOOM!

The sound echoed through the dense fog...the train forcefully collided with the driver's side...sparks flew from the undercarriage of the car...the metal grinding and screeching...

The back end of the car slid off the tracks...the car flipped several times...coming to rest on the grass...a trail of dislocated parts...glass...plastic...metal...tires....

Abraham pressed on. His concentration, breaking slightly. The emotional transference between him and Ray reached its threshold. *Just a little bit more...*

Ray struggled to crawl out of the car...blood gushing from a wound on his head...his white buttoned-down shirt drenched in red...a light shone in the distance...Exxon...Ray hobbled to a standing position...walking towards the light...stumbling every few feet...blood poured down the side of his face...

Abraham fought to hold the connection. A stream of tears dripped down his cheeks. *You can make it, dad. Walk to the light!*

"Almost there. I can make it." Ray stopped beside the tracks… "If I make it to the gas station, they'll go after my son." Ray dropped to one knee…his body collapsing to the ground…looking up at the stars…blood pulsed from the wound…dripping to the back of his head…staining the rocks under him… "The Little Dipper…I remember you showed it to me once, Aba…" His body relaxing in the quietness…dust, rocks, and patches of grass surrounded him… "He's always looking to the stars…a dreamer…my son."

Abraham broke. Gasping for air, tears showered his face. He could *feel* his father.

His hurt.

His sorrows.

His regrets.

His fear.

His love.

In that moment, Ray released himself from the grip of unnecessary evils that had plagued him for so long. The chains of ego, pride, and selfishness that hindered him from becoming the man God intended him to be. He had a few precious moments to rectify all that came before.

Abraham held on. Moans of grief overcame him.

The end was near.

"I know you can hear me, Aba. You're ready," Ray whispered, upward to the stars… "God, I give my life, my heart fully to you. In exchange for my son's safety…I give my life to you…in Christ Jesus."

LIX   NO WEAPON

Kay G. (10:33 a.m.): I'm sorry about your dad, Abe. Even though things weren't well, I know you loved him. Don't fall back into the trap of the Darkness. Don't forget how strong you've become. Proverbs 4:23 Above all else, guard your heart, for everything you do flows from it. If you need anything, I'm here for you. Love you.

> **Abraham M. (10:34 a.m.):** Thank you. How did you know?

> **Kay G. (10:35 a.m.):** Zander gave me the news.

How in the heck does Zander know? Nobody knows yet...

The war room provided a temporary sanctuary. Margie had adorned it with spiritual fervor. A wooden cross hung from the wall behind him, and a silver metal iteration of the crucified Christ was nailed to it. On the opposite side of the room, a white sign, almost as big as the window, floated with words painted in gold. The word "Faith" was written in cursive, nearly taking up half the sign. Underneath it, a Bible verse was also inscribed in gold, resembling an old typewriter font. It read, "Faith does not make things easy. It makes them possible. Luke 1:37." Close to Margie's chaise, there was a painting of a blue butterfly on a 16x16 white canvas. Butterflies were her favorite, and although purple held the distinction of her favorite color, she once mentioned that the blue butterfly symbolized love.

Abraham sat on the two-piece sectional couch, which was intended for occasional guests. He faced Margie, while she reclined in her chaise, reserved for the spiritual warrior herself. She lounged, read scripture, watched T.V., and held conferences in the magical chair.

"What's going on, little boy?" Margie noticed the shift in his demeanor. Since his outburst with Liv, she had been monitoring his spiritual well-being closely. Keeping him scripturally medicated was her top priority.

"A discrepancy," he said. "Someone already knows about my dad, and they shouldn't…at least not this soon."

"Well, guess what? I have a surprise for you…"

"The Empty Cross again?" he asked, mustering a halfhearted snicker.

Margie opened the door, barging into Grandma's sewing room.

"Is it a bottle of Crown?" he asked. "I could use a bottle of Crown," he whispered to himself. *What a good way to honor my dad…a glass of booze.* "Margie? Do you have Sprite? Coke is a no-go, for sure…all that corn syrup. Oh man, Crown *Apple* would be *really* good," he continued to converse with himself.

On the wooden end table, Margie's Bible lay open. Abraham peeked over to see which book of the Bible she had been studying. *1 Corinthians.* "Isn't this the love chapter? Corinthians?" He skimmed over several verses, waiting for her response. "Margie?"

He sensed a presence entering the room, a tangible yet supernatural human presence.

"Hey, love! Sorry, we don't have Sprite in stock," a sweet voice said. She giggled as she noticed the disbelief on his face.

It can't be her…

Abraham turned to see the surprise Margie had spoken of. It wasn't what he had expected, but the timing of her arrival couldn't have been better.

"Kay!" The two of them embraced, and she immediately noticed his renewed energy levels.

"You look good, babe! You're so different from the last time I saw you," Kay said, scanning the room. "So, this is it, huh? The war room…I can feel the energy in here."

Her aura harmonized with the surrounding energies. Through years of studying the Word, she had developed into a spiritually powerful force through discipline.

"But you *just* texted me…I had no idea you were literally in the next room!" he exclaimed, laughing.

"You're probably wondering why I'm here, and the answer is simple…"

"Yup, my thoughts exactly…"

"We're going to make sure you don't fall back into the dominion of darkness." Kay got straight to business. Critical matters were at hand, and she was aware the enemy was hard at work as well. "When the enemy loses a battle, it never retreats…it returns with full force."

"Wait, wait! So, you're telling me that you heard my dad died…in the wee hours of the morning, got on a plane at the crack of dawn…all within a matter of hours, just to pray over me?"

"Pretty much," Kay smiled.

Abraham placed his hand on her shoulder and nodded, glancing at the open scripture. *1 Corinthians 16:14 Let all that you do be done with love.* He looked at Kay. "Why would you do this for me?"

"You're my cousin, but more importantly, you're my spiritual brother in Christ. We are all part of one body. As Jesus said, 'whatever you do to the least of your brothers and sisters, you do unto me.' We're on the offensive now." Kay took out her cell phone. The only items she carried were her phone and wallet, and if he didn't know any better, he would have thought she came from Denver with just the clothes on her back. Her simplicity mirrored Margie's. Her presence radiated like a sunny day, and no one within a twenty-foot radius could escape her contagious shine. "Our goal is to prevent you from backsliding…this is spiritual warfare, and the only way it ends is when we welcome the return of our Lord Jesus Christ. Until then, I have a powerful sermon from Pastor Steven to share with you."

Abraham listened in silence. *I don't know what I'm supposed to feel right now. She's right…I don't want to relapse. I'm stronger, but am I really strong enough?*

Kay opened the video link, and Pastor Steven appeared on the small screen of her cell phone.

> *…The moment that you begin to fulfill the purpose God created you for, the enemy will dispatch special forces…*
>
> *…The reason you had some of your problems is because you are such a problem for the darkness because of the light that you carry…*
>
> *…my mom used to say the "proof is in the pudding." Well, I found out when it comes to the things of God, the proof is in the problem.*
>
> *How do I know that God is using me and that He has great plans for me? How do I know that God has put a big calling on my life? How do I know that God has something outstanding for my future? I know the size of my calling by the size of my problem…*
>
> *…The enemy sent special forces for you this year because you are right on the verge of breaking a generational curse and changing a bloodline. You're a problem for the darkness.*

They sat together on the conference couch as Kay prepared to orchestrate a counteroffensive. "The enemy has just attacked you where it hurts the most. You are now aware of the armor that God has instructed His children to put on. Now, you have to remember that no weapon formed against you will prosper." Kay proclaimed, unlocking her cell phone once again to read from the mystical device. "Isaiah 54:17 No weapon formed against you shall prosper, and every tongue *which* rises against you in judgment You shall condemn. This *is* the heritage of the servants of the Lord, and their righteousness *is* from Me, says the

Lord." She paused briefly before continuing, "Repeat after me, 'No weapon formed against me shall prosper.'"

"No weapon formed against me shall prosper," he said in a hushed tone.

"No weapon," she repeated.

"No weapon."

"No weapon! Say it like you're on fire for the Lord!" she encouraged.

"NO WEAPON!"

Margie entered the war room. "New levels, new devils, little boy. We're here to help you."

Kay stood up from the couch, her sandals never making a sound on the wooden floor. She favored comfy yoga pants, especially when traveling. A beige shawl covered her indigo tank top and the way she draped it over herself was indicative of an angel whose wings shielded itself for self-comfort. "Please stand," she requested. "Are you ready?" Kay asked, turning to Margie.

Margie approached Abraham's right side, while Kay stood on his left. Despite Margie's five-foot-six frame towering over Kay's five-foot stature, together they stood as formidable servants of the Lord. To Abraham, they were his personal guardians, earthly angels willing to do anything to protect him from foreign, domestic, or spiritual adversaries.

"Now you understand that spiritual armies are real, and you have a spiritual army right here on earth," Margie said.

"Like in Matthew 18:20, 'For where two or three gather in my name, there am I with them,'" Kay added.

Placing a hand on each of Abraham's shoulders, they extended their arms, forming a triangle of power.

Like the Jedi, their attire remained unchanged. Margie donned sandals, jeans, and a lavender blouse, while Abraham sported Air Force Ones, jean shorts, and a Carolina blue polo. And like the Jedi, they believed in a Higher Power whose energy flowed through and surrounded all things.

Abraham turned to Kay and asked, "Are you going to lead prayer?"

Kay laughed at the question. "No, I don't pray out loud. That's my Kryptonite. I get tongue tied," she confessed. "I can tell you a great tale of something I learned, but I can't pray aloud over people, so I asked Margie to lead us."

They stood together in silence for a few seconds, allowing the Holy Spirit to flow through them.

Margie began.

"Dear Lord, we humbly offer our gratitude and praise for gathering us here today. We seek Your divine protection from the forces of evil. Please watch over my nephew, Abraham, and accompany him on his journey, wherever it may lead. Grant him the wisdom to always keep You, our Lord and Savior, close to his heart, knowing that Kay and I are forever connected to him in spirit. Lord, bless his actions and guide his thoughts as he navigates through this this dark trial. We trust in Your unwavering presence, for You never abandon nor forsake us. Surround us with a shield of protection as we stand alongside Abraham in his battle against the dark forces that seek to harm him. Strengthen our faith, for it is through You, Lord, who will fight for us. May we remain still, witnessing Your miraculous work. In Jesus' name, we pray Amen."

"Amen," Abraham and Kay echoed in unison.

"You're going to be okay, Abe," Kay reassured him. "Margie and I will faithfully intercede for you each day until our last breath. And if you are ever struggling or hated in the world, just know that it hated Jesus first and that means you're in good company. This life is not easy and whatever battles you should face, know that you will never face them alone. We will love you always…in this life and the next."

LX PRINCES AND THIEVES

Zander M. (11:02 a.m.): Yo! I'm going to need your help tonight. Pick me up at 2 a.m. and wear all black.
Shit…I forgot I owed him a favor…

"Perfect for a stealth mission," Zander said, referring to the Stealth M3 as Abraham decelerated near the residence.

"At least it ain't a burned down house this time," Abraham said. Grandma Perla's dilapidated dwelling was still a fresh memory.

"This is my buddy's house. We're just gonna check in, hang out for a bit, make sure nothing's out of place." Zander pointed to the property. "There it is…turn off the headlights…the neighbors are assholes."

"Does your buddy know we're coming?"

"He's on vacation. We just here to house sit for a few," Zander said. He exited the car with his duffle bag. His garments blended nicely with the nighttime setting. A black extra-large t-shirt, black socks, black Nike's, and jean shorts draped to his knees. "I'll be back," he said in his best Arnold Schwarzenegger impersonation. He scampered away, crossing the street and into the shadows.

Abraham glanced at the clock display. *2:37.*

There were no houses and no streetlamp posts along the side of the street where he parked. A thick forest of trees blanketed in darkness lined the edge of the road. *The land that time forgot,* he thought.

Deep in the forest, a predator lurked. Its eyes, disguised within the forest, no earthly being could detect. A predator's ally, if used correctly, was patience. The skill allowed for the perfect time to strike, and it was only a matter of time before it had an opportunity to sink its teeth into its prey again.

Abraham stared into the dark forest.

Somethings not right...

His cell phone lit up, triggering his sixth sense. The sound waves of the notification alert tingled the hair on his arms and neck, signaling that his instincts weren't wrong.

Kay G. (2:41 a.m.): Something told me to send this to you. We do not wage war like the world does. https://youtu.be/_o-8OtHQFfo

Abraham clicked on the link. Pastor Steven appeared on the screen.

In 2 Corinthians, Paul is talking to the church about how we fight. Not "if" we fight. Everybody has a fighting style. But how we fight, he says "That though we live in the world, we do not wage war as the world does." We don't go to the Philistines to get our weapons sharpened, it's too expensive. We don't go to social media to get our emotional needs met, it's too expensive. We don't go to the devil for our dopamine hit, 'please devil give me some dopamine, make me feel good for a second, give me pleasure for a second, make me feel something for a second.' It's too expensive, because you can get it from the devil, but it's too expensive. How many of you have found out, it is too expensive to go to the world to get your weapons? It's too expensive. Because even if it works, it isn't worth it. That's why Paul says, 'We don't wage war like the world does. We have to fight these battles, we have to live in this world, we have to be realistic, but we don't have to fight it that way." The weapons that we have, have divine power to demolish strongholds. That is the spirit of Jesus inside of you. It is divine power to demolish strongholds. When you go to the world for your weapons, there's no power in them. When you go to the world for your weapons, it doesn't demolish strongholds, it creates strongholds. It creates dependence on the thing that you are going to, for the need you are trying to meet. Why would you go the devil for it when your Dad has it in abundance when you are a child of God!

The message resonated in his spiritual consciousness. *Break the cycle. It's too expensive. There's no power in this world.*

A loud knock on the glass startled him, breaking his thoughts away from the sermon. He rolled down the window to see his cousin clearly out of breath.

"Come inside real quick, Cuz," Zander said. His grin expanded his neatly trimmed goatee.

Abraham hopped out of the vehicle and crossed the street like a ninja. Black Timberland boots glided across the pavement. His dark jeans and black t-shirt reminded him of the scene that played out when he used tactical clothing and stealth moves to catch Liv cheating. *I'm not that guy anymore...*

They crept through the yard and onto the porch. On the front door was a wreath that said, "Welcome." Zander opened the door and the two men walked into the darkened house. Abraham turned on the lights so as not trip over anything or break any valuables.

"Turn 'em off!" Zander shouted. He ran over to flick them off himself.

"Dude...don't even tell me," Abraham said, shaking his head.

"Hey, this fuckin' guy robbed me first! He got me fuckin' fired, stole my job, and then lied about it. Fuck him! He deserves what's coming to him and I'm gonna make a fuckin' sandwich in his kitchen and I'm not even hungry, but I'm gonna eat his food because he stole my bread. Fuck it!" Zander whisked away to the kitchen, opened the fridge and threw sandwich meat down on the island counter.

"You know what, fuck it! Let's have a sandwich," Abraham said with a laugh.

"That's what's up Cuz! Here you go, have some bread!" Zander tossed two slices at Abraham.

Zander grabbed a few slices of bologna and slapped them on a bread. He grinned as he chomped on the sandwich. "I'm gonna take all this motherfucker's stuff!"

"What's he got in here?" Abraham asked.

"Dude, I've been scoping out this fucker's house for weeks and I know where his stash is at. It's not in his wife's walk-in closet, it's not in his secret safe, it's in his daughter's playroom underneath a floorboard. Jewelry, stacks of cash, and a key to a vault at his bank. Who knows what the fuck's in there, but I'm gonna find out!"

Abraham bit into his bologna sandwich. He grimaced as it smothered his taste buds. "I'm not that hungry." The stale dryness made him gag. He wanted to spit it out on the counter, but the detective in him sprung to life, so he forced himself to digest it. *No traces of DNA.* "I hope you brought bleach and gloves for all this evidence we're leaving right now." He knew full well how that process worked.

"I got a plan for that." Weeks of preparing earned him the right to proclaim a boastful statement. "No appetite?" Zander asked.

"Nah, haven't had one lately."

Zander glanced at Abraham, and it was obvious why he hadn't been stuffing his face. He'd seen his one-hundred-and-sixty-pound cousin devour a whole pizza at Incredible Pizza and eat a triple meat cheeseburger within minutes from Griff's Burgers. For him to take one bite of a sandwich and reject it was like watching Michael Jordan rejecting basketball for baseball.

"I'm sorry about your dad. The last time I spoke to him…it wasn't good."

"Same." Abraham kept it short. Conversations about Ray weren't on his chit chat list considering how things ended. Ray could have survived, but he chose not to. Guilt doused his flesh and he had grown tired of the feeling.

He didn't have to die…

His thoughts drifted to the future. He imagined facing the people responsible for killing his father.

Fuck them! They come after me and I'll beat the fuck out of 'em.

The realization struck him harder than a ton of bricks.
He was being hunted.
Pursued in the physical world *and* the spiritual realm.
Like a domino effect, thoughts trickled into his psyche.

Fuck it! Robbing this house will give us enough money for his funeral. Abraham smashed the plate onto the tile kitchen floor. Zander stared wide eyed at the display.

"Fuck it up, Cuz! C'mon, you know you want to take all this shit! Half of its yours for being the wheelman!" Zander laughed without a care in the world.

On the kitchen counter was a stack of plates. Abraham flung the top plate into the cabinet. One by one, he hurled plates from the island to the opposite end of the kitchen as each of them crashed against the wooden cabinets.

The open space of the kitchen and living room blended into one giant area. Abraham hopped over to the living room side.

The coffee table just behind the couch was the first to get upended. Abraham placed both hands on one corner of the sixty-inch T.V., ripping it off the wall. The screen cracked as it hit the floor and it looked as if veins grew on it instantaneously. Two six-foot bookshelves on either side of the T.V. toppled over. Trinkets and books splattered everywhere. Much like a caged animal wildly rampaging towards freedom, Abraham flipped, pushed, and lifted anything he could get his hands on. The rage garnered strength with each destructive act.

He shouldn't have died...

You took him because I beat you!

Books lay on the floor, some open with flaps bent. A few hardcovers absorbed dents on the corners while others stretched open with pages kissing the tile. Words adrift across the ocean of a cold hardened tile sea.

The end tables next to the couch suffered the same fate. Abraham threw them on top of the downed furniture. The gold frame of the end tables became unhinged, resting as a twisted heap of metal leaning on top of the distraught bookshelves. Picture frames that once rested on the end tables flew into the debris as well. They crashed on the bookshelves, shattering into thousands of pieces, exposing fragile family portraits.

Zander watched in awe as his cousin single handedly laid waste to the first floor living space. Broken gray marble cat statues lay on the floor. The color of them faded into the beige floor as paws, ears, and limbs lay scattered.

"Fuck yeah!" Zander yelled as he brushed crumbs off his protruding belly.

One 5x7 picture remained intact, glass pieces rested on it like twinkling diamonds. One glance at the family photo, and Abraham clamored an insistent urge to halt his upheaval. At first, the man and his wife didn't strike a sense of regret within him. It was the children that smiled innocently at him that caused the retraction. A little girl with dark brown hair, chubby cheeks and two missing front teeth caught his attention. *She's in Kinder,* he thought. Her sibling, a three-year-old boy smiled like a turtle, showing no teeth. From the looks of it, he would be starting Pre-K soon. The image reverberated in his moral conscious.

I can't do this…

The hair on his neck straightened. He sensed a presence he hadn't felt in weeks.

"Why stop now?" A growling voice boomed. "Destroy everything."

Abraham, you can stop, right now. Don't do this. You've come too far to go back.

His nerves calmed as he redefined his spiritual resolve.

"Cuz! I didn't think you had it in you! The savagery! I love it! Fuck it up! This dude is stacked…we'll leave here like royalty! The Prince of Thieves," Zander laughed, almost choking on his ham sandwich

Prince of Thieves…this isn't right…

"Why'd you stop? Fuck it up more!" Zander urged.

Abraham picked up the broken frame. The children looked happy, and he destroyed their home. *What would they think if they knew a teacher did this to them?* The thought brought clarity and utter remorse. *This is not who you are…*

"C'mon bro! Finish the job! I'll go get the goods," Zander declared.

The photo floated off his fingertips and onto the floor. He turned and headed for the door.

"Hey, where you goin'?"

"I can't follow you…I can't force myself to do this. You said you needed help house sitting, not *this*…not robbin' innocent people. I'm sorry, Cuz, but this is a place I can't be in anymore."

"Hold on, Cuz…you *owe* me! Go wait in the car…I'll be out in five." Zander sprinted up the stairs. Being light on his toes was an unprecedented feat, especially when he was ransacking a home.

Kay was right…don't fall back in…

"Release your anger," the voice growled with pleasure. "I told you…you can't get rid of me…"

The lies didn't make a dent this time.

You couldn't take my life…

So you took his.

I can't control who stays on the earth and who leaves…

But I can control myself…and how I react…

I have the power to choose who I follow…

…and I can choose to be at peace.

Abraham grinned, shaking his head in disgust. "You almost had me, but I know better now. I won't follow a prince of thieves…I follow the Prince of Peace…you have no power over me."

The Darkness snarled. "You have the power to take whatever you want from this house. You will have enough money to not only pay for the funeral, but to last you for a long time. Go get it…you earned it."

"I need to get back on track…to the things I love the most." Abraham calmly exited the house and walked across the street to the Stealth M3. It rested camouflaged with the background of the dark forest. Only the chrome rims shined in the moonlight and the glimmer of light was all he needed to remind him where he needed to be.

Abraham climbed in just as Zander rushed out of the house with the duffle bag in tow. "Cuz! What the fuck!" Zander backtracked to the front door. He reached inside the pocket of his zip hoodie and pulled out a candle lighter. He flicked the lighter and out sprung a flame. He lit the liquid trail leading into the house and up the stairs. The tiny flame blazed a trail along the soaked path and within seconds the fire consumed the house.

The playing field was now even.

Abraham countered the dark jabs. "The enemy will keep coming," he whispered. There was so much life left to live. God had spared him, and he relished the opportunity to make it count. Returning the favor meant he had to rise like the fire he was born to be. The fire he was *sent* to be.

With the wreckage in his wake, he sped off into the night, leaving Zander and the flames of destruction behind him.

LXI NEEDLE IN A HAYSTACK

A*ll those years of loving the world…*
And what did it get me?
…an empty house.

Regret was not a feeling he was used to.
The mistakes of a man broken by sin.

I can be good again. I can make things right…

The circumstances surrounding his failure were etched into his memory.
Psychological warfare.
Temptation.
Manipulation.
Control.
Ego.

Abraham stared into the mirror. The traits of a selfish narcissist stood in stark contrast to everything he had once believed in, yet somehow, he had become the enemy.
An enemy of the Lord.
An enemy to himself.

The existentialist within him refused to die.

What is the meaning of life? Are we not more than our mistakes?

He stripped away the layers of sin and deception, the lies and insecurities, leaving only an exposed version of his true self.

I am more than my mistakes.

Absorbing boundless vulnerabilities, Abraham studied his own circular black pupils, confronting the monster within. "I'm sorry…I'm sorry I failed you."

His eyes pierced into his own soul—a gateway between the person he had become and the man he could potentially be. "You can evolve to be better…"

There is no escaping the truth.

"I forgive you, Abraham. You are not perfect; you made mistakes, and I forgive you."

The metamorphosis had spawned the truest version of himself, regenerating his mind, body, and spirit, all converging on the one thing he yearned for the most…

Love.

Embracing this newfound truth, he quietly slipped into the bedroom. Settling into the office chair, he found himself swiveling from side to side, reminiscent of his carefree alter ego at four years old. Yet, the twenty-seven-year-old version of him longed for something beyond the simple amusement the chair provided.

"I don't want to go back to that life…I have to do things differently."

I have fallen harder than I ever have before. It's time to get back up. Remember you're training...everything you fought for. Go back to the beginning...

"All this means nothing if she's not here to grow old with."

This desolate place he called home once had a bright future. He wanted her, and more than anything in the world, he wanted her love.

She's the one.

The soulmate, the great love of his life, resided in his heart.

Liv.

She's never stepped foot in this house. I miss her...

Glancing at the pen and notepad on the desk, a thought emerged of what he could say to her. The idea made its way into the laboratory. The wheels turned, building momentum in the playground he called thoughts.

The thoughts multiplied - about her, to her, for her, and they were readying a launch onto paper...

She was the one he needed.

The one he craved.

The one he lived for.

The one he would die for.

His method of operation did not deviate, and his therapeutic tendencies began working their magic.

"I know what I have to do..." he announced.

Wasting no time, the pen raced across the paper, furiously capturing his thoughts and emotions. The years had hardened his heart, but he let love flow from the fragments of his shattered heart, trusting that the resulting creation would not disappoint.

Ideas took shape, transforming into letters, which in turn molded into words. Words danced together, forming stanzas that breathed life into his desires. It was an alchemical process, transforming mere ink on paper into living, pulsating flesh.

The ink came *alive*.

He allowed the monstrous surge of emotions to manifest, ensuring that he conjured the precise words he wanted to say. Nothing was left unturned or untouched, leaving behind an empty vault of sentiments.

The result, an ode to an ongoing odyssey, a testament to his belief that the journey was not yet finished.

Needle in a Haystack

I wasn't right and I lost sight
Fighting the wrong fight
Coasting through the night
With no light to guide me
For I lost her
and God you know
I nearly gave up.

And I know You are beside me
To help me stand up
And be the person
who loved the world.
I would give it all up,
for this one girl.

Lord, please bring her back,
for I love her so
She has my soul,
and I can't let go.
Love will take us to a place
we've never been before
Lord, please answer my prayers,
so I hurt no more.

The work I do for You
has been absent as of late.
But please give me another chance
with the most beautiful relationship to date.
I will make it up to You,
by loving her to the end of the earth
And I will let her know
how much she is worth.

Lord, please forgive me
for I made mistakes
I need Your guidance
to do whatever it takes.
I hurt her badly
and I was wrong.
Just give me a chance
to sing her a new song.

Lord, I promise to be
better than before
I was afraid to lose her
and I will fear no more.
Even as a superman
I need someone to save me
Because I can't fly
without my Beautiful Baby.

I found her
A needle in a haystack.
And my hardened heart
Only she could crack.
My heart turned black
But now it came back
And only my soulmate could
Get it back on track.

And all it took...
Was a needle in a haystack

Abraham placed the pen gently on the pad, his breath catching in his throat. His mind raced, fueled by a surge of adrenaline. He rested his hands and forearms, tingling from the rush, on the desk, his gaze drifting to the walls and ceiling as he contemplated his next move.

He had found her when she needed him most, but now the tables had turned, and he was the one desperately searching for her. The veil of egotistical pride had been lifted, replaced by a profound love that he couldn't conceal any longer, and he didn't care who knew or what he had to do to win her back.

Flipping the paper over to a fresh sheet, he began to pen a few words.

Liv,

> *I'm sorry for everything I did to you. I hope one day you can forgive me. I know you don't believe me, but I do love you. We have shared some amazing moments together and some that were not so great, but not for one second do I regret the day I "clicked" on you. You were a "Needle in a Haystack," and I found you. It took some time, and a trip to a darkened hell, but I see now I can't let you go. I never could.*

> *I never wanted to lose you and that forced me to evolve painfully, and even dangerously, to hold on to you, but I realize now it hurt us both. As I continue to grow, I hope you will see me as the man I once was, and the man that I know I can be and eventually become. I love you no matter.*

> *Love your Lion, your Sun,*
> *your Soulmate, Abraham*

LXII   RAY OF LIGHT

ll was quiet in the cemetery. The coffin hung suspended over the six-foot-deep hole, and it would be the final resting place that would soon house his father.

The black suit he wore rarely saw the light of day. The unpredictable South Texas weather reminded him of his hot-blooded curse—sunny eighty-degree days, drenching him in sweat. But it didn't matter. This was a celebration of life. The thought of Jedi Master Yoda's teachings popped into his head. *A transition into the luminous beings we are.* Perhaps Ray's body would vanish inside the black coffin just like a Jedi, becoming a permanent fixture of the Light.

He placed his hand on the coffin, while the workers in the distance held their shovels like canes, granting Abraham the courtesy of being with his father above ground one last time.

"Well, dad," he said, scratching the back of his head with his left hand. "You were an asshole," he laughed. "The last time we talked…it wasn't good. Having you as a dad was hard at times…but I know…deep down you meant well. Your intentions were for the good…even though they didn't always come off that way."

None are taken back from the Darkness. Not without giving one up in return.

"I thought the saying might be true, but I know now that it's not. What you did showed me the devil can't win," he paused, hoping that Ray could hear him. "I meant to give you this…" Abraham held up an envelope. "I wrote it for me…but I wrote it for you, too. I know that doesn't make sense…" He gently placed it on top of the coffin. "…maybe, if you get a chance, you can read it."

Abraham let out a heavy sigh. This was probably the most he had ever said to his father on his own, without provocation, in the last twenty years.

"Thank you for pushing me to go to the tournament. Because of it, believe it or not, I learned to embrace both the dark…and the light. We can't have one without the other…I needed that."

Abraham scanned the cemetery. The plots around Ray were covered with fresh grass. His neighbors had been there for some time now and in the coming weeks, Ray would have his own garden.

A few crows and sparrows perched in the oak tree to the right. The blue skies made for a glorious day to rise into the heavens. Abraham glanced down into the pit that awaited the coffin, and tears welled up in his eyes. He shifted his focus back to the coffin, and a little red bird landed next to his hand. Abraham grinned. "I guess you can hear me," he said. The bird, with its orange beak and black face, observed its surroundings for a few moments before turning its head towards Abraham and flying off to its next destination.

"I remember what you said… 'when these three meet, it will be more powerful than anything I've ever known.' I hope you're right about this next version of me." Abraham shook his head as he looked back down at the rectangular pit. The weight of the burdens of the next iteration of Abraham Moreno overwhelmed him.

More powerful than anything I've ever known…

Even in death, Ray had given him a specific set of expectations he wasn't sure he could live up to. "I have a lot ahead of me, a lot of…self-reflection, I guess. Deep down, I know I can overcome the thoughts holding me back." He nodded, agreeing with his own words, even though his thoughts hadn't fully embraced them yet. "I'll find a way," he reassured himself.

Finding oneself is challenging to say the least. Treasure is much more than material things. Some unseen things are more precious than gold...

"By the way, I did find it...the Codex. I'll do what the others before me have done...leave it behind for the next. These...extraordinary gifts, as Phil calls them, are recorded in this Codex. I have to do my part...I'm going to do my best to contribute, at least my portion. It reminded me that I shouldn't let anything go to waste...even the people in my life. I meant what I said...this cycle stops with me...and I'm sure as hell gonna do my best to make a difference..." He bowed his head.

A cool gust of wind blew against him, briefly refreshing his sweat-soaked face and drenched collar. He relished those few seconds of relief. *The breath of God,* he thought.

"I've been thinking...the day I meet God, I hope He's proud of what I've done on this earth when He calls me home. This test of mine was never about you. I did the best I could with the cards I was dealt. You work with what you've got, you know? I don't regret anything, and everything that happened was the way it was meant to be, and I played the hand I was given the best I could. I forgive you, and don't worry, I don't hate you." His voice shook as his words pierced the air. Another tear streamed down his cheek, mingling with the perspiration. The sunlight hit the coffin, creating a blinding white glare. Abraham reached for his sunglasses, shielding his eyes from the powerful beams of light.

"I love you, Dad. You're always gonna be my dad."

God, I humbly ask that You place Your hands on my dad and welcome him into Your kingdom. I humbly ask You to please comfort my family through their pain and grief. You always have a plan, and Your plan is always perfect. In Jesus' name, I pray. Amen.

Abraham made his way back to the M3, carefully navigating between the headstones. Liv leaned against the hood of the car, grinning and waving at him. He offered her a half-smile in return. She had shown up when it mattered most, and to him, that was all he needed.

Her red lipstick and light brown eyes captured his full attention, and his smirk transformed into a genuine smile.

Hope...

LXIII　　HOPE

"**H**ey, this is our third date!" he said, his smile stretching from ear to ear.

Liv did not disappoint. Her curvaceous figure had become even more alluring during their time apart. Abraham opened the moonroof of the Stealth M3. The cold December air seeped in, but it felt more like a refreshing breeze.

"It feels new, but familiar, if that makes sense," Liv smiled at him. Her eyes wandered to the stars through the moonroof. "Did you ever think…" she paused. "…that we might not end up back together?"

Abraham sighed. The loaded question couldn't be answered with a simple yes or no without explanation. "I did…I mean, it crossed my mind…and it wasn't a thought I wanted to believe."

"You never gave up hope?"

"Never."

"How can I forget," Liv said, laughing. "Mr. I Never Give Up Hope."

"Speaking of which…" Abraham opened the glove compartment and handed her a paper. "Read it."

"Is it going to make me cry?"

"It might, but I guarantee you it ain't gonna make you sad."

She unfolded the paper and glanced at the title. *Never Give Up Hope.* "I'll read it when I'm alone."

He stared into her light brown eyes and smiled, wishing this moment with her would never end. Minutes passed like seconds. The night sky shifted, and the stars along with it, as the Big Dipper descended closer to the horizon.

"That's good enough for me. I never thought I'd have the chance to give it to you, so I'll take that as a win. I wrote it when I was thirteen years old." Now, the poem carried a different meaning, yet somehow remained the same. "Hope…or my hope for *us,* never died. It might have faded or been lost for a little while, but my core is still filled with it." He grinned at her.

Liv studied her counterpart, noticing the changes the new version of him possessed. *He's sincere,* she thought. His smile had returned, and butterflies danced in her stomach. "Some things remain the same," she whispered. "You didn't take it off?" she asked, pointing to the Hawaiian ring on his left hand.

"No, I did not." Abraham turned his hand over, admiring the faint moonlight reflecting off the ring. "Not once." He glanced at her ring finger. The wedding band sat beautifully. A few months ago, he had desperately hoped she hadn't taken it off, and now, he had his answer.

✝

The sun descended toward the horizon, casting a golden glow where the vibrant hues of orange and pink merged with the vast expanse of the Pacific Ocean. Planning a matrimony in paradise wasn't an easy one, considering he had orchestrated it on a whim. He couldn't help but wonder if the man presiding over the ceremony was a genuine pastor, but it didn't matter though. He was going to marry the love of his life one way or another, even if it wasn't the real deal, at least he'd have this memory.

The ceremony was simple. Two people confessing their love for one another without the weight of legalities. Abraham had made it his mission to surprise Liv, with each surprise more extravagant than the last.

"Ladies and gentlemen, we gather here today to spiritually unite these two souls in matrimony," the Asian man smiled, his Japanese accent barely perceptible as he spoke flawless English. "Abraham, Liv, welcome to the beautiful island of Oahu and the sacred shores of Waikiki. This time-honored tradition has blessed countless souls who have sought to be one. Now, if you have prepared any vows, you may share them with each other."

Abraham locked eyes with Liv, and she nodded in affirmation. "I'll go first," she said. Retrieving a half sheet of notebook paper from her black shorts, she unfolded it with nervous anticipation. Adjusting her white shawl adorned with a red hibiscus print, matching the design on his button-down shirt he had purchased the day before at the International Market, she smirked and began to read, baring her heart to the world.

"Abraham," her voice quivered as tears welled in her eyes. "My faith in God has strengthened through you. In a new world of chaos, uncertainty, and darkness, yet full of dreams, ambition, and a shared future - we found each another. My faith teaches me to trust the Lord with all my heart. You make me feel safe and protected. With you, I have no fear. I trust you with my heart, soul, and mind. I promise to be faithful to you as I am to God. Put your hand in mine as you would put your trust in me, and together, we will walk the path that God unfolds before us."

A steady flow of tears streamed down her face. Her voice cracked every few words. "I can only hope that our future will be filled with joy, abundance, and happiness, but I know God has a plan for us. There will be challenges, trials, tribulations, and darkness. Through these storms, I promise to be hopeful, to be of light and calm, for hope is our anchor that will keep us together and weather the storms." She paused, gathering herself, hoping to steady her voice to read her final paragraph. "I have found the one whom my soul loves. You are my Sun, my Fire, my Superman, my Love, but most of all, my Soulmate. I prayed for you not knowing how hard the road would be. I know in my heart my soul has loved you many lifetimes before. All along, I believed I would find you, and now, time has brought your heart to mine. Little did I know the force that it would bring me as I stepped into the next chapter of my life. God has granted me many gifts throughout my life, but the greatest is our love. Although this chapter is just beginning, I promise to always love you in this lifetime and in the next."

Liv wiped away her tears and refocused on Abraham. Her emotional exchange flooded into his soul, and he pulled out his version of vows from his blue jean shorts. She had boosted his confidence enough for him to show more skin at her request, mustering the courage to reveal his vulnerability by unbuttoning his shirt, exposing the black ribbed tank top underneath. The colors of his outfit, coupled with his red and white Air Force Ones, created a complementary striking ensemble alongside hers.

"Liv..." His emotional reserve had been compromised, but he fought to hold himself together. "Little did I know that one click of a button would change my life. Your love has taught me so much, and it has taken me to places I've never known before. The result is me, here, standing before you. You have touched my soul in ways that I don't fully understand, but I do know this - it is not only my flesh that yearns to be with you, but also my soul as it craves to be unified with yours. Soulmate is a term that I had heard before, but I never understood it fully until now. This odyssey has led me from earthly confines to unexplained circumstances that I can only attribute to the spiritual supernatural realm. You have singlehandedly captured my heart, my soul, my entire being, just by being who God created you to be." A tear escaped his eye and trailed down his right cheek. His voice trembled as he recited the words he had written just hours before. He continued, "My love knows no bounds, but it would be meaningless without the ability to express it in the most intimate ways. You succeeded where everyone else failed. You broke through barriers that no one else could. Only a soulmate can do that. I love you."

A deluge of tears ran down her soaking wet cheeks. Her inability to contain them was characteristic of the water sign he fell in love with.

"Now, I ask each of you to take a handful of sand," the Pastor instructed, his bald head shimmering in the sunset.

Abraham and Liv bent down and scooped up a fistful of sand. The Pastor smiled, his eyes nearly closed, appearing as slits. He retrieved a quart-sized plastic bag from the left pocket of his silky blue shorts and a zip tie from his shirt pocket. The blue hibiscus print on his yellow short-sleeve button-down was an unconventional choice for a spiritual ceremony.

The Pastor opened the bag and held it between Abraham and Liv. "Together, pour the sand into the bag."

They watched the sand cascade from their hands into the bag until their palms were empty. The Pastor lifted the bag, securely fastening it with the zip tie. "This," he said, raising his right arm with the bag in his hand, "symbolizes the union of two individuals spiritually becoming one."

✝

"Necio! *Fool!*" she exclaimed, her laughter filling the air. "You always come up with these elaborate schemes."

"Hey, I made it happen...I mean, look who you're talking to," he said. Containing his laughter was futile when she praised and ridiculed him at the same time. "You do crazy things when you're in love, obviously."

"Obviously!" Her sarcastic tone was anything but subtle. "It feels like such a long time ago...another life ago," she said, her thumb and middle finger gently caressing the top and bottom of her ring. Her soft eyes fixated on the intricate carvings of the hibiscus, its ridges encompassing the entire circumference of the ring. Her mind raced back in time. "That ugly fight we had...that was the first time I could see the darkness in you. I never gave up on you, Abraham. Never. Even when you were super fucked up, I still stood by you."

"I know...I'm sorry. It was all my fault. All of it. I've been in the dark for two and a half years. Time has flown...but I'm trying."

"You were like the evil Superman. What's his name? Bizarre man?"

"Bizarro," Abraham chuckled. "Superman's evil clone. I'm transforming back into the good version. I feel I'm almost out of this mess, but I'm not quite there yet."

"The greatest apology is changed behavior," she said. Liv had a way of speaking undeniable truths when they mattered most.

"It's like being an alcoholic. Even if a person becomes sober and stays clean, they will always be an alcoholic. They just keep the urges at bay. It's no different with darkness. I'll always have darkness inside me, but I know now that I have to keep it at bay…so it doesn't take over. I've seen it firsthand my whole life…you know that."

Liv nodded in agreement. She fully understood what he was up against.

Abraham fixed his gaze back on the stars. They had a magical way of putting things in perspective. Perhaps it was the existential void that tinkered with his sense of purpose. "Thank you for being there for me when I told you about my dad. You didn't have to, but you were…'

"Even though y'all didn't get along, I know you loved him.'

"He did the greatest thing for me before he left. I didn't have to be there to see it. I just wanted him to change…fully. And he did that when it mattered most."

Liv placed her left hand on the back of his neck, gently stroking the back of his head. The soothing touch reminded him why he fell in love with her in the first place. "A simple touch has always calmed you down," she said.

He closed his eyes, allowing her hand to work its magic. The transference carried the weight of her sorrow, her sadness, and her heartbreak.

"I'm never going to hurt you like that again," he said. "I know what you're thinking…" Their eyes locked. She leaned into the passenger seat. "I can see it…the eyes never lie. But I promise."

"Don't make promises you can't keep, Mr. Moreno." Liv looked at him stone faced. She examined his face. She wanted to believe his confident proclamation. "I'm sure you have bigger fish to fry than keeping a promise to me. You're meant to do more with your life than just keep promises."

"You believe in me so much...even after all the destruction I caused."

"I still love you, Abraham. I always believed in you. Even though it didn't mean anything to you."

Abraham shook his head vigorously, disapproving of her claim. "Not true. It meant everything to me." He exhaled the burdens of a past he couldn't undo. "Your words kept me awake most nights. They helped me and haunted me at the same time. 'Meant to make a difference.' That statement brought shame and hope. If it weren't for you, Margie, and Kay, I'd be worse off, maybe even dead. Even my dad had a hand in helping, believe it or not. In all that chaos, I found so many things, especially within myself. I know what I'm meant to do now."

"And what's that?"

"When I was little, I always felt like I was 'sent.' It sounds stupid, but that's what I've always believed. Like I had a mission...and I wanted to save the world."

"Of course! You have to go and be Superman! Ugh!" Liv groaned playfully, though he knew there was truth in her jest. "More like Stupidman!"

Abraham laughed. "You know what I mean! I wanted to help people, and not just here, but people all over the world. I just didn't know how to do that until now."

"So how do you plan to save the world, Mr. Moreno?"

"I'm a writer. I've always been a writer. This idea that I've had for months is stuck in my head and it's turned into a story. What's the one thing that people across the world have access to?"

"Ummm, a movie? You're gonna be a movie star?" Liv asked.

"No, but close," Abraham laughed. He paused, waiting for her next guess, but all she could do was shake her head in anticipation of the answer. "Words! It's always been the words. And I plan to use them for God's glory."

"You're going to write a book?"

"I already started…"

"Wow. The great Abraham Moreno found his calling, huh?" Liv laughed.

"Well, that and early childhood," he said.

"Yes, and that too. How could I forget," she said, sarcastically. "Do you have a title yet?"

Abraham fell silent for a moment. "I haven't spoken this aloud to anyone, so you're the first to hear it. I felt it was an appropriate title after everything I've been through."

"Well...what is it?"

"Baptism of Fire."

Liv shook her head in awe, her beautiful light brown eyes widened with excitement. "That's really good. It suits you, because you've always been about the fire. Damn Leo," she snickered. "Seriously though, I love it. So, the goal is to write this book and then what? Get rich and famous? Live in Hollywood?"

"You've always supported me and my elaborate dreams." Abraham laughed at her presumptions. "No, I'm not writing it to get rich or famous. It's to help people...to inspire them...to help them believe...the ultimate goal is to make a difference. If I can inspire just one person with this book...then I've accomplished my mission. I believe this is why I was sent."

"You've figured it out. All those nights of tortuous thoughts and dreams...wondering what you're meant for. I'm proud of you. You're going to do great. I know it." She continued to caress the back of his head, her hand fitting perfectly on the nape of his neck.

As they sat in the car, Abraham reached into the compartment on the driver's side door and retrieved a weathered brown leather book.

"What's that?" Liv asked. "It looks old."

Abraham smirked. "That, my dear, is my little secret."

"Shut up!" Liv playfully backhanded his chest.

"I'm just playing," he said, laughing. "It's the Codex. I found it. It's pretty cool, right?"

"And a Codex is?"

"In this case, a book that's been passed down for generations. My uncle had it stashed away. I thought it might be a family tree kinda thing, but it contains handwritten writings from different people all over the world. They describe…certain characteristics."

"It sounds like a diary…and scary."

"It's a detailed account of people who have special abilities…"

"Like you…" Liv examined the cover, her fingers tracing the intricate indentations. "This is old-school," she noted, pointing to the quill etched into the leather, stretching from top to bottom. Her fingertips glided over the feather, feeling the delicate craftsmanship. She noticed a foreign inscription alongside the quill's shaft. "What does it say?"

"It's latin. *Scribere Cor Tuum*. It means 'Write with your heart.'"

"And what are you going to write in it, Mr. Moreno?"

Abraham drew out a pen from the right-hand pocket of his shorts much like a sword unsheathed. "You should know. For starters…I never-"

Liv interrupted him before he could finish his sentence. "Give up hope."

LXIV   PROGENY

This time, Abraham sat in the passenger seat as the sunset descended on Concepcion Park. Though he had always cherished its majestic view, it struck him differently now, with the news of a life at stake. His stomach twisted into a thousand knots, and even the beloved orange sun dipping below the horizon couldn't cheer him up. Still, he couldn't help but question the validity of such a predicament.

"The doctor says if we're going to do it, we have to do it now..." Avril said.

Abraham exhaled, feeling the weight of the world back on his shoulders. *Every time I feel like I'm one step ahead, I end up taking two steps back...*

"Abraham?" Avril's voice teetered. Wide-eyed, she stared at the side of his face, her trembling lips desperate for an answer.

"What is that?" Abraham asked, pointing to the bump on top of her wrist.

"It's been there for a couple of months, and it keeps getting bigger."

Abraham gave it a look over. "Can I try something?"

"What are you going to do?" she asked, her eyes growing wide. The circumstances had already put her on edge.

"Just let me see it."

The small bump protruded from the top of her wrist, devoid of any redness or discoloration. He placed his hand over it and closed his eyes, feeling the energy pulsate between his hand and her wrist. While he had absorbed an array of energies before, this one possessed a malignant property. Through his third eye, he witnessed the transference of energy as it flowed from the bump into his hand. Avril remained silent as he worked. Within two minutes, he completed the procedure and opened his eyes, signaling its completion. "It should go away in a couple of days," he assured her.

"The doctor told me it might not go away anytime soon, and if it doesn't, it could be cancerous."

"Just check it in a couple of days. Trust me."

Avril nodded. Trusting him was all she could do at this point. "I'm three months. If I need to schedule an appointment, you need to let me know now."

"I don't know, Avril. I don't know. How could this happen again? I used a condom this time. Are you sure it's mine?"

"Abraham, I haven't been with anybody else!"

This can't be happening. What the fuck! I can't take a life again.

Abraham searched the skies. Words escaped him, but his thoughts ran amuck. "I told you that this was over, remember?"

"I remember, but this was unexpected. I didn't plan for this to happen." Paleness covered her face, making her freckles more evident than ever. Faint red sprinkles spread across her cheeks and nose.

Why, God? I'm trying so hard to be good again and then you drop this on me...I don't know what the fuck I'm doing. I don't know how to be a father. All I know, is what not to be...and that's not good enough. I don't wanna fuck this up.

As the sun made its way to the other side of the world, leaving San Antonio in dusk, Abraham turned to Avril. "Not this time. Not again."

Avril nodded, though he couldn't discern if she felt relieved or frightened by his response. He opened the car door and leaned over to the side. Chunks splattered onto the pavement, staining the yellow parking line. Steam rose from the brown discharge. The burger he had earlier didn't taste so good on its way back out.

"Are you okay?" Avril asked.

"It's the energy transfer…sometimes I get a little bit of side effects. I'll be alright. I'm used to it. It'll wear off by the morning. Take me home before I black out. We'll talk tomorrow," he said.

LXV   THOUSAND YEAR CHAINS

The wooden bench creaked under the weight of a 167-pound apparition. Abraham had grown accustomed to the dream world, even becoming skilled at battling within its realm.

The darkened room triggered memories of a life he struggled to escape. A bright light from the adjacent room seeped through the crack beneath the door. Sitting upright against the cold brick wall, Abraham couldn't help but expect a more dramatic backdrop for his old nemesis.

The jail cell housed a bloodied and battered doppelganger.

"Welcome back, old friend," the grizzled voice sounded noticeably aged since their last encounter. The stagnant cell enveloped its occupant in darkness. The doppelganger occupied a chair across from Abraham, their interaction separated by black bars.

"No, this is my choice. You have no power. You think you know what I'm going to do, but you don't. I'm not going to take her life. I'll see this through, even if it kills me. I'll sacrifice everything if I have to, but you're not going get me to take a life. Not this time."

"Oh, you thought about it, alright. That's why you couldn't give her a straight answer. Avril might just decide to take matters into her own hands."

"She won't."

A faint snicker echoed within the cell. The doppelganger spoke with a weary voice. "There will always be new threats…distractions… tribulations. The earthly realm is my playground. One day, you're going to slip…and I'll be there. You can't keep me here forever." Chains draped over him in a suffocating pattern as he remained glued to a silver steel chair. His black jumpsuit blended into the background.

"What I did in darkness, God will use for good. You're the one in bondage now…" Abraham declared confidently to the tormentor who had beaten him down for so long. "…and you're the one who will be chained for a thousand years…"

LXVI

THE PROPHESIED DAUGHTER

The last time he walked out of Cristian's Tacos, he had sworn never to return. Fate had a peculiar way of coming full circle.

"You're early. That's a first," Abraham remarked, settling into the booth opposite Avril.

"You said seven thirty…and I'm hungry. Either I'll have to get used to eating more or, this is the last supper." Avril's attempt at alleviating the situation with a joke fell flat. Beads of sweat glistened on her nose and under her eyes.

"That's how you know something's wrong…when you show up early," he replied. "Let me see your wrist."

Avril rested her arm on the table. "The bump is gone."

"I told you it would go away."

"How did you do that? It had been there for months. You touch it once, and it disappears."

"Mind over matter, I guess."

The distraction did little to lessen Avril's concern about the life-altering situation. "Well, what are we going to do?"

"Do you know why I wanted to come to Cristian's Tacos today?"

"It's one of your favorites. I remember that much."

"Not after *that* day. I was sitting here and all I could think about was…what the hell are we doing? I went back and forth, and I felt so fuckin' guilty. We never gave Athena a chance…" Abraham's voice trailed off as he traveled back in time, pausing to compose himself before the tears overwhelmed him.

"Athena?" Avril asked.

"Our daughter."

"You named her?"

"Yes, I did. I knew she was a girl…I could feel it. I always knew my firstborn would be a girl. And she's a girl too." Abraham pointed to Avril's stomach. "The only thing I can tell you…is that I won't do what we did last time." Abraham reached for his sunglasses tucked away in his shirt pocket and placed them over his eyes. A tear escaped from underneath the lens. "I can't take a life…to correct my own."

The waitress appeared at the booth with her pen and pad ready. Abraham brushed away a tear from beneath his sunglasses before she could take their order.

"Hola! I'm Esperanza, and I'll be your waitress today. What would you like to drink?" she asked.

She took my order last time…what are the chances of her waiting on me again when I have another precious life in my hands? This time it's going to be different. This time…I don't have a choice.

Esperanza…hope…

LXVII CONFESSIONS

Liv darted out of the house, her senses finely tuned to his presence, and the unmistakable roar of the BMW reached her ears as she detected it two blocks away. A smile stretched from ear to ear as her face lit up at the sight of him, eager for another evening of heartfelt conversations about life, God, and their future together. She gave him a wave as she flung the car door wide open as it came to a stop.

"Hey! Aren't you a sight for sore eyes," Liv exclaimed, hopping into the passenger seat, ready to claim her throne. "Queen of the Beam," she chuckled, leaning in for a kiss. Abraham turned slightly, his lips barely grazing hers.

Returning his gaze to the windshield, he held his original position, staring straight ahead as far as the eye could see.

I don't want to lose her again.

Years ago, he confided in her before the Darkness took hold of him. Their conversations on this very street, in the same parking spot, filled with hope and goodness. But now, confessions of a shattered future loomed over them.

The Darkness was right…

It would never let him go.

I promised her I'd never hurt her again...

A rush of guilt washed over him, etching lines of anguish on his face. His heart shattered upon the sudden realization that he could never give her what she truly wanted: a life with him, free of any past engagements. The weight of his broken promises pressed down on him.

Liv sensed a shift in the atmosphere. It was unusual for him not to greet her upon her entrance. Just three nights ago, his smile had radiated the familiar light she'd known him for. The man before her now was starkly different. A frown creased her brow as she observed his trembling knee, a tremor distinct from his usual restless energy, to which she diagnosed as ADHD.

Amidst the sporadic movements, the wrenching in his gut, and the shattering of his heart, the task at hand was more than he could bear.

The arduous confession of betrayal.

Memories of confessing his sins to Father Frank when he was eleven flashed through his mind.

Reconciliation is what they called it...

The confessional room at St. Leo's housed his deepest, darkest sins, the remnants of childish mischief long gone. In their place were debaucheries that were no secret to the world. Unlike Father Frank, who remained on neutral ground, the confession to his soulmate was a time bomb strapped to both their hearts.

I failed her...

He had envisioned a life of success within the community, always striving to do things the right way, giving to those in need, and never causing harm. He even imagined coming home to a loving family. His accomplishments, despite his young age, were noteworthy, and he aspired to make world-changing contributions. Even death could not deter him. But despite his abilities and untapped potential, he couldn't escape the truth.

"Baby! What's wrong?" she said, playfully shaking his arm, trying to lift him from his melancholy. "Is it your grandma?"

"No," he said.

"Is it Margie?"

"No."

"Well, then what is it?" Concern filled her voice as she placed her hand on the back of his neck. But unlike the night before, her touch had no effect. "Talk to me…" Urgency spilled from her lips.

He glanced across the street at the vacant house, struggling to find the right words. The once familiar ritual of parking and conversing in front of her house had taken a turn for the worse. The visit now loomed over him like an impending thunderstorm.

"I can't do this anymore…" he finally confessed. He looked to his hands, tightly clasping them together.

"Okay, can't do what? Can't do *us*?" She turned her body to face him, her hand gliding against the back of his neck.

Abraham nodded slowly, his eyes wandering as he could only manage a peripheral view of her restlessness. Tears cascaded down his cheeks as he cradled his face with the palms of his hands. "I can't do this anymore." Only muffled words escaped his mouth. He groaned in agony, his torso jerking uncontrollably. Never had a single event caused such catastrophic heartbreak. All he had ever wanted was to be with her, forever, and now his chances of having a life with her were gone.

You have to tell her the truth…

Liv leaned over the console, resting her head on his shoulder. Physical closeness had always been a reliable way to restore his energy, and she had no reason to think it wouldn't work this time.

"Yes…we can do this. It's just me and you. You came back to me. I can see the man that I fell in love with. He's always been in there." She rubbed his arm, employing her calming techniques to their full effect. "We got this. It's just me and you."

Abraham moved his hands slightly, just enough for him to speak, but he kept his face hidden. "What about my daughter?" The knot in his throat distorted his words into a distressful slur.

Liv jerked back. "Huh? What are you talking about?" Wrinkles formed between her eyes, her head tilting slightly in confusion.

"You said if Avril and I ever happened, you'd leave." He sobbed his words onto her, his mouth dripping with the disappointment of breaking her heart.

"Okay…and?" Liv questioned his revelation, but as soon as the words left her mouth, she realized her greatest nightmare was coming true. "She's pregnant?"

Abraham groaned as tears gushed down his face.

Liv gently nudged his right hand with her left, attempting to clasp them together. "It's okay, baby, we'll make it work. Just don't leave me. We'll be okay." Her soft voice rendered the sentiment all the more heartbreaking, catching him off guard. Her maternal instincts kicked into overdrive. "We'll be okay. You had *hope* for us, right?"

Guilt swarmed him from head to toe. In his desperation, he wanted to believe Liv and trust her words. His gut churned into a million knots, and a flood of tears leaked down his cheeks. Her offer sounded appealing, but his heart and soul fought for what was truly best.

"Baby, it'll be alright," she said.

He sniffled as mucus poured out of both nostrils. Amidst his tearful eyes, he could only muster out a few words. "I can't do this anymore."

LXVIII OVERCOME THE WORLD

The scent of booze emanated from his breath as he exhaled. The whiskey sprite concoction Bartender Danielle was famous for amplified the molten manifestation of his anger. After consuming seven libations at On the Rocks Pub, he found himself heading towards the heart of downtown—the place where he and Liv had shared countless moments of happiness, peace, and life-changing conversations.

He knew better than to enter such an emotionally charged environment being spiritually unarmed, but it was the intensity of emotions that dominated the after-hours scene.

"Fuck you! Fuck everybody!" he yelled into the night sky, his slurred speech barely intelligible. The outburst sounded more like "luck you" and "luck everybody," but there wasn't a soul close enough to hear him.

I was fuckin' reckless...

Carelessness had caught up to him.

...and now it's the lives of innocent people I'm altering...unborn lives.

The Doppelganger he was certain he'd killed. But something else was emerging. A mutated darkness. One that was adapting to his new fighting skills.

Abraham limped his way across the street, relying on the store barriers of La Villita for stability. His footsteps veered to the left and right, unsteady. He extended his right arm, clutching a beer bottle.

"Cheers!" he said, pretending that someone was clinking their bottle against his in a congratulatory cheer for not falling to the ground.

The HemisFair Park sign came into view, triggering a flood of memories. As he stared at the letters in the archway, countless moments overwhelmed him. He had experienced various shades of happiness there with Liv.

Liv...

He pictured her smile, her laugh, her beautiful brown eyes gazing at him. He doubted there would ever be another moment with her in HemisFair again.

Choices...

Returning to his sinful, debauchery-filled ways crossed his mind. He entered the park, and with it, a temptation of a new, darker volatile version of himself. With each step he took, placing his foot onto Alamo Street, he treated the white crosswalk lines like a tightrope, focusing intently on his path as it led him deeper into the park. It reminded him of the final challenge Indiana Jones faced in the Last Crusade.

As his glazed eyes admired the Tower of Americas, he paused, taking a moment to collect himself.

First challenge complete...

A sense of darkness awaited him in the park, and he felt its presence. Its gravitational forces pulled him towards the heart of downtown, fueled by his reckless courage that sought out a battle he wasn't prepared for. While he aspired to be like the courageous heroes of his childhood

- Indiana Jones, Superman, and the Justice League, he had come to realize as of late, a painful truth he was now willing to admit.

I'm nothing like them...

Their values, he struggled to emulate.

I'm no hero. They fight monsters, but they never become one. They never went bad...I fought a monster, and I became one...that's the difference.

As he walked along the red brick path he had traversed many times before, he couldn't ignore the ghosts of his past, especially at 3:30 a.m. Shadows jumped out at him from behind the bushes and art pieces lining the path, as if taunting him.

I used to be a hero...tonight we can pretend that I am...this is the test of strength...and character. There are always three challenges. Always.

Crows cawed from the oak trees above, swooping down near him. Their attempts to instill fear only caused him to lose his balance. If it weren't for the alcohol, he would have plowed through the swarm. The crows darted in a calculated dive-bombing pattern, but their attack proved futile.

"That second challenge was weak! You're gonna have to do better than that to get me. I don't fear you...and I still held my beer!" He yelled defiantly at the trees above.

Abraham reached the water gardens that encircled the base of the Tower. Even in his drunken state, he scanned the area. A sign near the water garden read: "No Alcohol Beyond this Point." He grinned, looking at his beer. Compared to what he had done over the past two years, it was a minor transgression.

He stood in silence, waiting for the next challenge as he took a sip of his Dos XX. "C'mon motherfucker...whaddya got?" he shouted at the night sky.

Abraham glanced to his left, fixated on the grassy area on the edge of the walkway that sloped upwards at a forty-five-degree angle. The hill ascended forty feet, leading to a platform connected to the convention center at its end.

Jutting out from the hillside, rested a blue and white ceramic bench. It was where Abraham and Liv sat together many times and a place where their bond had been forged through frequent visits and profound conversations, even the ones regarding life and death.

✟

"Baby..." Liv stared at the side of his face, her fingers caressing his chubby cheek. "I'm glad you made it back home. Thank you for taking me to Hawaii and getting me this ring. I love it! Oh, and this one too!" she laughed.

"Wow, I guess the Hawaiian marriage one is clearly in second place," Abraham smirked.

"Shut up! You know I fell in love with the black coral diamond one first!"

"Duly noted. But this Hawaiian one is legit. Contractually binding, if you will," he laughed, attempting to make a point, but the Hawaiian ring stood no chance against the black coral counterpart that would never lose its first-place ranking.

"Well, if it's any consolation, Mr. Moreno, I still love you and I would love to start a family with you. Of course, I want two girls and I know what I'm going to name them."

"Hold on...what *you* are going to name them or what *we* are going to name them?"

Abraham raised an eyebrow.

"You heard me."

"What if we have a boy?"

"Ew, no! We are *not* having any boys. Period. Boys are just...ew!"

"Well, my sweet, unbeknownst to you, you don't really have a say or control over the baby's gender. Sorry to disappoint you," Abraham snickered.

"No, we're having two girls, Lily and Leilani, and that's that."

"Yes, your majesty."

Liv playfully swung her hand, lightly hitting his chest.

"What was that for?" he hollered, feigning offense.

"For disagreeing with your queen," Liv grinned.

"I apologize, my queen...I'm just a lowly peasant. It will never happen again," he said, and they shared a laugh at what he often referred to as his "afterschool special" acting.

Liv admired the pools below. "I love these water gardens. It just feels so refreshing."

"Water signs..." Abraham exhaled a heavily exaggerated sigh.

"I know, I know...your Kryptonite."

"Liv, little do you know you can reach out and break me anytime you want. You're dangerous. I guess it makes sense that a water sign has my heart. Let's just say, if we don't get married and have a family together, then it would break me apart. You know what I mean?"

"I do," she said.

Abraham grabbed her hand, clasping it in his. He pulled her hand to his lips and kissed the back of it. He smiled at her, and she rested her head on his chest as they admired the water together.

He had been different back then. He wanted to believe that he knew what love was, instead of the anger that consumed him. War had been his constant companion for far too long, and finding peace felt like navigating a treacherous minefield - cautiously advancing a few inches only to be blown back several feet with a single misstep.

Water splashed into the pools from Stonehenge-like pillars overhead. The calming sound of it relaxed him for a moment.

"4:09…witching hour is over, bitches!" Abraham taunted the Darkness and its minions.

He looked straight up at the Tower of Americas. The lights encircling the crown created an illusion of a flying saucer. His eyes lifted further, up to the stars. He could stare at them for hours, a reminder that God was bigger than any problem in the world.

In the solace of the stars, only One presence spoke to him. In past nights, he quoted a lyric from a song that reflected the relationship he had forged with the Light.

My best friend was born in a manger.

Just as it had been over two thousand years ago, their relationship had come full circle.

God and Abraham.

The Lord, the confidant of a thousand generations, never ceased to inspire questions.

Abraham began his drunken version of a methodical, emotionally charged search for answers. "Why did you give me this? What are you teaching me? How to fail? I know I shouldn't question Your plan. I have this, this urge to just…fuck shit up…and I don't wanna feel this anymore…I wanna break free from this darkness…free me…" The words slurred from his mouth, tears filling his eyes. "Please…"

Abraham stumbled to the pool's edge. The combination of liquor and beer mixed for the perfect abomination. Had there been onlookers in the park, they would have believed he had lost his mind, yelling at the sky.

There wasn't a soul in sight. Not one.

Conversing with the stars made him feel the loneliest he had ever been. One tiny speck in the vast universe, and the feeling spawned a terrible void.

Emptiness.
Nothingness.
Darkness.

"I love Liv...I really do. I never wanted it to be like this...I don't want to hurt people anymore..."

Thoughts of what could have been and what could never be overwhelmed him. Rage swelled within his gut. The reemergence of anger meant the Darkness was near.

"Don't go back to your old self...fight him hard!" In desperation, he coached himself, but vengeful emotions bristled around him.

The thoughts crept in like a thief. The struggle between tranquility and anger had consumed his heart. All his past wrongdoings came alive.

"You can move on from this...do better...it's you versus you!"

The thought of abandonment triggered the trauma of being left as a four-year-old.

"How can I be the man I'm supposed to be if I bail out on her now? I can't leave my daughter in her womb...what would that make me? I can't leave them..."

His words became more articulated, but his voice trembled. Releasing an honest confession shattered the last remnants of his pride.

"I promised You that I would never take a life again. I can't. I won't. So, I'm asking you...help me find a way through this. I'm not ready to be a father. I don't know what I'm doing. I don't know how to do this on my own...but it's the right thing to do. Show me the way..."

Abraham gazed at the night sky, waiting for God to respond. "C'mon, God, don't let me down..."

The internal conflict ripped him in two.

"Where are you? I can't hear you! Show me the way!" he yelled. "I've done everything You asked, and I still can't get above water!"

The booze hampered the rewiring process and although Kay advised him not to drink, he did it anyway, knowing the anticipated outcome. Defeat.

Fury encapsulated his flesh. His mind had been overtaken by thoughts of the wreckage he left behind and the possibility of failing to become a good father.

"Where the hell are You!?" Abraham hurled the green Dos XX bottle into the sky. It soared upwards before crashing against an archway hovering over the pool of water. The shattered pieces disappeared beneath the surface.

"Why have You forsaken me?" Tears showered down his chubby cheeks. He glanced back up at the sky, his eyes wandering the heavens. "Where are You? You promised…you'd never leave…"

Abraham, I will never leave you.

"She's all I needed…why would you take her away?"

My ways and My thoughts are higher than yours. All things work together for your good.

"Is that really You? Or am I just imagining things?"

Abraham stared deep into the night sky, listening, waiting, hoping the voice would speak to him again.

In the distance, a star moved from right to left.

A meteor?

Its erratic movements suggested otherwise.

Satellite? Moving all crazy? Is that a sign?

The object changed direction, descending vertically. It zoomed closer, seemingly zeroing in on him.

"What are you sending me, God?"

The object came into view, revealing enormous wings flapping with vigor.

"An angel…"

Abraham stood his ground, eagerly awaiting the miracle he had sought for so long. A mysterious being descended towards him, but it was far from what he expected. With its bizarre features and menacing glare, the winged creature made him take a few cautious steps backward, as he wiped his blurry eyes. As the winged anomaly drew closer, he recognized the monstrosity, causing him to wipe his eyes again in disbelief. It seemed to be a supernatural manifestation. To his horror, it was no angel.

The being possessed a distorted humanoid face, with leathery and wrinkled skin, and an open mouth that gave it a perpetual scream-like appearance, yet without any sound escaping.

"What the fuck..." he whispered, realizing that the liquor had muddled his senses, leaving him unable to comprehend the madness.

The creature continued its descent, and as it approached, the hair on the back of Abraham's arms stood on end. It was the creature Margie spoke of—the legendary winged owl with human features she claimed to have seen once. Its face resembled that of an old woman, while its talons were sharp enough to tear through flesh.

The Lechuza.

Above him, in the oak tree, the hoot of an owl spooked him, as the leaves rustled behind him. In the distance, a low cooing sound grew louder, capturing his attention. He turned in every direction, trying to locate the source of the baby's cry, stumbling slightly. When he refocused on the approaching bird of prey, the creature reduced its speed, flapping its massive wings above the pool. With a backward tilt, it raised its wings and its long, curved black talons gripped the pool's edge, resembling the razor-sharp claws of a velociraptor.

Abraham instinctively backed away from the pool's edge, frozen at the sight of this colossal creature. Even in his drunken state, he estimated its height to be at least five and a half feet. Its grayish face appeared distorted, while its wide-open mouth exposed corroded brown teeth. The stringy hair gave the creature a zombie-like appearance, and its glossy black eyes lacked any trace of white.

He backed away slowly, pondering the possibility of making a run for it. It was clear that the creature had come for him, and it was certainly not an agent of God.

He carefully maneuvered his foot, preparing for a quick turn and sprint, but as he did, the owl woman swung her wing at him. Though he anticipated the strike, he couldn't move fast enough to deflect it, feeling the stinging serrations in her feathers as they injected into his back. He stumbled headfirst into the exposed roots of the nearby oak tree, tasting the chalky dirt as it entered his mouth.

He turned over, and remained down for a moment, realizing he was too intoxicated to mount a serious fight.

I'm no match for this thing.

He couldn't run fast enough in his current condition, and facing the creature head-on was out of the question, even if he were sober. He scrambled away from her, using his palms and heels like a scurrying spider.

The Lechuza approached, raising a talon, ready to sink it into his chest. Abraham rolled over, evading the strike by spinning his body like a tire peeling out. He came to a stop on the cold concrete walkway beside the pool. In one swift motion, he propped himself up on one knee, attempting to sprint away. But before he could escape, the creature flanked him. The Lechuza flapped her wings and hovered, gliding toward him with her talons aimed. Her right talon tore through his shirt and into his flesh, leaving a seven-inch-long gash on his chest.

The strike knocked him off balance, and Abraham yelled out in agony as he fell backward into the pool. The Lechuza pursued him, flapping its wings above the water. The water blurred his vision, but he could make out the creature's movements.

Water rushed into his nostrils and mouth. The sensation spooked him every time. Chlorine-filled water flooded his lungs.

Water...

It was the perfect storm.
Kryptonite water.
A physical manifestation of evil.
No way out.

She dipped her talons into the pool, gripping his body and piercing his skin. The creature's strength dragged him deeper. Writhing in pain, he sent a flurry of bubbles rushing to the surface. The more he struggled to break free, the deeper her talons dug into him. The razor-sharp claws ripped into his side and lower back. Water continued to rush into his lungs, and his arms and legs thrashed in desperation. As he hit the pool's bottom, he grasped the floor, desperately hoping to find something to break free from the creature.

His frantic movements only caused the creature to press him harder and faster into the lagoon. One set of talons scraped against his rib cage.

He couldn't escape. Not this time. All the elements were against him. The harder he fought, the more ground he lost.

Unable to breathe and unable to break free, it was time to let go of the fight.

This is it...

Let go...

Let fate decide.

His hand grazed a peculiar object on the pool floor. His fingers found a smooth, sturdy cylindrical piece. The handle curved out to a thicker upper portion. He pictured the hilt of a magical sword lying at the bottom of the pool—a sword that would grant him the necessary power to slay the "mystical dragon" and emerge victorious from the water. He brought it within his line of sight. The emerald-green hilt had sharp, jagged edges. The bottleneck of the Dox XX survived the sacrificial destruction.

The Lechuza thrust Abraham above the pool, only to forcefully plunge him back into the water, leaving him gasping for a millisecond of air.

With the bottle neck in hand, he aimed for the creature's leg and rapidly stabbed at it. The water slowed his thrust, but he flung the weapon wildly.

The Lechuza momentarily lifted him above the water, countering his attempts to stab her. As soon as his arm was free from the water, Abraham softly cocked it back, aiming just above her talon.

The creature clasped harder onto him, and he could feel its claws dig deeper into his flesh.

After repeated stabs, the bottle neck struck the slender leg, slicing a piece of it. The Lechuza wailed in pain, its high-pitched shriek echoed throughout the park.

Abraham swung the green blade side to side, cutting the creature once more. The sharp edge of the bottle pierced the injured spot, severing her leg. The Lechuza squawked in agony, causing nearby crows to scatter into the sky.

Her talons released him, and his body splashed into the water. Ripples washed over the pool's bank.

As Abraham dipped below the surface, he watched the Lechuza fly off into the distance, despite the blurry view from the water.

Abraham drifted deeper into the abyss.

Death didn't scare him. At least not anymore.

Things are always meant to end…it is the way of life…

Peace settled over him, but not before a grizzled voice moaned in his ear. It was the voice that had haunted him every night—a voice he had learned to fight against and ultimately defeat.

I told you I would take away all that you love. Liv will never be with you. The Darkness snickered. Its deep voice burned the painful revelation into his psyche. *I will pound you until you break. I will hound you until you have no choice but to come back. You have to give up her life in order to live the life you dreamed…and only I can make that happen for you. Your progeny must die, so that you can live…*

Abraham shut his eyes as hard as he could. The crow's feet on the edges of his eyes stretched to his temples. He hoped that by doing so, he could shut out the growling voice. It was not the last voice he wanted to hear as he descended to the concrete floor.

Not my will…but Yours be done, Lord.

His third eye caught a glimpse of the Darkness writhing where Abraham had left him. The creature's chest remained chained the cell to the chair, but it had broken free from the chains around its feined

"*Ahhhhhh!*" the Darkness yelled; frustration evident in its voice as continued struggling to free itself. *I own this world…all these souls are mine!*

Those are lies…the world is already taken, but not by you…He who has risen, has already overcome the world…

Abraham meandered through his thoughts and dreams, but consciousness was fading fast. He sank deeper.

This is the only way…

His body hit the bottom of the pool.

My God, only You have overcome the world…

Abraham floated amongst the clouds. He envisioned what peace would look like. A gentle calmness washed over him as he replayed memories of Margie and Kay. He pictured them in their distinctive attire, speaking to him words of scripture.

Margie went first…

Her soft voice he could never forget, especially when he needed counsel.

Always remember that evil can never hurt you. Here it is in the Bible…Genesis 50:20…You intended to harm me, but God intended it all for good. He brought me to this position so I could save the lives of many people…

And then Kay spoke to him…

Her calmness always soothed him, even when was already at peace.

Oh, Abe. You forget...2 Corinthians 10:4...We fight with weapons that are different from those the world uses. Our weapons have power from God. These weapons can destroy the enemy's strong places.

And then Liv thrust out her words choked with tears....
I want you to always be in love with me...always...

His limbs settled against the concrete. *And I always will...I love you...no matter...*

His thoughts faded. In moments of consciousness, his mind had perpetually raced through countless thoughts, never finding solace.

The elements had beaten him.

The battle had taken his energy, and the water had taken his breath. His brain, finally forced to shut down. Memories became shrouded in the darkness of life's curtain call.

He could finally rest now.

LXIX

THE LAZARUS EFFECT

Just before dawn, darkness blanketed the park, casting a veil of shadows over the surroundings. The crisp sound of orange and brown leaves being crushed beneath the congregants' feet sent the squirrels scurrying away in surprise.

As the churchgoers arrived, preparing for a 6 a.m. mass, a small group veered towards the water gardens. The submerged lights bathed the pool in a serene, chlorine-blue glow, revealing a solitary figure nestled within.

"There's something in the water," a woman from the group exclaimed, her eyes fixed on the figure at the pool's bottom.

"It's a body!" a young man shouted; his voice filled with urgency. Without hesitation, he leaped into the pool. "Hurry, we have to get him out!"

Several members rushed into the pool behind him, their splashes mingling as they converged on the lifeless body. Reaching down, they hoisted the young man from the depths and carried him to the water's edge. They passed him to a man and a woman who stood by, waiting to resuscitate.

With great care, they laid the young man's body upon the stone walkway. An older woman among them checked for signs of life. "I can't feel anything," she murmured.

A short Hispanic woman leaned over and began administering CPR. She interlocked her hands for chest compressions, pausing intermittently to listen for any response from his chest. Placing her ear close to his mouth, she searched for any faint breath escaping his lips.

"Let's gather and pray for him," an elderly gentleman suggested to the group. They formed a circle around the young man, their hands joining together. Once their hands were clasped, the distinguished older gentleman, dressed in a navy-blue suit, led them in prayer.

"Lord, we humbly come before You today, seeking Your grace and healing for this young man," his voice resonated with reverence. "We entrust him into Your care, knowing that Your will, guides our paths and that Your perfect plans shall be unveiled on behalf of this young soul lying before us. Grant him blessings from this moment onward as we fervently pray and hold hope for the miracle of another day of life. You are never early and You are never late, and just as You raised Lazarus from the dead, we beseech You to resurrect this young man. In the name of Your Son, Jesus Christ, we pray. Amen."

LXX BREAKING BAD

I'm tired of fighting...

Fatigue lingered. Coming back from the dead had been exhausting. Recovery from the previous week's ordeal was like being in a state of suspended animation.

Time seemed to stand still.

The churchgoers insisted that Abraham had been mugged and beaten up in HemisFair Park. All he had were vague memories of an encounter with a creature believed to be a ghost tale.

The fight that never happened...

Nevertheless, the congregation saved his life. Little did they know, they had arrived just in time to rescue a man at the height of a spiritual war.

He was surprised by how well his lungs still functioned, considering he had now faced near drowning on two separate occasions. Scratches were visible on his chest and sides, but they were not as severe as he had initially thought.

God works all things together for our good...

"What now?" he asked.

God had been with him. Especially during whatever he battled that night.

I'm lucky to be alive...the devil's greatest deception is distraction. There's a mission in this life, and I need to finish writing the book...maybe, that's why God kept me alive...to fulfill the purpose...

The events that had led him to the park in the first place now resonated differently since coming back to life.

I love you, Liv. I'm sorry...

The anger subsided. He welcomed the calmness and the perspective that comes with a new life, but not without some doubts.

What if I can't be the man I need to be?

He needed the comfort of a sanctuary. A place to mend.

Abraham hopped into the Stealth M3. Spiritual allies were in short supply, but the advice from a member of his home congregation might speed up the healing process.

He noticed Gloria in her front yard and slowed the M3 to check on her. She peered into the driver's side window and handed Abraham an envelope. Glancing at the name written on it, he recognized the name his father had called him since he was a toddler.

Aba.

"When did he give it to you?" Abraham asked, placing the letter on the passenger seat.

"The same night he never came back," she replied.

Abraham nodded his head. "Do you know what it says?" He almost didn't have the nerve to open it, but it intrigued him. *What could he have possibly written to me for the final time?*

"Nope...he didn't tell me, and I didn't open it."

He didn't have the heart to press for more information. "I'll be back later."

"Where are you going?" Gloria's curiosity emerged. She was never one to pry. Perhaps it was because she was lonely, or maybe her concern outweighed all else. He decided to give her the usual vague answer which always worked to discontinue a prolonged interrogation.

"To see an old friend."

"Be careful."

"Sorry I'm late." Father Richard apologized as he slid into the fourth pew from the altar.

The last time Abraham sought counsel from Father Richard was before the fateful encounter in Los Angeles, and now, the residual effects from that event brought him back. He settled into his usual spot in the fifth row, and it instantly felt like home again.

Father Richard glanced at Abraham studying him discreetly. "You sure have some dark in you…that's obvious." Abraham was certain Father Richard had seen the look of darkness in someone a thousand times.

"You need to forgive yourself. God knew all the stupid things you would do…and He still loves you. He has forgiven you, and if He has forgiven you, you have the power to forgive yourself. You have the power to let go of anything that no longer serves you."

"But what if I can't?" Abraham questioned.

"You can. Trust me," Father Richard spoke with confidence. "You need to let go of your doubts. You *can* overcome the darkness. Believing fully…is the only thing that holds you back. You are a powerful servant of the Lord. Remember who you are and whose you are. You are a child of the Most High King."

Abraham stared at his clasped hands, deep in thought. "I'd forgotten, but I'm beginning to remember. The darkness did its work well…to the point that I didn't even recognize myself anymore. I'm not as strong as I once was, but I am stronger than I was a year ago…even two years ago. It's coming together. Slowly, but it's coming back."

"See," Father Richard raised both hands in triumph. "You *are* coming back. That's all that matters. You know all too well about coming back. Didn't you write about that when you were younger? A St. Leo's middle school standout if I recall?"

Both men laughed at the allegation.

"Now, you know that's far from the truth!" Abraham said. "Actually, I think I figured out what I need to do in this life. I feel that God grants us gifts, and we have to use them for His glory…to make a difference…to change the world. This spiritual battle has been eye opening, and it blinded me to who I really am, and what I'm meant to do."

"The light at the end of the tunnel is what you're looking for?"

"Yes."

"Abraham, you're looking for something that's already inside you. You *are* the light. Your spirit represents God's Kingdom, and nothing, and I mean nothing, can ever beat that! Ever!"

"And what if I can't be who God really intended me to be? I mean, I've had my doubts lately, and sometimes it's hard to see a way out."

"Let me ask you something," Father Richard began. "Do you lie awake at night, tormented by the feeling that you're not doing as much as you could be? That you're not fulfilling your purpose because you know deep down that you're destined for more?"

"Every single night," Abraham confessed.

"Then that's good! Because God is not finished with you yet! You need to surrender yourself to Him completely. This back-and-forth thing you got going on is not trusting God. Only when you go to Him in Praise, does He intervene in your circumstances with His power. You may have had wins, yes, but you need to give Him everything. Trust him, like you once did, and you'll find your way back. Don't worry, He'll give you everything you need, and He will provide when you need it. Just trust Him again. Fully!"

Abraham sped off towards the stop sign down the block.

It's okay to feel this way...to not be okay...to hurt...to be battered...to take heavy hits...

He'd lost something. Seven days ago, burdens and heartache had weighed him down. Now, he felt lighter, yet numb.

Have I gotten so used to carrying guilt? Pride? The unworthiness? The bondage of darkness?

Reflection had been a strength, especially in the face of adversity.

All this will pass. It won't be like this forever. Things fall apart, break away, pass on...only to come back again...stronger.

He fiddled with the radio dial. A song he hadn't heard in ages blared from one of the rock stations. Steely Dan played one of their classic tunes. The old rock band boomed in his car, just like it had in his father's.

"Reelin' in the years," he whispered to himself. The song triggered memories of recent losses.

Emotionally.

Spiritually.

Physically.

As a kid, he'd never truly listened to the lyrics before. For the first time, he paid close attention to the song. Each riff pieced together like a puzzle.

Your everlasting summer and you can see it fading fast
So you grab a piece of something that you think is gonna last
Well, you wouldn't even know a diamond if you held it in your hand
The things you think are precious I can't understand

I lost a lot this year. I was reckless. I let everything get out of hand. And now I hurt her severely…

> You've been telling me you're a genius since you were
> seventeen
> In all the time I've known you I still don't know what
> you mean
> The weekend at the college didn't turn out like you
> planned
> The things that pass for knowledge I can't understand

God, You sure showed me that my plans don't matter…they were altered on a whim. I can only hope the plan was to make me stronger…more knowledgeable…

> I've spent a lot of money and I've spent a lot of time
> The trip we made to Hollywood is etched upon my
> mind
> After all the things we've done and seen you find another
> man
> The things you think are useless I can't understand

I wasted so much and for what? I allowed the fight in Hollywood to alter my life. Liv will find another man one day…I'm gonna have to live with that…

> Are you reelin' in the years?
> Stowin' away the time
> Are you gatherin' up the tears?
> Have you had enough of mine
> Are you reelin' in the years?
> Stowin' away the time
> Are you gatherin' up the tears?
> Have you had enough of mine

Her thoughts swayed out of control. Liv lay sprawled out on the floor amidst tattered remnants of love letters from the past few years, crumbled and torn. Picture frames rested haphazardly, their shattered glass mingling with scratched photographs.

Liv glared at the picture of her and Abraham during happier times. The photo, taken at HemisFair Park, had been their go-to spot for romantic outings. She now despised his smile, and his beaming grin provoked a wave of nausea.

How could he do this to me?

A fountain of tears blurred her vision, leaving her eyes swollen and puffy. Countless hours of crying and vomiting had turned her left eye into a bloodshot mess. The silence of her room was deafening as she replayed the conversation in her head, trapped in an endless loop. Her gaze resembled that of a zombie, drained of all meaning and purpose. The life she had envisioned had been cruelly snatched away, and she refused to accept her fate.

"God, why would you do this to me? WHY? You took everything away from me! All I wanted was to be with him...to have our own kids, to build a family!" Liv screamed at the top of her lungs. Clenching her fists tightly, she pounded the hardwood floor. "Ahhh," she yelled. "I hate you! I hate you!"

Rolling over onto her side, she buried her face in her hands, consumed by thoughts of her shattered life. The soulmate that had promised her the world, was gone. He'd left her for another girl, one yet to be born. God had forsaken her, she believed. "I hate you!" Her body convulsed as tears streamed down her face.

Sadness and heartbreak collided, creating a medly of broken heartstrings. The emotions played in tandem, each taking turns to suffocate and wreak havoc on her spirit.

Liv rose to her feet, tearing through the pictures on the wall. Swinging her arms in a wild rage, she struck the air, imagining her opponent as the woman who had robbed her of her life, her dreams, and her great love. Her fist clipped the dangling ornament, a birthday gift from Abraham. Flames adorned one side of the circular trinket while the other half displayed a cool blue crescent moon against an orange-yellow backdrop. Together, both the sun and the moon shared one face. The ornament crashed into the mirror of her dresser, creating a spiderweb of cracks.

Liv tore the Hawaiian ring off her finger and flung it into the fractured mirror. With every fiber of her being, she screamed at the top of her lungs. "I HATE YOU!"

Bob cradled Charlie on the dirt patch in his backyard. He'd built a makeshift oasis amidst the grassy expanse. He had painstakingly crafted a dirt sea, transforming his yard into a semblance of a natural habitat for his cherished companion. Charlie's body lay on its side, as if peacefully slumbering. Though his eyes remained closed, Bob clung to him, unwilling to let go. Time was slipping away, and soon Charlie would drift into eternal slumber. Bob tightened his embrace, savoring every precious minute he had left to hold his friend.

Bob kept his promise to keep Charlie happy, reciprocating the love the loyal companion had given him, and as someone who experienced his own share of loss, Bob had made it his mission.

But now, the mission was done.

His arms enveloped Charlie's mane, and tears streamed down Bob's face unabated. He wept for hours, knowing that soon someone would discover them. Each anguished wail, punctuating the stillness of the air, was sure to bring attention, and it was the only way he would give him up after all these years—the animal being pried from his hands. Charlie could never fully embody his intended purpose, but he had fulfilled his own unique purpose. He gave Bob hope.

The gravesite had received a gift. A fresh tombstone, chiseled to perfection. Perhaps it was the illusion of the last remaining possession of the deceased that made it immaculate. Ray's tombstone was no exception.

Resting on the base of the headstone lay a branch from a mountain laurel tree, adorned with delicate seed pods. The intent of having the natural process take place is what Abraham hoped for, and maybe one day, Ray would have his favorite tree growing beside him.

Nestled beside the mountain laurel branch, an upright envelope leaned against the tombstone, supported by a smooth oval stone. Despite being weathered and stained with dirt, the envelope itself bore only slight creases from the rain. The name on it had smudged somewhat but remained legible.

Abraham didn't mind if Ray took his time reading it. After all, Ray had the luxury that everyone is granted one day.

Eternity.

✝

There was still some darkness left in him, but that's how it would always be.

He was human, and the Darkness made sure to remind him of that fact nor would it ever let him forget.

Counter the enemy...don't ever let him get the jump on you again.

Thinking in the dark had become second nature to him, but now he remembered what it felt like to think in the light.

In order for a prized stallion to reach its potential, it must be broken. Is that what you're doing to me, God? Breaking me, to better me?

Evening drives served as a stark reminder of his human vulnerabilities.

There's always going to be a dark side. I just have to make sure the light is stronger.

God's Word remained rooted in his soul.

Transform your mind.

The M3 Stealth sped down Probandt Street. His neighborhood, near the epicenter of downtown San Antonio, had always been his playground. The drive-bys, the hoodlums, the streetball, the drug dealers, the drunkards, the homeless, the overbearing neighbors, and the countless times he ran away were all a part of what made him who he was.

The good and the bad...

As he took a series of turns, he arrived back at his inner-city home, and an unexpected surprise awaited him. A radiant, silvery glow emanated from the driveway, and as far as premonitions go, he would take it as a win. Moonlight danced off the car, enhancing its brightness, reminiscent of its former glory. Davor must have brought the car back while he was at church. The man always returned the BMWs washed and gleaming.

The original BMW, M3 Steel, had returned home, and it brought the light with it.

6 months later

LXXI THE LETTER

June 2007

Abraham had lost.
He didn't mind losing to amateurs. The trip to Austin was never meant to be about winning.
He'd already won.

Instead, it was a tribute—an homage to the man who had introduced him to the world of darts. A man he knew loved him, even if he had a funny way of showing it.

As the sun's rays broke through the blinds, Abraham made it a ritual to bask in its energy every morning.

He lay in the hotel bed, his hands intertwined and resting upon his chest. Morning prayers had evolved into conversations.

> *Thank you, God, for everything…for all the good, the bad, the ugly and the indifferent. Thank you for guiding me and using the people in my life as instruments for Your Glory, and for bringing me back to the path I strayed from. Please place Your healing hands on me as I venture out into the world, again, in Jesus' name I pray. I love you, God. Amen.*

He crawled out of bed and sat upright for a few minutes. The letter Ray had written on the day of his death traveled with Abraham.

Glancing at the envelope peeking out of his backpack, he reached over and pulled it out. Opening the letter was the easy part. Reading the words written by his deceased father was another story. He took a deep breath and unfolded the paper.

Aba,

> *Responding to your last words is not something I can easily convey or express. It has become very complicated as I grow older, and because of that, my thoughts and feelings are seen with more clarity. Don't think for a second that I've forgotten to respond. I agree with 90% of what you said. I feel I could've done better spending more time with you, Abe. I was too harsh at times. I was so stupid to make you and Michelle sit on hot car seats in the Mustang. It kills me more so that you and Michelle couldn't or wouldn't say, "the seats are hot." How stupid could I be then. I think about these things and about the countless other horrible things I put you through. It hurts that I hurt you. I realize that now. There are times where I think about it quite often. I just want you to understand why things were the way they were back then. I couldn't tell you then because I didn't know. Never forget where you come from, even if it's not from a happy place. I love you, Dad.*

Teardrops splattered on the paper as he folded it and placed it in the envelope, tucking it into his backpack.

Conversations with his father were hard. They always ended in escalating tensions with no resolution. Perhaps writing to each other would have been the way to go. But it was too late for that now.

He spoke to the empty room, as if his words could reach his father's ears.

"I love you, Dad...you're always going to be my Dad. Always. I may not have come from a place of happiness with you, but all that matters...is that I'm happy today. I don't regret anything. I'm glad you made it to the light. That's all I ever wanted for you…I'm proud of you, Dad."

It took half a year, but better late than never…

Kay was right. Her sweet voice remained etched in his memory. "Death is not the end." He jumped off the bed, ready to start the day. A new life, yet to be born, waited for him in San Antonio.

I'll be a dad myself pretty soon…

He stretched his arms towards the ceiling, relishing the morning stretch. The transformation to the physical powerhouse he once was began six months prior. The knowledge of his progeny arriving sparked a new mission within him—to be better for her in every facet of life. Physically, he had shed ten pounds, transforming from flat to formidable once again.

Spiritually, he had reintroduced old rituals into his daily life. Reaching into his backpack, he pulled out the Jesus Daily book, using the ribbon bookmark to hold his place.

June 10.

Just as he began reading the verse of the day, his cell phone rang.
"Hello?" he answered.
"Abraham, my water broke!" Avril's voice echoed with urgency.
"What do you mean?"
"I mean my *water* broke!"
"Like, this is it?"
"Yes, hurry up and get over here!"
"I'm on my way!" He tossed the phone onto the bed and hurriedly packed his clothes into a suitcase.

Although the excitement of a newborn journey caught him by surprise, he couldn't deny his inner workings.

Mentally, he was a nervous wreck.

LXXII REBIRTH

Abraham hurried into the hospital room.

"Good, you're here!" Gloria exclaimed. "She's almost at ten centimeters…"

"How did you get here so fast?" Avril asked. "I talked to you forty-five minutes ago?"

"I booked it over here."

"Abraham, don't tell me you were speeding!"

"Nah, I didn't go over a hundred. I was pretty much at a hundred the whole way," he laughed.

"Aye, Abraham," Avril said.

"Dude! And if you were to get in a wreck? You need to stay alive for your daughter! Be careful, Abe! It's not just you anymore," Gloria scolded him.

"Too fast, too furious!" Abraham quipped.

"Abraham, please," Gloria shot him with a deadpan look, clearly unamused.

She was right. He hadn't fully grasped the weight of living for someone else. He had been reckless with his own life, but Gloria's words reminded him of the truth. Rewiring every part of his behavior needed to happen on the spot, which included speeding over the limit.

This dad thing is getting real...

The doctor rushed into the room to check on Avril. She assessed her progress. "Okay, it looks like we're ready!"

Avril grimaced and nodded in response.

Abraham observed the woman who would deliver his daughter. Her voice was gentle, and her blue-green eyes stood out against her blonde hair tied up in a bun. He glanced at her name tag. Glenda Rice, M.D.

"Are you the dad?" the doctor asked Abraham.

"Yes, I *am* the father!" Abraham announced, attempting a dramatic flourish like Maury Povich, but his ill attempt to settle his nerves with humor failed.

"Well, you've arrived just in time!" Dr. Rice seemed genuinely pleased that Abraham was present. Perhaps it was because most dads didn't show up, or maybe she was simply a kind person. Either way, his body and facial expressions froze. He acknowledged her with a slight smirk. The shock of his progeny's arrival caused him to go mute.

"I'll go get Mary!" Gloria said as she hurried out of the room.

"We can only have two family members in here when the baby comes," the doctor informed them.

"Mary is my mom, the baby's other grandma," Avril explained. "It'll be her and the baby's dad in here."

"Okay, no problem," Dr. Rice said, putting on blue latex gloves.

Mary entered the room in a panic. "I'm here, I'm here!" She beamed as she took her place on Avril's left side. Her flowing dirty blonde hair bounced with every step. Her cheerful demeanor and smile lifted her cheeks, emphasizing the black frames of her eyeglasses.

"Okay, grandma," Dr. Rice said to Mary. "You can hold onto Avril's hand. And Dad, hold onto her other hand. Are we ready?"

Everyone nodded in agreement. A nurse sneaked into the room at the last second, but no one seemed to notice. Lives were about to change trajectory in a matter of minutes, and nothing else mattered in the moment.

Here we go...

"Okay, Avril, push as hard as you can," Dr. Rice said.

Avril pushed. Drops of sweat trickled down her brow.

"You're doing good, keep pushing," Dr. Rice encouraged.

Avril continued, grunting with every push.

"Just a little bit more, Avril." Abraham did his best to support her, and he could only imagine the pain and emotions she was going through.

"Here she comes…we're crowning," the doctor said. "You're doing good, Avril. I just need you to push a little harder."

Avril gripped her mother's hand tighter. She pushed again as her face flushed red. She squeezed Abraham's hand, her fingers whitening at the tips.

"Keep pushing…just a little bit more," Abraham said.

"Almost there…" Dr. Rice announced. "Keep pushing."

The moment that scared him to death had arrived.

It was probably the shortest nine months he'd ever experienced. Water had been the only real fear in his whole life. Now, he had two.

The chances of him drowning in one of the two were great at this point. Overcoming the fear of being a father needed to start in the hospital room, and he psyched himself out for the most important job he could ever take on. There was a difference between the two potential drownings. Water would only take *his* life, but drowning in fatherhood would take his daughter's life as well.

Dr. Rice guided the baby out. "And we have a baby girl!"

She's here…

Abraham laid eyes on her. His daughter. In that moment, he recognized a distinct difference. His old life was gone.

I'm somebody's father…

Her newborn lungs breathed air for the first time. She was covered in slimy goo with traces of blood on her minuscule body.

"Time…2:42 p.m.," the nurse shouted, scribbling the time on a clipboard. Before whisking the baby away, the nurse handed Abraham scissors as she clamped the umbilical cord. "Dad, are you ready to cut the cord?"

Oh shit…time to suit up. This is the first dad thing I do…

Psychologically, he was seasoned. Relating the situation to basketball or superheroes made it easier to transition. He would have to perform in an area he had zero experience in.

Wide-eyed, Abraham pointed the scissors toward the cord. "Where should I cut it? I don't want to cut the wrong part," he said, his nerves working overtime as he steadied his hand.

"Right under the clamp. She'll be fine," the nurse assured him.

Abraham retracted the scissors, took a deep breath, and clenched the blades together. He proceeded to cut through the umbilical cord. It detached smoothly, and the baby didn't cry or wail.

The nurse scooped the baby from the doctor's arms and carried her to the weigh station. She bought Abraham a few moments to gather himself while the nurse documented the baby's weight and measurements.

"Congratulations, mom and dad!" Dr. Rice said to Abraham and Avril.

"Thank you!" Abraham replied, his voice filled with a mix of pride and relief.

"That might be the fastest delivery I've ever witnessed as a doctor! A new record!" Dr. Rice exclaimed.

I'm somebody's father, now…

He would never admit it to anyone, but the mixture of feelings jumbled up deep inside, where no one would ever witness, made him uncomfortable.

Feelings that made him vulnerable.

Their intensity rushed to the surface and flashed before his eyes in a whirlwind of thoughts.

The birth of my child...
Drastic life changes...
An heir...to pass on what I have learned...
The whole world, upside down...
Fear...I don't want to fail...
Love...I can't believe she's mine...
The Fire...you can pull off anything...you can do this...

Droplets of sweat accumulated on his brow, and his breathing became heavy and rushed. The shock of witnessing a life he helped create scrambled his thoughts, sending him into various eras of his own life—the future, the past, and the present.

What kind of man am I going to be?
What kind of father will I become?

The nurse wiped down the newborn before placing her on the weigh station. "Six pounds, seven ounces. Eighteen and a half inches long," she announced.

It wasn't until the nurse cleaned her off that the baby began to whimper, her first little cries echoing in the room.

I can never let her down.

She had a full head of hair, and it was dark, just like his.

If she's this tiny, she'll probably be short like me...

But none of that mattered. She was the most important person in the room, in the world, for that matter.

Everything has changed...I don't have a choice anymore. I have to be better.

Avril held her first as family members rushed in. Avril's father and grandmother, Doug and Maga, followed by Gloria and Grandma Marcella.

"She's here!" Mary announced.

Avril glanced over at Abraham. The nurse noticed the cue and she gently passed the baby to him.

"Dad's turn," the nurse said with a smile.

Abraham smiled back, his nerves on edge, as he made sure to cross his arms together to receive the handoff.

"You're okay, you've got it," the nurse reassured him.

The baby was swaddled cocoon tight, peacefully snoozing in his cradled arms.

I can't believe she's mine.

Abraham studied her features. He had seen plenty of babies before, but none carried his bloodline. He raised his arms enough to lean in and smell her cheeks. She had the distinct scent of being brand new.

His eyes scanned the room. Each family member engaged in conversation with one another, congratulating Avril as she lay on the hospital bed, exhausted from the pushing frenzy. Smiles graced the room as everyone eagerly anticipated greeting the first grandbaby on either side of the family.

Abraham focused his attention back on his daughter. He had her all to himself for a moment — father and daughter. He admired her, with thoughts alternating between excitement and panic.

As the room buzzed with conversation, he kissed her forehead and whispered words only she could hear. "I'll never leave you."

LXXIII MIRACLE

"**A**ww, my granddaughter!" Gloria smiled at her precious little grandchild.

"The nurse said we have to name her because we're checking out tomorrow," Abraham snickered.

"Y'all did good...she's beautiful," Gloria said. "You're a dad now, dude! You better get your act together because it's a lot of work, let me tell you."

Abraham stole a glance at his newborn daughter. Every feature of hers was delicate and pure. She inherited her father's eyes, not just the color but also their shape. Even the nurse had said to him on her second day of life, "You can't deny *her*!"

"She's going to be better than me...stronger...more powerful...*she's* going to be the one to save the world..." He envisioned the person she would grow up to be. "My baby..." He caressed her little hand.

The tiny child slept peacefully. Abraham braced himself for a life that included an Achilles heel, but also of a savior.

She was already born a hero.

The thought of an uncontrollable vulnerability scared him. He couldn't conceal it or alter it. This newborn baby single-handedly dismantled her father's entire defense mechanisms and protocols. She had the ability to touch him in a way no other human could. She was a living, breathing extension of himself.

> *Rewire…don't think that way…if you are willing to do anything for her, it won't be a vulnerability, it'll be a strength…to fight harder…to go farther than you've ever been…to show her anything is possible…to love her more fiercely than you ever were…to be there when she needs you the most…*

The pride of being mentally and emotionally strong dissipated. The trail of wreckage he left in the past few years created a void in his heart that could never be filled with debauchery, temptations, possessions, and recklessness. It was an endless cycle, and even the world itself was not enough.

But she was.

A single glance at her miniscule hands chipped away at the darkness within his heart. Her delicate, fragile feet uprooted the remnants of the rogue he had become.

The moment she arrived, his disservice to humanity was erased.

She was born, and he was reborn.

"I can't wait until she's older," Abraham said.

"Why's that?" Gloria asked.

"So I can train her in the ways of the 'Force'," he laughed.

"You need to work on yourself first, dude."

"I already started. The evolution has begun." Abraham glanced at his unzipped backpack. A notebook stuck out with words scribbled on it.

The Mission…

"Don't worry, Mom. I'm going to bring balance to the gifts that were given to me. I'm going to use everything I've got."

"You look better than you did a few months ago. How are your *abilities* coming along?"

"I feel stronger, more in tune. So much so, that I sense a storm coming…I can't pinpoint it yet. It's elusive," Abraham replied.

"Well, I can't help you there, but let me know if you need anything, dude. I'll help you in any way that I can. You need to be careful. It's not just you anymore," Gloria reminded him.

The toilet flushed, redirecting their attention to another small human emerging from the restroom.

"Paulina, do you want to give Abraham the gift you got him?" Gloria asked her stepdaughter.

"Yeah!" Paulina whispered. She retrieved a small box from Gloria's purse.

"You got me a gift?" Abraham asked his eight-year-old sister, surprised.

"Yeah, it reminded me of you and the baby."

She handed the box to Abraham. He opened it quietly, balancing the box in his hand. Inside was a statue resembling a wood carving, featuring colors of beige, tan, light shades of brown, white, and a touch of light blue. The sculpture depicted a man seated with a newborn baby in his lap, held upright.

"It's called the 'New Dad' statue," Paulina said.

He felt his eyes betray him as tears flooded them. He was more sensitive than usual the last three days. Perhaps it was evidence that his little girl instantaneously turned him to mush. "Thank you, Goose. It's perfect. I love it," he said to Paulina. She was like the daughter he never had before he actually had one of his own. "Are you excited to be an aunt at eight-years old?"

"Yeah!" Paulina giggled quietly.

"You and the baby are gonna be more like sisters when she gets older."

"Yay! I can't wait till she starts talking."

"Okay, dude, we gotta get going. C'mon, Paulina. They need to rest." Gloria looked to Abraham, pointing her finger at him. "You're going to need plenty of it."

Just then, the door swung open, and Margie entered with a delivery. "I brought your order," she said.

"Oh man, I'm hungry!" Abraham said, eyeballing the McDonald's bag.

"Just in time!" Gloria declared. "Okay, Margie, we'll see you later at the house."

"Tell Grandma I'll be there in about an hour." Margie made certain to make Grandma Marcella aware of her timetable, otherwise her phone would be ringing nonstop.

Margie placed the bag on the rollaway table and approached the baby, assuming her new role as "Great Aunt." Only a portion of the baby's head was visible in her pink cocoon as Margie gently rubbed her cheek with her finger.

"I'm proud of you." Margie placed her hand on his shoulder. Her purple blouse livened her aura. She was royalty, a child of the Most High. "There's your miracle," she said, pointing to the baby.

"You were right…I had another miracle coming. Not in the way I expected, but that's how God works, right?" he smirked, acknowledging her wisdom. Her guidance proved invaluable, especially in helping him bring back the practices of a faith-filled Christian man.

"You have someone to guide now, someone special. You're the one who has to lead her and show her what it means to follow Christ."

"I know." Reassuring himself was getting easier, but there was still plenty of work to be done. "I've been working hard to rewire…and now, a baby comes along. I'm not going to lie…I'm shell-shocked…I'm a *father* now. I don't deserve her…especially after Athena. I don't want to screw this up. But I don't believe in coincidence." He paused, exhaling a heavy breath. "I believe she was sent."

"She's definitely here for a reason…and now it's up to you to decide what kind of man you're going to be. Good or bad…you have the ability to change the world." Margie leaned in to hug her nephew. "It's going to be okay."

"Thank you, Margie. I don't know what I'd do without you. You are more than just an aunt. You're my mom too."

"We don't deserve second chances, but God always gives us plenty more. It's called Grace. Your baby is a blessing. You're making choices for two now, little boy."

"That's what freaks me out. I'm afraid I'll make the wrong ones, and I have a life besides my own that I'm responsible for now. What if I make a decision thinking it's the right one, but it turns out to be the wrong one…"

"It's called being a parent. You just do the best you can, just like anything else."

"Well, I'll give it my best shot. It might not look pretty. But one thing is for sure, she supersedes everyone and everything."

"Always remember that, and you'll be fine," Margie said.

The emotional roller coaster kept Abraham occupied for a few days, but in the back of his mind, a question lingered—one he was terrified to ask. He figured he'd get right to the point. "The cancer? Is it going away?"

"It's still there," she replied, her tone soft and without hesitation. She spoke as if carrying a plague was normal.

"What did the doctor say?"

"It hasn't gotten better…but it hasn't gotten worse. It hasn't spread…yet."

Yet?

It was a truth he couldn't handle. Although he gained strength in recent months, he wasn't ready to face this reality just yet, either. "Yet" was the key word.

"All we can do is pray, and whatever the outcome is, that's the Lord's plan. It'll be okay." He marveled at Margie's mastery of going with the flow. The good or the bad didn't affect her. She knew to Whom she belonged—the Lord of all. "Just know, when I leave you, you'll not only be able to take care of yourself in the real world, but you'll also know how to fight spiritually as well. Don't worry, you *are* going to do good. We're not done *yet*. Right now, your daughter is the most important person in your life," she said, directing her hand toward the baby. "You have to purge your old life. You have a new one now."

She's right…

"Get some rest, little boy," Margie said.

"You have to get healthy because I'm going to need you when I have a son," he replied, laughing.

"Cállate! *Shut up!*" Margie hollered. "You can barely take care of yourself, much less take care of two kids!"

He looked at his daughter. She was tightly coddled, and he wanted to grab her and hold her and kiss her, but she needed rest too.

Margie's words echoed.

My old life is gone…

The curvature of her button nose caused his heart to flitter. He focused on adapting to the new feelings rather than rejecting them.

Adapting means survival.

Margie crept next to him as he admired the baby. A book was plopped open in her hands as she read to him in a low voice. "For I know that good itself does not dwell in me, that is, in my sinful nature. For I have the desire to do what is good but cannot carry it out. Romans 7:18." Margie continued, "You are good, but sometimes we all need help from a Higher Power. Let God guide you, so that you can guide *her*. Your old life is gone."

Abraham never broke his gaze from the baby. He listened attentively to Margie's teachings. Her interpretation of the verse made perfect sense.

God will guide me…to help me guide her…

He caressed the baby's tiny cheek, and as she peacefully slept, she let him know that it was okay for him to drift off as well.

LXXIV THE SON

"Where am I?"

He blinked his eyes open to find himself lying beside a steep, rocky hill. The wall of rock stood at a near-vertical 90-degree angle, a formidable challenge that only an experienced rock climber could conquer. Its surface was smooth, adorned with dried weeds that clung precariously to the plastered facade. From this angle, the weeds seemed to cascade over an archway, serving as a makeshift entrance to what appeared to be a cave.

He made his way through the low archway. As he ventured deeper, a sight unfolded before his eyes—a colossal dome-like structure emerged, illuminated by a faint, artificial light emanating from an orange orb suspended high above. The contrivance simulated a sun, casting a muted glow that revealed the features of the cave's interior. Below the suspended orb, an expanse of green grass stretched out, covering the valley floor that extended into the unknown, fading away into darkness a thousand yards distant.

Thirty feet into the cave, a sudden drop opened up—a canyon that descended into the depths below. A tranquil river flowed silently through the chasm, unseen yet present. On the other side of the canyon, the land sloped down, significantly lower than the entrance. Standing at this vantage point, he peered over the edge, gazing down at the serene valley, its verdant expanse sprawling beneath him, at least fifty feet below.

What is this place?

Something in his gut told him he needed to reach the other side. He thought about backing up about seventy feet, sprinting at full speed, and attempting a leap across the valley. The canyon's width was a hundred feet across, rendering it impossible for a human to clear that jump.

In the distance, he noticed people walking barefoot along the cliff.

How did they get across?

He surveyed his surroundings, searching for any clues to get across and join them. The cave concealed an entire world within, and his curiosity got the best of him.

A powerful gust of wind burst through the archway. Within a few seconds it grew forceful, resembling hurricane winds. His balance began to falter.

"Let go," a gentle voice whispered.

He struggled to maintain his footing, but the force of the winds proved overpowering. The gust lifted him up into the air like a cannon shot, propelling him higher as he glided over the canyon.

Fear consumed him, his thoughts fixated on the perilous plunge that awaited him hundreds of feet below. Yet, as he soared through the air, the fear gradually subsided.

The winds began to die down, and at that moment, he dropped altitude. He found himself about fifty feet away from the grassy valley, panicking at the sight of the seemingly bottomless darkness below. Closing in on the grassy ledge, he continued his descent, arms outstretched in desperation.

I'm not gonna make it.

His body dipped below the edge of the canyon, and his chest slammed hard against the rocky cliff. His arms managed to make it over the ledge, but his body dangled helplessly on the cliffside. He reached out, grasping at anything within his reach, tearing out patches of grass, rocks, and weeds. His feet scraped against the edge of the cliff, causing the rocks to knock against his knees. Kicking away the protruding rocks, they clattered loudly into the stream below.

Slipping further, he made one last attempt, and this time, a hand caught his arm. The hand pulled him up and over the edge. Once safely on the ledge, he crawled along the grass, gasping for air. Taking a moment to gather himself, he finally managed to stagger to his feet, brushing off the dirt and grass from his body.

The stranger waited patiently for Abraham to regain his composure before heading in the direction of the group. In the distance, the group continued their journey deeper into the cave. The Man didn't seem too concerned with catching up. Abraham jogged over to Him.

"Thank you," Abraham said.

The Man walked alongside Abraham in silence, his hands clasped together as he studied the ground before them.

Abraham repeated his gratitude, "Thank you for saving me."

The Man remained silent.

Abraham attempted to catch a glimpse at the Man, but his neck refused to turn. An invisible force prevented him from swiveling his head, limiting his view to the periphery.

White garb.

Long brown hair to the shoulders

Tattered sandals.

Beard.

Dark complexion.

Five foot five or so.

The group had advanced a couple of hundred feet ahead, while the Man walked slowly. Abraham pointed towards the group. "Do you need to catch up to those people?"

"No," the Man finally spoke. "My father sent Me."

"Where is he? Is he here…in the cave?"

"I sit at the right hand of My Father."

Abraham knew now why he couldn't turn his head to see this Man. "Is it You?"

"I Am who you say I Am," the Man affirmed.

A sense of guilt washed over Abraham. "Why did you save me?"

"You came to Me. Your arm reached for Me," the Man responded.

"I'm sorry. I made mistakes. I did a lot of bad things…and I allowed them to break me. I should've turned to You," Abraham confessed, his voice laden with guilt. "I should've trusted you all along. I just got lost. All those years I counseled people, I always said that I'd stick with them through whatever they were going through until they were 'better,' no matter where that journey took us—the code of a counselor. I realize it should have been no different with You…to stick with You no matter what."

Abraham sighed as if a great weight lifted off him. "I had one foot in, and it got me by for a while…but then I was blindsided…by dark forces…and I couldn't beat them, until I put both feet in."

The Man continued to study the ground in front of Him, allowing Abraham to pour out his testimony. "I'm all in…with both feet. I trust You. I'm going to stick no matter what, no matter where that takes us. The Darkness will come after me again, but it won't matter…because I'm walking with You…"

To Abraham's surprise, the Man finally spoke. "I am the Light of the world. If you follow Me, you will not walk in darkness but will have the light of life. Take up your cross and follow Me. If the world hates you, remember that it hated Me first."

"I wasn't used to being hated…I felt so alone…and there was a time when I couldn't feel Your presence anymore…" Abraham confessed.

"Don't let your heart be troubled," the Man calmly reassured. "I am with you always, even until the end of the age."

"Yes, You've always been with me. My faith was tested…and I failed. You were always there, but I didn't take the time to listen…"

"You heard My teachings but did not keep them. I do not judge. I did not come to judge the world," the Man responded.

"You came to save it. I know the mission now, and I'll do my best to give it everything I've got…to give *You* everything I've got."

"Truly I tell you, if you have faith as small as a mustard seed, you can say to this mountain, 'Move from here to there,' and it will move. Nothing will be impossible for you."

The Man continued walking alongside Abraham.

"I don't fear death anymore…I just don't want to die right now…I know it's not up to me…" Abraham confided in the Man. The power of death He held in His hands.

"I am the Living One. I was once dead, but now I am alive forever and ever. I hold the keys of death. Those who believe in Me will live, even though they die…and those who live by believing in Me will never die. Do you believe this?" the Man asked.

"I do," Abraham whispered.

"I have shared these things with you so that you may find peace in Me. In this world, you will have trouble. But take heart…I have overcome the world."

Abraham fell silent. The magnitude of such a profound statement calmed his conscience. The emotional wreck he'd been in the past dissipated. Mortality and purpose prompted his next question. "Did You break me…in order for me to become who I'm meant to be?"

The Man responded, "In the same way I will not cause pain without allowing something new to be born. You do not realize what I am doing but later you will understand."

"Thank you for guiding me. I will always welcome You into my home, my heart, and my life."

"I stand at the door and knock. If you hear My voice and open the door, I will come in, and we will share a meal together as friends."

"As friends, and brothers. I know in the end…everything will be okay. Margie and Kay spoke truth over me…over the lies that infiltrated my mind."

"And the truth will set you free."

They walked together deeper into the cave, and the light from the orb followed them. The dreamlike tranquility comforted Abraham, and even through the soles of his shoes, he could feel the softness of the cotton candy grass. It was a place where the ills of the world did not exist. A place where the Darkness could never reach him.

The Man continued as if reading Abraham's thoughts. "Your accuser has no power here. The work has been done at the cross. You shall no longer walk in darkness but have the light of life. Your faith has saved you."

"The Darkness can never hurt me…"

"No. It is finished. Today, you will be with Me in paradise."

LXXV   BAPTISM UNDER THE GUN

Awakened by the nurse, Abraham jolted upright from the chair, startled. She had come to check on the sleeping baby and Avril. The leather seat beneath him emitted an uncomfortable heat, drenching his backside with sweat from his upper back to his thighs. His eyes were moist, not from perspiration, but from something else.

Soul travelers were never meant to retain memories of the realms they visit.

But he did. At least this time.

"Oh, I'm sorry," the nurse said, glancing in his direction. She was a young girl with brunette-colored hair.

Abraham widened his eyes, allowing the emotional discharge to escape.

"It's okay…" Abraham muttered in a muffled voice. His eyes felt heavy. He strained his blurred vision, adjusting to the familiar world he knew. The journey back had left him groggy, as if he had been abruptly pulled from the cave. "Is the cafeteria open?"

"Yes," the nurse replied, stealing a glance at her watch. "It just opened for breakfast."

Abraham limped into the hallway. Fragments of the dream came to him. He replayed them, desperately trying to etch as much as possible into his memory. He had ventured to a place that few ever go, and he was grateful for a second chance.

He was alive.

The conversation played in his head, serving as a constant reminder of the truth.

He didn't come to judge…He came to save the lost…

Those words re-instilled a powerful belief, one upon which he had built his code around.

Hope.

Looking back, the Man had given him confirmation of the one thing he had lost sight of.

The Truth.

Building himself back up required the most important piece of his foundation.

The Cornerstone.

The Man who had brought him to converse in a place between life and death.

The Son of Man.

He found comfort in knowing he was never alone. All he needed was a whisper of reassurance. "My God is the God of the comeback."

"Room 237," he said, repeating the number to himself, determined not to forget it. "Hopefully they aren't awake yet."

Breakfast didn't quite live up to his five-star expectations, but who was he kidding. Hospital food had never been known for its culinary delights. Still, he devoured every crumb.

Just as his hand reached for the doorknob, a chime from his cell phone interrupted him.

> **Kay G. (6:06 a.m.):** Congratulations, Abe! You're a dad! Blessings and prayers for your baby girl. Life is a gift. The darkness can never win. The Light is peeking through, and it reminds me of Romans 13:12…The night is nearly over; the day is almost here. So let us put aside the deeds of darkness and put on the armor of light. I love you!

> **Abraham M. (6:07 a.m.):** Thank you, love! Miracles never cease! We'll visit as soon as we can. Baby needs to know who her Aunt Kay is…because you're more than a cousin. You're my sister. I love you!

Kay never failed to bring a smile to his face. Their bond had solidified as siblings in Christ.

He opened the door slowly, careful not to disturb Avril and the baby. The sunrise was still thirty minutes away, yet the room appeared darker than when he had left it. As his eyes adjusted to the darkness, he sensed a new presence, one he hadn't felt in years. The malevolent energy emanating from the being sliced through the room, triggering his internal alarms. He froze, trying to pinpoint its location.

"I've been waiting for you," the stranger declared, his deep voice piercing the air. "You didn't think I forgot about you, did you?"

"Who are *you*?" Abraham asked sternly. The voice was unfamiliar, not originating from his own thoughts. This new adversary was human.

By the window, the intruder stood, gazing out at the imminent sunrise. Clad in a black wind jacket, his hair was slicked back, with the sides and back buzzed to a subzero fade.

The imposing figure turned one hundred and eighty degrees to face Abraham. "Good to see you, Super One."

Abraham straightened his posture, his brow furrowing. There was only one man who had ever called him that nickname. The towering six-foot-five giant loomed over him. "Tommy?" Abraham said, his voice filled with surprise.

"It's been a long time," Tommy acknowledged.

"What are you doing here?" Abraham asked, his confusion evident.

"I heard you were having a baby, so I thought I'd drop by," Tommy replied with a sly smirk. "You know, congratulate you and shit."

Abraham glanced over at Avril and the baby, while keeping a close eye on Tommy's movements. Tommy slowly inched closer, his boots gliding silently across the tiled floor. His stealthy actions resembled that of a predator stalking its prey.

"How did you hear about that?" Abraham asked, moving closer to the baby. The unexpected confrontation, just a few feet away from his newborn daughter, caught him off guard.

Tommy circled around Abraham.

Abraham's mind raced, realizing that he couldn't risk a fight in such close proximity.

I can't fight in here…Avril and the baby will get hurt…

Adrenaline surged through his veins. It had been a long time since he had been in a fight.

There's no way I can fight him in here…

"I heard from Adam…he gave me the news," Tommy said in a low, almost whispering voice. He glanced over Abraham's shoulder to catch a glimpse of the baby.

"That's not true. Nobody knows. I didn't tell anyone about her…" Abraham sensed the lies emanating from his dangerous adversary. Despite Tommy's attempt to sound genuine, he failed to conceal his malicious intent.

Tommy snickered; a conniving chuckle escaped his lips as he lowered his head to his chest.

Abraham quickly recalled the last encounter with Tommy Gun. "The last time I heard from you, you were in Ohio…getting arrested for attacking my sister. How was jail time over there? Good?"

Tommy ignored the question and continued with deliberation. "You've gone through dark times recently, I heard. You and me both. It's dark in this room. Take away that lamp, and you have total darkness…just the way I like it. Three years…that's how long it's been. And in that time…I've embraced the darkness. I've evolved, as you used to say. I've become even more…dangerous. You won't be able to beat me. I've grown too strong for you."

"What do you want?" Abraham interrupted, determined to cut through the veiled threats.

Tommy paused, tucking his right hand away and avoiding eye contact. He looked up, his face contorted with a grimace. "Revenge…for what you did to me."

Before Abraham could react, Tommy pointed a 9-millimeter directly at his forehead.

"Do you remember this gun? You should. It's been pointed at you before…"

A fleeting faded memory resurfaced. Only one person had ever held a gun to his face.

Abbadon.

Tommy continued circling until his back was against the door. "You think you live in peace, thinking no one watches you, no one studying your every move. You're wrong. Abbadon was my friend, and he left because of you. He valued your friendship…over everything…he stopped helping me get my money because you thought it was wrong. He chose *you*!" Tommy trembled, his hand shaking as the gun rattled on his ring finger. Each word fueled his anger, his face shifting from pale to tomato red. "We would ve made a good living, but you always have to be the fuckin' good guy, right? Fuckin' pathetic."

"I should've known better…spying on me won't get you what you want." Abraham thought back to the people he had encountered in the past year. One person stood out, and he couldn't shake the feeling that her appearance in his life was a mere coincidence. "Elida…I know you sent her…"

Mentioning the past only served to infuriate Tommy further. His voice seethed with disgust. "All I have to do is pull the trigger. I *am* gonna fuckin' kill you. That's what I want. You can't run and you can't hide from me."

Abraham stood his ground, protecting the baby as Tommy continued his tirade. "And then you do this to Abbadon…you let him die, and you have me arrested." Tommy inched the barrel closer to Abraham's face. "One wrong move and you're *dead!*"

I won't be able to take him down in here…what if the gun goes off? I can't take that chance.

Taking down Tommy seemed almost impossible without putting Avril and the baby in harm's way.

It's too risky…

Tommy advanced, closing in on his new enemy. The barrel landed on Abraham's forehead, and the threat of imminent harm sent a shudder down his spine. The touch of cold steel ignited a wave of fury, causing his brow to crease around the hollow exit point.

Get him out of the room with minimal damage…

Abraham eyed the barrel. Using his peripheral vision, he noticed Avril rolling over to her side, causing Tommy to freeze.

The feelings of rage ballooned, threatening to overcome his resolve. The vow he made to himself, to never succumb to anger, was on the verge of breaking. But this time, Abraham channeled it for the love of his newborn daughter. In that moment, he remembered his father's question from long ago.

Is there anything you wouldn't do for your family?

Adrenaline surged through his veins. Goosebumps erupted over his head, traveling down his arms and legs.

"You ever been baptized by fire?" Tommy snarled.

Abraham focused on Tommy's shoulders, trying to anticipate his movements. If he acted quickly enough, he might be able to disarm him. Deflecting Tommy's arm and delivering a swift punch to the groin was a risky gamble he wasn't sure he could pull off.

"Soon you'll know what it feels like to be hit by *Gun* fire...when you least expect it."

Abraham pressed his forehead against the barrel, hoping to push Tommy out of the room. Tommy stepped back, inching closer to the door.

C'mon, you can do this...be super fuckin' quick...move your head and grip the barrel hard...

Mentally preparing himself to take control of the gun, Abraham readied his hand to strike. But it was too late.

A scream echoed through the hallway. The nurse peeked in, witnessing the chaotic scene. Avril awakened, her eyes wide with fear.

The nurse ran to alert the front desk, shrieking in panic. Tommy took advantage of the distraction and scurried out of the room.

"Abraham, what's going on?" Avril asked, traces of worry evident in her voice.

"Stay there!" Abraham shouted, his urgency growing. Avril leaned forward, grimacing in pain. She was half-asleep, but panic was quickly overtaking her.

Abraham rushed out of the hospital room, pausing for a moment to reconsider his actions. *Shit! I don't have a choice...I have to go after him...*

The consequences of such measures carried a hefty price. Tommy Gun had threatened his family, his newborn daughter. The choice to pursue Tommy had been made for him the moment the gun touched his skin.

He glanced left and right, struggling to recall the direction of the stairwell. His dormant tactical training skills started to awaken.

Abraham sprinted down the hallway, pushing his legs harder as doubts flooded his mind. *I'm in no shape to take him on...*

Tommy glided effortlessly down the stairwell, skipping multiple steps with his long legs. The sound of the door opening two floors above echoed through the space.

Leaning over the guardrail, Abraham and Tommy locked eyes, the latter smirking and taunting Abraham for his failed pursuit.

Abraham assessed the stairs, realizing that skipping a few steps wouldn't be enough to catch up in time. Hesitation cost him precious seconds. Psyching himself up, he knew he had to skip entire floors if he wanted a chance at apprehending Tommy Gun.

Fuck it! Abraham hopped onto the guardrail, finding his balance. Gliding down to the stairwell below, he landed safely on two different steps. *I made that one without busting my ass.* He leaped over the next guardrail, aiming for another successful landing on the level below. *A couple more.* Mid-air, he carefully tracked his movement to avoid injuring his ankle. *I'll have backup by the time I catch up to him...*

Arriving at the second-level stairwell, Abraham could hear Tommy's footsteps racing toward the first floor.

Almost there...

Abraham peeked over the edge and jumped onto the handrail, carefully balancing himself while surveying the floor below. To his surprise, Tommy had vanished.

Puzzled, Abraham leaned further without tipping over, straining to detect any hidden adversaries. He paused, anticipating an unexpected encounter.

Tommy reappeared, sprinting up the stairwell from below. Reacting swiftly, Abraham settled back onto the second-floor stairwell, his feet landing on separate steps. Bracing himself, he prepared as Tommy dipped his shoulder and rammed into him. The force sent Abraham sprawling onto his side, his body resting at an awkward angle on the stairs.

Tommy discreetly withdrew the firearm from the back of his pants. Without giving Abraham a chance to defend himself, he struck him on the side of the head with the handgun. A thin stream of blood trickled down Abraham's face as he became disoriented, desperately crawling up the steps. Hovering over him, Tommy taunted his weakened adversary.

"You can't stop me!" Tommy jeered, seizing Abraham by the collar and dragging him to the upper level of the stairwell. With both hands, he forced his former friend to stand. Abraham struggled to maintain consciousness, leaning against the wall lethargically.

Tommy tightened his grip around Abraham's throat, his massive hand squeezing tightly. He hoisted Abraham off the ground, sliding him up the wall until he dangled twelve inches above the floor.

"This time, you're the one who's gonna die!" Tommy bellowed. Abraham gasped for air, attempting to break free from Tommy's grip, using both hands to pry apart the fingers constricting his neck. His vision grew distorted, with black and white specks clouding his sight.

"There he is!" a doctor shouted from three floors above. Tommy released his hold, emitting a growl before sprinting down the remaining stairs and out the door. "It's not over!" he shouted.

Abraham collapsed to the ground, his body hitting the floor like a sack of potatoes. He rolled onto his side, struggling to breathe. Blood pooled on the concrete, staining his Superman t-shirt on the left shoulder.

Two nurses rushed to his side and knelt beside him. "Stay down," one of them advised.

"I'm okay," Abraham said, attempting to pull himself up. The two nurses flanked him, supporting his weight. "Let me go. I have to go after him!" With a faltering step, his knees buckled, and the nurses gently guided him back to the ground.

"Who?" one of the nurses asked.

"He's back..." Abraham gasped, fighting to remain conscious. His breath came in ragged gasps as the name of his new enemy echoed through the stairwell. "Tommy Gun, he's back."

"We need to get you to a bed," one nurse asserted, while a group of nurses and doctors hurried toward them. "We need to get him upstairs now!" another nurse urgently called out.

"Please...don't tell...my family...please..." Abraham pleaded, his words escaping between labored breaths. Gradually losing consciousness, he was haunted by a single thought that lingered as he succumbed to darkness—an old friend turned nemesis had returned.

LXXVI REINSTATEMENT

The secret remained safe for now. Typically, countermeasures would have already been set in motion, but this was different. He was different.

Closing his eyes, he practiced the breathing techniques Margie had taught him. As he delved deeper into meditation, the vision grew clearer. The future had been his enemy. He'd lived in it for far too long.

His spiritual resolve spoke supernatural wisdom.

Take things as they are, not as you'd like them to be...
Enemies will always be there. Threats will always reveal themselves.
I have God on my side...

This supernatural power invigorated his soul, granting him the strength to face the impending battles. He knew he wasn't alone, and he allowed spiritual power to flow through him.

A faint rattling disrupted his concentration. A click echoed from the keyhole, and the doorknob turned slowly. The visitor silently entered the house. "You're always in the dark," Margie said. Abraham sat on the red futon in the living room, engulfed in darkness.

"That way, I can truly appreciate the light," he responded.

"How's your head?" Margie asked.

"Better. No more headaches. The stitches will be out tomorrow." The fabricated story of falling down the stairs seemed believable enough, as the nurses had lied to cover for him. Everyone bought it, except Margie. She wasn't easily deceived. Just like the time he claimed to have been in a car accident with his then-girlfriend, Laura. After breaking up with her, she scratched his face and bit his cheek so hard that it bled for hours. He thanked God that the wounds hadn't left lasting scars. Margie was the only one who ever knew the truth.

"It's finally happening, you know. The new you is forming. You're about to become the best version of yourself…"

"But not without sacrifice, not without trials," he interjected. The confrontation with Tommy Gun was only a matter of time, but he didn't disclose that to Margie just yet. There was a more pressing battle that demanded their attention.

"Of course. That sort of thing is never in short supply. You needed a battle in order to be blessed. Now it's time to show the world who you really are." Margie positioned herself near the door, aware that his meditation ritual was in progress.

"And for you too…you're going to be okay. I believe that…in the name of Jesus." He wanted to speak words of life over her, just as she had done for him.

"God's plan, little boy. What are you going to do now?"

Abraham sighed. "I don't want to go back to old habits. If I'm going to go places, I've never gone before, I need to do things I've never done before. And I know what I need to do first…" he paused. "…exile."

✟

Kay G. (7:23 a.m.): It's been over a month since I last heard from you. I hope that all is well. Been praying for you. My prayer is that God has gifted you with the words to move His Kingdom forward and that He would fill you with perseverance to finish the job He has called you to do. John 4:34 Then Jesus explained: "My nourishment comes from doing the will of God, who sent me, and from finishing His work." Acts of the Apostles 20:24 "But my life is worth nothing to me unless I use it for finishing the work assigned me by the Lord Jesus – the work of telling others the Good News about the wonderful grace of God." 2 Timothy 4:7 "I have fought the good fight, I have finished the race, and I have remained faithful."

Can't wait to read the book when you finish. Your words will change lives…love you.

Kay G. (7:23 a.m.): This sermon by Pastor Steven reminded me of you. It has all the markings of a journey you are about to embark.

Abraham M. (7:24 a.m.): Your words always come in at the right time. I'm grateful God brought you back into my life, especially when I needed you most. I love you.

Abraham clicked on the link and immersed himself in the sermon from Pastor Steven.

Because after you've been through all that hell has to throw at you…

After you've survived the worst possible assault on your faith, and your mind, and your sanity…

After people have left you, after circumstances have drained you of your human energy, there remains a promise in the word of God, and this is not Peter's prediction, this is God's promise. He said never will I leave, and never will I forsake you. The Greek word is Ou mē…they might, but I won't!

Never, no, never!
When will I withdraw my love from you?
Never, no, never!
When will I change my mind about you?

Never, no, never!
When will I walk away and give up on the plans I made for your life?
Never, no, never!
When God says never, He means never! There's nothing you can do about it devil! I got a living hope!

✠

The cool breeze gently kissed his cheeks. He had never experienced the luxury of sitting on a porch and enjoying the stillness of a dew-soaked morning. Once upon a time, he would rise at the crack of dawn to train his body to become one of San Antonio's Finest.

Now, he trained his entire being—mind, body, and spirit. On the porch, he sat on an old concrete bench that Margie had given him from her home to his. There, he immersed himself in reading scripture.

Every morning, he read aloud to himself. "This day I call the heavens and the earth as witnesses against you that I have set before you life and death, blessings and curses. Now choose life, so that you and your children may live. Deuteronomy 30:19."

Scripture, he was learning, was perhaps the greatest teacher. Each verse he read offered a new understanding and a reinstatement of the spiritual being he truly was.

Hope had been restored.

"Now hope does not disappoint, because the love of God has been poured out in our hearts by the Holy Spirit who was given to us. Romans 5:5." He bowed his head and closed his eyes, meditating in the light.

The sound of a clanking motor disrupted his meditative state. A yellow car appeared, fishtailing onto the street, and screeched to a halt in front of Abraham's house.

A young woman jumped out of the yellow Ford Focus and rushed to the porch. Her long black hair swayed from side to side, and her fresh white complexion stood out against her eyeliner. "Abraham, I have something to tell you…" Elida shouted.

"I already know what you're going to tell me…"

"I know Tommy. He wanted to keep tabs on you and—"

"I know it was you…" Abraham interrupted calmly. "That's how he found out about my daughter."

"What? How did you know? Did he tell you?"

"Why would you do that to me? That's not what a real friend does."

In an instant, tears streamed down her face. "I'm sorry. I needed to pay for my dad's surgery, and there was no way I could afford the hospital bill. I was desperate…and that was before I really knew you."

"It doesn't matter now."

"Abraham, you have to believe me. I would never try to hurt you."

"Not intentionally, right?"

"I didn't know he would do this to you." Her voice cracked. "Please, believe me."

"I'm on a different path."

Elida lowered her head, her tears flowing uncontrollably. For a moment, he almost believed her. Across the street, neighbors peered out, captivated by the unfolding drama. "I'm really sorry, Abraham."

"Why did you come here? To ask for forgiveness?"

"I came to warn you…to tell you to be careful."

"I'll be all right. No thanks to you."

"Abraham, he's dangerous…" Elida wiped her face with her hands, smearing mascara under her eyes. She locked onto his eyes in hesitation of her next words. "You don't have a chance…of surviving this. He's going to try to kill you any chance he gets."

His eyes wandered to the street, to the neighbors, and then back to her. She wasn't lying.

He sensed her aura, and his feelings confirmed his suspicions.

The truth scared her.

A truth evident in the confrontation with Tommy Gun. A life force doesn't lie, and Tommy's emanated a malicious intent.

"Why don't you come away with me?" she pleaded, desperation in her voice. "We can leave the city. I have enough money to take us somewhere far, where he won't be able to find us."

Abraham laughed at her offer, seeing it as a poorly thought-out solution driven by self-redemption. "You're crazy! You think I'm just gonna get up and leave with you, especially after what you did to me? I have a daughter now. I'm not going anywhere."

"Abraham, he has too many forces working with him, too many weapons…"

"So…what you're saying is I'm outmanned, outgunned, and I have no chance to get out of this alive?"

"There's no way you can pull this off!"

Abraham cackled at her assumption, recognizing that she had no clue about his seasoned battle experience against far more superior supernatural forces. "A long time ago, I told Gun something…something he probably doesn't remember…but, one day he will."

"And what's that?" she asked, her voice muffled from sobs and sniffles.

"I have God on my side…"

"You can't win!"

Abraham snickered. "Oh, you know me…" he said with a smirk. "I never give up hope…"

"Now it came about after these things, that God tested Abraham, and said to him, "Abraham!" And he said, "Here I am!"

Genesis 22:1

AFTERWORD

River City Rage was an extremely difficult book to write. The previous book, Baptism of Fire, was 50% based on true events and 50% fabrication. In the case of River City Rage, over half was based on real life events. That said, traveling back in time to remember certain instances was spiritually taxing. Many of the moments in darkness were hard to write. In some ways, revisiting those moments brought back the feelings of what it felt like to be in darkness, hence, I faced something I did not expect...

...to heal all over again.

The dilemma was twofold. Margie, who served as my spiritual advisor in this life, and who also plays a major role in this story of spiritual warfare, passed away 43 days after Baptism of Fire was published. She was an integral, important piece of my life and this story would not exist without her. Even before her death, this book was always going to be dedicated to her.

The opening chapter of River City Rage was written back in January 2007, while I was in the beginning stages of working on Baptism of Fire. As I knew what was going to happen already at the end of the first novel, I imagined what it would be like to lose a brother, a best friend, and I wrote what I thought that pain would feel like. Ultimately, I fully experienced the feeling of losing someone close to me the following year after Margie's death, with my brother of 22 years, Jason. As fate would have it, Margie and Jason married into the same family, and I was deeply close to both. Jason knew what Margie meant to me. He helped me carry her to her final resting place and in 22 years Jason had never seen me cry until the day we carried her. The last year of his life, he did the greatest thing for me as he stood by my side, the one time I needed him the most. And then…

…Jason passed away.

Just as I was beginning to heal from losing Margie, I lost Jason 10 months after her, unexpectedly. I had just started to write again, focused on bringing River City Rage to life. After Jason passed, I stopped writing for nearly two years. When I began again, I went back to the first chapter and modified it as I now had firsthand experience of what it felt like to lose a brother.

In the wake of unexpected grief, this was the first battle in spiritual warfare where I felt broken, scattered, and uncharacteristically - an emotional wreck.

As all things are intertwined, I used that pain and heartbreak to deliver the innermost feelings of spiritual warfare. In doing so, I invested further. As time passed, new obstacles emerged, some I would say possessed supernatural qualities, but I know that the enemy wouldn't fight so hard if it wasn't for a greater purpose, and that purpose has always been for God's glory. He deserves all the credit, for this story is His.

Lastly, I cannot have this novel published without mentioning my father. The story is a mixture of reality and fabrication, and as always, it's up to the reader to decide which is which. Although I would say my father has been my cross to carry in this life, as of this writing, I have spoken to my dad more this past year than probably my entire life. On October 4, 2020, I personally handed my dad a letter explaining why things were the way they were between us, as he questioned the reasoning. In the letter, a short and sweet testament, I explained and reminded him that I had no regrets nor was I perfect by any means, but that I tried every day to be like Christ even though I fail horribly at times. I prayed that he would incorporate the same practice, not for me, but for himself. For the first time in my life, my father did not discount my feelings or my words. He agreed with 90% of my letter and that was the beginning of my father and I having a real relationship.

The power of words *can* make a difference.

So, if my dad should ever read this I just want to say:

Dad, you helped make this story possible. As I have said for a lot of years now, I don't hate you nor do I resent any circumstance. Not for one second do I regret growing up the way I did. All I ever wanted was for you to accept accountability and you have done that. The first step in growing and changing is admitting a wrong, and you have done that. To me, that is the greatest thing anyone can ever do for me. We can't go back in time, and I wouldn't change a thing if I had a choice. You mentioned you'd go back and do things over if given the chance, but I wouldn't let you because it wouldn't make me who I am today. I would do all those yesterdays over again, just so I can be glad that I have a dad today. I love you, dad. You're always going to be my dad.

Your son, Abraham

The real-life spiritual advisor, my aunt/mom, Margie.

ACKNOWLEDGEMENTS

G od deserves all the glory! There is no other reason why I write as much as I do, and without Him, I would never be able to accomplish the mission. Thank you, Lord, for everything!

A huge thank you to my support system of my mom, grandma, and my aunt Margie. I know I was not easy to handle when I was younger, but you three have always supported me. Thank you for loving me unconditionally.

A big thank you to my beautiful daughter Maddy for being the amazing daughter that you are! I thank God that he chose me to be your dad! When I was in darkness, you were the light I saw at the end of the tunnel. I could never be the best version I am today without you. I love you so much!

Thank you to my dad. The greatest apology is changed behavior and I appreciate the man you are becoming. I'm proud of you, dad.

Thank you, my brother Jason, for always being there, especially in the last year of your life. You stood by my side on the hardest day of my life, and I will always be grateful for your brotherhood. When you went home, I used the grief and the heartbreak to help me focus on what this story would eventually become. I miss you, Aquaman, but I find comfort in knowing I'll see you when I get there, too. I love you, J.

Huge thanks to my developmental editor and friend, Amy Acuna-Fuentes. I can't thank you enough for stepping up at the last minute and helping me refine the story and, more importantly, the mission. You are the first person to read the book in its entirety and I am honored and blessed that you spent so much time with my story. It meant more to me than you will ever know. You are a lifesaver, or should I say "booksaver!"

Thank you, EAM, for being my muse, inspiring me, and giving me great ideas. I can't believe we have known each other for 20 years! After all that time, you still manage to love and believe in me. I thank God for our "chance" meeting. Thank you for still being a part of my life. I hope you know how much I appreciate you and am grateful for you every day.

A special thank you to Kristy Grace. You have always been my sister rather than a cousin. Reconnecting with you in 2011 has been one of the greatest treasures of my life. Our spiritual conversations and our faith foundation connect us deeply and for that I am grateful. God knew I would need you down the road and your spiritual inspiration, as usual, did not disappoint. Thank you for being my spiritual warrior who fights with me, side by side. As you always say, "I leave you with this verse," so now I leave you with one – because you help to remind me that what is unseen is eternal – "Therefore, we do not lose heart. Though outwardly we are wasting away, yet inwardly we are being renewed day by day. For our light and momentary troubles are achieving for us eternal glory that far outweighs them all. So we fix our eyes not on what is seen, but on what is unseen, since what is seen is temporary, but what is unseen is eternal." 2 Corinthians 4:16-18 NIV.

I must thank Levi Lusko and Steven Furtick. Although I do not know you both personally, your sermons every Sunday gave me a whole lot of inspiration. So much so, that some chapters were created because of the messages that resonated so deeply, especially regarding spiritual adversity. The spiritual evolution of the main character, combined with your sermons, led the character arc in a direction that I am certain God wanted me to incorporate. I know the Lord was working through you both, my brothers in Christ, to help guide this story to what it needed to be for His glory. Thank you, again, brothers, for your inspiration.

I would be remiss if I did not mention the wonderful staff at Halcyon Southtown in San Antonio. I spent many a days and nights in the coffee shop (I'm here right now writing this) for hours on end. They have taken care of me, gotten to know me, and went out of their way to make sure I had a fresh cup of coffee or glass of water. Cat, Hailey, and the rest of the team – thank you!

Thank you, Rasel Khondokar, for taking the time to help me create the book exactly as I wanted it. Your kindness, dedication, commitment, and constant communication made a huge difference in bringing this book to life. Thank you!

I thank you, the reader, for continuing this journey with me and allowing me to share these stories with you. Thank you for your love and support! I truly hope you enjoyed this story, and hopefully are deeply invested with the characters so far. An author is nothing without the readers. The goal, for me as a writer, has always been to take you on an emotionally invested journey, not only to inspire, but to also let you know you are never alone. With any luck, you'll stick around with these characters for one more adventure in the "Fire" trilogy.

The journey continues in Fire Rises Free…

SPIRITUAL APPENDIX

"Worship That Hurts Like Hell" – Pastor Levi Lusko –
Fresh Life Church
October 3, 2021

"My Maker is My Mirror" – Pastor Steven Furtick –
Elevation Church
April 30, 2019

"Stop Making Agreements With The Enemy" – Pastor
Steven Furtick – Elevation Church
July 27, 2021

"You're a Problem For The Devil" – Pastor Steven
Furtick – Elevation Church
July 15, 2021

"No Weapon" – Pastor Steven Furtick –
Elevation Church
February 13, 2022

"God Will Never Leave You" – Pastor Steven Furtick –
Elevation Church
April 10, 2020

RIVER CITY RAGE PLAYLIST

Reelin' in the Years – Steely Dan – Album: Can't Buy a Thrill (1972)

Rapture – Iio – Album: Poetica (2006)

Hate It or Love It (G-Unit Remix) – 50 Cent – Album: The Massacre (2005)

Go! – Common – Album: Be (2005)

Forbidden Love – Madonna – Album: Confessions on a Dance Floor (2005)

Jesus Freak – DC Talk – Album: Jesus Freak (1995)

Lose my Soul – TobyMac – Album: Portable Sounds (2007)

Luv U Better – LL Cool J – Album: Ten (2002)

What's Left of Me – Nick Lachey – Album: What's Left of Me (2006)

Clocks – Coldplay – Album: A Rush of Blood to the Head (2002)

Printed in the USA
CPSIA information can be obtained
at www.ICGtesting.com
LVHW040949090324
773861LV00006B/28